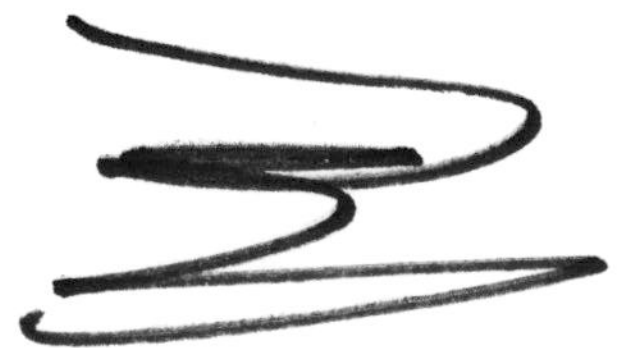

ALSO BY CHITRA BANERJEE DIVAKARUNI

One Amazing Thing

Shadowland

The Palace of Illusions

The Mirror of Fire and Dreaming

Queen of Dreams

California Uncovered: Stories for the 21st Century

The Conch Bearer

Neela: Victory Song

The Vine of Desire

The Unknown Errors of Our Lives

Sister of My Heart

The Mistress of Spices

Leaving Yuba City

Arranged Marriage

Black Candle

The Reason for Nasturtiums

OLEANDER GIRL

Chitra Banerjee Divakaruni

Simon & Schuster

New York London Toronto Sydney New Delhi

Simon & Schuster
1230 Avenue of the Americas
New York, NY 10020

First Simon & Schuster hardcover edition March 2013

Book design by Ellen R. Sasahara

Manufactured in the United States of America

1 3 5 7 9 10 8 6 4 2

Library of Congress Cataloging-in-Publication Data

Divakaruni, Chitra Banerjee, date.
Oleander girl : a novel / by Chitra Banerjee Divakaruni.
p. cm.
1. Fiances—Fiction. 2. Family secrets—Fiction. 3. Fathers and daughters—Fiction. 4. Calcutta (India)—Fiction. 5. United States—Fiction. 6. Domestic fiction. I. Title.
PS3554.I86O44 2013
813'.54—dc22
2012025671

ISBN 978-1-4516-9565-6
ISBN 978-1-4516-9569-4 (ebook)

For my three men:

Murthy

Anand

Abhay

And for my grandfather,

whose life inspired this story

Oh love is the crooked thing,
There is nobody wise enough
To find out all that is in it,
For he would be thinking of love
Till the stars had run away,
And the shadows eaten the moon;
Ah, penny, brown penny, brown penny,
One cannot begin it too soon.

—"The Young Man's Song," William Butler Yeats

OLEANDER GIRL

ONE

I'm swimming through a long, underwater cavern flecked with blue light, the cavern of love, with Rajat close behind me. We're in a race, and so far I'm winning because this is my dream. Sometimes when I'm dreaming, I don't know it, but tonight I do. Sometimes when I'm awake, I wonder if I'm dreaming. That, however, is another story.

I smile and feel my mouth filling with cool, silver bubbles. Rajat's fingers brush the backs of my knees. Even in my dream I know that if I slow down just a bit, he'll grab my waist and pull me to him for a mischievous kiss. Imagining that kiss sends a shudder of pleasure through me. But I don't want it yet. The chase is too much fun. I surge away with a splashy kick. *Hey!* he calls out in spluttering protest, and I grin wider. Competitive, he slices through the water with his fierce butterfly stroke and lunges for my ankle. I wait for his strong, electric grip to send a current through my veins. My mouth floods with anticipation of our kiss.

Then out of nowhere a wave breaks over me. Salt and sand are on my tongue. I try to spit them out, but they fill my mouth, choking me. Where's Rajat when I need his help? Gasping, I thrash about and wake in my bed, tangled in my bedsheets.

In my mother's bed, I should say. The bed I used every year when I came home from boarding school for the holidays. The bed that's made with the same sheets she covered herself with as a girl.

As my eyes adjust to the darkness, I know at once that someone is in the room. My heart flails around. It's impossible. I always lock the door before going to sleep, and the window is barred. But there it is, in the armchair in the corner of the bedroom: a still female form, black against the darkness of the room, looking toward me.

"Mother?" I whisper, my fear replaced by a yearning that's as old and illogical as anything I can remember.

I know so little about my mother, only that she died eighteen years ago, giving birth to me—a few months after my father, an ambitious law student, had passed away in a car accident. Perhaps she died of a broken heart. I never knew for sure because no one would speak to me of them. My grandparents had to put aside their own broken hearts to care for me, and I'm grateful: they did it well. Still, all through my years growing up, I longed for a visitation from my mother. The girls in my boarding school whispered stories about such occurrences, deceased parents appearing to save their offspring from calamity. I prayed for it in secret and, when that didn't work, tried to put myself in calamity's way, figuring either my mother or father might appear. But I only ended up with bruises, sprains, a case of the whooping cough, and, finally, a broken ankle. My adventures led to detentions, confiscation of pocket money, and a somewhat exaggerated reputation as a daredevil. They also resulted in numerous tongue-lashings from our harried principal, which didn't matter to me, and, finally, a long-distance phone call from my grandfather, which did.

"Korobi," Grandfather said in that stern, grainy voice that I had adored from babyhood, "I'm too old for this. Besides, why would a smart girl like you do a stupid thing like walking on the upstairs window ledge?"

The canny old rascal. He knew me well enough to appeal to my three major weaknesses: my vanity, my guilt, and, most of all, my love for him. He was, to me, father and mother rolled into one, and the thought that I had distressed and disappointed him made me burst into tears. Thus ended my attempts at forcing my parents into making an appearance.

Now, years after I had armored my heart and accepted that my mother was gone from my life, here she is.

How can I be sure it is her? There are some things we know, in our breath, in our bones.

It makes a certain sense that she should visit me now. Tomorrow I am to take my first real step into adulthood: I will be engaged to Rajat and thus begin the journey away from this family into another one. Perhaps my mother has come to say good-bye, to give me her blessing? Is she concerned? A strange tension seems to emanate from her. Perhaps she can't go to her final rest until she's certain that I am loved. I think I know why.

Some years back, during one of my vacations, I'd been going through Grandfather's library looking for something to read. I finally chose an old book of poems, its pages thumbed soft with loving use. As I flipped through it, a thin sheet of blue paper fell to the floor. Someone had left a half-finished letter inside. As I read it, my heart beat so hard I thought it would break through my chest.

Dearest,

You are in my thoughts every minute. I can't believe that only three months have passed since the last time I held you in my arms to say good-bye. I thought I could handle this separation, but I can't. Each day I ache for your touch. Each night I think of the way I felt complete in your arms. I talk to the baby inside me—I'm sure it will be a girl—about you all the time. I want to make sure our child knows how your love surrounds her even though you are so impossibly far away, in a whole different world—

It was beautiful and heartbreaking, this note from my mother to my dead father. It brought them close to me, made them real in a way none of my imaginings had. I couldn't share it with either of my grandparents, but I memorized every word on the page. I hid the note carefully in the bottom of my trunk—my first, cherished secret—and took it back to boarding school with me. Nights when I couldn't sleep, I would hold it in my hand and wish that someday I might find a love like theirs.

"Rajat is a wonderful man, Mother," I say, throwing off the bedsheets and sitting up straight in my excitement. "How I wish you could have met him, and Father, too. Then you'd have no doubts that I'm making the right choice. He's smart, funny, and caring—not only to me but to my grandparents. I've loved him from the moment I met him—it sounds silly, Mother, but it's true. At first I didn't think it would work. He comes from such a different kind of family. They're so rich and modern and fashionable that it's a little scary. And you know Grandfather—proud to bursting of our heritage, of the old ways. But I was amazed at how well they got along from the first. Maybe it's because Grandfather saw that Rajat loves me just the way I am, that he never wants me to change. And I—I feel complete in his arms, Mother, just like you'd written in your letter. Why, I love him so much, I could die for him!"

My mother makes a small, agitated movement, as though distressed at something I've said. She turns toward the window. Is she leaving? Desperate to recapture her attention, I blurt out something I haven't confessed to anyone else.

"The real reason I love him isn't his good looks or charm—it's because underneath it, I can sense a secret sadness. No one else can see it. No one else can cure it. But I'm going to find out what it is, and I'm going to make him happy!"

I'm breathless from my confession, but still the air in the room hangs uncertain, incomplete. My mother continues to look out the window. Why will she not speak to me? Where is the blessing kiss I've wanted all my life, cool as a dew-drenched breeze on my forehead?

A terrible thought strikes me: Has she come, like ghosts in tales, to warn me of an impending disaster?

I struggle to get to my feet, but my body is suddenly too heavy.

I *will* go to her. I *will* find out what she isn't telling me.

Suddenly the window behind her is filled with light. Outside I see an ocean, over which a sun is setting. Have I fallen, then, from one dream into another? She points over the ocean, leaning toward it with such sad longing that sorrow twists my heart. I understand.

She hasn't come to learn about me. All the things I said to her—she probably knew them already, being dead. She has appeared now, instead, to tell me something.

But what?

"Talk to me, Mother."

This time when she turns to me, I notice that my dream mother has no mouth. She points again.

"There's something out there you want? Beyond the ocean?"

She nods. Her face is glowing because I've finally understood. Now she points at me.

"You want me to go and get it?"

She nods.

"Where must I go? What am I to look for?"

My mother's frame shivers with effort as though she longs to speak. She begins to dissolve. I can glimpse the ocean through her tattered body, waves breaking apart on rocks. An urgent sorrow radiates from her disappearing form. Then she is gone, and I am finally awake, blinking in the first rays of the sun entering the room through the bars.

I need someone to interpret this dream. It means something, I'm sure of that, coming at this crucial moment in my life. I can't go to Grandfather. When my mother died, he destroyed all her photographs because he couldn't bear to look at them. When I was six, he told me never to bring her up. It was too painful.

I imagined it at night when I lay in bed, alone with my longing: that sharp, silver word, *mother*, like a chisel, chipping away at Grandfather's heart.

Perhaps I can tell my dream to Grandmother. She, too, is reluctant to speak of my mother—but she can be cajoled.

The household at 26 Tarak Prasad Roy Road has been abustle since daybreak, preparing for the engagement. The maid has ground the spices for the celebratory lunch and chopped a mountain of vegetables. The yawning cook has cut up the rui fish and marinated it in salt and turmeric. In the Durga mandir, the family temple established over a hundred years ago, old Bahadur yells threats at the gardener boy until the cracked marble floor is mopped to his satisfaction. There Sarojini hurries to arrange lamps, camphor holders, incense, sandalwood powder, marigolds, large copper platters, fruit, milk sweets, rice grains, gold coins, and multicolored pictures depicting a pantheon of gods. Is she forgetting anything? She loves the temple, but it also makes her nervous. Too many memories lurk in its sooty alcoves.

On one side she has unrolled mats for the priest and for her husband, Bimal Prasad Roy, retired barrister and proud grandfather of the bride-to-be; on the other she has placed four low chairs. The chairs, which have been the cause of some contention, are for the Boses, family of the groom-to-be, because they are modern and elegant and thus unused to sitting cross-legged on the ground.

Bimal had been dead set against such westernized nonsense. "For generations we've been praying on the floor. They can't do it for one day? Sacrifice a little comfort for the goddess's blessing?"

But ultimately Sarojini, who has had ample opportunity over fifty-five years of marriage to perfect her cajoling, had prevailed.

Reentering the house, Sarojini is swept into a sea of commotion. The milkman is rattling the side door; the phone rings; on the Akashbani Kalikata radio station, the newscaster announces the date: Feburary 27, 2002; Cook berates the neighbor's striped cat for attempting to filch a piece of fish. Bimal summons Cook in querulous tones. Where on earth is his morning tea? His Parle-G biscuits? Cook replies (but not loud enough for Bimal to hear) that she doesn't have ten arms like the goddess. The commentator on Akashbani, who is discussing the growing tension between India and Pakistan since the testing of the Agni missile, is interrupted by a news bulletin: over fifty people dead in a train fire in Gujarat.

So many disasters in the world, Sarojini thinks as she climbs the stairs to Korobi's bedroom. A pity that one had to happen today, a day of more happiness than their family has seen in a long time. She opens the door to Korobi's room to help her granddaughter get ready for the ceremony.

There's the girl, dawdling on the veranda in her thin nightgown for all the world to gawk at! Sarojini is about to scold her, but, leaning over the rail toward the row of oleanders that Anu had loved, Korobi looks so like her dead mother that the words die in Sarojini's throat. Not her face or fair skin—in those Korobi resembles Sarojini herself, but that posture, that troublesome yearning toward the world, that radiant smile as she turns toward Sarojini.

In any case, Sarojini is no good at scolding. Bimal has always complained that she spoiled the girls—first Anu and then little Korobi—and thus did them a disservice. Sarojini admits he has a point; girls have to be toughened so they can survive a world that presses harder on women, and surely Bimal does a good job of that. But deep in a hidden place inside her that is stubborn as a mudfish, Sarojini knows she is right, too. Being loved a little more than necessary arms a girl in a different way.

"Come on now, Korobi, bathwater's getting cold."

Not that Sarojini had much of an opportunity to spoil Korobi. As soon as the girl was five, Bimal made arrangements with that boarding school in the freezing mountains. Sarojini begged to keep the child at home. She even wept, which was uncommon for her, and mortifying. After Anu's death she had vowed to keep her griefs to herself.

"Look what happened the last time I listened to you," Bimal said.

A rejoinder shot up to her tongue. *Whose fault is it that my daughter's dead?* At the last moment she pulled it back into herself. If the words had crystallized into being, she couldn't have continued living with Bimal, she couldn't have borne it. But she didn't know any other way of being. Also this: she loved him. His suffering stung her. Yes, he suffered for Anu's death, though he would not speak of it. Even now he startles awake at night with a groan, and lying next to him, Sarojini hears—sometimes for an hour—the ragged, sleepless thread of his breathing.

But this is no time for morbid thoughts. Luncheon smells rise from the kitchen—khichuri made with golden mung and gopal bhog rice from their ancestral village, sautéed brinjals, cabbage curry cooked with pure ghee and cardamoms. Sarojini will have to supervise the fish fry. Last time Cook, who is getting old, scorched the fillets and collapsed into tears. But first Sarojini must get Korobi dressed. The child is always dreaming. Listen to her now, singing with abandon in the bathroom as though it were a holiday.

Sarojini knocks on the bathroom door. "Hurry, hurry, so much to be done. Sari, hair, makeup, jewelry. The mustard-seed ceremony to avert the evil eye. If you're not ready by the time Rajat's party arrives, your grandfather will have a fit."

While Korobi was away at school, all year Sarojini would hunger for winter break, when icicles hung from the eaves of the old school buildings and the children were sent down to the plains. But somehow when Korobi came home, the two of them never got to do the things Sarojini had planned. To share the special recipes that she was famed for, to pass down secrets her own mother had given her. It seemed that whenever she tried to teach Korobi how to make singaras stuffed with cauliflower, or layer the woolens with camphor balls to save them from moths, Bimal called the girl away to play chess or accompany him to the book fair. In between, armies of tutors invaded the house, dinning the next year's curriculum into Korobi so she could be the top student in her class. Korobi didn't complain; she adored her grandfather and wanted him to be proud of her.

When Sarojini ventured to suggest that Korobi needed time to be a child, Bimal said, "You want to ruin her brain quite completely?"

Only at bedtime did Sarojini get her granddaughter to herself. "Tell me about Ma," the girl would whisper in the dark, the forbidden request forging a bond between them. Sarojini would swallow the ache in her throat and offer Korobi something innocuous: a childhood escapade, a favorite color, a half-remembered line from a poem that Anu liked to recite.

"Why did she name me Korobi?'

"Because she loved oleanders so much, shona."

"But they're poisonous! You told me so. Why would she name me after something so dangerous?"

Sarojini didn't know the answer to that.

Now Korobi is getting married, leaving Sarojini struggling under the weight of unsaid things, things she had promised Bimal she would never speak of.

She pushes the thought away, unfolding the stiff pink silk sari she had bought, so many years ago, for Anu. She tucks it around her granddaughter's slender waist, admonishing the girl when she fidgets, making sure the pleats are straight and show off the gold-embroidered border. When Sarojini is satisfied, she starts on the jewelry—her beloved dowry jewelry, which she made Bimal get out of the bank vault, even though he had fussed and said it was quite unnecessary. She pins the gold disk in the shape of a sunburst to Korobi's braid and stands back to evaluate. The girl has lovely hair, not that she takes care of it. Mostly it's left untied, a mass of tangled curls cascading down her back. Where she got those curls, Sarojini can't figure out. Everyone else in the family has stick-straight hair.

The long necklace with a crescent-shaped diamond pendant, the earrings so solid they have to be supported by little chains that hook to Korobi's hair. The two-headed-snake armband fits perfectly around her upper arm. Sarojini had hoped to do this for Anuradha at her wedding. But Anu had married in America, and Sarojini's going there had been out of the question. Each piece has its name: mantasha, chandra chur, makar bala. Not many people know them anymore. Sarojini had tried to teach Korobi, but the girl wasn't interested.

Rajat, though, surprised Sarojini. Last week he had come to take Korobi for a ride in his new BMW, but he ended up sitting on Sarojini's bed for a half hour, touching each piece, listening to its story. That disk belonged to my widow aunt, who left it behind when she ran away. My father gave this necklace to my mother when my oldest brother was born. My great-grandfather the gambler won the snake band from a neighboring landowner while playing pasha.

That evening when Korobi returned from the ride, Sarojini said, "You're lucky to get him for a husband. He cares about history and tradition, about spending time with an old lady."

"Excuse me, I thought he was the lucky one!"

Sarojini laughed along with her granddaughter, but secretly she hoped Rajat would cancel out all the tragedies that had piled up in the girl's life already.

Asif Ali maneuvers the gleaming Mercedes down the labyrinthine lanes of Old Kolkata with consummate skill, but his passengers, occupied as they are with the day's engagement festivities, do not notice how smoothly he avoids potholes, cows, and beggars, how skillfully he sails through aging yellow lights to get the Bose family to their destination on time. This disappoints Asif only a little; in his six years of chauffeuring the rich and callous, he has realized that to them, servants are invisible. Until they make a mistake, that is. Let Asif jerk to a halt because a brainless pedestrian has suddenly stepped in front of his car, and he would hear plenty from Memsaab right away.

Not that Asif is complaining. The Boses are a definite improvement from his previous employers. For one, they aren't stingy. (It is an unceasing wonder to Asif how ingeniously tightfisted the rich can be toward servants.) He gets overtime if Barasaab comes back from a business trip at night, or if Memsaab stays late at a party, both of which happen with heartening regularity. They might grumble a bit, but they never cut his pay when he asks for time off on Muslim holy days, and they tip handsomely when they're pleased about something. Especially Rajat-saab, though since he acquired his BMW, Asif hasn't seen much of him. Rajat-saab gave him five hundred rupees the night he proposed to Korobi-madam.

"She said yes, Asif! How about that!"

Even in the car's subdued interior light, Rajat's eyes had a naked shine to them. It made Asif feel ancient, though he is at most five or six years older than Rajat.

"Congratulations, Saab. I am wishing you two will be very happy together."

He meant it, too. He liked Rajat-saab, who was always kind and considerate, even in his wild days, before meeting Korobi-madam, when he used to go clubbing every night with his crazy friends and that Sonia woman, who was the craziest of them all. But Asif didn't blame him. If Asif had that kind of money, he would be doing a few crazy things, too, instead of spending his off-evenings playing teen patti with the other drivers in the building, watching them get drunk on cheap beer.

But Asif's favorite person in the family is Pia-missy, whom he drives to and from school each day, and who reminds him—though it's illogical of him to think this way, and perhaps presumptuous—of his younger sister.

Although no one will ever know, Pia is the reason he refused when, last year, Sheikh Rehman's men tried to lure him away with the offer of a higher salary and the opportunity to drive a Rolls-Royce. For a moment, he had weakened; more than the money, it was the car; and more than the car, it was the sheikh's reputation.

Sheikh Rehman is a legend in the Muslim community. He's known for hiring young Mussulmans of promise and taking an active interest in their welfare. He's generous with bonuses and overtime pay. He houses them in staff quarters that are downright luxurious. They eat for free, delicious halal meals prepared in a communal kitchen in the back of the sheikh's own mansion. Last year, when some of them told him that they wanted to visit Mecca, he paid all their expenses and gave them extra vacation time. It is said no servant has ever quit his service, though several—because the sheikh is a stickler—have been fired.

But then Asif thought of the way Pia-missy would look if she found out he was leaving, and he said no.

Pia-missy has a secret name for him, which she only uses when no one else is within earshot: A.A. It's a name with style. "A.A., do you want some Wrigley's Doublemint?" "Can you go faster, A.A?" "Tell me again who you have at home in your village, A.A." "Turn up the volume, A.A. More!" She likes American music, earsplittingly raucous; it mystifies him, but he has decided it is his favorite, too. When they are alone in the car, Pia-missy holds up an imaginary mike as though she were a rock star and shakes her shoulders as she sings. Asif hums under his breath, accompanying her.

Being invisible, Asif knows things. For instance, the argument Rajat-saab and his parents had had after their first visit to Korobi-madam and her grandparents. Memsaab wondered if Korobi wasn't too young, only in her first year of college. Plus she'd been tucked away in that boarding school all her life. Rajat insisted she was more mature than most of his friends—a statement with which Asif silently agreed.

"Aren't you rushing into this too soon after Sonia?"

"This has nothing to do with Sonia," Rajat said coldly, but Asif thought he detected a slight tremor in Rajat's voice.

Barasaab was worried that Korobi didn't have enough in common with Rajat. She came from such a different background. Rajat insisted that he found those very differences fascinating. The culture and history that surrounded her every moment in that wonderful old house. How much he learned every time he visited her there.

"Her upbringing is quite unique," Memsaab admitted. "But would that be enough for you? I just don't want you to be unhappy and bored in a couple of years—"

"Mother, if you knew Korobi better, you'd know that I could never get bored with her. I haven't ever been able to talk to any woman the way I talk to her. She understands me, sometimes even without my having to say anything. I love her more than I ever thought I'd love anyone."

Memsaab had sighed. "In that case, Son, we'll support you."

They arrive at the Roys' house right on time, though no one commends Asif for it. He pulls the car into the tamarind-shaded driveway of 26 Tarak Prasad Roy Road, steps out smartly, and opens the door with a flourish. Pia-missy is the last to get down. A deep blue georgette zip-up sari is pinned to her shoulder with a brooch. Solemn and formal, she inclines her head regally. "Thank you, A.A.," she whispers. But then she can't stand the excitement. She grins at him and rushes ahead of her parents, pulling the sari up to her knees, swinging her new Kodak camera by its strap. Yesterday she explained to Asif how special that camera is.

"It just came out, A.A.! Dada asked one of his friends who went to America to get it for me. See, it's digital. You can view the photo as soon as you take it. If you don't like it, you can erase it and take it again.

After the engagement, I'm going to take a photo of you. Maybe standing against the car, what do you think?"

"That would be very nice, Missy," he said, touched. No one had ever thought to take a photograph of him.

Asif's sister had been the same age as Pia the year he left the village. She had cried when she learned he was going away. In spite of the difference in their ages, they'd been close. Asif would listen tolerantly as she prattled on about things girls were interested in, and if none of her friends were around, he would allow her to cajole him into playing five stones or ekka-duka. A few years later, she was married off to a man in Ghaziabad. Asif had been upset when he was informed of it. He thought she wasn't old enough to take on a wife's duties, but it was too late to do anything. The marriage had already been arranged. Afterward, he had gotten her address from his mother and written to her several times, even sending her some money, but she had never written back. Probably her in-laws kept the rupees he'd enclosed and didn't give her the letters. He wanted to call her, but the in-laws didn't have a phone. He thought of asking Barasaab for some time off so he could visit her, but the days passed, as days tend to do. Then last year his mother wrote that his sister had died of pneumonia. Reading the letter with its crooked lines and misspellings, Asif had felt sorrow and guilt tear through his heart. He remembered how his sister had looked at the wedding, bowed unhappily under a heavy bridal veil. She had died of neglect, he was sure of it, and he had done nothing to help her.

Now he tenses as he watches Pia wobble on her high heels. Allah, he finds himself praying, don't let her fall.

I am trying not to fidget against the itchy, heavy silk that Grandmother is draping me in, or the even heavier jewelry she's attaching to various parts of my body. I don't like the scented oil she rubbed into my hair before she imprisoned it in a braid, or the large bindi she's painted on my forehead, like an astonished third eye. But I can tell it makes her happy. Maybe it brings back memories of my mother's wedding day—

my mother, whose visit I need to ask Grandmother about as soon as I can find an opportune moment. So I summon as much patience as possible. Anyway, I'll get to shampoo out my hair before the engagement reception this evening. And tonight I'll get to wear my perfect outfit, the one hidden in the back of my almirah, which only Rajat has so far seen.

The reception will be held at the Oberoi Grand, fanciest of the Kolkata hotels. Rajat's mother, who likes me to call her Maman, told me that 350 guests are coming. The chief minister himself might stop by.

"Remember, dear, you're going to be the center of everyone's attention!"

Nothing like this has ever before happened to me. Because I grew up at boarding school, my birthday parties were muted affairs executed in the refectory: balloons, a lumpy cake made by the cook, a few minutes of birthday song and scattered applause. The thought of tonight's festivities is a bit alarming, but mostly it's exhilarating. I draw in a deep breath and square my shoulders, ready to take my place in the world as Rajat Bose's fiancée.

"Why are you all puffed up like a bullfrog?" Grandmother says. "How do you expect me to hook the komarbandh around your waist if you do that?"

Since the party is expected to continue late into the night, Papa Bose has booked three suites at the hotel—one for him and Maman, one for Rajat, and the third for me and Pia, Rajat's eleven-year-old sister, whom he calls Sweet P. Grandfather didn't care for the idea one bit. He scrunched up his face and started on how girls of the Roy family don't spend nights away from home. But Papa, bless his heart, said in his soft-spoken way, "Bimal-babu, isn't Korobi also my daughter now?" Papa's words sent a surge of joy through me. I wanted to tell him, *Yes, I am. And you and Maman are parents to me.*

Grandfather had finally barked his acquiescence at Papa, but he would never have given in if he knew what Rajat has planned for tonight, which is to smuggle me into his suite once his parents are asleep. He has sworn Sweet P to secrecy. That wasn't hard; she adores her brother. Thinking of Rajat and me, just the two of us together, privacy like we've rarely been allowed, intertwined on a blue velvet couch—that's as far as I let my guilty imagination go—makes my stomach feel wobbly. Yes, I'm scared, but in a delicious kind of way. My breasts tingle, and I breathe carefully so that Grandmother will not ask me, *What's the matter now? Are you feeling light-headed from fasting?*

But even my fantasies of Rajat can't keep me from worrying over my mother's visitation. I've got to bring it up soon. We're almost done.

Grandmother adjusts the armband one last time and tilts her head to give me an appraising look.

"Beautiful!" she proclaims. She rises on tiptoe to give me a kiss, and then, after a small hesitation, another one, as though on behalf of someone else.

I guess this is as good a time as any.

"Grandma, can I ask you something?"

Right then Cook calls from below to inform us that Bimal-babu is dressed and waiting in the foyer, pacing up and down and none too happy that we're still dawdling upstairs.

"Let's go," Grandmother says.

I grab hold of her arm. "I need to talk to you."

"Not now, my dear. You know your grandfather, how he can get if people are late."

"It's really important!"

There must be something in my voice, because Grandmother peers into my face, her eyes clouding with apprehension.

But Cook's raspy yells assail us from downstairs. "O Ma, O Korobi-baby, babu has already walked off toward the mandir in a huff. You'd better hurry, else you know what's going to happen."

Grandmother sends me ahead to pacify Grandfather. She will join us as fast as her bad knee will allow. She promises to talk to me right after the ceremony. For now, I have to be satisfied with that.

I run down the gravel path and catch up with Grandfather. I slip my hand into his as I've done ever since I was old enough to walk. I don't expect a response; he's never been demonstrative. But he surprises me today by squeezing my fingers. The frown on his face dissolves into a smile, and I feel a moment's pride knowing only I am capable of working this magic on him. He looks me up and down and gives a small, approving nod, and that means more to me than the most fulsome of compliments from someone else.

In the temple, I sit on the cool floor next to Grandfather, beneath the stern benevolence of the goddess's glance. Grandfather is clad in only a traditional silk dhoti—no fancy modern clothes for him, not even for a special occasion such as this. That's one of the things I admire about him: how he is always unapologetically, uncompromisingly himself. His spine is erect and impatient; white hairs blaze across his chest. From time to time, he intimidates the priest by correcting his Sanskrit, but in between mantras, when he places his palm on my head in blessing, his touch couldn't be gentler. How I love him, with all his bluster, his exasperating prehistoric notions, his tenderness that he tries so hard to hide.

Across from us, Papa and Maman, unaware of the battles waged over the seating arrangements, are poised splendidly on the wicker chairs. Rajat, however, has chosen the floor. From the other side of Grandfather, he sends me a quick, wicked glance; the private, scandalous things his eyes say bring a rush of heat to my face. A truant lock has fallen over his forehead. It's all I can do to stop myself from leaning over and smoothing it back. When at last he clasps my hand to slip on the diamond ring we chose together, joy balloons in my chest until it's hard to breathe. Rajat has made me a believer in miracles. How else could we have fallen in love?

Three months ago, I had gone to my college friend Mimi's birthday party—a minor miracle in itself. Usually Grandfather refused to let me go out so late, but that night I'd pushed back. Grandmother had taken my side, too. "She needs to meet other young people," she'd said. Finally, he'd nodded in grumpy agreement. When I walked into the flat, the party was in full swing: the lights low, the music deafening, the adults inexplicably absent. Crowds of people I didn't know were downing suspicious-looking drinks and smoking what clearly weren't cigarettes. I looked at the girls in their glittery tank tops and stretch jeans and felt antediluvian in my gold-worked kurta. I was about to make an excuse and leave when Mimi said, "Oh my God, is that Rajat Bose at the door? You don't know about him? His parents own that swanky art gallery on Park Street. He just broke up with Sonia Gupta, whose dad owns a Hyundai factory. Wow, I never thought he'd come to my party!"

I'd peered through the smoky dimness and seen Rajat. Backlit by the door, he appeared to be shining. A glass was already in his hand, a leather jacket slung over his shoulder. He leaned against a wall, holding court, nodding at acquaintances who rushed up to offer homage. He allowed Mimi to pull him to the dance floor, where he performed with loose-hipped, dismissive grace, smiling a little when more girls mobbed him. Weeks later I'd be astonished when he confessed that upon walking in and seeing all those people milling about, he, too, had wanted to escape.

"Thank God I didn't, Cara," he added—he'd given me my special name by then—touching the bones of my face as though he needed to memorize them. "Are you glad I stayed?"

I nodded; I wanted to tell him that he had transformed my life, bringing Technicolor to my sepia world. But I was afraid I'd sound stupid.

"You were standing in a corner, remember? There was something about the way you held yourself that set you apart from all those gyrating girls. Like you belonged to an earlier era. It made me curious. When I asked you to dance, you told me, quite unapologetically, that you didn't know how. I admired that."

He had offered to teach me. While the entire female contingent stared with envy, he asked the DJ for a slow song. Then he took me in his arms. I was nervous and awkward. To help me relax, he asked me questions. He had a way because I found myself telling him things about myself I didn't share with anyone else. My answers seemed to interest him. We spent the rest of the evening on the balcony, talking.

What could have caught his fancy? Wasn't my life most unadventurous, deeply ordinary?

"Are you kidding!" Rajat says later when I ask him this. "The way you've grown up, orphaned at birth, hidden away in some mountain valley, and now guarded in that ancient, beautiful mansion by your ogre of a grandfather—why, just listening to you was like entering a fairy tale!"

"Grandfather isn't an ogre!" I counter, laughing. "He and Grandmother brought me up so carefully that I never felt I was an orphan."

When it was time to leave the party, Rajat asked for my phone number. I didn't give it. Grandfather had informed me a long time back that the daughters of the Roy family did not have boyfriends. Rajat didn't argue. I think he took my refusal as a challenge. A couple of days later, returning from college, I was shocked to find him at our home, having tea with Grandfather. I still don't understand why Grandfather allowed Rajat to see me. Or why, three months later, when Rajat requested his permission to marry me, Grandfather said yes.

"It must have been my innate charm," Rajat says, laughing. But at other times he says, "I think your grandfather, who's nobody's fool, saw that I'd do anything to make you happy."

Pia, who has slipped down to sit beside me, kisses my cheek, bringing me back to the temple, where the ceremony has ended.

"The ring's gorgeous, Korobi-didi! Oh, you are so lucky! Dada has the best taste. Doesn't he, Maman?"

"Yes, of course," Maman says. She looks at us, and the love on her face makes her even more beautiful.

Now Papa and Maman give me their present: an exquisitely designed diamond set—necklace, earrings, a pair of bracelets—to match the ring. When I saw the price tag at the jeweler's, I was scandalized and begged for something less costly.

"Absolutely not, my dear!" Maman said. "You're worth every rupee of it. Besides, all the guests at the reception will be waiting to see what the Bose family gave their only daughter-in-law!" She smiled to show me she was joking. "May I get you your outfit, also? I know just the right boutique—"

I wouldn't let her do that—I was Bimal Roy's granddaughter, after all. I would pay for my own clothes. But her words lodged somewhere within me. When I went shopping, I kept in mind that I was the only daughter-in-law of the Boses and bought an off-the-shoulder kurti in maroon chiffon with slim-fitting pants, embroidered over with crystal teardrops, more expensive and daring than anything else I'd ever purchased. Rajat loved the ensemble and gifted me stiletto heels studded with fake diamonds to wear with it. But once home, I lost my nerve and hid it in the almirah behind a stack of cotton saris. From time to time, I imagined—with a mix of horror and pride—what Grandfather's reaction would be when he saw me in it.

We're not done with gifts yet. Ceremoniously, Papa hands us a large parchment envelope. I know what's in it: the deed to the flat Papa and Maman have bought us as an advance wedding present. The flat is located in a gated high-rise near Rabindra Sarobar Lake, in a neighborhood favored by models and playback singers and newly minted millionaires, only minutes from where the Boses live. This way, Maman says, Rajat and I can be close to them yet have our privacy.

Thinking of managing my own home, my own servants, fills me with a heady unreality. How wondrous to be expected to perform such adult acts! But I'm thankful that I don't have to worry about that for at least another year, that I have one more year to spend with my dear grandparents. A year—that's when we plan to have the wedding. It's going to be the most wonderful year, a sweet year of courtship, of enjoying the envy in the eyes of my college-mates, of evening forays into the glittering world of clubs and parties to which Rajat has promised to introduce me. A year of play before we take up the serious business of being married. I plan to enjoy every moment.

The flat is still in its early stages, but I've seen the sales model. It looks like a set in a movie. In its media room, the TV screen takes up an entire wall. Bidets gleam in every bathroom. Could anything be further from this dear old house with its water-stained plaster walls, the banyan saplings growing between cracks in the terrace bricks? When Rajat drives me from the crooked alleys of North Kolkata to check on the progress of the flat, I feel disoriented, like a time traveler.

After the ceremony, at Pia's insistence, the group gathers on the veranda overlooking the garden. Pia arranges everyone on chairs: Bimal and Sarojini in the center, Rajat and Korobi flanking them. (Boy-girl-boy-girl, Pia instructs.) Mr. and Mrs. Bose stand behind. Pia is a finicky photographer. People must angle their heads according to her dictates. They must either gaze into the distance, faces benevolent as buddhas, or look meaningfully into each other's eyes. She tells the grandparents to hold hands; taken aback by her demand, they do as she says. Under the pretext of bringing lime sherbet and cashew nuts, the servants venture into the frame, for how can there be a family portrait without them? Pia lets them stay. An ice-cream man passes by the gate. The tinkle of his cart bell becomes part of the picture, as do the smells of the engagement lunch: cauliflower khichuri, sautéed pumpkin (Cook is given to sudden, wild improvisations), rice pudding sweetened with palm molasses, and, yes, scorched fish-fry.

Pia will be particularly proud of this photograph. She will make her father mail copies to all their relatives, even those she will never meet. She will hang an enlargement in her family's drawing room, next to their Jamini Roy original, despite her mother's remonstrations. A copy will go on the first page of the new photo album that Rajat gave her, along with the camera. She will title it *Happiness*. Even after certain events come to pass and Mrs. Bose removes the enlargement from their wall, Pia will keep her copy. Late afternoons, when her mother thinks she is doing homework, she will remove the album from the back of her closet and run her fingers over the photograph, over the minuscule, innocent smiles fixed on the faces of her subjects.

After lunch, the adults rest under the fan on the veranda. Grandmother passes around a crystal dish holding silvered cardamom seeds, specially ordered from Bara Bazaar, to freshen the breath. Pia disappears into the overgrown garden to take more photos. For the moment, Rajat and I have no further duties and are free to walk up and down the oleander drive.

"Cara," Rajat says, "there's something I've been waiting to tell you. I've come up with an exciting idea for the business. I want you to know before I tell anyone else."

Rajat works for his father, managing orders, doing the accounting, handling the fancy clients. He's been doing it for the last couple of months. He had another job before that, business development in a big multinational, but then his father needed him.

"I want to start a website where customers can see the entire range of our products and buy them online. What do you think?"

I don't know much about websites—I'm studying history—but I'm touched that Rajat trusts me with his vulnerable, newborn vision. That he's watching me with some anxiety, waiting for my verdict. It means more to me than all the love words he's spoken.

I reach for his hand. "It's a wonderful idea." We walk for a while that way, fingers clasped, too happy to need to speak.

On the veranda, the men discuss politics. At another time, I'd be more interested, but right now, walking hand in hand with Rajat, I feel too complete to care much. Grandfather says that it's a good thing our city's name has finally been changed back to Kolkata from that anglicized version the British saddled us with. But Papa points out the change is costing the state millions of rupees because all the documentation has to match the new name. It's more important to deal with the unrest in the city—there's certainly been a lot of it lately. Remember last month when militants attacked the American Center?

"Ah, yes, those Muslims. A violent lot. Did you hear about the incident on the train today in Gujarat? All those Hindu pilgrims they burned to death?"

"Tragic," Papa replies. "I hope it doesn't lead to more bloodshed."

Rajat, who hasn't been paying attention to the conversation, says, "It's going to be a challenge. People here aren't used to buying things over the Internet. We'll have to make the website attractive and easy to navigate. Do you think you could help me? Maybe take a graphics course?"

"Of course!" I am flattered at being asked. I imagine the site I'm going to create, vibrant with flashing images of art. As soon as I can, I'll study all the details of the Boses' business so I can do a good job for Rajat. Maybe I'll pay a visit to their Park Street gallery, as Maman has been inviting me to do.

Farther down the drive, Pia makes Asif pose against the Mercedes for a photo.

"Your driver—isn't he Muslim?" I hear Grandfather say. "If I were you, I wouldn't have him taking my family around, nights and all."

I cringe. I can feel displeasure emanating from Papa. But he says politely, "Asif is very trustworthy."

"You think I'm prejudiced, don't you? You're too young, you haven't seen what I saw—the Partition riots, right here in Kolkata, men chopped to pieces on the streets with hansulis—"

"Please!" Grandmother entreats. "Let's not discuss such bad-luck matters today."

Grandfather looks thunderous at being interrupted, and Papa says quickly, "Roy moshai, do consider attending the party tonight."

Grandfather shakes his head. "I told you, Bose-babu, all that singing-dancing-alcohol-drinking—you know I don't approve. You're better off without me. But there's something I do want to tell you before you leave. I asked our family priest for an auspicious wedding date for the children—and there's a perfect one, the stars well aligned, in three months. I'd like the marriage to take place then."

I stare at him in shock. He wants us to get married in three months? Has he gone crazy? That's far too soon, and besides, he hasn't even consulted Rajat or me! Glancing at Rajat, I see that he, too, is taken aback. Beneath the surprise, is he delighted or distraught? I can't tell. It strikes me that perhaps I don't know my fiancé as well as I thought I did.

"Are you sure you want the wedding to take place so quickly?" Papa says. "I thought we'd decided that Korobi should finish another year of college first."

Grandfather sounds tired. "Bose-babu, I'm an old man. Who knows how long I'll be around? I want to see my only granddaughter settled before I go. You'll let Korobi continue her studies after the wedding, will you not?"

I want Papa to argue, to declare that this is a terrible idea, but for some reason I can't fathom, he merely says, in his courteous manner, "Of course we will." When Maman starts to protest that three months won't give her enough time to plan a proper wedding, Papa lays a gentle hand on her arm.

"I want you to announce it at the reception tonight," Grandfather says.

"It shall be as you wish, Bose-babu."

I stare at them all, outraged. Do they think that they can pick up my life like a ball of dough and roll it into whatever shape they fancy? I'm about to speak out, but just then Rajat pulls me behind the leafy cover of the oleanders and clasps me close for an audacious kiss that leaves me breathless.

"That was a bombshell, wasn't it? But Grandfather's right! Now that we belong to each other, why should we put off our happiness?"

My heart knocks about like a caught bird. In the face of his obvious joy, I don't know how to explain to Rajat that although I love him, I'm upset at being pushed into something I'm not quite ready for.

"We'll celebrate at our own private party tonight after the guests leave," he whispers against my throat. But I suddenly feel I'm not ready for that, either.

As soon as the Mercedes backs out of our driveway, I confront Grandfather. "How could you do this without checking with me!"

"It is a very auspicious date. That's important. I want to make sure your marriage is luckier than your mother's."

"But, Grandfather, surely there are other auspicious dates later. I need more time!"

He shakes his head and starts to turn away.

I put my hand on his arm, unwilling to give up, but he says tiredly, "Not now, Korobi."

His skin has a yellow cast; his eyes are red-veined. He lists a little as he makes his way into the house. Worry pricks me, and I swallow my anger for the moment. I'll let him rest. But I'm not going to let him rush me into the biggest event of my life.

Grandmother looks concerned. "I had better get your grandfather his heartburn medicine. You lie down, shona, and get some rest before your big party." She picks up the crystal dish of cardamom seeds. In a moment she, too, will disappear after him.

"Grandma, wait! I've got to talk to you!"

"I know you must be taken aback by your grandfather's decision. I was, too. Maybe we can discuss it with him after he wakes up—"

I blurt out the words because there's no good way to say them. "Someone was in my room last night. I think it was—my mother."

I wait for Grandmother to dismiss my foolish notions with a laugh and send me off to bed, but she pales and takes a step back. The crystal dish falls from her hand and shatters; tiny silver balls go flying over the veranda.

"Why do you think that?" she whispers.

"I felt it." Even to my ears, my answer sounds weak. But Grandmother accepts it. Her hands are trembling.

"Did it—she—say anything to you?"

I shake my head, disconcerted. I had no idea that my pragmatic grandmother believed so strongly in ghosts. But even if she did, why would the thought of her dead daughter's spirit agitate her like this? I realize that I don't want to know the answer.

"Maybe I imagined it."

"Maybe you did," Grandmother says, but without conviction.

"I'll go lie down now."

"You do that."

"You rest, too."

"Yes."

But when I look back from the doorway, she is still standing among the broken glass, scattered cardamom seeds surrounding her like a field of frozen tears.

TWO

In the white marble hall of the hotel, I'm waltzing with Rajat. The music is a river and we're dancing in it. It winds against our bodies, muscular as a serpent. Rajat holds me close, palm pressed against my chiffon back. And that is good because I might otherwise float away. On my own I am a clumsy dancer, but Rajat makes me feel elegant and unabashed. Wherever my eyes fall, guests are appraising us. Beside the piano, the diaphanous windows, the sleek, polished bar, the hand-painted urns crowded with blossoms, the overflow of gifts on tables inlaid with ivory. Guests whisper to each other as they raise their glasses and smile. I'm unused to such scrutiny, but I hold myself tall and allow Rajat to twirl me around. My long hair, which I shampooed and powdered with glitter and left loose, streams behind me. My collarbones rise like wings from the daring neckline of my kurti. My shoulders shine. Some of the smiles are serrated as knives. I feel them on the nape of my neck.

There is in particular a slender girl in silver with a beautiful, pale face, an intense mascara glare. I've never seen her before, but I know right away who she is. Sonia. Mimi, seething when she discovered that Rajat was seeing me, had told me about Sonia.

"He used to be crazy about her, and no wonder. She's the most gorgeous girl I've seen—and she has style! Buys all her clothes abroad, belongs to the most expensive clubs. We'd see them together at parties and think how perfect they looked together. I bet he's sorry he broke up with her." She looked at me and shook her head. "You were just lucky you caught him on the rebound."

The venom in her voice had startled me. It was my first experience of being hated because of good fortune. I walked away with what dignity I could muster so Mimi—who had been the closest I'd had to a friend—wouldn't see how hurt I was. Not just by her words—but also by Rajat's silence. Over the next month, I waited for him to bring Sonia up, but he said nothing. When I asked about old sweethearts, he kissed me hard and said they weren't important.

I can tell that Rajat has noticed Sonia, too. He pulls me closer. Against my forehead, his cheek is hot. I can feel the uneven jerk of a pulse. Should I say something? Is it better to pretend I don't know what's going on? I'm saved from making a decision: by the time we swing around again, she is gone. But I know I can't afford to forget her.

The party has just begun, but already it is a success. Many celebrities have arrived and seem in no hurry to leave. Maman is pleased, though she is too sophisticated to exhibit this. She beckons to me as soon as the music ends. I can feel the satisfaction in her fingertips as she straightens my diamond necklace. She leads me to a prosperous-bellied man in a Nehru suit.

"Korobi, I want you to meet Mr. Bhattacharya. He has been a most generous supporter of Barua and Bose Galleries."

From her tone I understand how important he is. I keep still as he holds my hand in his fleshy one a little too long.

"Charming girl. Almost as beautiful as her mother-in-law!"

"Mr. Bhattacharya! The things you say! But I believe congratulations are in order for you, too. I hear that you've been named as a candidate of the Akhil Bharat Hindu Party for the upcoming elections. We must have a celebration."

Mr. Bhattacharya gives a deprecatory shrug. "Nothing is official yet. It would be unwise to celebrate prematurely. But tell me more about this lovely young lady. Is she really the great-granddaughter of Judge Tarak Prasad Roy, the one who had a street named after him?"

"She is, indeed."

"Excellent match, Mrs. Bose. So important to create alliances with the right kind of people."

I am beginning to feel a little like a prize dog, but I valiantly hold on to my smile.

"People who uphold our sanaatan Hindu traditions," Bhattacharya continues with enthusiasm. "Exactly what my party is working to promote. Don't the Roys have an ancient Durga temple on their property? I heard that Netaji himself is said to have visited it to get the goddess's blessing in his battle against the British. Oh, Mr. Roy is not here? I must meet him. You will arrange it?"

"Of course, Mr. Bhattacharya. We'll do it as soon as possible."

They go on to discuss business matters—something about new investments. Mrs. Bhattacharya, a thin woman with darting eyes, reaches out to touch my necklace. Her fingers remind me of pincers.

"Lovely, lovely. Where did your mother-in-law-to-be get this? . . . Of course. Nothing but the very best for our Mrs. Bose." She moves closer and speaks in conspiratorial tones. "Mrs. Bose must be so relieved. Our Rajat was getting to be quite a handful. Running around with the wrong crowd. Drinking, gambling, who knows what else! My husband was ready to speak with Mr. Bose about it. He's an important man, after all. He has to be careful about who he associates with. Now, if I were you, I'd keep close tabs— Oh, here comes your sweetie! Hello, dear Rajat! I was just congratulating your betrothed on her good fortune."

Rajat's smile matches Mrs. Bhattacharya's in affability, though his eyes, like hers, are cold. "The good fortune is entirely mine."

Further pleasantries are exchanged; Mrs. Bhattacharya skitters away in search of more promising bait. Waiters in turbans surround us with silver trays of shish kebabs and samosas and Western delights I don't recognize. Rajat fills a plate for me, but I can't eat; that awful woman has stolen my appetite. More waiters come by, carrying drinks. Thin wine flutes on long stems, pale yellow, deep maroon, hoarding the light that spills down from the chandeliers. Squat crystal glasses filled with whiskey, sweating amber. I've never drunk alcohol—Grandfather would have had a fit at the very possibility—so Rajat waves the waiters away. But tonight, contrarily, I want something.

Rajat looks surprised, then amused.

"Bring the lady a piña colada."

I'm enchanted by the sweet, smooth taste, the pineapple flavor so unlike what my friends led me to expect. I ask for another, and then a third, but Rajat stops me.

"Easy, Cara! It's more potent than it seems. Try a little of this quiche instead."

Through the pleasant buzz in my head, I appreciate his caring. I could go through all the time allotted to us like this, my sheer chiffon back pressed against his solicitous palm. Mrs. Bhattacharya is a shriveled gossip, jealous of our happiness. And as for Sonia, now that I'm engaged and have the right, I'll ask Rajat for the full story on her as soon as we're alone.

But that will not be for a while, because Papa is on the dais, calling us. The clapping sounds like a thousand small explosions. I climb the steps, wishing my grandparents were with me at this special moment. With the wish comes a stab of guilt.

Before leaving for the reception, I'd gone to see them to say good night. I was feeling happy and excited—in my bedroom mirror, the off-the-shoulder kurti, glittering like gossamer, made me look more sophisticated than ever before. I'd decided to wait until tomorrow to bring up the issue of pushing back the marriage date. I didn't want an argument to mar the evening, my special, magical party. I expected a tart comment from Grandfather—he liked me to wear saris. I wasn't too worried, though. I knew he was proud of my looks, and tonight I looked my best. But when I went up to hug him good-bye, the fury on his face floored me.

"Are you planning to go out wearing that—*thing*?"

Grandmother jumped in, attempting damage control. "Why do you say that? It's what young people wear nowadays. Shona, you look like an oleander in that deep red."

"No, she doesn't!" His lips were a pressed white line. "She looks like a—call girl."

Perhaps it was the accumulated stress of the day, the unanswered questions from last night. Perhaps it was because he had snatched away my simple joy in my new clothes and made me feel cheap. Suddenly, I was furious, too.

"It's always what you want that's important—do you ever think of what might make other people happy? Like moving the wedding day forward—did you even think to ask me before you made such a big decision? I was going to beg you to reconsider. But now I'm actually glad. This way I can get away quicker from you!"

He'd been shocked at my outburst—we'd argued before, but never like this. For a moment, his face was drained of color. Then it turned dark and he shouted back, "Go, then! Go right now. And don't you dare come back. Why, you're no different from—"

Grandmother, her voice unsteady, interrupted, "I hear Bahadur calling. It's time to leave for the hotel. Go on down." She pushed me toward the door.

The memory of the fight floods my mouth with its bitter, burnt taste even as I stand on the dais beside my new family, smiling for the cameras. I wish I hadn't lost my temper. Grandfather only wanted to protect me, to make me do what he thought was the right thing. But now it'll take me forever to cajole him out of his bad humor because he isn't one to forgive transgressions easily. I find it hard to concentrate on Papa's speech, and even Rajat's, though once in a while unexpected words leap from him like sparks. *Deeply grateful. Soul mate.* He must feel my tenseness because, as he speaks, he gives my fingers a reassuring squeeze to indicate I'm not alone. Whatever I have to face, he'll face with me.

When Rajat holds my hand like this, all my problems recede. I think, Mimi was right about one thing: I really am lucky.

Rajat ends by announcing that we're to be married in three months. As the room erupts in applause, he turns to me and bows. Most men would not be able to pull off that bow, but Rajat does it regally.

At least one good thing has come out of my fight with Grandfather. I'm no longer upset at the thought of getting married so fast. My place is with Rajat, and I'm ready to take it.

Mrs. Bose sweeps down the hall resplendent in her brocade designer sari, greeting her guests. She inclines her head gracefully and speaks in an attractive, raspy voice that makes each person feel essential to the evening's success. They have no idea that inside her head the elegant Jayashree Bose is far away.

Mrs. Bose is remembering her own engagement party—the one she never had. Mrs. Bose's father, who owned a failing handicrafts store, could not afford one, and Mr. Bose's father, who was one of Kolkata's leading surgeons and could have afforded a score of parties, was furious that his son had chosen—no, had been *entrapped* by—a girl so far beneath their station. *A shopkeeper's scheming daughter.* If she shuts her eyes, Mrs. Bose can still see the distaste that had twisted her father-in-law's handsome mouth as he spoke the words.

They'd been waiting outside his chambers because her fiancé wanted her to meet him, insisting that once his father saw her, he would come around. It had been an ill-advised move, to face him in his stronghold. He walked past them even as Mr. Bose was talking to him. Shaking off his son's grasp, he spat on the sidewalk, close enough to Mrs. Bose's feet that she jumped back in shock. None of the words of love and apology that Mr. Bose offered her afterward could keep her from feeling besmirched.

So many years, and Mrs. Bose hasn't been able to wash away the memory of that spit. Every designer outfit she has bought since then, every grand party she has thrown, every expensive flat she's moved to, every risky maneuver she has undertaken to push their business up another rung on the slippery ladder of success—it's all been to show that man, though he's been dead for years, what a shopkeeper's daughter can achieve.

"Lovely decor, Mrs. Bose!" Plump Mrs. Ahuja, wife of a textile tycoon, breaks into her thoughts, waving emerald-studded fingers. "But then, you always have such good taste. Is it true that you've designed the young couple's flat, too? I'd love to take a look!"

"Of course you must, as soon as it's completed. But I can't take any credit for tonight. My decorator did it all."

Here Mrs. Bose is being disingenuous. This last month, she has spent several evenings closeted with the decorator, reducing the woman on more than one occasion to the verge of tears.

"You wouldn't . . . ?" Mrs. Ahuja pauses. In their milieu, the names of decorators are almost as secret as those of plastic surgeons.

Mrs. Bose smiles magnanimously. "I'd be happy to give you her number. Your niece's marriage is coming up, no? She'll be perfect for that."

Mrs. Ahuja gushes with gratitude until Mrs. Bose adroitly steers her toward a group of chattering women and takes her leave.

Mrs. Bose is ashamed of her obsession with proving herself. She wishes she could get past it, let it go, but she also recognizes that without it she couldn't have turned their business around. It fueled her through those exhausting early years when she toiled at her father's store. It helped her develop a sixth sense as to which artists were up-and-coming, and the charisma to sweet-talk them into signing exclusive agreements with her. Slowly, the Boses began to sell Bengal art—first across India, then to Europe and America. They developed a reputation for dependability and quality. Look at the properties they own now: the Park Street gallery, the warehouse near Sealdah, the New York operation. Their penthouse occupies the entire top floor of a building bordering Rabindra Sarobar. From her bedroom window, Mrs. Bose can see the lotuses on the morning lake, the long, low boats filled with rowers.

When Mr. Bose's father was dying, he sent word. Could he see his son one last time? He didn't mention his daughter-in-law.

"I won't go unless you agree, Joyu," Mr. Bose said.

Mrs. Bose, who does not believe in self-deception, knows she has many flaws. She drives a hard bargain. She cares too much for social acclaim. She is quick to take offense though smart enough to hide it. She seldom forgets or forgives and rarely trusts. But on that day, looking at the painful pucker between Mr. Bose's brows, she was surprised to discover something new about herself: for her family's happiness, she was willing to sacrifice her pride.

She had taken him by the hand and led him to the door. "Go, Shanto. I don't want you to have any regrets."

For her family's happiness. Isn't that why she has thrown this lavish party today, in spite of certain recent financial problems, to welcome the girl Rajat has chosen to be his wife?

Deep down, Mrs. Bose has her reservations about Korobi. Not that she dislikes her—she's a sweet girl, charmingly unspoiled. But it's as though she's been living in a different century. Mrs. Bose will have to invest significant energy in molding her to fit into their milieu. Sonia, now, she thinks with a pang of regret—she was stubborn and spoiled, so that sometimes Mrs. Bose wanted to shake her, but she comported herself perfectly. And she knew everybody worth knowing. In the few months that she had been with Rajat, she had brought several of her parents' friends over to the gallery, which had led to a number of big sales. Moreover, she had spirit. When she and Rajat quarreled, she held her own. Korobi, Mrs. Bose fears, will crumple like tinfoil.

But it's no use moping over what might have been, Mrs. Bose thinks as she continues greeting guests with her best smile. Something had occurred between Sonia and Rajat, something he wouldn't talk about. It had pushed him into a period of black moods and huge risks that had terrified Mrs. Bose. She'd been at her wit's end when he met Korobi. What spell did the girl cast on him? Within weeks, he stopped spending his evenings with his drunken, club-going friends. He quit a job that looked fancy but was going nowhere and started working for the family business. Most of all, he was happy again. Just for that, Mrs. Bose is grateful to Korobi.

The waltz has ended; in a few minutes, the guests will be seated and the toasts will begin. Mr. Ghosh, the hotel manager, is waiting for her at the entrance to the dining hall. Mrs. Bose is distracted by a twinge of disapproval—she has just glimpsed Rajat pulling a laughing Korobi to the dark privacy of the terrace. But she collects herself and compliments Mr. Ghosh on the tables, which are just as she wanted, sophisticated without being showy: rich, white tablecloths, gold-edged plates, white-orchid centerpieces sending a faint sweetness through the room.

Then she sees Shikha, her personal assistant, hovering behind him, and feels a frisson of worry. Shikha, who has been with her for over a decade, does not hover without cause.

"Phone call, madam."

She takes the cordless hotel phone from Shikha, who is biting her lip. Mrs. Bose wonders if it could be Sonia. She had noticed her earlier this evening in the dance hall—she must have slipped the checkers at the entrance a hefty bribe. Mrs. Bose, angered by the girl's audacity (but a little impressed, too) had been about to instruct Mr. Ghosh to alert the security guards, but then Sonia had disappeared.

"Hello? Hello? Calling from Pantheon Hospital. Trying to reach Miss Korobi Roy."

The connection is bad. The words rise out of a roar of static and plunge back into it. Grandfather. Heart attack. Unconscious. Must come soon.

Mrs. Bose disconnects the phone and hands it to Shikha. She looks longingly at the stage in the front of the room, a gorgeous construction of silks and crystal beads, from which the family is to offer toasts. Pia has been practicing her speech for days, raising a champagne flute filled with apple juice with a jaunty flourish. The apex of the evening—and now it's ruined. Oh, why couldn't the old man have given them one more hour!

Shikha holds the phone, waiting; her eyes glisten intently as she watches Mrs. Bose. Mrs. Bose suspects Shikha knows what is going on inside her head—the girl understands her even better than her husband does. Ever since Mrs. Bose discreetly helped out with a certain situation that Shikha's unmarried younger sister had found herself in, Shikha has been bulldog loyal to Mrs. Bose. She pauses a moment, wondering if she could ask Shikha to bring back the phone after the toasts are done so that Mrs. Bose can pretend she just received the call from the hospital. Shikha would certainly comply. No one would ever learn the truth. Imagining the look of disappointment that will crumple Pia's face if her toast is canceled, Mrs. Bose is tempted. After all, the old man is already unconscious. What difference would it make to Korobi?

But Mrs. Bose can't do that to her. The child is devoted to that difficult old man. She draws in a deep breath, pulls herself up tall, makes her decision with some regret.

"Inform Mr. Bose of what has happened. Tell him he should ask the guests to begin dinner. Then have Asif bring the car to the side entrance. I'll go and find Korobi."

I protest as Rajat pulls me into the seductive darkness of the terrace. "Stop! We have to go back to the guests. What will your parents think?"

"It was pure self-defense. Didn't you see all those aunties, closing in on us like barracuda?"

I can't help laughing. That's one of the things I love about him—he makes me laugh more than anyone else ever has. As though it were a signal, Rajat begins kissing me. I give myself over to the pleasure of those kisses—I'm not sure for how long. Those rash piña coladas have skewed my sense of time. But slowly I begin to feel that something's different. Rajat is more aggressive; his tongue parts my lips expertly and explores my mouth. His hand caresses my breast, and it's as if I were driving fast along a road that has suddenly, sharply dropped out of sight. Even as my body responds, I'm disconcerted. Something has changed between us.

I remember the kiss that had begun our courtship. It was a couple of weeks after we'd met at Mimi's. Rajat had been in a pensive mood that evening, perhaps because of the rain falling around us, misty, silken. We were walking in the Victoria Memorial gardens among the white roses, almost alone because of the weather.

"I shouldn't have brought you here," he said. "Look at your clothes, your hair—soaked."

I told him I didn't mind.

"That's what I love about you. You're so easygoing." Then he kissed me.

Later, Mimi said that he must have been thinking of Sonia, who never liked the outdoors, not even in good weather, and could you blame her? The outdoors was infested with spiders and wasps and snakes, everyone knew that. But Mimi was wrong. Rajat couldn't have been thinking of another woman, not when he kissed me like that.

He had pressed his lips to my forehead, just below the hairline, the gentlest gesture, as far from passion as a sunset is from fire. He kept them there for a long time. I held my breath. I could see him kissing me like that when we were old. That was the first time I was able to imagine a future for us beyond what the girls in college whispered about, gorgeous trousseaux and movie-style honeymoons. That vision had made me fall in love.

This change tonight—is it because we're so close to getting married? Or did seeing Sonia trigger something in Rajat?

I take a deep breath and plunge in. "Was that Sonia in the silver outfit?"

In the dark, I can't see his expression. He's silent for so long that I expect him to say he doesn't know what I'm talking about.

At last he exhales heavily. "I've done some stupid things in the past, Cara. One of these days I'll tell you about them. But I don't want to ruin this evening. I still can't believe that we finally belong to each other. That we'll be married in just a few weeks. This means we need to decide where to go for our honeymoon. What would you like? Mountains? Foreign cities with lots of shopping? Casinos and nightclubs?"

He's changing the topic, I see that. I let him. It's a once-in-a-lifetime evening. I don't want to ruin it any more than he does.

"How about the ocean? I've never been to the ocean." Am I thinking of my dream? I don't know.

"Okay. We could fly to Goa. Lovely beaches there, and lots of nightlife, too. Or there's Lakshadweep, quite spectacular. And very private." He kisses my hand, lips lingering on my palm, then takes my fingers into his mouth, sending a shiver through me.

"I don't want anything expensive. Your family has already spent so much on this reception, and now the wedding's coming up sooner than we expected. Just a couple of days someplace close would be fine." I search for a name I heard Mimi and her friends mention once, when they were talking about fun weekends. "How about Digha? Isn't that just a few hours' drive from Kolkata?"

"I hate that place! It's low class."

I'm startled by his vehemence and mortified as well. Mimi had said she'd found Digha charming. Apparently I'll have to learn to evaluate things more stringently, now that I'm about to become a Bose.

"I'll let you choose," I say, and am rewarded with a hug.

"I'll pick the perfect honeymoon spot. You'll love it, Cara. And you'll love tonight—our own little after-party."

His lips are hot on my bare shoulder. He presses into me. I'm suddenly afraid of what tonight might hold.

In the darkness someone clears her throat loudly, announcing her presence. Startled and embarrassed, I try to pull away, but Rajat holds me to his side.

It's Maman, just as I'd feared. Even in the half dark, I can see how rigidly she holds her body. I can't blame her for being angry. But when she calls Rajat's name, her voice is weighted down with some larger problem.

"What is it, Maman?"

She tells us. Her words slash to pieces the world I've known.

Rajat clenches his teeth as the Mercedes hurtles down the night streets toward the hospital, bucking and rattling across potholes because he has impressed upon Asif that speed is more important than comfort or even the welfare of the car. Bands of light from the street shiver over them, followed by striations of darkness. Glistening with tears, Cara's face materializes in the corner, then disappears, then materializes again in a beautiful, hypnotic pattern. "Why is there so much traffic this late at night?" she says, clenching her fists, when they are forced to slow down behind a truck loaded high with bales of cotton. But Rajat guesses that she's really asking another question, *Why should this terrible thing happen to us?* He doesn't know how to answer it because it is his question, too. *Why should this happen to us today of all days?* Her distress fills the car. When he glances at her, his chest feels as if someone were squeezing it in an iron fist. For the first time in his life, he's learning one of love's tragedies: no matter how much you want to suffer in your loved one's stead, you cannot take away her pain.

Earlier, when he helped her into the car, Cara said, "It's my fault. I fought with him and brought this on." He told her it wasn't true, she wasn't thinking straight; but he was shaken by the conviction in her voice. He tried to put his arm around her to comfort her—then, and later again. On each occasion she moved it politely away. It was the politeness that defeated him. Had she pushed his hand off, had she screamed at him to leave her alone as Sonia would have done, he would have been able to gather her to his chest and hush her.

He tries to imagine Bimal Roy lying in the hospital close to death; he tries to summon up concern for his helpless, furious pain. He knows how terrified Sarojini must be, handling the crisis all by herself. Rajat has always respected the stubborn old man for his crusty intelligence. He holds Sarojini in genuine affection. But today he can't seem to feel anything except a baffled anger against the universe that it would ruin the happiest occasion of his life like this—and that, too, after he'd prayed in the temple, asking for forgiveness and promising to be true to Cara.

The car jerks to a stop at an intersection. The sudden movement makes Rajat dizzy. He hasn't eaten properly all day. At the engagement lunch he had pushed the food around his plate, though usually he loves the traditional dishes that Cook prepares. Since morning, Sonia had left five messages on his mobile; anger at this invasion had curdled his stomach. That woman, why couldn't she take no for an answer? In her last message, she said, "You're rushing into a mistake you'll regret all your life." Now random thoughts assail him. The memory of other things she had said to him in that husky voice, how much he'd loved it once. And was it a bad omen, this heart attack occurring in the middle of the engagement party? Oh, he's being as superstitious as a peasant! He shouldn't have had so many drinks. But it had shocked him to see Sonia at the engagement party, that she'd managed to get in.

The car jolts to a standstill again. A group of partygoers, young men in narrow pants and shiny nylon shirts, has wandered into the middle of the street, making Asif miss his green light. Cara makes a panicked sound in her throat that leaves Rajat feeling helpless.

"Come on, Asif!" he exclaims in annoyance. "Can't you do better than this?"

The news of the heart attack must have shaken up Asif, too. Uncharacteristically, he rolls down the window to shout at the young men. They shout back expletives. One of them thumps the hood. Another one grinds out his cigarette on it. For a moment Rajat is afraid that they'll be embroiled in a fight.

That would not be good. In Communist-run Kolkata, the pedestrian is king. Public sentiment against cars—especially expensive foreign ones—runs high. If there's a fight, onlookers would automatically take the side of the partygoers. Just a month ago an acquaintance of Rajat's had been in an incident. His car had stopped at a busy intersection when a woman walked too close to it. Her dupatta got caught on the side mirror, and when the car moved forward, the dupatta slid off the woman's shoulder. She accused him of harassing her; a crowd gathered immediately; they pulled him out of the car and, chivalrously, beat him up.

But today they're in luck. The partygoers are distracted by friends yelling from the opposite pavement for them to hurry. With a last belligerent thump, they move on.

Relief mingled with anger makes Rajat's voice sharper than usual. "That was a stupid thing to do!"

"Sorry, Saab."

In the rearview mirror, Asif flashes Rajat an accusing glance. Rajat knows Asif blames him for forcing him to rush, for the ignominy of rabble handprints on the Mercedes, for the cigarette that might as well have been ground out on Asif's skin. Why does he care so much? It's not as though it were his car.

At the other end of the seat, Rajat's fiancée is sitting straight, not crying anymore though her face is still wet. She wouldn't let him wipe it for her or even take the handkerchief he offered. Rajat wants to conjure up the tenderness he feels for her and her alone, the tenderness that is the best part of who he is. But in the colored neon lights from an electronic billboard, she is no longer his Cara. She has gone back to being Korobi, the enigmatic stranger he saw across the room at a party. Is Sonia right, has he made a mistake, rushing to tie his life to this girl? He tries to push the insidious thought away, but it circles back. It frightens him so that he has to open the window and gulp in the smell of the city, flowers and fried pavement-foods and exhaust fumes from buses with people hanging from them even at this hour. Rancid and jubilant, the city comforts him.

Tomorrow, things will look better. Tomorrow, the choices he has made will make more sense.

In the hushed ICU corridor, the lights are dim and splotchy. They must slip blue plastic covers over their shoes, spray disinfectant on their hands. The smell makes Rajat gag. Cracks in the plaster, like veins in a drunkard's eye. He tries to keep his attention on Cara's back as she hurries down the corridor, but his disobedient mind flits to the huge sum of money his mother had poured into making the evening perfect for them. Money he hadn't wanted her to spend, money they couldn't afford right now. But he always found it hard to talk to Maman about money trouble. It was the thing she was prickliest about. In all this rushing, he didn't have a chance to tell Pia where he was going. He remembers the toast she had practiced so carefully, and a sadness overtakes him, the sadness of aborted things. He sees the old man's face, crumpled around his oxygen mask. Tubes hang from his flaccid arms. How spiritedly he had argued with Papa only a few hours ago! They would all come to this, even Korobi in her agitated beauty, leaning over his bed.

Before entering the room, she asked Rajat if she could wear his jacket over her kurti.

"I should never have bought it. That's what made him so upset. And now he's in the hospital."

"It isn't your fault!" he protested again as he draped the jacket over her shoulders, but she only threw him an agonized look and retreated into that inner territory that baffled him. With Sonia there had never been this distance. With her, the lack of distance had exhausted him.

Rajat seats himself on the wooden bench beside Sarojini. Bowed into a comma, she suddenly looks frighteningly old. She rests her head against his chest and weeps a little. Rajat strokes her hair, grateful at finally being needed. Oh, the women of this family. How he loves them, with a pure and helpless love.

"Grandfather refused to give permission for an angioplasty," Sarojini says. "As soon as the medicines made him feel well enough to talk, he told the staff that he was a lawyer and he would sue them if they did anything to him against his will. All my life he's plagued me with his stubbornness! He ordered the nurses to get out. 'I'll call you if I think I'm dying,' that's what he told them. To me, he kept saying, 'I've got to see her.' But I didn't know how to get hold of you. I didn't have your phone number with me. I was so panicked, it took me a while even to remember the name of the hotel."

Leaning over in the too large jacket, Korobi looks like a child playing dress-up. She strokes the old man's ankles, blackish and puffy. In the ice-blue night-light, she is lovelier than she has ever been, and more remote.

"Grandfather, I'm here. I'm so sorry. Does it hurt a lot?"

High and shaky, her voice, too, is that of a child on her way to tears. The old man does not respond. His eyes are shut. His thin chest barely moves. The machine to the left of the bed displays waves of green and yellow on its screen. To the right, an IV stand dispenses liquid into a tube attached to the old man's arm. The steady drip of the translucent fluid is strangely comforting. Watching it, Rajat feels that something, finally, is working right. And not just here. On every floor of the hospital, in every room darkened for rest or blinding bright with emergency, the machines, untiring, so much more reliable than the frail human body, are doing their job. He allows the IV's rhythm to pull him into an amphibious space between sleep and waking where nothing is required of him.

Suddenly Sarojini gives a cry that startles Rajat into consciousness. He sees the old man struggling with his oxygen mask, trying to pull it off. Sarojini rushes to the bed.

"Stop it, you! Stop it right now. Hei Bhagaban, he'll be the death of me yet."

She jabs at the button for the nurse, shouts to Rajat to help her. Still in a daze, Rajat makes it to the bed and pins down the old man's wrists. The old man is no match for Rajat, but his eyes plead so furiously that Rajat's hands slacken. The old man needs to say something crucial to Korobi before he dies. Rajat knows he has no right to keep him from that.

The oxygen mask is off now and dangling from a tube. The old man fights to sit up, gasping, choking. Korobi hurries to kneel at his side. She tries to smooth the wrinkles from his forehead.

"Please don't strain yourself, Grandfather. You'll have another attack. Please lie down. You can tell me later, when you're stronger."

The old man whispers something that Rajat can't hear.

A guilty look flashes across Korobi's face. "Oh, no, don't say that. I'm the one who's sorry. The engagement ceremony put too much strain on you. And then I upset you with my clothes. I'll never wear this outfit again. I promise. And I didn't mean what I—"

But the old man keeps mumbling. His eyes seem to have lost the ability to focus. They stare blankly past Korobi's shoulder at the wall's grayness. His lips open and close stiffly, like a marionette's. Then his gaze fixes on something, making Korobi glance nervously over her shoulder. By the time she turns back, his head has lolled forward like a flower on a broken stalk. Two nurses run in; a doctor follows. They try various resuscitation procedures that Rajat watches in horrified fascination. But they all know it's too late. Bimal Prasad Roy, barrister, whose acerbic words had, for so many years, intimidated family members, clients, and those lawyers foolhardy enough to oppose him in court, has relinquished speech forever.

Death demands certain homages from the living, and into these Rajat dives with relief. He chastises the medical staff for negligence; makes arrangements with the funeral service for the body to be picked up the next day; calls his mother to inform her that he will stay at Korobi's tonight; and phones Sarojini's home to sternly order a blubbering Cook to get some food ready. In the car, he sits between the two women. Sarojini sobs into the fisted edge of her sari until, exhausted, she lays her head on Rajat's shoulder and closes her eyes. Korobi sits upright, staring mutinously out of the window. But after an hour of being stalled in a traffic jam by road construction (at midnight!), she wilts against him. Now she is asleep, head wedged under his chin, mouth slightly open, a hand clutching his coat lapel. A sudden pothole causes her to butt her head against his chin, making him bite his tongue. He can taste the salt of blood. He doesn't mind.

Sleep, Cara. I'll take care of you.

THREE

Stillness has invaded 26 Tarak Prasad Roy Road, the stillness of a fairy tale where dark magic has cast the kingdom into a waking dream. In all the fifty-five years Sarojini has lived here with Bimal, she can't remember feeling adrift like this, not even after Anu's death. The others, too, seem to be lost. Cook stands at the kitchen karhai, staring at the potato curry until it grows charred. Bahadur watches the gardener boy overwater the oleanders, but where are the succulent curses into which he would usually have launched? And Korobi, who has not been to college since that night of death, spends her days in bed, leafing through the musty books she has taken from her grandfather's library. The household has given up on breakfast, even the sacrosanct cup of morning tea. If Rajat, who comes by each evening, hadn't insisted on having dinner here, that meal, too, might have disappeared.

If it weren't for Rajat, what would have happened to them? Sarojini wonders in gratitude. Each evening he enters the house brisk as a sea wind. He plans the next day's menu and gives Bahadur shopping instructions. He checks whether the utility bills have been paid, whether Sarojini has enough diabetes medicine. He cajoles the women into walking around the garden with him. Best of all, he doesn't try to fill the silence with small talk.

The newspapers that Bimal Roy scrutinized each morning have piled up, unread, on the drawing-room table. Cocooned in shock, the household remains ignorant of the Godhra riots and their aftermath, raging along the western edge of the country. Even if they had known, would the incidents have penetrated their numbness? The sorrows of others seem so distant compared to our own.

Among all this torpor, Sarojini alone cannot seem to rest. She opens the doors of spare rooms she has not visited in years. She peers into the dark, cool pantry that smells of palm-date molasses, which Bimal had loved. Tonight, once the rest of the household has collapsed into sleep, she goes into the bedroom she has shared all these years with Bimal, removes his clothes from the almirah, and searches under the newspapers lining the shelves.

Sarojini knows, guiltily, that Rajat would be upset if he knew what she was doing. He has asked her to stay away from this room, to sleep with Korobi. Much as she loves Korobi, Sarojini dislikes this arrangement. The girl is a restless sleeper, kicking her own pillows off the bed and then reaching for Sarojini's, jolting her from uneasy dreams. Once awake, Sarojini cannot fall asleep again because the room is too quiet, devoid of Bimal's disruptive snores.

There's nothing under the lining. A disappointed Sarojini turns, then catches her reflection in the floor-length, oval mirror. It startles her: a woman so colorless that she is almost transparent. White sari, bereft of the bright borders that she has always favored. Bare forehead, wiped clean of the vermilion of wifehood. Bare wrists, ears, neck, the jewelry jumbled into a drawer until someone—but who, now that Bimal is gone?—remembers to take it to the bank. Out of old habit the woman in the mirror pushes phantom bangles up her arm, then shakes her head with an embarrassed laugh.

If Sarojini stands in front of the mirror long enough and unfocuses her eyes the right way, the woman's image fades. Instead, Bimal appears in front of her. Sometimes he is knobby and querulous, as in recent months, waiting for her to peel him his after-dinner oranges. Sometimes he gives her a lopsided, newly married smile that takes her breath away. Today he is dressed in a cream kurta with an elaborate paisley design. When she sees that, Sarojini begins to shake. That was the kurta he had worn the night their daughter died.

What's the right thing for me to do now, Bimal? Should I tell Korobi?

She wants a sign to guide her. But his face is frozen into the shocked expression it wore eighteen years ago. His eyes are furious with loss.

The truth is like a mountain of iron pressing on my chest. Still, I'm willing to bear it. If only I could be sure that it's the best thing for Korobi—

He had thrown away the kurta after that night, in spite of its having been one of his favorites, and expensive. He wouldn't even let her give it to Bahadur.

Tell me! All my life you insisted on making the decisions until I forgot how to think for myself. And then you leave me like this?

Tears fill her eyes. That's always been Sarojini's problem—she cries when she gets angry. When, having blinked away the wetness, she looks again, the mirror holds only her bleached, blanched self.

An unexpected by-product of Rajat's nightly visits to the Roy household is that Asif has struck up a friendship with Bahadur.

At first Asif had looked upon the Nepalese gatekeeper with disdain. Dozing by the gate in a frayed khaki uniform that had not encountered an iron in years, the old man clearly belonged to that obsolete generation of retainers whose dowdy servanthood was their entire identity. His face wreathed in a gap-toothed grin, he salaamed Rajat entirely too many times as Asif pulled onto the gravel driveway. Bahadur embodied everything Asif detested about working for the rich, everything he was determined to avoid. So he would give a curt nod in response to the old man's effusive greeting, refuse his offer of garam garam chai with spices from Kathmandu, put on a pair of fake Armani sunglasses, and pretend to sleep. Through the rolled-down window, the scent of the tea, brewed with generous helpings of milk and sugar on a kerosene stove outside the gatehouse, assailed him. A nice, hot cupful would have improved the quality of these boring, mosquito-infested evenings. But Asif didn't believe in being obligated to people unless he liked them.

One evening Bahadur knocked apologetically on the windshield. Would Asif mind moving his car? Bahadur needed to take the family vehicle out to make sure everything was working right. Asif reversed the Mercedes, scowling to make sure the old man registered his irritation. But when he saw the car Bahadur brought out of the garage, he couldn't help loping over.

"You have a Bentley! How old is it? Looks like an antique."

Bahadur scratched his head. The car had already been in the family when Bahadur was hired—what was it?—forty-four years ago. He didn't get to drive it for a long time, even though he had a license from Park Circus Auto School. The Roys—richer then—had a chauffeur just for the Bentley, a military-looking Sikh whom everyone called Sardarji. He drove old Tarak-babu wherever he needed to go. If Bahadur wasn't on gate duty, he would sit up front with Sardarji, jumping out to open the door. When Tarak-babu passed away, Bimal-babu, too, insisted on being driven only by Sardarji. Relegated to taking Sarojini-ma shopping in a cumbersome Ambassador, Bahadur began to despair of ever being allowed to handle the Bentley. He confessed that he would wish for it at night: just once to feel that steering wheel in his hands, that accelerator under his foot.

And it did happen, but not the way he had wanted it. When Anu-missybaba died, Bimal-babu went a little crazy. He cut himself off from his friends and sent Sarojini-ma and Korobi-baby to the village home, along with Cook and Bahadur. By the time they returned, the other servants—including Sardarji—were gone. Bahadur was put on double duty, both gatekeeper and driver. But guilt (had he wished this tragedy into being?) kept him from enjoying his elevated position. The first time he drove the Bentley, to take Sarojini and Korobi to the doctor, his hands shook so badly that he almost landed them in a ditch.

Asif wasn't interested in this ancient ramble, but he loved the Bentley. He'd never seen an old car that had been taken care of with such diligence. When Bahadur, noticing how reverently Asif ran his hands over the car, asked if he would like to drive it, Asif was ambushed by a boyish delight he hadn't felt in years. Seconds later, they were on the street, Asif pressing cautiously on the accelerator, Bahadur urging him on. The car ran as smooth as—Asif couldn't even imagine a simile for it. When they returned, he asked Bahadur, a trifle shyly, if he might take him up on that offer of chai. Soon they sat on the porch of the gatehouse, sipping, fanning themselves with old copies of the *Telegraph* and cursing the mosquitoes.

Over the next nights, they shared dinner—the dal and coarse chapatis that Bahadur cooked, the fancier meal that Sarojini sent out to Asif. They told each other about their faraway homes near Kathmandu and Agra and commiserated on the vagaries of fate that had landed them here; they described their loved ones—a son in Bahadur's case, a dead sister in Asif's; they fantasized about returning to their families, rich and plump, though they knew they probably never would; they listened in consternation to Bahadur's small transistor as it spouted news about the continuing massacres in Gujarat; careful not to offend each other's religious sentiments, they discussed the tragedies, concluding that it was madness. Ultimately—because that's what servants do, sooner or later, willingly or otherwise—they talked about the people who controlled so much of their lives.

Thus Asif learned that the Roy household was in trouble. The family lawyer was closeted for an entire morning with Sarojini, emerging frazzled, his thinning hair limp over his sweaty forehead. Sarojini-ma wasn't sleeping well. Often, late at night, she went into Bimal-babu's bedroom. Cook said she'd taken to talking to herself in there. They were afraid Ma was losing her mind, and then what would happen to the lot of them?

Asif, too, had news to offer: the Bose household was facing its own challenges. They didn't discuss it in front of the help, but servants always know. The expensive new American gallery they started just a year ago in New York was having money troubles. Something significant, otherwise why would Rajat-saab have sent his beloved BMW back to the dealer? And Pushpa, Memsaab's maid, who was sweet on Asif, told him the phone rang at the oddest hours, early mornings, or during dinner. If Pushpa picked it up, there was only a click.

Tonight Asif says, "I think it's Rajat-saab's old girlfriend, Sonia."

"What does she look like?"

"Expensive. Too thin, though those people think that's glamorous. Foreign-bought clothes, showing legs and all. Eye makeup that makes her look like a witch—but one of those enchantress witches. When he was with her, Rajat-saab acted like he was half-drunk all the time."

"I've seen a girl like that outside our gate," Bahadur says, startling Asif into sitting up straight. "She was driving a little foreign car, silver color."

"A Porsche. Yes, that's hers all right."

"She stared at the house a long time. I got up to ask if I could help her. But she turned those eyes on me. And then she roared away so fast, she frightened all the street dogs."

Driving Rajat home, Asif considers telling him about Sonia. Then he remembers what Pia-missy said after she met Korobi for the first time: "A.A., I think Korobi-didi is a good person. Her face has a shine to it." That was enough to put Asif, who believes Pia to be rather resplendent herself, squarely on Korobi's side. No, Asif's not going to say something stupid that might start Rajat thinking about Sonia again.

In the backseat, Rajat closes his eyes and sighs. He looks tired. Cheering up this household day after day is taking its toll on him.

"Take the Strand Road."

Asif hesitates. "Saab, that river road is empty so late at night. I hear some bad things happened there last week. One saab was driving when two cars came in front of him and two came behind. They blocked him off and forced him to stop. Broke his windows and—"

"Nonsense, A.A. Nothing will happen to us."

Hearing his secret name on Rajat's lips startles Asif into compliance. He is sure Pia-missy has never called him that in front of her family; she understands that they would frown on the casual intimacy the nickname implies. Does Rajat-saab, too, have his sources of knowledge? What else might he have learned about Asif? Concern distracts the chauffeur, who had until now believed himself to be invincible in his invisibility. He presses down on the accelerator, turning onto the deserted riverfront, into the night wind.

I lie in bed with Palgrave's *Golden Treasury of English Songs and Lyrics,* which I brought up from Grandfather's library. The funeral was three weeks ago, but it feels as though it were just yesterday Grandfather exited my life like a bullet, leaving a bleeding hole behind. I swing between numbness and grief, preferring the former, which stuffs my head with cotton wool. The hours blur together. How could they not, when Grandfather is no longer there to order each one into its slot? Who will knock on my bedroom door now, to wake me early so I'll have enough time to join him for tea before I go off to college? Who will keep track of every test I take and glow with pride when he finds out I topped the class? Who will ask me to play chess and vainly try to hide his delight when I back him into a corner? Who will ask me to light the lamp for his evening worship and then sit by him in companionable silence? Bereft of his fierce energy, the entire household has grown dim. I can sense, vaguely, Grandmother and Rajat, like moths hovering in the half dark. I know they're anxious about me. I know Grandmother is struggling with her own sorrow. But I can't seem to reach her from this deep hole into which I've fallen.

Now I understand the calamity my mother's ghost had come to warn me about.

Only Grandfather's books, their solid heft in my hands, comfort me a little. I open this one and run my finger over his name on the title page, tracing the bold slashes made by his fountain pen. I wish I could find something of him in those pages, like the letter from my mother so long ago, but there is nothing. Still, it's a comfort just to hold it—almost like touching him. I press the book to my cheek. It smells of a faint, wild sweetness, like the fennel seeds that Grandfather liked chewing after meals.

In the wake of that memory, a tide of others sweep in, tugging me toward happier times. How much clearer they seem than my present life. Sitting on his lap as he told me why volcanoes erupt. Holding his hand on our way to a rerun of *The Sound of Music,* him explaining the history behind the movie. The pride in his eyes the first time I beat him in chess. His waiting at the airport gate waving a bar of chocolate, face wreathed in smiles, when I returned from boarding school. I had never seen him smile at anyone else like that, not even Grandmother.

I close my eyes, allowing the book to grow heavy in my hand. I yearn for blessed sleep to carry me away. But Grandmother's voice intrudes into my cocoon.

"Get up, you can't sleep all day like this, you'll make yourself sick. Clean your face and change your clothes; remember, Rajat will be here in just a while." Determined to revive me, she refuses to leave until I splash water on my face and pull on a fresh salwar kameez.

Downstairs, Rajat is already waiting. He asks the same questions every day. I have nothing to offer him but the same desultory answers. I'm fine, everything's okay. At the dining table, it hurts my eyes to look at Grandfather's empty chair.

He had wanted his body cremated under an open sky. That's why we ended up at the old-fashioned burning ghats at Keoratala, the sulfuric smell of ignited flesh all around us. Framed by garlands, Grandfather appeared mild and saintly, so unlike himself that I felt only unreality—and a slight outrage. Someone had tied a strip of cloth around his face and knotted it under the chin, as though he were an old woman with a toothache. The priest dipped a stick of wood in ghee and called for a son or a grandson. When Rajat stepped forward, I elbowed past him angrily. But I wasn't as strong as I'd thought I was. When the priest lit the stick and pointed to Grandfather's mouth, asking me to set him on fire, I couldn't do it. Rajat had to take the flaming wood from my hand and begin the ceremony.

It had been terrible to see his body burn. Yet now, beside me, Rajat and Grandmother eat their dinner and discuss various mundane matters. Things have been a bit tense at the Boses' warehouse between the Hindu and Muslim workers since the religious riots in Gujarat. The garden has been invaded by slugs. They're eating even the oleanders. Grandmother wonders if an exterminator should be called.

Slugs! I push the food around on my plate. They're talking about slugs.

I can't keep my eyes from Grandfather's chair, its vast emptiness. Passing by his bedroom on my way downstairs this evening, I noticed that his clothes had been taken from the almirah and stacked on the bed.

The untidiness of the heap bothered me. He was always so exact. Why would Grandmother do such a thing? The last time I saw him as himself, he'd been sitting on that bed. I remember again the fight, my last, unforgivable words. Why had he apologized in the hospital, just before he died? Why had he looked beyond me at the door, as though someone else were standing there? Had it been my mother's ghost, come to help him on his final journey?

Once, feeling guilty about the precariously piled newspapers that Grandfather had loved to pore over, I looked through one. The news in it horrified me. Ordinary people, people just like our family, were killing each other in the streets. Without Grandfather in it to maintain equilibrium, the world had gone mad. I threw the rest of the pile in the garbage.

Grandmother says, "Korobi, shona, listen to Rajat—he wants to take you for a drive." She eyes my plate. "Looks like you're not going to eat any more. In that case, go ahead now. I don't want you to be out too late."

My body feels heavy with resentment. Why won't they leave me alone? I tell them that I would rather stay home.

"You must go! You need the fresh air."

"If fresh air's so good," I find myself retorting, "why don't *you* go with him instead."

"There's no reason to be rude to Grandma!"

The crackle of Rajat's voice makes me jump. He's never spoken to me like this. In a way, I'm thankful. Since Grandfather's death, everyone has been tiptoeing around me, and I'm sick of it. I'm ready for a good fight. But I don't want to do it in front of Grandmother.

Rajat dismisses Asif and takes the car down toward Victoria Memorial, driving fast with the windows open. The night wind whips my tangled curls into my face. My skin smarts; I welcome the pain, clean, immediate, a good distraction from the muddled ache inside me.

A little distance from the lit white dome with its dark angel, where on a very different evening he had kissed me into love, Rajat stops the car.

"We have to talk." His voice is measured. He's trying to be calm, reasonable. "I'm concerned at what's happening with you. I understand that you've suffered a great shock. But lying in bed all day is no good for you. It's been three weeks. You've missed a lot of classes. You can't just—"

I don't let him finish. I remind him he hasn't had anyone close to him die. How can he presume to understand how I'm feeling? What am I? A clockwork doll that he can wind up and say, *Three weeks have passed, enough moping, now smile and dance?*

His jaw tightens. He takes a deep breath but doesn't say anything.

Something has come over me. I tell him he's insensitive. A tyrant. He wants to control my life. In the closed car, my voice ricochets like bullets. I keep saying these things though they're making both of us feel worse.

He turns the car around. "You're not yourself," he says. "We'll talk when you can see sense." He's upset. I can tell that by how he drives. He runs a red light, but luckily no one's at the intersection. At the gate he lets me out, says he won't come in.

"Try to remember that Grandma's going through as much as you, if not more." His voice sounds tired.

His words are like a slap. The worst part is I know they're true. A tightness is growing in my chest like a giant abscess. I wish he'd fought with me. A fight would have burst it and let the poison out.

When Cook opens the door, I slam it behind me. I hear Grandmother asking what's wrong. I push past her up to my room, to my almirah, where my chiffon engagement kurti hangs. I pull it out, rummage in my drawer.

"What are you doing?" Behind me, Grandmother is breathless, having hurried up the stairs. "Have you gone crazy?"

The scissors snag in the soft, thin material. They refuse to slice through it as I would like them to. I have to grab the kurti in both hands and tear it.

"Stop! Stop! Oh, your beautiful outfit. Why did you do that?" Her face is stricken and scared.

"Grandfather hated it. It brought on the heart attack, the fight we had about it."

"That's ridiculous. He'd been sick for a while."

I shake my head. I don't believe her.

"He's gone, Korobi." She clears her throat, though it still sounds rusty. "We loved him, but he's gone, and we have to continue with our lives. Did Rajat talk to you about going back to college?"

But I'm stuck on her earlier words, the traitorous finality of the tense she used. *Loved.*

"Is that why you've started removing his things?" I cry. "I saw it when I passed by the bedroom. His clothes in boxes. His books off the shelves—"

Guilt flits darkly over her face. "It's not what you think. I've been looking for—oh, you won't understand."

"No, I don't understand!" A wild abandon has taken hold of me. I notice how pale her face has become, like a wraith's, but I can't stop. "Don't you have any respect for Grandfather's memory? Don't you care at all?"

Grandmother grasps the bedpost. "How easily you say that," she whispers. "All my life I've cared only about what he wanted. Obeyed him even when my conscience cried out against it."

"Grandfather had the highest principles," I say coldly. "I don't believe he would ever tell you to do anything against your conscience."

"No, of course you wouldn't!" I hadn't known she was capable of such a bitter, rasping laugh. "You were always his golden child. You weren't the one who had to put up with his black moods. You weren't the one he dragged to the temple on the night Anu died, insisting that the baby never learn about her father. He made me promise in front of the goddess that I'd never tell you. He was determined that you would grow up believing that he's dead."

I can barely understand her as she gasps for breath. I know that her blood sugar has been erratic lately. She's panting so hard that my anger turns to concern.

"Grandma, calm down! Here, sit beside me. I'm sorry I fought with you. Did you take your medicine today? You're getting confused. My father died months before my mother, remember?"

"No, Korobi . . . that's what I'm saying . . . It was a lie," she says slowly and clearly, looking in my eyes. "Your dear grandfather lied to you—and forced me to do the same. Your father's alive. His name is Rob. Yes, Rob. He lives in America."

Sarojini lies in her marriage bed, vast as a desert, with a damp cloth over her throbbing forehead. It is perhaps two in the morning, perhaps three, she isn't sure; the bedside clock that Bimal used to wind up every night before he slept has stopped working. Her mind will not stop replaying the quarrel, the look in Korobi's eyes when disbelief was replaced by the shock of betrayal. The girl had made a choking sound and stumbled from the room, not looking back, though Sarojini had begged her to stop. She had heard the front door slam. Terrified at what she might do, Sarojini had sent Cook after her and had paced the bedroom until the woman returned to report that Korobi-baby was sitting on the temple steps. She wouldn't answer Cook, not even to tell her to go away. It was as though she didn't see her. Swarms of mosquitoes were attacking her, but she didn't seem to care. Finally Cook lit a couple of mosquito coils, wrapped her in a shawl, shook awake a snoring Bahadur and told him to keep an eye on her, and came back to ask Sarojini what terrible thing had happened. Sarojini didn't want to lie to Cook, who had been with her for so many years, so she closed her eyes and shook her head until Cook went away. Now she presses the wet cloth, hot and salty with tears and no longer comforting, against her throbbing eyes and thinks, Bimal was right. By breaking her word to him, she has lost her granddaughter.

The bed is filled with memories. Of Bimal, of Anu. But it's the memory of Korobi that comes to Sarojini now. Born prematurely, she had been kept in the hospital incubator for weeks. How tiny she was, how frighteningly fragile when Sarojini finally brought her home, her skin like thin porcelain with the blue veins showing through it. Terrified that she would die, Sarojini had sent Bimal off to the guest bedroom and kept the baby in this bed, shored up by pillows. She checked on her breathing every hour, fed her milk from a dropper, held on to her as though she were afraid that any moment she'd slip away. With her eyes closed and hand cupped, she can even now feel that silky newborn skin. It comforts her, pulling her finally into sleep and thence into a dream.

It is late morning on the last day of her daughter's life. Sarojini the dreamer knows this already, and unease pulls at her heart. The Sarojini in the dream doesn't know, but she, too, is sad because she is getting ready to say good-bye. Anu has asked her mother for a head massage, her last one before she returns to America tomorrow. She sits on this very bed, holding her distended stomach, while Sarojini fetches the perfumed hibiscus oil. Pregnancy has been good for Anu. Her hair is thicker than before, her complexion luminous. Except for the few times recently when she's argued with her father, she has been as serene as the goddess.

"I wish you could stay until the baby arrives," Sarojini says, but without much hope. She knows her daughter intends for the child to be born in America, in the presence of the mysterious Rob, the husband she never mentions, and that is a reasonable desire. But Sarojini the dreamer knows that her wish will come true, tragically, perfidiously, that very night. This knowing-yet-not-knowing is a strange sensation, like being split in two.

"Oh, Mother, let's not think of all those complicated things right now. Let me just enjoy my head massage. It makes me feel like a girl again—and I want that so much today."

Sarojini pours the fragrant oil into her palm and rubs it into her daughter's scalp, feeling that beloved body relaxing against her with a sigh. She wishes again: if only she could be around to do the same thing for her grandchild as the baby grows up! She closes her eyes and imagines a beautiful girl—and look, hasn't that longing been fulfilled, too? If she were wiser, thinks the Sarojini of the future, she would never wish for anything again. But the foolish heart doesn't know how to stop.

Anu turns, tilting her head up at Sarojini, smiling without a hint of rancor. Looking at her, Sarojini remembers that she had always loved this quality about her daughter—this sweet quickness to forgive. To trust. Sarojini wonders if Anu would still be alive if she had been a little more hard-hearted.

"You must tell her everything," Anu says in the dream.

"There's so much I don't know. So much your father kept from me."

"Tell what you can. Imagine the rest. I'll fill in the gaps."

"But it'll be so painful, Anu-ma. For myself and Korobi both."

"Ah, pain," Anu says with that heartbreaking smile. "Mother, who among us has ever escaped it?"

I stumble through the overgrown tangles of bramble bushes behind the house, pushing away vines that hang like snakes from the old trees. I throw myself down under an ancient banyan, barely missing a fire-ant hill, and press my knuckles into my eyes. How could Grandfather, to whom I'd given my entire child-heart, who had taught me how important it was to be truthful, have perpetrated such an enormous, criminal lie? All night I paced the temple veranda, trying to make sense of Grandmother's confession. It couldn't be true. I had my mother's note, mourning her dead husband. But how did I know that? Could I have been reading it wrong this whole time? What if *impossibly far away* hadn't meant he was dead, but only that he was in America? I tried telling myself Grandmother was confused. She was old and under a lot of stress. But deep down, I knew. It isn't always possible to discern a lie, but truth has an unmistakable ring, and that is what I'd heard in her voice.

How will I ever trust anyone again?

I hear footsteps behind me and stiffen, but it's only Cook, blundering through the bushes, carrying tea and biscuits.

"I've been looking for you all over the place! Oh, goodness, look at those horrible ants! If they get hold of you, you'll be swollen like a balloon. And the itching—I'm telling you, you can't even imagine how terrible it can be."

She squats down, holding out the steaming cup of tea and my favorite cream-filled biscuits.

"Here, have some tea, baby. Tea always makes you feel better. And then tell old Cook what's wrong."

I'd expected to be too upset for hunger, but I find that I'm ravenous. I'm touched, too, by Cook's efforts. I'm about to give her a hug. Then I remember that Cook has been in the family since before I was born. Was she, too, part of this deception? Each time she saw me, did she think, *Poor girl! She doesn't even know her father is alive!*

I turn my face away until Cook leaves the food on a pile of bricks and

goes back to the house. Then I dip the biscuits, innocent and delicious, in the tea, so they melt effortlessly on my tongue. A breeze blows through the neem tree, bringing me its clean, therapeutic odor. A dragonfly made of shimmery gauze alights on a bramble. Two crows are building a nest in the crook of a branch, their movements an intricate, precise dance. Yes, it's terrible, what my grandparents did. It'll take me a long time to recover from that blow. But the fact I learned last night—isn't it also a miracle of sorts? A dead father brought back to life? And along with him, a way to finally know my mother, that silhouette forever glimmering at the edge of my mind, those few scribbles of love on a page?

Eighteen years lost already—I can't waste any more time. The need to find out everything about my parents, suddenly, is like an ache in my bones, a deep deficiency. So much that I've been deprived of all this time. I run back to the house, ignoring the thorns that catch at my kameez.

I find her in her bedroom. She has opened the windows so the room is full of the wild, enigmatic odor of oleanders.

"Tell me everything," I say.

"Sit down," she says. "You'll need it."

"Your mother came late to your grandfather and me, after three miscarriages. The doctor had warned us not to try again, but your grandfather couldn't bear the thought of the family name dying with him. When I got pregnant a fourth time, he was delighted—and terrified that something would go wrong again. At the delivery, he insisted on remaining in the birthing room of the hospital, something men never did in those days. When Anu was born, he took her from the nurse even before I'd had the chance to hold her. Maybe that was why they loved each other so intensely and later hurt each other so bitterly.

"Your grandfather brought Anu up as the son he never had. But he could never forget that she was a girl. Thus his two main passions—that Anu should excel in whatever she did, and that she should be brought up as befitted a daughter of the Roy family—crashed constantly against each other. When she was chosen for her school's national debate team,

he took a week off from court so that he could take her to Delhi for the tournament. But if they were in a gathering of his friends, he expected her to be respectful and silent. If she expressed her views—and like your grandfather, she had strong views—he subjected her to a chill silence. His approval was important to Anu, so she learned to live a double life, assertive and competitive at school and college, compliant and voiceless everywhere else.

"When she was about to complete college, your grandfather found a match for her. It was not difficult. She was beautiful and accomplished and sweet-natured, and many people were keen to form a relationship with our family because of your great-grandfather Tarak Roy. Your grandfather was partial to the son of one of his colleagues. Anu didn't say no, but she asked for time. She told him she had applied for an American scholarship. If she was lucky enough to receive it, could she please go? It would be only for two years.

"Your grandfather was angry that she had taken such a big step without consulting him, but I could understand her longing to see the world before wifehood bound her with its responsibilities. Finally he agreed to wait until the results were announced. It was a very competitive scholarship; we didn't expect her to receive it.

"But your mother must have been even smarter than we realized—or perhaps a bird of ill luck had flown over her head on the day when she mailed the application. She received the scholarship, all expenses paid, to study international relations at the University of California in Berkeley. The delighted principal of Anu's college announced her success to the newspapers. The phone wouldn't stop ringing as friends and relatives called to congratulate your grandfather. How could he refuse to let her go after that? Still, he hesistated until she agreed to go to our temple with him and swear, in front of the goddess, never to marry without his approval. That put him at ease. He knew she wouldn't make such a promise lightly.

"Anu settled into the university quickly, doing well in her classes. In Kolkata she had been reclusive, preferring to read or listen to music in her room. In America she grew adventurous. She would tell us in her letters about folk-dance lessons and plays she had seen in San Francisco.

She visited the giant redwoods and saw migrating whales. People in California, she said, were kind and friendly and very interesting.

"'When does the child study?' your grandfather grumbled. But Anu must have found time for that, too, because at the end of her first semester, she received As in all her subjects.

"'One and a half years more,' your grandfather said, sighing. He missed her even more than I did. 'Then she'll be back, and all this foolishness will be over with.'

"'Don't forget,' I said, 'she'll be married soon after that, and no longer ours.'

"Your grandfather waved away my words. 'She's always ours, no matter whose house she lives in.'

"A week after that, we had just sat down for dinner when the phone, which was kept in his study, rang. I went and picked it up. You know how your Grandfather didn't like to be disturbed at dinner. It was Anu.

"'Are you all right?' I asked, worried, because she only phoned us on special occasions—calls were too expensive. She said she was better than all right. She was in love. My mouth grew dry. I knew Grandfather wouldn't like this.

"'He's a wonderful man,' she said, 'sweet and intelligent. You couldn't have found a better person for me in all of India. His name is Rob.'

"'He's American?' I said in horror. But before I could ask anything else, your grandfather took the phone from me, telling her how nice it was to hear her voice, and asking what was the occasion. Then his face changed. He gestured to me to leave the study and shut the door.

"I stood in the passage, petrified. After a few minutes he hung up the phone, but he didn't come out. When I knocked, he told me to go to bed. The next morning, he sent Anu a telegram ordering her to return to Kolkata immediately. If she did not obey, she was not to ever contact him—or me—again. He would cut her out of his heart as though he never had a daughter.

"He insisted that I, too, swear not to contact her. When I protested that I couldn't do that to my only child, he told me that in that case he would send me to live by myself in his ancestral village.

"'I will have nothing to do with a wife who does not stand beside me in a crisis,' he said.

"I begged him to reconsider, but he was adamant. Finally, I gave in. I wasn't strong enough to stand up against his will. And though I asked, he refused to tell me anything more about the man Anu loved.

"I heard nothing more from Anu after that. Your grandfather opened a post office box, and all our mail went there. Any letters she might have written to me—and I'm sure there were several, at least in the beginning—did not reach me. He changed our phone number. About a month later, he came home in a cold rage. He took all her photographs out of their frames and burned them. I understood then that she had chosen love over duty, the American over her parents. Could I blame her for that? What she felt inside her as she made that choice—of that I had no idea.

"Every day when your grandfather was at work, I wept, certain that I would never see Anu again. But I said nothing to him. That was the way I had been brought up. If he noticed my swollen eyes when he came home, he said nothing, either. Perhaps that was the way he had been brought up.

"About six months later, your grandfather came home, highly agitated. Anu had written that she was expecting a baby. The pregnancy was not going well. She was often sick and missed us terribly. Would we allow her to come and see us?

"All the feelings I'd dammed up for so long burst over me: joy at the news, anxiety for Anu's health, sorrow that she had to beg to visit her own home. I told your grandfather that this was our chance to make up with Anu. We had to put the past behind us and welcome her back. I was prepared to fight him as I'd never done before. I was even prepared to go to Anu if he refused to let her visit. But your grandfather surprised me. He phoned her the very next day and said she could come and stay as long as she liked. His only stipulation was that she come alone and speak to no one, not even me, about her husband while she was here.

"Anu must have missed us more than we guessed. She agreed to your grandfather's terms. Two weeks later, she flung herself into my arms at the airport, her face thinner, darker, with worry lines between her brows that she hadn't had when she left. Her belly pushed against me—I guessed her to be at least five months along. As I kissed her, I felt you kick. That night, after she had eaten a good dinner of rice and Ilish fish and gone to sleep in her childhood bed, your grandfather said, 'We should never have let her go.' But I was silent. I had felt that kick and fallen in love already. I couldn't wish you into nonbeing.

"The next two months were the happiest in my life. Your grandfather had made it clear that he didn't want Anu to leave the house. I thought she might chafe at such a restriction, but she didn't seem to mind. In those months, to keep Anu company, I, too, stopped going out. We were suspended in a magical space into which the outside world could not intrude. She followed me around contentedly, chatting about her childhood, small incidents from long ago. Once in a while, she would start to speak and then stop, a shadow passing over her face. I guessed she had been about to say something about Rob, your father. I longed to know what it might be and tried, gently, to get her to tell me. I wished she would break that ridiculous promise your grandfather had exacted from her, but she never did. That was the kind of person she was.

"In the third month of her visit, the problems began. Your grandfather started to inquire into hospitals, though Anu had told him that she wanted to have the baby in America. Every night at dinner he would try to persuade her to stay, while she maintained an increasingly stubborn silence. The glow that had come upon her faded. She ate less; at night I could hear her pacing in her bedroom. Finally she told us she had fixed the date for her departure—it would be in three days. She couldn't delay any further; the airline had restrictions on how far along a pregnant passenger could be.

"Now it was your grandfather who refused to speak. He was the one who paced the bedroom, keeping me awake. I told him we had to accept Anu's wishes. She was grown and married now. He turned on me with frightening fury, telling me to shut up.

"Next morning, however, he had calmed down. He took a day off from work and took Anu shopping. Although she protested, he went into Mallik's and bought an entire layette for you. He chose the softest, most expensive things and had the towels embroidered with flowery *K*s because she had already told us the names she had picked out: Kartik for a boy, Korobi for a girl. Anu, on her part, was at her sweetest, hugging us and thanking us for everything we'd done.

"'Thanking your parents!' your grandfather said gruffly. 'Don't talk like an American!' But he hugged her back, and I was grateful that he had accepted the inevitable.

"The night before she was to leave, however, while I was in the kitchen supervising a special dinner, they had another fight. I couldn't hear the details above the whistle of the pressure cooker. I know there was a cry, a series of thuds. By the time Cook and I came running from the kitchen, your mother was crumpled at the base of the stairs, unconscious, with you folded helplessly somewhere inside her. Your grandfather stood on the landing above, frozen. All he would say in answer to my anguished questions was that she had tripped.

"It would take me a year to get more than that out of him—he was a lawyer, after all. Even then, all he said was that he had gone into her room and asked her one more time to put off her journey. She had refused and, when he persisted, rushed from the room in anger. I guessed that he must have said other things—perhaps something against your father. Maybe he had followed, haranguing her. In her haste to get away, she had pushed past him and fallen."

"It was because of him she fell, wasn't it?" Korobi whispers, words Sarojini couldn't bring herself to say all these years. "If it wasn't for his stubbornness, his inability to accept a no, she might have lived. Did she say anything to you before she died? About my dad, about me?"

Sarojini shakes her head. "We rushed her to the hospital, but she never did regain consciousness. By the time the doctors operated on her and got you out, she was dead."

"Dead!" Korobi echoes. "Just like that?"

Sarojini nods, wiping her eyes. "When we came back to the hospital after the funeral, you were in intensive care, inside an incubator, a bandage tied over your eyes, tubes sticking into you. Oh, how frighteningly small you were. We weren't allowed to touch you for fear of infection. Looking at you, I couldn't stop crying. I was so afraid you would die, too, and we would have no one, nothing to tie your mother to us. That night your grandfather took me to our temple and told me that your father must never learn you were alive. If he did, he would take you away.

"'We'll grow old in an empty house while she is brought up in another country without culture or values,' he said. 'Do you want that?'

"I shook my head.

"'Then swear on the goddess that you'll never contact him—or tell her about him.'

"I felt only a moment's compunction. I had no love for the stranger who had snatched our daughter from us. And I agreed with your grandfather: it would be the best thing for you.

"Later, as you grew and began asking about your mother and father, I would have my doubts, but I couldn't say anything, not until I became the only keeper of your secret."

The two women sit in silence, musing over the words that reverberate around them, words that have been waiting all these years to be born. What emotions are going through Korobi? Sarojini wonders. She tries to look into her granddaughter's face, but Korobi keeps it carefully turned away.

"Tell me about my father now."

Sarojini shakes her head helplessly. "I've told you everything I know. That's why I was going through your grandfather's things. I thought there might have been a letter or photographs. Maybe a copy of a marriage certificate. But if there was, he destroyed it long ago."

"But didn't my father come to India, looking for my mother? For me? They were in love!"

"No. Your grandfather sent him a telegram saying you were both dead."

"He told my father *what*?" Korobi's voice is furious.

Sarojini looks shamefaced, as though she herself had initiated the falsehood. "He told him not to come, that we were barely able to cope with the tragedy and to talk to him would only increase our distress. As an extra precaution, as soon as the hospital released you, he sent you and me to our village home along with Cook and Bahadur and moved into a hotel himself, closing up the house. The story he gave out to his friends and even to our servants was that your father—a certain Bhowmik, a brilliant young law student in America—had died tragically in a car crash some months back. A pregnant Anu had come home to be comforted by us. Brokenhearted, she had shut herself up in the house, refusing to meet anyone, begging us not to inform anyone of what had happened. She couldn't even bear to mention her husband's name. And then, just as she was feeling better, fate had struck her down, too.

"For the first year of your life, you and I lived in the village, in our ancestral home, which was falling to pieces. When it rained, Cook had to place buckets under the leaks. We never left the house. Bahadur spread the rumor that I was recovering from tuberculosis. That kept the curious away. Once a month your grandfather came to see us. He spent most of his visits holding you, just looking at you. The pent-up love he had for Anu, I think he transferred it all to you during those days."

Korobi looks away. Sarojini knows that this is what hurts her granddaughter the most. Not just the deception, but that it came from the man she'd trusted more than anyone else in her life.

"I don't expect you to forgive us for deceiving you. All I can say is that we did it out of love—and fear. And once we had woven the story, we, too, were caught in it. We didn't know how to cut ourselves loose."

The day is gone. Sarojini peers through the gloom of evening at Korobi, hoping for a sign of pardon. But her face is dark and hard, closed up tight like a walnut. Silence stretches between them, punctuated only by the call of birds returning to their nests. Sarojini thinks this silence will go on forever, until she crumbles into dust. She would welcome that: to disintegrate, to blow away in the wind, to never have to answer the look in her granddaughter's eye.

Downstairs, the phone rings.

Neither Sarojini nor Korobi moves. Finally, Cook hurries from the kitchen, grumbling loudly, and picks it up.

"It's Rajat-babu," she yells up. "Calling to talk to baby. What shall I say?"

Sarojini puts her hand on her granddaughter's arm. "Don't talk to him right now. Don't say anything until you've calmed down. Maybe it's best not to tell him any of this. It'll do no good. And it might lead to a host of problems."

The stiff angle of Korobi's neck. Anger, sorrow, disappointment, distaste—Sarojini can't count all the things it conveys.

"You want me to hide such a big thing from the man I'm about to marry? You want me to perpetuate the lie you and Grandfather concocted? You want me, too, to deny my father?"

Korobi rushes from the room as though she can't bear to be near Sarojini. Almost as though she wants to tumble down those same stairs to join her mother, Sarojini thinks, holding her breath until she hears her granddaughter pick up the phone and say hello.

By the river in the yellow light of the deserted streetlamp, Rajat holds his sobbing fiancée and tries to comfort her. But he can't find the right words—he's too shocked by the astounding news she's just told him. He starts to say that he can imagine what she must be going through, being lied to like this, but then he stutters to a stop. The truth is, he can't imagine it at all. It chagrins him, this failure of empathy. Perhaps it's because the news ambushed him so unexpectedly. He'd called the Roy home to tell Korobi that he wouldn't be able to see her tonight. He needed to spend some time with his family, whom he'd been neglecting shamefully since Bimal Roy's death. Even at the height of his infatuation with Sonia he had managed to carve out more time for them. His mother hadn't complained—that was not her way. But last night he got home to find Pia lying on the sofa, where she had fallen asleep waiting for him to return. Awakened, she had rubbed at her eyes plaintively and said she never got to see him these days. Struck by compunction, he promised her that he would have dinner at home tonight, maybe even play a game of Scrabble afterward. He was surprised by how happy it made him to plan a relaxed evening with his family. But when he'd talked to Korobi, the feverish intensity of her voice had worried him. He had come—as she requested—as soon as he could.

"I'm very sorry. . . ."

Even to his ears, the words sound inadequate, equivocal. What exactly is he sorry for? Sorry that her grandfather had betrayed her, that he might have contributed to her mother's death? That she'd been lied to about her father for all these years? Yes, of course. But isn't he also sorry that she has now found out about her father? Certainly it would have been simpler had Rajat not been handed this strange, sudden father-in-law, a foreigner shrouded in a conspiracy of silence. He can't help wondering what reason Bimal Roy, a canny man if ever there was one, might have had for cutting Rob out of Korobi's life so completely.

"It's hard for me to believe that Grandfather was so harsh to my mother. If only he'd accepted my father—or at least not pressured her to remain in India—she would still be alive. And I'd have grown up with both my parents."

Rajat makes a sympathetic sound. *If only* is a dangerous path to travel. But it's no use trying to tell Korobi that right now.

"What hurts even more is knowing that my grandparents—whom I loved more than anybody—would deceive me like this! It hurts so much."

Something twists inside Rajat. He thinks, unwillingly, of Sonia. How well he knows, from his own life, what Korobi is describing, that feeling as though the solid earth has turned to shifting sands beneath his feet.

"Plus I feel stupid for being so gullible."

He takes a deep breath. His job right now is to comfort Korobi. She is his heart, his breath, the way out of his own abyss. "You can't blame yourself for believing them. You had no reason to think it could be a lie. I would have done the same."

"Well, I've learned my lesson. I'm never going to trust anyone so blindly."

The weary bitterness in her voice troubles him. "Cara, surely you can trust me."

She raises a mutinous chin, her body hard, her eyes narrow and so angry he hardly recognizes them. It strikes him that he doesn't know her as well as he'd thought. But then she gives a giant sigh and crumples against him.

"You're right. You're the only one I can count on. That's why I had to tell you. Grandma said I shouldn't, that it might change things between us. But I had to. I can't lie like that to the man I love."

That word *love*, it comforts him. "You did the best thing."

"Was Grandma right? Do you feel differently about me because of what I just told you?"

"Of course not." But a part of Rajat is troubled. One of the things that had always charmed him about Korobi was her background. Old Bengal through and through, her great-grandfather the judge, her grandfather the barrister, her father the brilliant law student cut down tragically in his prime—khandaani, something with heft, something you could never buy your way into. As different from Sonia as handloomed silk from glittery synthetics. Marriage to Korobi, he had hoped, would initiate him into the mysteries of this life.

Now she isn't quite the person he had believed her to be.

Can she read his thoughts? Because just then she says, "I'm so confused. All the things I was so proud of, my family, my heritage—they're only half-true. The other half of me—I don't know anything about it. Except that all this time my father was alive, and in America."

In the light of the streetlamp Rajat examines his fiancée's distressed expression, the slight tremble of her lips, the hair escaped from its braid to curl untidily around her face. For a heart-stopping moment, he feels nothing. Then, thankfully, love comes rushing back like the ocean after low tide. It's in her eyes, the real reason he loves her, and nothing can take it away: her forthrightness, her unspoiled enthusiasm—and now, courage and honesty in the face of the unexpected. At the moment, those eyes are swollen from crying and clouded with distrust. He vows that he'll bring the shine back to them. He, Rajat, will be 100 percent dependable. He feels again that overwhelming desire to protect that he has never experienced with any other girlfriend. He kisses her with great relief.

"You're still my Cara, and I adore you. What you learned today doesn't make the slightest difference to me. Don't think about it anymore. We'll get married in a couple of months, just as we had planned. With time, what you heard will fade away—"

She shakes her head impatiently as though she didn't even hear his declaration of love. "Rajat, you don't understand! I don't *want* it to fade away. I'm shocked and hurt, yes, but I'm excited, too. Do you see? I have a father now! I can meet the man my mother loved so much! All my life I longed to understand my parents. Now fate has given me a chance."

Rajat doesn't like the sound of this, but before he can respond, a car door slams, startling him. A trio of men has stepped out of an Ambassador, carrying bottles of beer. They see Rajat and Korobi, and one of them says something. The others snicker. The group begins to walk toward them.

"Cara, we have to leave."

"I need to find him, talk to him. I need to know who he is. And he can finally tell me about my mother—the things that no one else knows. My mother in love. Won't that be wonderful, Rajat? Then I'll know who I really am, too. But how will I find him? I don't even have his name. And America is such a big country."

He hears the words, but they are too much to process right now. He grabs her hand and hurries her to the car.

"Will you help me, Rajat?"

The men are closer now, goonda types, he can see: flashy nylon shirts, thick chains around their necks. One calls out, "Come on, bhaiya, join us for a drink. And your girlfriend, too."

Korobi doesn't notice. "Until I find him, Rajat, I'm not sure I can get married."

He pushes her into the car. Locks her door. At least she knows enough to lean over and unlock the driver's side.

As he slips inside the car and locks his door, too, the man sneers, "Looks like the bhaiya got scared! Eh, bhaiya, we were only being sociable."

Heat pulses inside Rajat's head. The city is going to the dogs, even this beautiful riverbank. He wishes he carried a gun, like some of his friends do. He has a flash vision of pointing it at the man's face, seeing his features crumple. In his mind he says, *Let's see who's scared now, bhaiya.*

He takes a deep breath. Back away from trouble, Rajat. You need to be Cara's support right now. Plus, Papa and Maman have enough problems—the gallery in America, their money troubles here. And now this news about Cara's father. He needs to figure out how to contain it, like a radioactive leak. As for that daft notion of hers that she can't get married until she finds Rob, Rajat hopes that a good night's sleep will rid her of it.

"We've got to tell your parents." Korobi puts a hand on his arm. "I know they will want to know. They are like parents to me already, but they will understand I need to find my own papa before the wedding. . . . Will you tell them for me? Right now, it's too painful for me to go over it again."

He inclines his head, a motion that could be a yes or a no, and turns the key in the ignition. The last thing his parents need right now is to have to deal with this disconcerting development. He's going to do all he can to keep it from them.

The car roars to life, gratifyingly obedient, carrying them to safety.

I sit on the edge of my chair in the investigator's office, hands clasped tight, watching the man's face. Mr. Sen does not look happy; his brow is creased as he hands back the photograph I gave him at our last meeting. It's an old Polaroid, the colors faded. In it, two young women dressed in jeans and sweatshirts stand in front of a tall, pointy tower. A shadow has fallen over one woman's face so her features are blurred, but the other woman can be seen quite clearly.

The night I told Rajat about my father, I found the photo on my bed, with a note attached:

> *I found this tonight, searching through your grandfather's papers. I'd been hoping he loved Anu too much to destroy every single image of hers. She sent us this photo to us just a few months after she went to America.*
>
> *There's something else I remembered: A week or so before her accident, I had asked Anu where she planned to live when she went back to America. She was careful not to mention your father, but she did tell me that they were thinking of moving to the East Coast because of a job opportunity.*

I lifted the photo with shaking fingers. At last I was to see my mother, my real mother and not the mournful, mouthless silhouette of my dream. I knew her right away—those serious, straight eyebrows were the ones I saw whenever I looked in the mirror. But she was her own person, too, with her generous, strong-willed, beautiful mouth. She smiled with such vivacity into the camera that I was sure my father had been the photographer. Indeed, when I turned it over, a bold script stated, *To lovely Anu*. My heart raced. Halfway across the world, before I had even been imagined, my father had handed this piece of paper to my mother. Perhaps their hands had touched and she had shyly smiled—it would have been in the early days, soon after they met. I ran my fingers across the back, over where their fingers had rested. It was as close to touching the two of them as I had ever been. In a strange way, it made my father possible.

How could I remain angry with a grandmother who had given me such a gift? Now that I was calmer, I could see how impossible it would have been for her to stand up against Grandfather. His will, which I had always thought of as protecting and supporting me, would in this case have been an avalanche, crushing everything in its path.

I went into the bedroom. She was sitting by the shuttered windows in the melancholy, slatted moonlight. I sat by her. We didn't speak, but I leaned into her and felt something begin to mend, as when one blind end of a fractured bone finds its partner under the skin. And here's something strange: I was still furious with Grandfather, but a question rose up through my anger. Of all the photos of my mother, why had he chosen to save this one? Had some subterranean part of his mind recoiled from cutting me off totally from my father?

Now I knew what my dream-mother had wanted. She wanted me to understand that I had a future across the ocean, someone waiting there for me, although he didn't realize it yet. The photo had cemented my decision to find my father, the man who had shared my mother's smiles, the unwritten half of her tender letter, the presence at the other end of the camera. But I wasn't sure how to go about it.

Filled with a restless hope, I started searching the Internet that same night, typing random words into the browser, peering hopefully into the infinite blue of the computer for a directive. *Rob, Anu Roy, University of California, Berkeley, International Relations, marriage records, East Coast,* the approximate dates of my mother's sojourn in America. But though the machine spewed up an enormous number of entries (were there really sixty-two men at the university during those years nicknamed *Rob?*), it was unable to offer me a definitive lead. I would need professional assistance.

That night I slept fitfully with the photo under my pillow, dreaming of my parents walking down an oleander pathway arm in arm, my earnest mother, the blank, white oval of my father's face. As soon as it was morning, I called Rajat's mobile.

"Will you help me find a private detective?"

I must have startled him from sleep, for he blurted what was on his mind without attempting diplomacy. Had I gone crazy? Didn't I remember what he'd advised last night, that I should let things be? In any case, he didn't know such men. Decent families didn't have anything to do with them.

I held on to my temper. He had been my anchor the night before, and I was grateful for his strength. But I couldn't so easily give up the possibility of finding my father, not even for the man I loved.

"I'll find a detective myself, then."

"How?" He sounded annoyed and amused at the same time—as though I were a child to be humored.

"I'll ask Mimi. Just last month during lunch break she said her cousin had hired someone to find out if her husband was cheating on her—"

He groaned. "God, no! Don't say anything to Mimi! It'll be all over Kolkata within a week, and we really need to keep this inside the family. You understand that, don't you?"

I didn't respond, and finally he sighed. "Very well, I'll ask around discreetly and see what I can come up with."

When Rajat sets his mind on something, he doesn't waste time. Within a couple of days, he had found Mr. Sen, explained my situation, hired him, and given him the photograph. That is why we're here today, sitting side by side, watching Mr. Sen slide the photo back across his gleaming mahogany desk and shake his head.

"I'm sorry. That photo doesn't help much. The other woman—I'm guessing she was a friend of your mother—her face is too blurry to follow up on. And there's too little information on your father. I need a last name, at the very least. I searched on the Internet, even called overseas, but that first name is too common. We don't even know if he was a student at the university, and that really widens the field. I searched for marriage records for Anu Roy, but nothing came up there, either. They might have gone to another state—or maybe even another country—Canada perhaps. Some private religious organizations don't post their records on the Web. The possibilities are just too many. My advice to you is to forget about it. Don't waste any more of your money and your time. Besides, in old cases like this, it's very possible that the man has gone on with his life and remarried. Even if you found him, he might not be happy about it. He might even refuse to see you."

My heart plunges. I think about telling the detective about my mother's note and her ghostly visitation, but I know they don't prove anything. Besides, those secrets are too close to my core. I'm not ready to share them yet—not even with Rajat.

Rajat is nodding, his face bright with relief.

"That's exactly what I've been thinking! Cara, you must listen to Mr. Sen. He has years of experience in such matters."

I know Rajat is right, finding my father seems impossible, but I can't give up so easily. Stubbornness rises inside me like a wall. "I don't care how hard it is! I must do everything I can to find him. He's my *father*, for heaven's sake!"

"In that case," Mr. Sen says mournfully, "I'd recommend that you work with an investigator who lives in the United States. Such a man might be able to access old records that aren't on the Internet. He could send someone to the Berkeley campus to talk to people who knew your mother, who might remember—"

"Do you know someone like that?" I interrupt.

"As a matter of fact, I do. It'll cost a lot, though. You'll have to pay him in dollars."

My heart sinks. I know Grandmother has been worrying over our finances. Still, I say, "I don't care!"

Rajat looks over at me but says nothing.

Mr. Sen searches through a large box of alphabetized index cards and writes down details.

"His name is Desai. Unfortunately, he lives in New York, not California, which would have suited you better."

Perhaps it's a sign. I tell Sen what Grandmother had said about my parents' plans to move to the East Coast. Sen looks doubtful. But he informs me that Mr. Desai is good at what he does. He doesn't take many new clients. However, Sen will ask him to help me.

We're barely in the car when Rajat bursts out, "You heard it! Even Mr. Sen advised you against searching further. You need to put this obsession aside."

Perhaps something of the dark insurgence I'm feeling is in my face, because he takes my hand in his and adds more placatingly, "At least wait until after we're married, Cara."

I try to explain to him how I feel one more time. "I need to understand my parents' marriage before I can enter my own. I've got to contact Desai, see if he can find out something. If I need to"—the idea comes to me in a flash, an icy exhilaration down my spine, an understanding that this is what my mother wanted all along—"I'm even prepared to go to America."

He ignores that last bit the way one might disregard the ramblings of the delirious. "Who knows what you'll uncover if you keep digging? There must have been a reason why your grandfather was so insistent about keeping you away from your father. Cara, my parents can't afford a scandal just before the wedding—"

I want to say hotly, *There won't be a scandal. My mother chose a good man! She loved him!* But Rajat's words remind me of something else.

"What did your parents say when they heard about my father? I'm surprised Maman didn't call me. Are they very upset?"

He's silent for a moment, then says, "I didn't tell them."

"What? Why not?"

"They're going through a difficult time. They've suffered a big financial loss, and they're in the midst of negotiating a major deal that might help them recover. I don't want to stress them right now. Why do they have to know, anyway? You've told me, and I'm the one you're marrying. It doesn't concern anyone else."

I stare at him in angry disbelief. "You want me to go through my whole life with my in-laws pretending that my father is dead? That he was Indian? Why? Are you ashamed of who I am?"

"Korobi, don't put words in my mouth. I never said that. But you know how highly they think of your heritage. Maman has been talking about it to all her friends. Don't take that away from them!"

I understand where he's coming from, but I can't agree. "Each time I look into their faces, I'll think, They love me only because I deceived them. I'll know I'm living a lie. No, Rajat! I've seen how harmful secrets can be. I refuse to start my married life with a sword hanging over my head. I'll meet with your mother tomorrow and tell her myself."

"Please don't! You'll be unburdening yourself at the cost of her peace of mind—"

I can feel anger uncoiling inside me, but right now I don't want a fight. I need to save my energy for the search. Luckily, we've reached home. I get out of the car before I say something I'll regret.

Behind me, I hear Rajat say, "You make such a big deal about being honest and open. Do you think there's anyone in the world that doesn't have a secret?"

I don't respond. I don't trust myself to. But all the way to the door, the gravel of the driveway crunching under my shoes, I wonder what secrets my fiancé is harboring.

FOUR

Barua & Bose Art Galleries sits between a nationally famous restaurant and an imported-car showroom on a prime piece of Kolkata real estate. I pause outside its massive, gleaming glass-and-wood doors, at once impressed and uneasy. Though Maman has invited me several times, this is my first visit. I would be excited if I weren't so nervous. I've heard so much about the gallery from Rajat—how Maman bought a run-down storefront and remodeled it herself, how she launched the careers of several major artists from here, how the guest list for her show openings reads like a who's who in Kolkata. Sometimes I imagine working here alongside her after Rajat and I are married. In my daydreams, Maman—who is as close to a mother as I'll ever have—hugs me, telling me how proud she is of me.

The interior of the gallery is elegant and understated, stretches of white wall and dark granite flooring that allow the paintings to leap to life. I find it hard to pull my eyes away from the pictures on the wall—sumptuous women with the faces of animals, geometries of rainbow color. This is a side of Maman I haven't seen, eclectic and adventurous. I'm filled with new admiration.

A sinuous young woman in a black georgette sari eyes my cotton salwar kameez with a dubious look, asking how she may help. When I tell her who I am, her eyes widen in disbelief. She hurries me through a passage studded with jewel-like paintings to a huge back office, its windows opening onto a courtyard garden, a rare luxury in the heart of the city. Maman's desk looks out on a flame-orange Krishnachura tree. Dressed in a beautifully embroidered silk sari that makes me feel doubly dowdy, she's on the phone, frowning elegantly, taking notes, giving instructions in between to a woman with her hair pulled into a severe bun. I feel guilty because I'm about to disrupt her day.

The matter on the phone is clearly urgent, but when she sees me, Maman cuts the conversation short and waves me over.

"How are you, my dear?" she says with a warm smile, tucking back one of my stray curls. If she's surprised at my sudden visit, she doesn't show it. "You're looking much better than the last time I saw you. I'm delighted that you decided to drop in today. We're about to install a new exhibition of urban landscapes—"

I hate to interrupt Maman's enthusiasm, but I must. "Maman, there's something I have to tell you."

Maman's eyes fly to my face. "Leave us alone, please, Shikha," she tells her companion. I recognize the woman with the no-nonsense hairdo; on the night of the engagement, she rushed us out of the hotel and instructed the Boses' driver to take us to the hospital. Now she asks, in some agitation, "What about lunch, madam? You haven't eaten since morning, and you'll have meetings all afternoon. Let me at least bring you some—"

"I'll be all right, Shikha."

Shikha flings me a displeased glance as she closes the door soundlessly.

Alone with Maman, I suddenly wish I'd asked Rajat to come with me. What if Maman's furious when she hears my news? What if she feels she's been handed flawed merchandise? It strikes me more than ever before that the approval of this woman whom I've already been thinking of as my new mother is crucial to me.

But when I've let the words tumble from my mouth, she only pauses for the briefest moment before giving me a hug. "What a shock, dear! You must be devastated."

Her sympathy makes me tear up. I hold on to her. She smells of pomegranates. I'm lucky to have such an understanding mother-in-law. I'm glad I didn't let Rajat persuade me into deceiving her.

"Does anyone else know about your father?"

I'm a little surprised by her question, but I answer dutifully, "Only Grandmother and Rajat."

Maman lets out a sigh of relief. "Thank God! Because we're going to have to keep this very quiet."

My face must have expressed my uneasiness, for she adds, "No, no, don't look like that! The news about your father hasn't changed anything between us. I won't pretend I like what I learned, but it's not your fault. We'll have to bring the marriage forward, though, maybe to next month. We don't want to take any chances with the news leaking out."

I feel as though I've fallen into a river that's rushing toward the edge of a precipice. I have so many astonished questions, they jam my mouth.

"I can't get married yet, Maman," I finally manage to say. "I need to find my father first. I think I have a good chance. I've located an investigator in America. He'll start work as soon as I make the first payment. It's going to be expensive, but he said if I travel to America and do some of the legwork for him, following up on his leads, it'll cost a lot less. So I'm planning to—"

Maman grips my hands. "I understand how agitated you must be, my sweet. Under normal circumstances, I would never deter you in your search. But we're in a tough situation here. You see, Mr. Bhattacharya—you remember him from the engagement—wants to play a part in the wedding ceremony. He's very impressed by your family background. I suspect it'll look good to his voters as well—him upholding the sanaatan Hindu tradition and all that. He asked me if he could have some publicity photos taken at your temple before the ceremony. If he learns of your mixed heritage, and the fact that you aren't even really a Hindu, he'll be most upset. He's likely to distance himself from the whole thing."

Something sharp is in my throat, making it hard to swallow. I try to control my voice, but it comes out both shaky and belligerent.

"Why? Surely it isn't a crime to have an American father! And does it matter that much if Mr. Bhattacharya doesn't participate in the wedding? I know he's a good friend of yours, but this—forgive me, Maman—but this is really crucial for me."

"I'm afraid he's not just a friend, Korobi. Listen, sweetheart, this isn't public knowledge, but we're negotiating with him right now for him to become the chief investor in our business. There's a chance that news like this might make him pull out of that as well. The members of his party are very conservative. They even frown on intercaste alliances, so you can imagine what they would think of someone who marries outside the Hindu faith. With the election coming up, he can't afford to lose their support—and we can't afford to lose his."

I try to make sense of all this, but my confusion must show, because Maman gives a deep sigh. "Under normal circumstances, I wouldn't care what Bhattacharya—or anyone else—thinks. I wouldn't let them dictate my actions. But—" She hesitates, then plunges in. "Oh, I might as well take you into my confidence, you're part of the family now. Barua and Bose is going through a really rough financial patch. Our gallery in New York was vandalized soon after September eleventh last year, and some very expensive paintings were destroyed."

I stare at her in shock. "I'm so sorry to hear this," I finally manage to say. "I had no idea."

"We've been careful to keep it under wraps. If the public came to know, it might affect our sales. People don't like to have anything to do with victims of bad luck. It's as though we're contagious. Anyhow, we'd taken on some big loans to open the gallery. The market was great at the time, and there was a lot of interest in Indian art in the West. Paintings were being auctioned at Sotheby's at record prices. But now we're losing money there every day. We're fighting with the insurance company to recover a portion of the price of the paintings. In fact, I was just on the phone to Mr. Mitra, our manager in New York, getting an update. Things don't look good. The insurance company claims this happened during a crisis situation that isn't included in our contract. Meanwhile, sales there are down to zero. Mr. Bhattacharya's investment will make the difference between life and death for our business. So this is why I need your help, my dear."

I'm torn. This is the first time Maman has asked anything of me. Her situation is precarious—I can see that. My immediate instinct is to put my arms around her and tell her that I'll do as she says. But I remember, too, my mother, my real mother, dream or vision, and her wordless pleading as she pointed across the ocean toward my father.

Maman's pacing now, counting off items on her fingers. "This is what we'll do. We'll get the wedding performed as soon as possible—just a quiet ceremony in your family temple. We'll say we're honoring your grandfather's last wish, but keeping it simple on account of his passing. Bhattacharya would love it—he's fascinated by that temple. Should the news about your father by some chance come to light, your grandmother will have to state that she alone knew this secret. Since she'd sworn an oath in front of the goddess, she could not divulge it. Even the staunchest Hindu wouldn't fault her for that."

I'm touched at being taken into Maman's confidence. Flattered, too, I admit it. She doesn't let many people in under that elegant guard. But I'm also worried. A woman such as Maman rarely asks for assistance; if someone turns her down, I suspect she doesn't take rejection well. I want to help my future family, these wonderful people who have been like parents to me already. But if I give up on my father, it would be a further betrayal of my mother, who has been so terribly wronged. Confused thoughts battle inside my head. Maman is smiling at me. Part of me wants to collapse against her strength and let her make the decisions. Everything would become so easy then. The Boses take care of their own—they would protect me, and Grandmother, too. Rajat would be delighted by the early wedding. I remember the firmness of his palm against my back as we danced, and it is so sweet a memory that I almost say yes.

But I can't. It would be cowardly, for the sake of security, to relinquish this chance to find and to know the man my mother loved so deeply that she couldn't give him up though it tore her heart in two. It would be a betrayal of myself to go through life pretending to be what I'm not.

Maman is smiling already in anticipation. I take a deep breath, hoping she will not hate me for what I'm about to say.

"I'm sorry, Maman. I can't stop my search. I owe it to my dead mother. If Mr. Desai finds a lead, I will follow it to America. But neither do I want to be a trouble to you. I understand how much of a problem for you my heritage has become." I swallow and clear my throat. It's hard for me to say the next words. "If it is so important for your business, I'm willing to release Rajat from the engagement."

Maman's face turns white. "What are you saying? You don't want to marry Rajat?"

"Of course I do, Maman! But I'm a liability to you at this time, I can see that. This way you can tell Mr. Bhattacharya that you broke off the alliance because you found out about my father not being a Hindu. That should please him and make him want to invest with you. Once the investment goes through, and some time has passed, Rajat and I can get back—"

But Maman isn't listening to me. A cold, closed look has descended on her face. "Rajat would give his life for you—and you're prepared to throw his love away like this?"

"I'm not throwing away his love!" I cry, trying to hold back my tears. Oh, why won't she understand me! "Don't you see? I'm offering to do this for him and for you!"

Her nostrils flare with suppressed anger. She goes on as though I haven't spoken. "It's best you discuss this matter directly with Rajat." She presses the buzzer on her desk to indicate the visit is over.

Shikha shows me out in frigid silence. Everything I wanted to say has come out wrong.

Although it is only 4:00 p.m., Mrs. Bose has left the gallery. She sits on an old marble bench across from Rose Aylmer's tomb in the Park Circus cemetery, trying to calm herself as she waits for Rajat.

After Korobi's visit, she couldn't concentrate. She forced herself to meet her next appointment, a potential buyer for a high-end restaurant, but she was too distracted to make an effective presentation. Mortifyingly, she had to plead ill health and hand him over to Shikha. She canceled the rest of her appointments—something she had never done—and called Rajat to say they had to talk.

"Right now? Mother, I have a lot of work. The billing has piled up over the last two weeks, and—"

"It's urgent. Meet me at the cemetery, where we won't be overheard."

"It's that girl, isn't it, causing trouble?" Shikha said with a frown as Mrs. Bose left. Mrs. Bose didn't answer; she didn't have to. Shikha always knew.

Mrs. Bose has chosen the cemetery because it's halfway between the gallery and the warehouse, and because the tales of untimely death etched on the crumbling tombstones usually put her own troubles in perspective. But today they don't help even though it is quiet and cool in the shadows of the palms, beside the worn path lined by moss-encrusted mausoleums. Impossible to sit still any longer! What on earth is delaying Rajat? She paces up and down, startling pigeons into flight. By the time Rajat appears, apologizing about traffic snarl, her patience is at an end. She launches into a tirade even though she knows she shouldn't.

"Why didn't *you* tell me about Korobi's father? I shouldn't have had to hear it from her—"

He sighs. "I'd hoped to get her to keep it to herself. I didn't want to worry you with one more thing on top of all the problems you're handling right now."

Mrs. Bose forgives him immediately, even though he has caused some of those problems. It's always been this way with her firstborn, brought up in those early, difficult days when she had so little time to give him. Her mother would put him to sleep long before Mrs. Bose returned home, but somehow, no matter how quiet she was, he would hear her and lurch from his bed, rubbing his face into her neck with his smell, a mix of milk and earth and sweat, clinging to her. The memory of that embrace, a balm on her aching mother-heart, would keep her going all next day.

He looks so tired, she thinks now with a pang. He's taken on a lot recently. In addition to handling their failing finances, he's offered to be in charge of the warehouse operations while Mr. Bose is traveling. Lately a spate of incidents have occurred there—small, like ant bites, but enough over time to wear one out. He must also feel guilty about the losses at the New York gallery—he had urged them into opening it. And Korobi—she's been a weight on him ever since her grandfather died. All this time, Mrs. Bose has tried to sympathize with Korobi's sorrow, to be patient about how for three weeks Rajat hasn't been home once for dinner. But today, in the gallery, the girl had pushed her over the edge.

Calm down, Joyu, Shanto would have told her if he were here now instead of in Bardhaman, checking on an overdue order of weavings. *Wait and see how the two of them work things out.* Mrs. Bose imagines it: She could say, *It's okay, Son. We'll handle it somehow.* Then Rajat and she could walk the grassy pathways, reading their favorite memorial inscriptions aloud to each other, the poem Walter Savage Landor wrote to his too-soon-withered Rose. They could buy brightly colored ices from the vendor outside the gate, the way they did when he was a boy. They would remember the afternoon only for the way the clouds draped themselves like gray shawls above the pipal trees, for the pair of shalikhs that scolded them from the top of Hindoo Stuart's tomb.

But a part of her will not let things be—the bulldog grip that has led her all these years to succeed when everyone else was waiting for her to fail. She describes the afternoon meeting in passionate detail: how she had put aside her shock at Korobi's news to express her sympathy; how she had confided their difficulties to her; how she had thrown her pride by the roadside and requested her help. The girl had fixed those wide eyes on her and stated, without a trace of hesitation, that she would rather break off the engagement than not go to America.

"She said that?"

"That's right. As if you mattered less to her than this stranger who might not even want to meet her."

Rajat's face is pale and stricken, sharp lines bracket the corners of his mouth. He's taking it harder than she expected.

"Maybe it's best this way," she says consolingly. "You've only known each other a few months. A clean break will hurt for now, but it'll heal fast, and then you can both be free to—"

"But I don't want to be free of her! She's the most precious thing in my life. And she doesn't care? She doesn't care at all for my love?" His voice breaks on the last word.

Mrs. Bose's heart constricts. She can't stand to see her son suffer like this, not even for the good of Barua & Bose.

"Maybe she didn't mean it quite like that," she says, putting an arm around her son. "We were both overwrought. Discuss it with her tomorrow. Come home with me. Pia must be back from school already. We'll order pizza and sit around the table and chat. Put aside our problems for a while—"

Rajat declines. He has to get back to the office, he says curtly. He left some urgent business unfinished there. But at least he sounds calmer.

In silence they walk back to the entrance, past the ironic, ebullient orange of the Gulmohur trees.

"Take the car if you're going to be late," Mrs. Bose says. "I'll catch a cab." From the taxi, she calls Shikha to tell her she's going home. "I don't think I'm up to doing any more work today. Can you handle things?"

"Not a problem, madam. I'll take care of it all. You rest. Maybe take a long soak in the tub with those Yardley bath salts Sir bought you for Valentine's Day."

"I'm so glad I can count on you, Shikha," Mrs. Bose says gratefully.

"It's nothing, madam."

Then, as Mrs. Bose is about to hang up, Shikha adds, "Miss Korobi never did fit in with our family."

Mrs. Bose's body jerks upright in surprise. Why, it's the very thought that has been swimming through the dark part of her mind that she doesn't want to acknowledge.

"Enough, Shikha," she says, but without heat.

"Forgive me, madam. It's just that it pains me to see you upset."

Mrs. Bose is touched, though she doesn't respond. It isn't appropriate to discuss family matters with retainers, no matter how loyal. But Shikha's words have sparked a new thought inside her. As much as she had begun to warm to Korobi, bringing her into the family confidences, the child is clearly not as dependable as she had thought. Perhaps allowing Korobi to go away to America might not be a bad idea after all. If the girl does find her father and decides to remain there, perhaps it would be for the best in the long run.

Late at night I'm jerked awake by a loud, confused commotion. I push up reluctantly through viscous layers of sleep, still exhausted by the events of the day, by the argument I had with Grandmother upon my return from the gallery.

"You told her *what*? You want to break off the engagement and go to America? Are you crazy? Don't you understand how lucky you are that Mrs. Bose is willing to go through with the marriage even after knowing about your father? You should have accepted her offer of an early wedding."

I should have held my tongue. Grandmother looked so distraught. But I was feeling frightened, and so I shouted, "I'm tired of people treating me like a charity case, acting like they're doing me a great favor by having this wedding take place. I'm not ready for it, anyway!"

"Not ready?" Grandmother's mouth fell open—in surprise or outrage, I wasn't sure which. "You're talking as though we forced you into this engagement! I remember the day you came to us, all shiny-faced, begging us to let you marry Rajat. Didn't you say you were surer of your love for him than of anything else in your life?"

I reached back, trying to recapture the feel of that day, but the memory came to me in dim sepia, leached of emotion. I felt sad for the innocent girl I'd been then.

"I'm sorry for causing you so much grief. I'm no longer sure about anything. Except that my mother would have wanted me to find my father. That was what my dream meant, Grandma, I'm sure of it."

Rajat didn't come for dinner. We waited for him until the curry was cold and the rutis hard and dry, but he didn't even call.

The commotion is louder now, someone shouting, someone pleading. It's coming from the entrance. I don't want Grandmother to wake—she has a hard time getting back to sleep. I throw a shawl over my nightgown and hurry to the stairs.

I recognize Bahadur's voice, then Asif's.

"Please, Rajat-saab, it's very late. You'll wake Ma."

"Saab, let me take you home. You can talk to Korobi-memsaab tomorrow."

"No. Now! I'm going to talk to her right now! How dare she say she wants to break off the engagement? That she doesn't care about me?"

Rajat's voice is loud, his words slurring. He pounds the door with both fists. In all these months, I've never seen him drunk like this. I rush down the stairs, aghast. Oh, Rajat! What have I done?

Cook, cowering at the foot of the staircase, tries to hold me back, but I move her aside and unbolt the door. The blood pounds in my temples, but I must face Rajat. I owe him that much. I'm shocked by his face, splotched with red, his unfocused eyes. His clothing is rumpled. I force myself to take him by his upraised arm. Faking a confidence I don't feel, I tell Bahadur and Asif, who look distraught, that I'll take care of him. I pull him into the house and shut the door. Rajat follows me, surprisingly docile. But just when I let out a relieved breath, he grabs my shoulders. His nails dig into my flesh, making me cry out, more in shock than pain.

"Stop! You're hurting me!"

His grip doesn't slacken. "No more than you've hurt me. Why do you want to end our engagement? Don't you love me anymore? I trusted you. I thought you would be different from—from the others."

I pull at his hands, but he's too strong.

"What is it? Have you found someone else? Have you?"

With each question, he shakes me so that my head snaps back and forth. Somewhere to the side, I hear Cook's terrified whimpers. Why, I don't know this man, don't know him at all! Despair rises in me, a molten red wave.

Help! I cry inside my head. I'm not sure whom I'm calling. I think it's my mother. With that thought, time seems to slow down. How much courage it must have taken her to stand up to Bimal Roy, of whom half of Kolkata was afraid. She'd refused to be bullied into giving up the man she loved, though it eventually cost her her life. I'm her daughter. I can handle this.

I stop struggling. "I can't talk to you unless you calm down," I say, trying to keep the gasp out of my voice.

I must sound different because Rajat lets go and slumps onto the sofa. I tell Cook to bring a wet towel and some food. I wipe his face with hands that are still trembling. "Eat," I say as though to a child, and like a child he opens his mouth obediently. I feel tenderness rise in me as I feed him the Parle-G biscuits Cook has brought. When he buries his face in the towel, I rub his back.

I can feel our relationship shifting, plate by tectonic plate.

"There's no one else," I say when Rajat looks up again. "Only you."

"Then why do you want to be free of me?"

"I don't want that! But I also don't want to bring financial disaster to your family. I refuse to be the reason for Bhattacharya backing off from investing in Barua and Bose. Your mother told me how crucial his support is right now—"

Rajat holds me tightly. "Bhattacharya can go to hell. But it's not just my mother—I don't want you to leave, either. I love you, Korobi. Don't abandon me and go to America!"

I want to say *Okay*. I want it so badly, I can barely breathe. But I can't. If I do, I know I'll never feel complete, in his arms or anywhere else. I have too many unanswered questions to just let this go.

"If I can conduct the search from here, I'll certainly do that. But if Desai says I need to be in America, I'll have to go."

"I'm afraid to be without you, Cara." Rajat's voice is muffled against my neck.

"I'll come back as soon as I can. I promise."

"I'm trying hard to change my life," Rajat whispers against my throat. "I want to be a good person—like you. But I'm not skilled at handling temptation. What if I backslide? What if I do something stupid?"

An image flashes in my brain, Sonia in her silver dress at our engagement party watching us with her intense silver eyes, more glitteringly beautiful than I'll ever be. My mouth goes dry. Is she the temptation Rajat is thinking of?

"I trust you." I look into his eyes and want him to know I mean it. "Just hold on for a little while."

Our kiss is long, passionate, laced with desperation. When he pulls away, his voice is sober.

"All right, I can manage one month without you. If we pull the right strings, it'll take about three weeks for you to get your travel papers. That'll give Desai enough time to do the groundwork. You can search for one more month after that in America. If you don't find your father by then, you have to promise to return. That way, we can still make the wedding date your grandfather set."

Misgiving stirs in my heart. A month seems like too little time to find a father who has been lost for eighteen years. But Rajat's making a compromise, and so must I.

"Very well." In a way, it's a relief, knowing that this will all be over, one way or another, in two months' time.

Asif Ali drives the Mercedes up Nazrul Islam Road, taking the family to the airport. Tonight he has a full load, Rajat-saab up front, Pia-missy between her parents in the back. Usually when the family gets together, there's laughter and jokes, teasing comments flung back and forth, but this time the car is silent. This is because they are going to the airport, to say good-bye to Korobi-memsaab. She's going off to America, and no one is sure what will happen next.

Though the family is careful not to speak of such things in front of Asif, he knows more than they suspect. In fact, he might know a few things that they don't. Madam's maid, Pushpa, has told him, over samosas and chutney at a chai house, that the Boses' financial situation is worsening. Their only hope is that fat, khadi-wearing politician who comes around late at night to discuss a possible business deal. Memsaab is polite to him, offering the imported Scotch they only take out for special guests. Saab and he have spent hours going over stacks of accounts, but he hasn't bitten yet.

And, yes, the calls from Sonia continue.

From Bahadur, Asif has learned that Korobi-baby is going to New York City to look for someone—a long-lost rich uncle who can help the Roys out of their troubles, Bahadur guesses. Sarojini-ma must be anxious. She hasn't left the house this last week, not even to cut oleander sprigs for the temple. Can you blame her for worrying, with all those terrorist bombs going off nowadays in America?

The night he'd been drunk, Rajat had let some things slip, too, as they drove to the Roy mansion. He had punched the back of the car seat repeatedly, ranting that Korobi-memsaab wanted to break off their engagement. After six years of living in the city, not much surprised Asif anymore, but this had. Korobi-memsaab didn't seem the flighty type. At the mansion, he admired the way she had come to the door herself, quite unafraid, and taken Rajat by the hand. It must have been a miscommunication, because by the time he left her a couple hours later, Rajat was calm and—thank Allah!—sober. Not that Asif was one of those fundamentalists who believed that alcohol was the gateway to Jahannam. Still, seeing Rajat so out of control made Asif give serious consideration to the offer that Sheikh Rehman's man had made to him again recently.

"A solid young Mussulman like you, with a reputation for being discreet and loyal, can rise far higher with his own people. The sheikh is making you a better offer than last time. But he may not make another one. He doesn't like being turned down."

Memsaab's increasing ill-temper in the last month has also made Asif consider a change of employers. He still thinks about the afternoon when he was driving her to the Park Circus cemetery. A truck carrying a load of furniture swerved suddenly into their lane, inches away from their car. Asif had to wrench the wheel to the side, slamming his foot down on the brake and barely missing a cyclist. Memsaab had slid across the seat and hit her head on the window. Not hard, but she'd gone on and on about his carelessness, though clearly it wasn't his fault.

"I hope you don't drive like this when Pia's in the car!" she'd ended.

The unfairness of that had pricked him. As though he'd ever do anything to endanger Pia-missy. Why, that child was the reason he was finding it so hard to leave. She talked to him about everything and trusted him to keep it secret.

"A.A., I think Korobi-didi is breaking up with Dada. Why would she do that? They're both such amazing people. I was sure she loved him."

"Dada is always sad nowadays. He used to be such a good sport, but now he snaps if I ask him anything. Of course he won't tell me why. Everybody thinks I'm too young to know what's going on."

"Is this what love is, A.A.? People are crazy for each other, then it's gone, and you're left feeling terrible? I don't think I want it to ever happen to me."

"Mama and Papa were talking about selling bonds. When I came into the room, they covered up the papers and asked me about school. As though I'm a moron!"

"Our class is going to Darjeeling over the summer holidays for a week. They'll see the sunrise from Tiger Hill and ride horses and visit a tea garden. It'll be such fun. But I didn't even tell Maman. I know we don't have the money."

"Yesterday I was playing basketball in the schoolyard, and I saw Sonia watching me from across the street. I recognized her silver car. Why would she be there, A.A.? She doesn't even like me, not really."

Pia was the only person, other than Asif's sister, who had ever asked his opinion, who listened to his halting answers with complete absorption. He wished he could solve all her problems. Recently, protectiveness rose in him like a wave when he had her in the car. He drove with extra caution, even though she complained that he was turning stodgy like the other adults she knew. When he heard about Sonia stalking her, his mouth filled with bile. Allah help him, if the woman tried to hurt Pia, he'd—he'd ram the Benz into her little car until it was a junk heap with her in it. Even now, driving, his hands clench as he remembers. He'd know how to find her, too, because a couple of days earlier, she'd stuck a note on his windshield giving him that information.

He had come back from lunch and discovered it.

Phone me—I'll make it worth your while.

He wishes he had someone he could confide in as Pia does with him.

Memsaab leans forward. "Asif, why are you going so slow? The road's not even crowded. Pick up the speed. We should have been at the airport by now. We'll hardly have time to talk to Korobi before she has to go into the security area."

"Yes, Memsaab."

He'll call Sonia tomorrow. Better to know what that Jezebel is planning than be ignorant of her schemes.

At the security gate, I turn for a last look. They stand in a line behind the metal barricade: Papa, Pia, Maman, Rajat, Grandmother—and Cook, who to everyone's surprise threw a fit just as Bahadur was loading the car, insisting that she accompany us. I stare until my eyes burn, trying to memorize their faces. Three people stand out: Maman, Rajat, and Grandmother. In the last month, all three have surprised me.

After I had a long phone conversation with Desai and concluded that I must go to America, I informed Grandmother, hesitantly, of what I wanted to do. Now that my grandfather was gone, I was her whole existence. I felt guilty at the thought of her wandering alone through the big, empty house.

She wept a little when I told her, but when I asked if she would rather I didn't go, she scolded me away from guilt. "Of course I'd rather you didn't go. Of course I'm sick with fear because of how dangerous America is, especially for you. You don't know much about surviving in the world on your own—you've never had to do it. But I understand how important it is for you to find your father—and that I have no right to stop you. I believe your mother's spirit will watch over you, and that makes me feel better. Don't you dare worry about me! You think I can't manage this household on my own for a month? What am I, senile?"

When she realized how much the search was going to cost, Grandmother brought out the casket containing her dowry jewelry and handed it to me.

"We'll sell them. Ask Rajat to help—he'll get us a good price."

"But, Grandma," I said, at once grateful and aghast, "these pieces have been in the family for generations!"

She shrugged. "They're only metal and stone, in the end. Less important than a living person's happiness."

Before we left for the airport, she kissed me on the forehead and said, "It'll be a great adventure. Look carefully at everything. Feel. Enjoy. Remember."

A great adventure! Caught up in the gravity of what I was doing, hobbled by Rajat's reluctance and Maman's disapproval, I hadn't thought of my journey as an adventure. Grandmother was giving me permission to do so. "It's so easy to let the days slip through your hands," Grandmother continued. "Sometimes I look at myself and wonder, how did I become this Sarojini, so staid and responsible, so different from that girl who liked to climb guava trees in her parents' home and play tricks and burst into laughter for no reason? I don't want that to happen to you."

I felt a pang of regret. There was so much I didn't know about Grandmother, so much that, distracted by Grandfather's leonine aura, I'd never bothered to notice. If I come back, I promised myself, I'll do it differently.

Then I was shocked. *If I come back*. Where had *that* come from?

Next to Grandmother stands Maman, waving cheerily. After our ill-fated encounter in the gallery, I'd been reluctant to face her. I dreaded the weight of her disapproval and feared that she would pressure me to give up my journey. But she was unexpectedly pleasant when she came over to the house a week later to discuss wedding plans. The marriage would be held in three months, she said, honoring the date set by Grandfather. That should give me enough time for what I needed to do. When I stammered an apology at having hurt her by offering to break off the engagement, she said she understood. She only asked for one thing: that we keep my reason for going a secret. Perhaps we could drop discreet hints in the right places, indicating that I was going to meet a long-lost relative who had been estranged for decades from Grandfather? It wouldn't be too far from the truth.

"Of course," I said, thankful that she was being so reasonable, but inwardly I was baffled by this magical change. Then I figured that Rajat must have explained my motives to her.

Before leaving, she added that, while in America, I could stay with the Mitras, the couple who managed their New York gallery. She would speak to them if I wished. I breathed a sigh of relief. I had been worrying about where I would stay. Every place in New York was so expensive, even the run-down weekly rooms that Desai had suggested. In my gratitude, I agreed to let Maman buy me an overcoat, though I feared (and rightly so) that she would choose something far too expensive.

Once in a while, though, I am reminded that the polite, friendly woman I'm seeing is not the real Maman. The warm woman who had begun to love me as a daughter, who might have scolded and cajoled me the way she would have with Pia, who had once demanded my help the way one can only with family, had receded from me after our argument and soundlessly shut a door. It'll be a long time before she emerges again.

Finally, Rajat. I've held off on looking at him because I want him to be the last, for his face to remain imprinted on my retinas like lightning. He has lost weight in the last month. It makes him more attractive in a haggard, hungry way. He stands with an arm looped around Grandmother; he has promised to take care of her while I'm gone. Since the engagement, not a day has passed when we haven't spent at least a few hours together. Now we'll be halfway across the world from each other. So far! How will I handle it? How will he? And what of those temptations he had mentioned that drunken night?

That night had changed something between us, though not quite in the way I had hoped. Yes, he let me in on his vulnerabilities a little more. He told me when he had had a hard day at work and how the negotiations with Bhattacharya were going. He confided that he felt guilty about the money they were losing in New York because he had urged the family to open the gallery there. From time to time he stopped what he was doing to grip my hands and look hungrily into my face, as though he were trying to store up our moments together. But he still guarded his past. Anytime I asked about Sonia, he deflected my questions and focused instead on the details of my journey. He made sure I had everything—passport, visa, tickets, medical exams, traveler's checks. He even wired money to Mitra so he would have a mobile phone ready for me.

"Call me every day, okay?" he said last night when I walked him to his car. He clutched me as if he were drowning and only I could save him. It frightened me a little, how important I was to him. A swell of tenderness came over me. I held him close and stroked his hair.

"Promise you'll be faithful?"

For a moment I was outraged that he should doubt me, but I couldn't keep it up. Not when he was vulnerable like this.

"I promise."

"Promise you'll return in a month and marry me?"

"I promise."

Even as I said the words, I remembered a story Grandmother had once told me about an enchanted land. When people went there, they forgot the loved ones they had left behind. They forgot themselves, too. No one returned from that country, although they weren't unhappy there in their bewitchment. What if America turned out to be like that?

"A month without you will seem like a lifetime, Cara!"

I said nothing. The issue of time was murky. A month without him, on my own, would be torturous for me, too. It stretched forth lonely as an ice field at the edge of the world. But what if I was close to finding my father when the month ended? Would I be able to give up that chance?

Rajat must have sensed my hesitation. He said, "In today's world, if you can't find someone in a whole month of searching, you'll never find him. Maybe a man like that doesn't want to be found."

Looking back at him now, his free arm raised in a solemn wave, I think how people are full of contradictions. Rajat loves me, I have no doubt of that, and I love him. But here I am, hurting him, maybe even jeopardizing our relationship by going off on this crazy hunt. And he—he's done everything for me to succeed in my search, but deep down I suspect he'd rather I failed so that things could go back to how they were.

The monitor flashes. It's time for me to go through security check. As I turn, behind Rajat's head I see two ovals of light. Is it just a trick of my tear-filled eyes? I want to believe it's my mother. And, next to her, Grandfather. Are they blessing my journey, or battling over my future, the different outcome each wishes for me? I want to keep looking, but my disobedient eyes will not obey. They blink. The lights disappear. Only a whitewashed wall, discolored from the seepage of rain, remains.

I walk into the women's booth, where a security officer pats me down. Ahead, in the waiting lounge, a gallery of uninterested faces. No one knows me. I know no one. This is my life now.

FIVE

I stumble out of the customs area of Kennedy Airport exhausted and dizzy and search the mass of milling humanity for a face that matches the one on the photograph I carry. The flight, where I was crammed into a corner beside an overweight man who spilled onto my seat, snoring energetically, had seemed interminable. The recycled air made my eyes itchy and dry. Unable to sleep, I had obsessed over all the things that might go wrong in America—and it seems that already the first of them has come true. Mitra, who was supposed to pick me up, is nowhere to be found. Minutes pass; half an hour; my flightmates reunite joyfully with their families and go off to their various destinations. Panic forms a lump in my throat. What if Mitra has been in an accident? What if he's dead? I force myself to breathe slowly; I get coins from a money changer and phone Mitra's home and then his cell phone. No one picks up. I long to call Rajat. But it's 2:00 a.m there. I push the thought out of my mind before it can take hold. He can't help me from halfway across the world, and it would only make him crazed with worry. I'm not such a weakling as to subject him to that, not this soon.

Finally I see Mitra—but I wouldn't have recognized him without the makeshift sign he's holding up, a sheet of paper with my name untidily scratched on it. The photo that Rajat had given me—taken less than a year back in India—was of a confident, good-looking man in a designer shirt, shoulders thrown back, smiling infectiously. This person, though his features are still handsome, has circles under eyes that dart back and forth. He wears a suit that must have, at one time, been expensive but is now only crumpled. His hair hangs dispirited over his forehead as he apologizes about the traffic. Following him to the taxicab stand, I wonder how America the Beautiful could have wrought such a change on him.

Once in the taxi, my spirits lift. We cross a bridge, the mysterious water colored like steel. In the distance, buildings rise imposingly into a gray sky. My heart expands as I look at that famous skyline. Grandmother is right, this *will* be an adventure. For the first time, I feel ready.

I want to tell someone this, but Mitra stares out the window, lips pressed together, clearly preoccupied. He breaks his silence only when I ask the driver, a dark man with an unfamiliar accent, where he's from. In low, rapid Bangla, Mitra tells me that it's dangerous to ask questions of strangers in America. Chastised, I lapse into silence until we pass a Ganesh temple—the last thing I was expecting to see!

"Is this close to your apartment?" I ask. Unexpectedly, I find myself missing our temple back home, though I rarely visited it on my own.

"Not too far."

"I'd like to visit it. Have you been in there?"

"I have as little to do with this neighborhood as possible."

I look around. Why, then, is he living here, among modest halal restaurants that are a hair's breadth from being run-down, and sari shop windows crammed with mannequins in garish sequined chiffons? Especially since the Boses' gallery is some distance away in Chelsea?

When we arrive at our destination, I make a polite offer to pay the fare, which is alarmingly large. In India, a host would have refused, but Mitra only looks away when I put a stack of my dollars—limited and precious, for Grandmother's jewelry had brought less than we'd expected—into the driver's hand. I'm both worried and annoyed. If Mitra wasn't planning to pay, he should have chosen a cheaper form of transportation. I'll have to insist on that from now on.

Already I'm losing my Indian courtesies; I'm thinking in terms of survival, like an immigrant.

Mitra's apartment sits above a karaoke bar, its windows plastered with gigantic Bollywood posters. We climb a dingy stairwell, passing an Indian woman who stares at us but doesn't greet Mitra. He is obviously not popular with the neighbors. He unlocks his door, hands me over to his wife, a pregnant young woman who has been waiting with a hesitant smile, and tells me that he must be off, sorry to rush, but he's already late. He's gone before I get a chance to ask about the cell phone he is supposed to give me, or about visiting Desai, which I hoped to do today.

Fortunately, Mrs. Mitra, a sweet-faced woman not much older than me, is more welcoming. She apologizes for the smallness of the apartment, which is cramped and dark, with paint peeling in corners, brings out hot tea and spicy snacks, and entreats me to call her by her name, Seema. When I ask if I can phone India, she tells me sorry, their line is set up to make only local calls. No, no e-mail, either—the laptop is with Mr. Mitra at work. But, yes, I can phone Mr. Desai.

Desai informs me that he's made good headway and has a possible lead—he'll explain when he sees me. When I tell him I want to come over right now, he advises me to wait for Mitra as his office is not in the best part of town.

Disappointed and a little taken aback, I gulp down my watery tea and stalk impatiently around the apartment, which is crammed with expensive furniture that looks as if it was bought for somewhere else. With a sigh Seema puts her swollen feet up on a large and elegant coffee table and barrages me with questions. What news of Kolkata? Have I seen the latest movies? Which are my favorites? What are the new fashions, and have I brought any with me? (Here she tugs self-consciously at her cheap smock, which is already too tight.) In between, she glances nervously out the window, which is covered with a thin fabric that allows her to look out without being seen. She seems sweet, if nervous, so I curb my frustration about wasting time here when I should be starting my search—and respond as best as I can.

What has brought me to New York? she finally asks.

I stave off this one with a vague reference to a lost relative. I have some questions of my own. What happened to the Mitras to reduce them to this state? Are the Boses aware of the situation? Maman certainly hadn't warned me. I wonder how to ask about this, but I don't have to. Seema, starved for conversation, has already launched artlessly into the story of her life.

They had met two years ago in the Kolkata call center, where she was a new employee, freshly arrived from a small town, and he the hugely popular manager, famous for throwing pizza parties when they exceeded their sales quota. He'd been quite the man-about-town, clothes from New Market, haircut from Park Street, and his cologne—always foreign. You wouldn't know it, looking at him now, would you? Seema still can't believe that he fell in love with her, little brown mouse from a suburb-town. When Mrs. Bose approached Mitra because she needed a manager for their new art gallery in the United States and promised him a job for his wife, too, if he had one, he proposed to Seema.

Seema was thrilled and relieved. She'd been afraid he was only slumming with her, that one day he'd move on. She was delighted, too, at the prospect of living in America, of having the chance to walk the magical streets that had popped up so many times on her screen in the call center.

At first all had gone well: a grand opening at the Mumtaz, positive write-ups in the papers, several exciting sales. They rented a charming apartment on the edge of the Upper West Side, in a building with a doorman, like in the movies. They worked well together, she handling the accounts and reception, and he taking care of marketing and customers. When work was done, they plunged into the heady life of New York—restaurants, plays, museums, shopping. Even walking in Central Park or people-watching around Times Square was an adventure. They began to make friends, though generally they avoided the Indian set. They hadn't come to America, Mr. Mitra reminded her, to stay closeted with their own kind. Seema agreed, though sometimes she missed having friends who would have understood her pangs of homesickness, who could have taught her easy American substitutions for Indian dishes she hankered for, who could have explained how to navigate through the dangers of America she was always hearing about. But in the early days, neither she nor Mr. Mitra considered America dangerous. They often exclaimed how much safer it was than India—no pocket-maars snatching your wallet, no burglars breaking into your apartment, no corrupt police who showed up at your store for monthly "tea money."

Then the Twin Towers fell, and everything changed.

When Seema mentions the Towers, her face caves in like an old woman's; her mouth moves as though the words she needs have suddenly gone missing. The abrupt change startles me. Though I want to hear what happened, I take her hand and tell her she doesn't have to talk about it if it upsets her.

"I'll tell you tomorrow," she finally says. "If I start on it now, I won't be able to sleep, and that would be bad for the baby."

We wait up late for Mr. Mitra, but he doesn't return, and finally, exhausted, we go to bed. Seema sighs and tells me this has been happening lately. Since the vandalism, he works too hard, trying to make up for the losses they encountered. She shows me to a tiny room with a mattress on the floor. Cardboard boxes are stacked along one wall. Some are filled with Indian groceries, stockpiled against a future the Mitras no longer trust; some hold unexpected, elegant decorations: crystal candlesticks heavy enough to be real; a hand-painted Japanese plate wrapped in damask napkins. The room is bitter cold; the window doesn't close all the way. Seema stuffs a blanket into the opening, but I don't think it will help much. When she leaves, I take out my mother's letter and her photo from my suitcase and huddle with them under a surprisingly beautiful satin quilt. What a contradiction this apartment is! Noise from the karaoke bar below hits me in sudden blasts as guests enter and exit. Bollywood songs, nostalgic old favorites, the immigrant's longing to capture home. In India, I never cared for this kind of music, but now as I hear it, homesickness twists my insides. Before bed, I called Kolkata collect and talked to Grandmother, but only for a minute because it was dreadfully expensive. She sounded sad and worried. I called Rajat's mobile, too, but no one picked up. I lie on the lumpy mattress, clutching the letter and the photo as though they were talismans that might lead me to my father. I am as far from my loved ones as it is possible to be while still remaining on this planet. Loneliness falls on me like snow over an empty field.

A cockroach scuttles from one box to another, startling me. I hadn't thought there would be such creatures in affluent America! The roach rubs its serrated legs together and watches me from the edge of its cardboard fort. It's a fitting emblem to end my first disconcerting day. I pull the quilt over my head, tucking it in carefully to prevent unwanted night visitors, and stifle a wild laugh against my knuckles. I'm afraid if I get started, I may not be able to stop.

It is a beautiful afternoon, with a crisp, cool breeze unusual for Kolkata in April, but Asif is sweating. His ironed shirt is limp and dark at the armpits as he waits outside the closed gate of Miss Sonia's mansion. He's angry with the young woman for making him wait, but also with himself because after seeing the palatial mansion in which she lives—you could fit the Boses' flat into this compound eight times over—his brain started calling her Miss Sonia.

The gate is made of solid, black iron, embossed with some kind of family crest. It has a small window cut into it at eye level, which the guard on duty opened to question Asif, rudely, on his business. When Asif told him that Miss Sonia had asked him to come here, the man lifted a disbelieving eyebrow and said he would check. Asif took great pleasure in telling him not to bother, he had Miss Sonia's mobile number and had called her already. But that was fifteen minutes ago, and his pleasure had faded, especially as the guard had just opened the window again and said, "You still here?"

Bitch, he thinks. Forcing him to wait like a beggar outside her gate when she was the one who needed him. Because of her he's wasted his off-duty afternoon, the only one he got all week. He could have been at the zoo, his favorite spot. Right now, he could have been sitting on a bench outside the aviary, munching on crisp, hot bhajias from the vendor, watching the bright birds flit from branch to branch inside cages so large that they probably didn't know they weren't free. They reminded him of his sister and of Pia-missy, the way they cocked their heads to look at him curiously. Often he found himself smiling back at them. From there he would go to the elephant compound, where he fed peanuts to the big, lumbering beasts, enjoying the feel of their raspy, inquiring trunks in his palm. It always put him in a good mood when the elephants trumpeted and salaamed him after the peanuts were gone. Animals were superior to most humans. Men would have turned away once you had nothing more to give them. If Asif hadn't dropped out of school in sixth class, he would have written a shayari on the subject.

Asif decides he isn't going to waste any more time on Sonia. Let her go to hell. He strides down the street, shouldering roughly past other pedestrians. He's almost at the bus stop when he hears the horn and knows it to be hers, slicing powerfully through the other street sounds, tempting him like a siren's song. Against his will, he looks.

The breeze from the open window has tousled her hair just the right amount. Or maybe there are things—shampoos, gels, he's seen them on TV—that make her look this way. He has to admit that she's attractive. The mocking expression in her eyes says she knows it, too. *Look but don't touch. I'm not for your kind.*

"Impatient, aren't you?" she says casually. She gestures for him to climb into the passenger seat.

He'd love to turn his back on her and keep walking, but he does as she says. He's curious about what she's planning—and about the Porsche. He'll never get another chance to sit in a car like this. Owners of foreign-model two-seaters liked to show them off by driving themselves around. The leather is silken, the skin of a princess. She's dressed for tennis in a tight blue top and a short, white, pleated skirt that exposes unseemly amounts of thigh and sends evil thoughts careening through his mind. The outfit is what he expected, but the perfume she's wearing startles him, floating its light, flowery innocence through the cool air of the car. It seems like something Pia-missy might have chosen.

Sonia weaves deftly through the unruly Kolkata traffic, one hand on the wheel. When she needs to honk, she uses her elbow, a fluid jab that Asif vows to try for himself as soon as he has a chance. Not that Memsaab would allow it. He can just hear her: *Asif, what kind of crazy bug has got into your head? You want to land us in the hospital?*

With her other hand Sonia takes a sealed envelope out of her purse. "Give this to Rajat-saab. Today. Make sure he's alone when he gets it."

She drops the letter in his lap and digs in the purse again. This time she takes out some rupee notes and holds them out for him to take. The three notes are each for a thousand rupees. His heart gives a jolt, as if the car had just hit un unexpected pothole. It's almost a month's salary. Does so much money mean nothing to people such as Sonia? How much more did she have in that purse of hers? A fantasy unspools with dizzying velocity through his brain. A lonely stretch of road—maybe near the river. He leans over and flings open her door. Grabs the purse and pushes her from the car. Maneuvers himself into the driver's seat. Ah, the feel of that hard, gleaming steering wheel under his fingers. The acceleration smooth as butter. It was a big country. He could go far away, sell the car, start a new life. There were people who bought things like that. He was confident he could find them. Meanwhile he'd use the money in the purse, change his name, dye his hair, lie low like a wild animal. He'd never work for another rich bastard again.

"What's wrong with you?" Her voice, raspy with too many late nights in too many immoral places, jerks him back to the present like a fishhook. "Take the money!"

The fantasy hangs around him like hashish smoke, which he tried when the other drivers prodded him, but only once because of how disgusted it made him feel later. He cannot quite reach past the haze to formulate an objection. So he takes the notes, though a warning jangles through his system.

What could be in that letter?

She gives a small, satisfied smile. Her teeth are white and straight. She pulls over smoothly to the curb, motions to him to get out.

"Make sure you give it to him as soon as you can. Believe me, I'll find out if you don't. And don't even think of double-crossing me."

"Oh, no, madam, never-never." His voice is obsequious yet steady, a loyal, trustable voice. He has already resolved to steam open the letter and read its contents, then decide what to do.

Late afternoon of my second day. I lie on the couch after lunch, gripped by the tentacles of jet-lag sleep. When I awoke around noon, to my dismay Mitra was nowhere to be seen. Seema told me he left for work, but I'm suspicious. Perhaps he never came home last night. She told me also that Rajat had called, but I was sleeping so soundly, he told her to let me be. I was furious with her for not waking me. I was starved for the sound of Rajat's voice, for a word of love. But now it was too late at night there for me to call him.

I'm dreaming of the Towers, which Seema talked about a little while ago. When I'd seen the disaster on Indian TV, sitting beside Grandfather in our living room in Kolkata, I'd felt only a mild sorrow. They had been icons of another world, tiny and distant and beheaded already. But in New York their absence saturates the air I breathe. In my dream they loom, bigger and bigger still, unharmed and shining in the midst of a perfect autumn day. The jaunty silver clouds are reflected on their thousand glass windows. I know I'm about to witness their destruction. I try to wake up, but though I thrash and moan, I can't.

The first plane is slender and graceful, arrow straight. It enters the building smoothly, pauselessly. Only a Medusa smoke, curling thickly everywhere, gives away that this wasn't meant to happen. By the time the second plane hits, the screams are so loud that I can't hear the crash. Floors crumble, one collapsing onto the other, a vertical domino set. Chunks of buildings fly at me, malignant comets. They set other buildings afire.

Then the people start jumping. Aghast, I try to turn away, but I can't climb out of my dream. Around me, white ash drifts like bitter snow. It coats my mouth, it makes me blind. I taste on my tongue hatred for those who could have done such a terrible thing.

Afterward, Seema said, many South Asian businesses were boycotted, especially those with Muslim names. Others were attacked. The Mitras had arrived at the Mumtaz one morning to find the plate glass cracked, paintings slashed, the floor filthy with urine and feces, threats scrawled over the walls in terrifying red letters. The shock had almost caused Seema to have a miscarriage. And worse: when Mitra went to the police to complain, not only were they unhelpful, but they detained him for two days for questioning. Seema had been in the apartment alone all that time, crazy with worry. No, she didn't know where they'd taken him, or what exactly they did. When he returned, haggard-eyed, Mitra refused to talk about it. Those two days had changed him, made him bitter and silent the way he'd never been. That was when she developed her fear of strangers. When they had to move out of their Upper West Side apartment because they could no longer afford it, she insisted on living here, among her own kind.

My dream shifts. In it, I hear Seema's voice, arguing urgently.

"It's four p.m.! Where were you all this time? Why don't you pick up the phone when I call? You know that makes me ill with worry. Especially when you stay out all night."

"I told you, I'm busy with a project. Can't be disturbed in the middle of business dealings."

"Not gallery business, I can guess that much—"

"Quit nagging! I'm doing this for you—you know that. Haven't you been begging to go back to India to have the baby? Where do you think the money for that will come from? You know Mrs. Bose has refused to advance us any more, the bitch!" His hisses the words, which reverberate in the small room.

"Shhh. Korobi-madam will hear you."

"Are you kidding? Jet lag's like chloroform. Just look at her, slumped over."

"Please don't do anything dangerous! I don't want anything to happen to you."

Mitra gives a bitter laugh. "You're like the cat in the proverb—want to catch the fish, but don't want to touch the water. Everything comes with a price. Did you find out why she's here?"

"I asked, but all she said was she's looking for a relative. She doesn't want to talk about it. I'm sorry! I'm no good at things like that."

It sounds as if Seema is tearing up.

He gives a sigh. "Never mind. Come here. Let me rub your back. Is it aching a lot? Did you have heartburn again?"

Even in sleep, I can feel her snuggled up against him. My body aches with memory.

"Remember how the baby wasn't moving, the last couple days? Well, he kicked again today, thank God!"

"He did? How about that!" A smile fills Mitra's voice.

In my dream, they kiss. Mitra bends over Seema's stomach to whisper to the baby inside. After a while, she serves him lunch. He tells her everything tastes excellent.

"Korobi-madam helped me."

"Don't call her madam!" He's angry again. "She's not your boss. And you shouldn't have taken her help."

"Why don't you like her?"

"Because she's one of them. And because Mrs. Bose practically ordered me to put her up." He puts on a posh, clipped accent. "'Mitra, Rajat's fiancée is coming to New York. I'd like her to stay with you.' Not a single *please*, and certainly not a *thank you*."

"But Korobi-madam—uh, she—can't help that. And she seems kind. She asked about the baby and my health, telling me to eat on time. I can't tell you how nice it is to have someone to talk to."

"I hope you didn't tell her anything important?"

"What can I tell her?" Seema says petulantly. "It's not like I know anything about what you're doing."

"The Boses can't be trusted. Anything they know, they'll use against us. Have you forgotten how Mrs. Bose acted after the gallery was broken into? When the police took me away? Like it was all my fault. Then when I asked for an advance because you were pregnant and we hadn't been able to sell any paintings, she wanted to know what I'd done with the earlier commissions. That's none of her damn business!"

Seema makes soothing sounds, but Mitra ignores her.

"And how about when I said I wanted to quit and return to India because of your depression?"

"She told you that we couldn't leave now, because they'd have to close down the gallery."

"Is that all you remember? You're such a simpleton, it's good you have me to watch out for you. She said you needed to pull yourself together, and added that if I quit now, she'd make sure no one in Kolkata ever gave me another job again. For all you know, she's put the girl here to spy on us."

"Okay," Seema says in an abashed voice, "I won't tell her anything else."

"There's something fishy going on. This Desai, whom I'm supposed to take her to see, is a private detective. Korobi must be looking for someone important. Otherwise she wouldn't have traveled halfway across the world on a shoestring budget—I saw how she counted out her dollars. Whatever her secret is, it's clearly something the Boses want to keep private. If I can figure it out, maybe I can get some money out of them, and a good reference as well. Together with the deal I'm working on, that'll be enough for us to get back to Kolkata and on our feet again. The Boses owe us that much, at the very least, for all the trauma they've put us through."

Seema whispered something I couldn't hear, but Mitra answered vehemently, "Oh, they'll pay! And if they don't, I'll make sure to crush that family reputation they're so proud of. Trample it into mud."

His voice is so vicious, I cringe in my sleep.

"Go wake her. I'll take her to that detective now."

When the kettle begins to hiss, Asif turns off the gas burner and holds the letter in the steam billowing from the spout, as he had once seen in a spy thriller. In the film, the hero had peeled the flap open in one smooth move. This letter turns soggy and refuses to cooperate. He should wait for the paper to dry some, but he's desperate to read what's inside. He pulls the flap, and it tears. Asif swears. He'll have to buy another fancy envelope for the letter. It won't have Rajat's name on it, but that would be believable, won't it? It's a secret letter, after all. He'll just have to hand it to Rajat with the professional chauffeur's expressionlessness.

The single sheet inside is filled with English words. It takes him a long time to unscramble the bold handwriting with its slanted slashes, the unfamiliar vocabulary.

Rajat,

I need to see you—even if it's for the last time. I need to sit face-to-face and talk things out. I made some mistakes, I admit it. I hurt you. And I'm willing to apologize—something I've never done for any man. That should tell you how I feel about you.

Before you crumple up this letter and throw it away—see, I know you and your temper, because mine is just like it—I want you to remember all the things that were good between us. Remember when your company sent you to Delhi? When I flew up there without telling you and bribed that clerk to let me into your room, so I was naked under the sheets waiting for you when you came back from making that disastrous sales pitch? How magical those three days were. Those hours between meetings, and in the evenings, wrapped in the sheets . . . We hardly slept. You were afraid you wouldn't get the account, you were so distracted, but I coached you, and it worked out. Remember how you said I was your lucky charm?

But sex wasn't the only thing that made our relationship special. We could talk to each other, express our anger and frustration with the world, or even with our families. We could show each other our dark sides and know that we'd be understood and not shunned. You told me things that you said you'd never shared with anyone. Can you do that with that bland pretty-face you have now? How soon before you get tired of acting the virtuous husband for her?

I can help you, too, far better than she can. I know about your family's financial problems, the failing gallery in New York. Yes, I've made it my business to know. My father would give me the money you need in a moment, if I tell him it's for the man I love.

Understand, I'm not trying to bribe you. I just want to meet you once. Then you can do what you want.

Call me if you have the guts to face who you really are.

Sonia

Asif lies back on his lumpy mattress, exhausted and shocked. He's had to spell out some words and guess at the meanings of others, but he understands the gist of the letter. He's surprised that Sonia would give him a letter with such private details in it. She must have thought he was illiterate, at least in English. Or maybe she couldn't believe that a mere servant would dare to open her letter. His eyes burn as though he, too, stayed up for all those sex-soaked nights. When he read that part, he could feel himself hardening. He wanted to spit at Sonia for being a whore. He wanted to tear her clothes off. He was disgusted at her and himself. But then came that last part. The way she accepted Rajat's shortcomings—and her own—with a shrug and didn't try to pretend, as most people would, at a virtue she didn't possess. There was courage in that. He could see the lure of being with such a woman. To be accepted not in spite of your vices but because you had them. The great relief of that.

She seems to really love Rajat, too—something else that Asif hadn't expected. It bothers him. He was much more comfortable with the notion of Sonia as a millionaire's spoiled daughter who only cared for her own pleasure. Then there's the money. If she could get it from her father (and Sonia wasn't the kind to make promises she couldn't keep), that would change everything for the Boses. Pia-missy wouldn't have to give up any of the things she deserved to have. She could go to Darjeeling every year if she wanted. And Asif is the one—the only one, at this point—who can make it happen for her.

Then he remembers how, on those occasions when Pia accompanied Sonia and Rajat someplace, she would sit silent in a corner of the car while Sonia chattered on gaily, waving her flamboyant hands, pressing up against Rajat to give him a kiss. Sonia was never mean to Pia; Asif had to admit that. But where Korobi showered Pia with affection, Sonia merely tolerated her. Could Asif condemn Pia-missy to a lifetime of that?

Asif's head swims from the lateness of the night, from having stared at the letter for so long. Just when he thought he had figured out what to do, he's confused all over again. He goes to the shelf where he keeps the Quran his sister tucked into his bag when he left home. He takes the scuffed volume from the shelf and presses it to his forehead, hoping for guidance. But the book offers no answer. Instead, an image rises in his mind: himself down on the ground, face encrusted with blood, ribs broken, teeth knocked out. It isn't difficult for a moneyed woman to hire thugs to beat up someone in this unforgiving city. He feels that might be Sonia's style when people refuse to do what she wants.

The prudent decision would be to take the letter to Rajat, as she wants. Let them fight it out among themselves. Why should he put himself in danger by opposing a spoiled rich girl's stubborn whim?

He thinks all this. Then he folds the letter and slips it inside the Quran. Before replacing it on the shelf, he kisses the book for luck, because surely he'll need it now.

SIX

Rajat sits in his office, which is on the upper floor of Barua & Bose's warehouse, massaging his throbbing head and cursing last night. His table—a beautiful carved mahogany affair chosen by his mother—is stacked with notices and invoices that have piled up over the last month. They require his immediate attention, but he's having a hard time focusing, in spite of several cups of tea and more aspirin than was good for him. What makes everything worse is that he hasn't been able to talk to Korobi since she left India.

He had called Mitra's apartment before he went out last night. Mitra's wife said Korobi-madam was still sleeping. It was early morning in America, plus she hadn't slept well the last night. Mitra's wife had heard her moving around even after midnight. With the pregnancy, she didn't sleep so well herself. Her back ached all the time.

Mitra's wife talked too much, Rajat thought in annoyance. He interrupted her to say he was going to let Korobi sleep in, but she should call him as soon as possible.

"Surely, of course," Mitra's wife had gushed. "How lucky she is to have such a considerate man to be her husband."

"Where's Mitra? I tried his mobile, but he didn't answer."

"Gone to work," Mitra's wife said—which was what Rajat had expected, except there was a little hitch in her voice that worried him. In retrospect, he thought that Mitra had behaved strangely the last time they spoke, answering in monosyllables when Rajat asked him to take good care of Cara.

"Tell him to call me," he instructed Mitra's wife. "And tell him to get Korobi to the investigator as soon as possible."

Now Rajat wishes he had been less magnanimous. If he had heard Cara's voice, cool as salve on burned skin, maybe last night would have gone differently.

Last night, while he was trying to catch up at the office, Khushwant had called. It was his birthday, he was turning twenty-nine, in a year he would be thirty and over-the-hill, my God, it was depressing beyond belief. A group of friends were getting together at the Pink Elephant, that new club near the race course, to help him overcome this tragedy. Rajat must come, too!

Rajat wished him happy birthday. But he excused himself; he was tired and had to check on a set of orders that should have been sent to Kanpur yesterday.

"Yaar, I can't believe what a limp noodle you've turned into." Khushwant's voice went tinny with outrage. "You used to be the coolest guy even just at my birthday last year. Remember, how we were at the Taj, with you and Sonia dancing on our table. She ruined that tabletop with her stilettos! And when the manager complained, she threw down a stack of rupees, enough to buy two new tables. That girl had class! I never did understand why you guys broke up. And the weed we had afterwards in my flat? People were so wasted they couldn't even make it home. That was some party, if I do say so myself! And now listen to you. You sound like some forty-year-old father of two. Makes me think your engagement's been a bad influence. That Korobi, she's beautiful and all, but she's too serious, man. And her family—don't they have like a temple in their house? That's just insane! I'd think twice before marrying into shit like that."

"That's enough about Korobi, Khush!"

"Okay, okay, sorry! Forgive? Anyway, hasn't she gone off to America or something?"

Rajat was shocked that Khushwant knew about Korobi's trip already, in spite of all the efforts to keep it quiet. That was Kolkata for you. He wondered who else—all right, he might as well be honest with himself—he wanted to know if Sonia had found out. He wanted to know if she would decide to do something about his being on his own now.

He ducked away from the thought. Sonia was like an infection in his blood, rising up to attack just when he believed he was cured.

"I bet she's having a good time there," Khushwant was saying. "So why not you come and keep your old friends company? The guys are all complaining that they haven't seen you in months."

Rajat felt himself wavering. He missed his friends, too, and the giddy, adolescent fun of drinking too much and watching the girls and guffawing at puerile jokes, the music thrumming all the while through your blood. He said weakly, "I really have too much to do, yaar."

"What good is it working for your parents if you can't fall behind once in a while? They can't fire you, can they? You just have to put up with a bit of bad-mouthing. Hell, my old man yells at me every week."

Rajat wanted to say that his parents would never yell. In fact, if his mother knew of Khushwant's invitation, she would tell him to go. *You've been taking on too much, Son. You need a break.* That's why he had to be sure to do the right thing himself.

But Khushwant barreled on, "Listen, yaar, come for one hour only. Hang out, have a couple beers. Then you can go back to work, mother-promise! You don't even have to dress up. It's just the boys tonight. Girls are too much maintenance, man."

It would have been churlish to turn Khushwant down, after that.

"Okay," Rajat said. "Just for an hour."

But it hadn't turned out that way.

Rajat dials Mitra's mobile, gets a recording again. Is Mitra avoiding him? This hangover is making Rajat paranoid. It's night in New York. Where on earth is Korobi? He resists the urge to call the number again, the way Sonia would have done, and leave a blistering message. Instead he dials Mitra's home and speaks to Mitra's wife, who sounds scared. A sound in the background, like a man's voice, abruptly cuts off.

"They went out together," she says. "I'll tell Korobi-madam to call as soon as she gets back. Thank you, thank you." She hangs up before he can ask anything else.

The music hit him like a fiery blast as soon as he stepped into the Pink Elephant. His ears, accustomed to 26 Tarak Prasad Roy Road through the many evenings he'd spent there, to its few, nuanced sounds, had grown unused to this kind of loudness. Light pulsed green and red across the room, then turned itself off, creating a moment of disorienting darkness lit only by small, pink fireflies that bobbed erratically through the room. It took him several minutes to locate his friends—six of them, huddled at a table on the other side of the dance floor. Wishing he hadn't come, he threaded his way through couples gyrating with abandon, past a wild-haired, gesticulating DJ immured behind a glass wall like a sci-fi character, past waitresses in tiny skirts and dangly, pink, glow-in-the-dark elephant earrings. In the strobe flashes punctuated by darkness, he saw his friends, who had not noticed him yet, cruelly captured: a foolishly open mouth, a gesticulating hand sporting a Rolex, grinning lips that exposed expensively straightened teeth. The offspring of fathers who had fought their way into mansions and millions where these children now floundered. He was one of them, too, wasn't he?

Then they noticed him and gave a great cheer, rising to their feet as though he were a Bollywood star. He was engulfed in hugs redolent with Johnnie Walker, that old, comforting smell. Such stupid thoughts he'd been having! See how they loved him. They were his people, they understood the challenge of languishing in the shadow of titans. He should not have stayed away from them for so long.

Still the image of that desk, piled with responsibilities, would not leave him.

"Just one beer, yaar, in honor of your birthday," he told Khushwant. Jaikishan—Jay for short—pushed a plate full of shrimp kebabs at him. Rajat took one, suddenly ravenous. He needed this respite, this sinking into camaraderie as into velvet cushions. He'd slip away after this drink, catch a cab back to the office, call his mother, tell her he would sleep there tonight. She would protest that he was ruining his health, but underneath she'd be proud he was working so hard, shoring up the family finances. How good it would feel tomorrow, the clean desk, the orders sent out, the invoices responded to. Maybe he'd even get started planning the

Barua & Bose website, surprise Korobi with a preliminary design when she got back.

The shrimp kebabs were excellent. Likewise the beer, steaming cold in the bottle he raised to his lips.

Then he saw her walk into the room, dressed in a silver mini and tall silver heels. He was surprised at how long her hair had grown. She'd put something sparkly in it, and it swung about her face like satin.

The beer tasted flat, corrosive. He put it down and tapped Khushwant's shoulder, pointing.

"Shit! I swear, yaar, I didn't tell her anything. Didn't even talk to her." Khushwant was speaking the truth. Rajat could hear it in his slurred, shocked voice. But Rajat couldn't believe it was mere coincidence.

"Looks like she has other fish to fry anyway." Khushwant was pointing. A man had walked in behind Sonia, American, Rajat thought from the clothes, expensive but too casual. He was tall and blond, with that irritating American expression of trustfulness. He bent his face to say something, and she threw back her hair and laughed, her eye makeup glittering. He was no match for her. She would chew him up and spit him out within a week.

Rajat ordered another beer. He waved away the paneer pakoras that were going around. The two were seated at a corner table, heads close together, whispering. What did the blond fool have to say that was so interesting?

Khushwant must have seen something on his face because he grabbed Rajat's elbow. "Ignore her, yaar. It's not worth getting into trouble."

Khushwant was right. Rajat turned toward his friends, raised his bottle, and drained it. Jay was telling them a joke. His jokes were so stupid, they cracked everyone up. But after a few minutes, Rajat couldn't stop himself from glancing back. They were dancing. She moved her body in that fluid way Rajat knew so well. Half the room was watching her. He closed his eyes, tried to call up Korobi's face, but the features kept shifting. Sonia tapped on the glass and said something to the DJ, and the music turned soft, slow. She was in the American's arms now. If she'd noticed Rajat, she gave no indication of it. Rajat reached over and took one of the glasses waiting on the table. The whiskey went down his throat smooth, making him feel a little better.

A few dances later, Sonia left with the American. Where had she gone? Rajat would bet anything it wasn't home. Was it to another club? Or one of the fancy hotels where they knew her well enough to let her have a room, even though such things were not done by women from good families?

He didn't remember much after that, except that the jokes stopped being funny. At some point, Khushwant put him in a taxi and gave the driver his address. Fortunately, everyone was asleep when he got home, and he could stumble into bed without having to face questions. Now here he is, with the grandfather of all headaches splitting his skull, cursing himself for his stupidity in letting a woman he doesn't even care about rile him like this.

We had to take a taxi, even though I didn't want it, because Mitra warned me that changing buses would take too long and Desai's office would close. Another handful of my precious dollars gone. Now Mitra and I negotiate a street as narrow as the old Kolkata alleys, making our way past carelessly dumped garbage and people curled into blankets in random doorways. The chill evening wind flutters abandoned newspapers and sets me shivering in spite of my coat. The distaste on Mitra's face mirrors my own misgivings. What kind of investigator would have his office in a neighborhood like this?

In the taxi, Mitra made an attempt to be friendly, asking about my life in Kolkata and pointing out notable landmarks. But I no longer trusted him and responded warily. When I asked about my cell phone, he said he was working on it, but it was hard for tourists to get phones because of tightened security. I didn't believe him. Was he trying to keep me from talking freely to Rajat? This much I knew: I needed to become less dependent on him. Tomorrow, I promised myself, I'd buy a map of New York, ask Desai about buses, learn to get around.

Ahead of me, a man with a pale, shaven head and tattoos on his neck slowly pushes a rusted metal cart piled with plastic bags. I try not to stare, but I'm disconcerted. Maybe he senses my attention. He suddenly turns and lumbers toward me, mumbling, hand outstretched. His nails are bluish, dirt-encrusted. His eyebrows look scorched. In Kolkata I'd have known how to ignore a beggar, how to drop coins into an outstretched palm if the case merited it. Here I'm unsure. I look for Mitra, but he's gone ahead around the corner of the building. I have no choice but to face the man, who's almost upon me.

Heart thudding, I square my shoulders and yell, "Go away! Stop harassing me!" To emphasize my words, I clap my hands. The sound echoes eerily down the street like a shot.

The man doesn't leave, but at least he stops advancing. That's victory enough. I run and catch up with Mitra, stumbling in my unsuitable Kolkata sandals. He gives me a brief, appraising look. Was he watching to see how I'd handle myself in a dangerous situation? Was he hoping I'd break down? I'm happy to have disappointed him.

Desai's building, a once-ornate Victorian, has been sectioned into apartments. As we enter the corridor, dimly lit by a grease-covered bulb, the smell of stale cooking assails us. Behind the doors, strange sounds coil and churn: arrhythmic thumps, a woman weeping, flute music. Bypassing an elevator that looks too ancient to be trusted, we climb three stories to the top floor. Desai's office is at the end of the corridor and protected by a collapsible gate. Approaching it, I hear male voices raised in argument. One has a distinct Indian accent and sounds angry. The other is American and defiant. When Mitra knocks, there is sudden silence. After a minute, the door is opened by a man in his sixties wearing an old-fashioned suit. His lank hair reaches his shoulders in a style reminiscent of biblical movies. He's taking deep breaths in an effort to calm himself. Behind him, leaning back nonchalantly in a swivel chair, is a young man in jeans and a leather jacket. He sports an ear stud and a short, stylish haircut. He's distinctly good-looking and bears himself in a manner that suggests he knows this. He stares at me with frank curiosity.

Desai pulls himself together and greets us. Introductions are made.

The young man, who is Desai's nephew and part-time assistant, bows mockingly and offers me his chair. The computer on Mr. Desai's desk is unexpectedly sleek and modern. Indeed, the entire office is filled with sleek and modern gadgets I don't recognize. I feel a little better; clearly, Desai takes his work seriously.

To my dismay, Mitra pulls up another chair and sits beside me, peering with far too much interest at the computer screen.

Perhaps to make up for his earlier lapse, Mr. Desai launches immediately into business.

"As you know, we're handicapped by our lack of information about the subject. Still, I've located a couple of promising leads." He points to the computer screen.

My pulse speeds up. The blue screen with lines and lines of text on it makes the prospect of finding my father more real than ever before, and I am newly afraid. But I also need to get Mitra out of the room.

"There are also some possible sources that will have to be questioned over the phone. That's where you come in. But first I need to get a few more details about your mother—"

Mitra's posture is still and intent. Panicked, I blurt out, "Can we discuss this in private, please?"

The words come out louder than I intend. Everyone stares. Then Mr. Desai motions with his chin to his nephew, who raises an ironic eyebrow and goes through a side door into another room. Mitra stands up with a sudden, offended motion, pushing his chair back so hard it almost topples.

"We'll be done in an hour or so," Mr. Desai says, his tone placating. "If you'll wait next door, Vic can get you some—"

"I'm going to leave, since Miss Roy obviously doesn't want me to be here. I have many other responsibilities, I'd like you to know."

I hadn't expected such an extreme response. I stare as he stalks to the door.

"Wait a minute!" Desai exclaims. "She can't go back to your place alone after dark. You know this area."

I'm worried, but I refuse to beg Mitra to stay. "I'll manage," I say with more confidence than I feel. "Please go ahead and take care of your business."

After Mitra leaves, Desai purses his lips in a silent whistle. "He certainly took it personal. Hopefully he'll get over it soon."

"I didn't mean to be rude to Mr. Mitra or your nephew, but this is a confidential matter. My fiancé's family is particularly concerned to keep it—"

Desai raises his hands to halt my excuses. "You have every right to privacy in a matter as delicate as this. It was my fault for not taking precautions. But when Mitra called for directions, he implied that he was a friend of the family and already knew what was going on. As for my nephew—you needn't be concerned about him. The rascal has a thick skin—thicker than is good for him! I'll ask him to give you a ride home, so don't worry about that, either."

This small generosity—the first since I arrived in this country—pushes me perilously close to tears. But Mr. Desai is discreet as well as kind. He rummages busily in his file cabinet until I've recovered enough to continue with business.

Someone is knocking loudly at Rajat's door and won't go away. The noise pounds his skull like a jackhammer. The door swings open, even though he hasn't given permission. He glares at the intruder. It is Subroto, the foreman. Rajat is about to reprimand him when he notices how distraught Subroto is. Rajat has never seen him this way, half his shirt hanging out, hands shaking.

"Babu, come quickly! A fight has broken out on the packing floor."

Rajat has never faced a problem like this. His job is to take care of accounts and handle customers. His father is the one who deals with the workers. But right now his father is in a remote village in Medinipur. Rajat runs with Subroto all the way to the packing area, trying vainly to remember if his father had ever mentioned a fight at the warehouse. He sees packing tables turned over, the floor littered with shards of earthenware and splinters of wood. The workstations have been abandoned, and a crowd mills around in the middle of the hall. Some of them see him, and a shout goes through the crowd.

"Rajat-babu is here! Babu is here!"

Faces turn toward him, men old enough to be his father, lined and work-worn, but filled with innocent hope, as though he were their savior. They don't know that he has no idea how to handle such a situation. A panicked nausea swirls inside him. But he knows that the first step is to get to the fight, which, from the yelling and thumping, is still going strong. He begins to push his way through the crowd, which parts for him like the Red Sea so that in a few moments—too soon—he is at the epicenter, the floor under his feet horrifyingly sticky with blood.

Luckily for Rajat, Subroto's second-in-command, Abinash, the burly assistant foreman, has things almost under control. Under his direction, workers have separated the three men who must have been the perpetrators. They yell curses at each other, all of them bleeding—heavily, it seems to Rajat's inexperienced eyes—one from a head wound, one from a slashed arm. The third looks as if his nose might be broken. Rajat knows their faces, though not their names. He does not recall having had trouble with them before. Or with anyone else. The Boses' workers are paid at a higher-than-average rate; tea and snacks are provided to them free of charge from the canteen; each year, their families are gifted with new clothing. Why then, suddenly, this?

Rajat swallows the bile that floods his mouth and tells Subroto to phone for an ambulance. He yells for someone to run and get the first-aid box. But no one remembers where it's stored, so Rajat must ask Abinash to cut up one of the expensive embroidered bedspreads from Assam into strips. The tea boy runs to fetch a kettle of hot water. In this way the injured men are patched up as well as possible. As they wait for the ambulance, Rajat tries to piece together, from a chorus of contradictory voices, what has occurred.

The packing room had a radio, usually tuned to upbeat Bollywood songs—the men liked to listen to these as they worked, and sing along, too. Subroto monitored the radio and changed the station as necessary. But today he had gone to the toilet when the music program was interrupted by a news bulletin: Just when the authorities were hoping the Hindu-Muslim riots in Gujarat were at an end, another outbreak had occurred in Ahmedabad. The announcer described some of the atrocities. One of the men on the floor, an older Hindu, had made a remark about Mussulmans always causing trouble, ever since Partition. The man working next to him, a Muslim, had taken strong objection and reminded him that the Hindus had torched Gulburg just a few weeks back. Voices had risen, tempers had overheated, words had been slung back and forth until a last incendiary one had come up: Godhra. With that, the men—some of whom had worked side by side for decades—had begun to shove and punch one another. A Muslim pushed a Hindu, who fell backward, cracking his head on the concrete. The sight of the blood drove the Hindus wild. Several of them rushed the Mussulman, punching and yelling, breaking his nose and throwing him down, oblivious of the foremen, who were ordering them to stop. What happened next was not clear, but at some point one of the Muslims had taken a box cutter and slashed at a Hindu, slicing open his forearm.

Just as the ambulance's keening announces its arrival, Rajat's cell phone rings. It is a collect call from Korobi, at this, the worst of times! He whispers that he will call her back as soon as he can. Yes, he knows it is late in the United States, and, yes, he understands that she doesn't want him to disturb the Mitras. But he's in the middle of an emergency. No, he isn't hurt, but he can't talk now. He puts the phone away, feeling angry and afraid and churlish. His headache is worse. He'll have to take another dose of aspirin as soon as he gets back to his office.

The injured men are taken to an emergency clinic, and now Rajat must make some difficult decisions. Certain individuals must be punished, others reassured. A significant amount of inventory has been ruined, including some expensive terra-cotta statues, and appropriate people must be fined. It must be done right, so the workers see that he is both just and firm. But how to achieve this tricky balance? Rajat doesn't know. So he sends the men off for an early lunch and asks the managers to meet him in his office in half an hour. Meanwhile, he tries to contact his father. But Mr. Bose must be in a village without mobile access; he doesn't answer. Rajat doesn't want to call his mother, who will ask a million frantic questions. Though generally levelheaded, she tends to panic if she thinks her children are in danger. She might insist on coming over, and he isn't up to handling her right now. There's no way around it. He'll have to take on the role of leader.

When Subroto and Abinash come to his office, Rajat tells them this must never occur again. To that end, they'll have to change the way things are done on the floor. Hindus and Muslims must be separated into different areas and given different tasks. Abinash nods, but Subroto is hesitant. He points out that they will have to reorganize the entire work area, moving around machines and workstations. It will be complicated. Not only will they lose days' worth of work and money, but the men will not like it. They've become used to doing certain tasks. Each one has his expertise—unpacking, cleaning, polishing, touching up paint, loading. They'll resist learning new skills. They'll resist working with new people. Some of them have been with the same teammates for years. Subroto is confident that today's incident is an isolated one. The management shouldn't overreact. Abinash and he will make sure it doesn't occur again. They'll monitor the radio more carefully, maybe bring in a CD player with movie songs. Subroto does have one suggestion: Perhaps Rajat-babu can hire another supervisor—a Muslim one this time? There's a good man, Faizal, whom they can talk to.

Rajat shakes his head. He can't pull his mind from the blood on the floor, that unreal red on his shoes, sticky and slippery at the same time. It nauseates him all over again.

"I don't want to take chances. Just separate the men. Also, I want you to make a list of all the people who were involved in the fight. Fine them a day's pay. And the man who slashed open the other one's arm—fire him."

Now both Subroto and Abinash exchange uneasy glances.

"Babu," Abinash says, "it's hard to tell who was in the fight, and who wasn't. It was all mixed up in there. And the man who used the box cutter, Alauddin Miah, he's been with us a long time. He's high up in the union and has a lot of influence on the Muslim workers. It might cause trouble if we fire him."

"He's a good employee," Subroto adds. "Never done anything like this before. They were beating up his nephew, broke his nose, maybe that's why he went crazy."

"Whatever the cause," Rajat says, "he attacked a man with a weapon that could have killed him. What if he *had*? Can you imagine the trouble we'd be in now if a man had been murdered in our building—especially a Hindu?" Rajat thinks of his parents' tenuous relationship with Mr. Bhattacharya and shudders. "How can we allow something like that to pass without serious punishment?"

"Please, maybe you should check with barababu first?"

Rajat sighs in frustration. "I can't reach him. We can't put off our decision for too long, otherwise it'll send the message that the management is weak."

"Couldn't you wait until next week? He'll be back by then. He can talk to the men. Most of them were hired by him. They'll surely listen to him."

The headache is worse now, slicing through Rajat's brain like a buzz saw. Even though he, too, has been longing for his father to take care of this mess that's been shoved at him, he is suddenly furious.

"Barababu left me in charge. Are you saying I'm not capable of handling this problem? That I don't know how to talk to the men?"

"No, Rajat-babu," the managers stammer.

"Then do what I said. Go on!"

When the door closes behind them, he kicks off his shoes—he can't bear their touch on his feet—and goes to the small bathroom attached to his office and splashes water on his face. How he would love to go home and lie down. But he can't. He's in charge. He has to prove—maybe more to himself than anyone else—that he's capable of leadership. He considers trying his father's number one more time, but after a brief look at the clock—it's past midnight in New York—he calls Mitra's home.

Korobi picks up the phone on the first ring, thank heaven! She must have been sitting by the phone, waiting on his call. He pictures her running her fingers through those unruly curls he so loves, dead tired but forcing herself to stay awake because she can't let another day pass without talking to him. The inky surge of anger inside him recedes. Its place is taken by fear and loneliness, and though he hadn't intended to, he finds himself telling Cara everything that happened at the warehouse.

"Oh, Rajat! That's a horrifying load to be thrust upon you!"

He relaxes a little. Her sympathy is like fresh air blowing down a mine shaft. But then she adds, "I hope you can get in touch with Papa quickly and get some advice."

Does she, too, doubt his ability? Angrily, he notices that her voice, far and muted, is not as distressed as he would like. And was that a yawn? Their worlds have split apart already, she in a land of night while he is in daytime, each unable to truly gauge the other's suffering heart. He is reminded of an eerie tale out of his childhood, a prince and a princess who were kept captive in an enchanted palace. The curse laid on them was that whenever one was awake, the other would be asleep. Although they fell in love gazing at each other, they could never convey how they felt, nor understand what the other was going through. That story had a happy ending, thanks to a pair of matchmaking genies. But where are the genies that will travel the dusty distance that stretches between Rajat and Cara?

To my chagrin, I find myself drifting off as I listen to Rajat. I shake my head, even pinch my arm. I stifle a yawn, hoping Rajat hasn't noticed. I'm worried about the troubles in the warehouse, worried that Rajat is making a dangerous mistake, but never have I experienced such lassitude, descending on me like an evil spell. Perhaps my body longs to escape, in the only way known to it, from this country where I'm unloved.

Now, brusque and impatient, he asks, "Did the investigator find anything yet?"

"Yes!" Enthusiasm surges through me, but I keep my voice low. The Mitras are asleep, and that's how I want them to stay. "Mr. Desai has narrowed our search down to about thirty people with the same first name who were at the university or employed there around the same time as my mother."

"Thirty!" He sounds incensed. "It'll be impossible to follow up on them all."

"Yes. We'll have to select carefully. I'm going to call and locate my mother's professors, or maybe a secretary or adviser who might lead us to my father—or at least to some of my mother's friends."

"Speak up! I can hardly hear you."

"I don't want to wake the Mitras. We're following up on that photo, too—I wish it wasn't so blurred."

"Doesn't sound like you have anything solid," Rajat says heavily.

"It's not so bad!" I say, more to myself than to him. "Mr. Desai has already picked out a prospect for me to visit. This man went to Berkeley and had a girlfriend who was Indian, though later he married someone else. He lives relatively close to New York, in Boston. Remember my mother had mentioned plans to live on the East Coast?"

"Boston isn't close!"

I'm disappointed that he's not happier for me. "He's an architect. I'll go and see him as soon as we can set up an appointment."

"Don't you think you should call him before you go all the way up there? Ask him a few questions on the phone?"

"Mr. Desai doesn't think I should. Often people won't answer sensitive questions over the phone. Maybe they have a new life and don't want to admit to old ties. Or they're afraid someone might bring a paternity suit against them or try to blackmail them. Once they get suspicious, it's almost impossible to get them to meet you face-to-face. And face-to-face is the only way you can tell if someone's lying."

There's a pause. Then Rajat says, "That doesn't always work, not even for people more experienced than you."

"Vic will be with me. He says he's a pretty good lie detector."

"Vic?" Rajat says in a tight voice. "Who's that?"

"He's Mr. Desai's nephew—and his assistant. Mr. Desai has arranged for him to drive me to Boston and back. He brought me back from the office tonight."

"Why didn't Mitra do that?"

The suspicion in Rajat's voice annoys me. I remind myself that he's had a stressful day.

"Mitra had to go somewhere, so Vic gave me a ride."

"Vic! What kind of a name is that for an Indian?"

"I don't know!" This time I can't suppress my exasperated sigh. "Why are you so interested in him?"

There's a pause. Then Rajat says forcefully, "I'm not interested. I'm worried because you trust everyone too easily."

"I do not!" I retort, stung.

"Mitra shouldn't have left you alone in their office. And why hasn't he given you your phone so you can talk from your room? Maybe *he* should be the one going down to Boston with you."

I suppress a shudder. "He can't!" I whisper. "Remember, your mother doesn't want him to know what's going on. Besides, he's been kind of—difficult. I'll call you from Desai's office tomorrow and explain."

"Are you okay, Cara?" Rajat's voice is concerned. "Is he treating you badly?"

Now I've gone and worried him on top of his other problems. "I'm fine, I really am."

After a long, disbelieving pause, he says, "What good will it do for you to know if the man in Boston is lying, if he's your father but doesn't want to admit it?"

The question that has crossed my mind, too. I don't have a good answer, but finally I say, "Then I'll know not to search any further. Then I'll know to come back to Kolkata."

Rajat waits for Korobi to say that she loves him, but she merely claims she's exhausted and hangs up. He sits in the sudden silence with his head in his hands. The idea of some unknown man taking her to Boston worries him. She said Mitra was being difficult. What did that mean? Rajat will have to have a talk with him, straighten things out. She said, if she knew her father was lying, she'd come back to India. Why hadn't she said, *I'll come back to you?*

But what's bothering him most, what's gone deep into him like a poisoned thorn, is her comment *face-to-face you can tell if someone's lying.* Because he hadn't known with Sonia, even though people had warned him about her. She'd looked him in the eye and run her fingernails over his bare chest and sworn she loved him, and he had believed her completely.

He can hear sounds below: the hall being cleaned up, the worktables pushed around, voices raised querulously. He must go down soon and explain to the men. He must make them see the changes are for their benefit. He must reassure them that the Bose family will take care of them as always. But the words he requires for this enormous task have fled from his mind.

There's a knock. Will they never leave him alone!

"Who is it?"

No one answers. His heart beats erratically. Is it one of the workers, a relative of the man he fired, come to get revenge?

"Who's out there?" he yells. *"Who?"*

The door opens a crack. It's the tea boy, looking fearful, holding a tray with a cup of tea and a plateful of glucose biscuits.

Rajat expels his pent-up breath. "For God's sake, come in. I won't bite you."

The boy advances hesitantly. When he sets the tray down on the table, his hands shake, so that some tea spills onto the saucer.

"Sorry, Babu." The boy wipes at the tray nervously.

"Who told you to bring me this?"

The boy backs toward the door. "No one. You didn't have lunch, so I thought . . ." His voice fades away.

"Stop." Rajat takes a sip. "Good tea!" He bites into a biscuit and realizes how hungry he is.

A grin, exposing crooked teeth, appears on the boy's face as he watches Rajat eat. He is thin and wiry and wears shorts that have faded to no color and a cotton shirt that lacks a couple of buttons. "Glad you like it, Babu." He opens the door to leave.

"Wait, let me pay you." Rajat pulls out his wallet.

"Oh, no, Babu, no charge for you! You're the owner!"

Rajat holds out a twenty-rupee bill. "This is for you, then. For being so thoughtful."

The boy shifts from foot to foot. "No, Babu, I just wanted to do something for you."

Oh, this boy, sent to him like a fresh breeze in the middle of a suffocating nightmare.

"What's your name?"

"Munna."

"How old are you?"

"Twelve. At least that's what my mother thinks."

With a little nudging, Rajat learns that Munna lives in the slums beside Sealdah station. His father died some years back. His mother and two sisters work as housemaids. Munna went to school until class four; then he had to start working. He can still read a little.

Rajat thinks of Pia, who is the same age as this boy, of all the affluence that cushions her against disaster.

"What do you like to eat best?"

Munna grows animated. It seems that Rajat has hit upon his favorite subject. "Mughlai parathas from the corner shop. Kesto fries them so crisp. The bread fluffs up like this, and he puts eggs inside, and green chilies and onions, extra if you ask. He'll even give spicy tomato sauce to eat it with. If you want, I can run and get you one."

"How much?"

"Four rupees each."

Rajat takes out a hundred-rupee bill. "When you get off work today, I want you to buy parathas for your whole family. And sweets. Tell them it's a gift from me. Tomorrow you can tell me if they liked it."

The boy protests, but only a little this time. Rajat presses the bill into the boy's hand. How big his eyes are, sparkling! When was the last time Rajat saw someone so completely happy?

When the boy has gone, he finishes the tea and the biscuits and rises to his feet. He can handle things now, he thinks.

SEVEN

We are in the office, strategizing: Desai, Vic, and me, an unlikely, ebullient triumvirate, all of us excited because Vic and I are to meet Rob Evanston, the Boston architect, tomorrow. In a few minutes Vic will call his office to confirm Evanston's appointment with Mr. and Mrs. Vic Pandey. We'll drive down in the morning, be back by evening. No one outside this room—except Rajat—will even know. And perhaps, just perhaps, my search will be over.

Vic is part of the show now. When Desai asked him to drive me to Boston, he said, "Only if you tell me what's going on." In a way it was a relief because now we can talk openly. He's kind in an offhanded way. The first night, he figured out the situation at Mitra's and offered to give me a ride whenever I needed it. I appreciated the offer, but I didn't want to be beholden. We finally reached a compromise: I'd take the subway to the office in the daytime, and he'd take me back at night.

I'm thankful for this upcoming meeting because nothing else has been going right. All week I've been phoning the university from Desai's office, trying to find people who knew my mother. Several have retired or moved away. Others are suspicious or just plain busy. Some hang up. Those who are willing to talk mostly don't recall Anu Roy—so many foreign students have passed through International Relations in twenty years. A few remember her as polite and smart, but quiet. They were sorry to have heard of her death. No one recollects seeing her with any young men. No one knows where she had lived. Student Services has Anu Roy on the computer as a past student, but no other information saved from so long ago. Vic has been equally unsuccessful in his search for marriage records. Nor has anyone responded to the advertisements Desai has placed in the Indian American papers, requesting people who knew Anu Roy to step forward, and promising a reward. Whatever tracks my mother left behind have been effectively obscured by the dust of time. I'll need a miracle to find my father.

Sometimes, to take my mind off my troubles, I watch Vic, who works in the same room when he's not off reconnoitering. I find him intriguing. He navigates the labyrinth of America with such seeming ease. He told me that the restaurant business he owns along with a couple of friends is failing; that Desai is the only relative with whom he's on speaking terms. What allows him to so easily slough off troubles that would have dragged me under?

One of my troubles is my situation at the Mitras. The night of my unsatisfactory conversation with Rajat, after I hung up, I noticed that Mitra's bedroom door was slightly open. I thought I could see a shape hovering behind the door, in the dark. I was sure it wasn't Seema. Furious and frightened, I'd hurried past, wondering how much he'd overheard. How much had I given away? Why was he watching me? In my room, I shoved the biggest boxes against the door in a barricade, not caring if he heard the thumps.

Since then we mostly avoid each other, though his displeasure at my presence permeates the apartment like the smell of burnt food. At night he returns late or spends his time in the bedroom, from where I sometimes hear the indistinct booming of his voice on the phone. He still hasn't given me my cell phone. When I confront him, he says he's working on it. He uses terms such as *homeland security* and *Patriot Act*. I don't believe him for a minute. I'd love to tell him that and storm out, but where would I go? I don't have the money. Plus, there's poor Seema, who follows me around the house like a lost puppy. "Are you leaving already?" she asks each morning, plaintive. "Don't be late coming back now. I'm cooking something special for your dinner."

But now, finally, there's a glimmer in the darkness. We go over the plan one more time. Vic and I will pretend to be rich newly-marrieds wanting to build a house. We need an architect; that's why we're meeting with Evanston.

"Remember to act privileged and pouty, like a rich man's daughter, now a rich man's wife," Desai tells me. "That way, Evanston will be willing to answer your questions, even randomly curious ones about his past. Give him the impression you're used to throwing money around."

To Vic he says, "You shouldn't have any problem with that! What car is it you're driving nowadays? That BMW convertible that's going to land you in the poorhouse?"

Vic throws him a wounded look. I laugh; I love it when they banter. It makes me a little jealous, too. I've never had a relationship like this with anyone in my family. In a corner of my mind I place a small hope, like a candle on an altar: that my father will turn out to have a sense of humor.

"Let her do the talking," Desai says to Vic. "You watch Evanston, for when she says her mother's name."

"What if he doesn't have any reactions?" I ask.

"Everyone has reactions," Desai says. "You just have to know how to read them." He grabs Vic by the jacket sleeve. "You! Come with me. I'm going to fix lunch for us all today—your mother's pau bhaji recipe—in anticipation of your Boston adventure, and I need someone to chop the onions."

Vic grumbles loudly, but he allows his uncle to pull him along.

I watch with a smile until they disappear through the side door. Recently, I find myself thinking of Vic at unexpected moments, perhaps because he's a bit of an enigma. That first night, when he was about to give me a ride to Mitra's, Desai had pulled him aside. "Careful now," I heard him whisper. "Keep it professional." What had that meant, anyway? But I'm not going to think about that now. Now it's finally time to call Rajat.

The day after Mitra's eavesdropping, I asked Desai if I could use his phone. I'll pay, of course, I added awkwardly. In India I'd never had to ask for favors. I had demanded, as people do with persons tied to them by blood and love, not realizing how fortunate I was.

I don't know what Desai saw in my face, but he agreed without asking why. He told me he'd add the amount to my bill, though I suspect that he isn't doing that. How strange the world; you never know who will extend you friendship, and who will hate you.

I long to talk to Grandmother, alone in that big house with Grandfather and me both so suddenly gone. But it's too late, past midnight in India. I don't want to disturb her rest. Fortunately, Rajat isn't an early sleeper. I hope he's in his bedroom, though. Or else Maman will ask to speak to me. The last time, when I confessed that we hadn't found anything yet, her wordless *I-told-you-so* hummed through the phone line.

The phone keeps ringing, which surprises me. Rajat is conscientious about picking up if he sees it's a call from America. Is he out someplace noisy, with friends? I hope so: he needs something to cheer him up. He's been depressed about the tensions at the warehouse. The phone rings and rings, a futile, faraway sound. Just when I've resigned myself to leaving a message, he picks up, his voice slurry with sleep.

"Hello? Sonia?"

The corridor is dimly lit and stretches beyond his vision. He walks along it, dragging his feet. He is so tired nowadays. Unfair that in his dream—for that's what this is, he knows it—he should be as exhausted as while awake. He recognizes the corridor, distorted as though seen through a fish-eye lens: he is at the warehouse. It is night. The place is closed. He is alone.

No, Rajat. Observe the shadows on the wall, moving toward you, a group of workers. They look away as they pass, mumble in response to his hello. That's what they've been doing all week. He has come across knots of people at recess, discussing in fierce whispers. When he's near, they stop, wait for him to move on. They won't meet his eyes. Before the incident, they pushed past each other to come and offer salaams, or to say, "Namaskar, babu, are you well today?" Why do they refuse to understand that the changes he instituted are because he wants to keep them from hurting each other? Instead, they argue with Abinash, saying the new tasks are too difficult to learn.

What are these shadows that shudder along the ground toward him? The group that passed him in the corridor is returning. The shadows reach for him, fingers pull at his shirt. What impertinence! Is he not Rajat Bose, their employer? Drenched in sweat, he swings his fist, connects with flesh. Don't you dare touch me! Will the phone never stop ringing? Will she never leave him alone? He wakes with Sonia's name on his lips.

"It's me, Korobi." Her voice is small and upset.

"Sorry, I was having a nightmare."

"About Sonia?"

He is tempted to assent, to be absolved. A jealous woman, on top of all his other problems, is too much to handle right now. But he stops himself. His relationship with Cara is the purest thing in his life.

"Actually, it was about the warehouse."

She's immediately contrite. "I'm so sorry. Tell me everything."

"I deal with it all day. I don't want to go over it again."

"But, baby, I need to know. I feel so cut off from you."

Something about what she said bothers him. But she's right. He sighs and gives a brief summary, skipping over the more painful parts: How, when he told his mother what had happened, he saw in her startled eyes that he had made a mistake. How his worried father has cut his trip short to return from Medinipur tomorrow, with only a portion of the merchandise he went to purchase. How each day more workers are calling in sick, causing the warehouse to lose money. He feels that he needs to reverse course, but how to do so without appearing weak? With an effort, he forces his mind to concentrate on Korobi's voice, that fragile link between them. "Tell me about you."

"I'm going to Boston tomorrow to meet the architect."

"With that Vic?"

"How else would I go?"

He stops himself from saying, *Make sure he doesn't try anything funny*. Instead, he asks, "Why are you calling so late?"

"I'm calling from Desai's office. We just finished going over our plans."

"Mitra still didn't get you that cell phone? I'm going to call him tomorrow, give him a piece of my mind!"

"Please don't! It'll just annoy him further, and I'll have to deal with the fallout. I'll talk to him once more—"

"Cara, you can't let people push you around. They'll think you're weak, and they'll push you more the next time."

She's stubbornly silent. He can feel her disagreement shimmering like heat through the airwaves, so he adds, "Okay, I'll give him a couple more days."

"Did you find out why the Mitras are so short of money? The other day, Seema was complaining that he barely gives her enough to buy groceries."

"I can't understand it. Mama's been sending them supplemental pay. And I know she sent him money for your expenses. Plus I paid up front for the phone. Something strange is going on."

"I'll try to find out once I return from Boston. Maybe I can get Vic to take me to see the gallery."

Rajat grimaces. Vic again! "Call me from Boston as soon as you've met with the architect. No matter how late it is here. Maybe I should call Desai. Ask him to warn his nephew to take good care of you—"

"Please don't! That would be insulting. You have nothing to worry about. Really. I'd better go now. Love you!"

After she hangs up, he sits with the mobile in his hand, all vestiges of sleep vanished. Her declaration at the end seemed rushed and perfunctory. He remembers now what had bothered him earlier. *Baby,* she had called him, a term she had never before used. It's only been a few days. How did she pick up that American endearment?

He can't rest. The bedclothes are heavy as canvas. He wanders out into the living room, pulls out a writing pad. Starts sketching the website. Here in the center he'll put the slide show; here on top, the name in calligraphy. Reviews from satisfied customers will float up from the bottom of the page. People can click on the sidebar to get a history of the gallery, the famous painters his mother has launched.

He doesn't know when she came out of her bedroom. He didn't hear her. She still moves lightly, like a far younger woman. Cool on the back of his neck, her hand doesn't startle him. He knows it well from fevered childhood nights.

"What is it, Son? Can't sleep?"

He considers telling her all that's on his mind. His chagrin at the troubles at the warehouse, which he, with the best of intentions, has brought on them. Mitra's indecipherable behavior. Cara's receding from him, caught in some other, more magnetic orbit. But it's so peaceful here, the light of the lamp pooling over the pad on his lap, illuminating possibilities.

"You have a few minutes, Maman?"

"For you? What a question!"

"Then let me show you what I've planned. It's starting to come together, better than in my earlier drafts. Customers can click here to place online orders. Here they can chat with a representative. And here they can go to 'About Us,' where I'm going to upload your photo and bio."

She brings tall glasses of cool, clean water. She sits by him, leaning her head against his shoulder. He remembers he used to do that as a child, listening to the stories she read to him, his head reaching only halfway up her arm.

"It looks perfect, Son. I know you'll make it into a great success."

The love he feels for her is calming and simple and true, untouched by mistrust or irritation. Why can't he feel that way toward Korobi?

It has been a bad day. A statement arrives from the bank in the afternoon. The account has less money in it than Sarojini had realized, and she hasn't even paid all the bills related to Korobi's trip to America. Along with the statement, the manager has sent a note reminding her that property taxes are due soon. Soon after the postman departs—too soon for it to be a coincidence—Bahadur knocks to announce an unexpected visitor. He's waiting outside. Sarojini steps into the courtyard to find a squat, sweating man in a white polyester suit examining the house and jotting down items in a thick black book. From time to time he swabs at his neck with a large, checkered handkerchief.

He tells her he is Mr. Saxena of Saxena and Sons Developers, and he's interested in purchasing the Roys' property. He would like to build a high-rise here and will give Sarojini a flat on whichever floor she wants. In addition, he will pay her a substantial amount of money up front.

The idea of selling the home that has belonged to the Roys for generations makes Sarojini's heart tighten in repugnance. "You want to buy this house so you can tear it down?" she asks.

Saxena nods, watching her with his shrewd eyes. She need not worry about the temple, he says. It won't be touched. He's a good Hindu, and luckily it's in the far corner of the compound, not in the way of the plans he's drawn up. He shows her problems she hadn't known to look for: loose bricks along the roof's parapet, cracks in the foundation, appearing aboveground like roots gone wrong. Here and there, where the stucco has crumbled, the walls are damp with rot. A woman on her own, getting on in years, without income or know-how, would have a hard time repairing all this.

He has a point; Sarojini can't deny that. She hides the stab of fear she feels and takes his card, telling him that she isn't interested in selling right now. But she'll keep him in mind if things change.

The man gives her an appraising look that makes Sarojini wonder how much he knows of her financial situation, and how he might have found out. "Do think about the offer, madam," he says as he leaves. "Our company will give you a fair deal, not like others, who might try to cheat you."

All day Sarojini frets about how she will come up with the extra money for the taxes and the repairs. Will she really have to sell the house she has lived in since she was a teenage bride? If the dead know and feel what goes on in the world of the living—and she believes they do—how distressed Bimal would be. He loved the old house as if it were a second body. Korobi loves it, too—and Rajat. If she can't hold on to the mansion, she'll be failing all three of them.

By dusk, when the bruised light wavers and the world seems to collapse upon itself, Sarojini is exhausted and fretful. She ignores Cook's pleas to eat a little something and retreats to her bed. That is a mistake. The bed reminds her of Korobi, who had crept into it the night before she left for America and in silence put her arms around her. Sarojini is annoyed at how keenly she feels her granddaughter's absence. She reminds herself that the girl will be away only for a few more weeks, but her body refuses to understand. Her insides feel distended with loss; no wonder she has no space for food. It is beginning to feel the way it did when Anu left, that gaping hole, that feeling as if her heart had gone to America with her child. She hasn't spoken to Korobi in a week—something to do with the time difference and Korobi not having a phone of her own and staying in a place where she can't talk freely. Though Sarojini gets news of her from Rajat, it doesn't quite assuage her anxiety or slake her longing to hear her granddaughter's voice. Now she lies on her vacant marriage bed, which seems as vast as the ocean and as unstable, and contemplates the unexpected turns her life has taken. Who would have thought, on that beautiful engagement morning filled with songbirds and swaying oleanders, that in less than two months their little family would be scattered like this?

Fast on the heels of that thought comes another, one that she has been pushing away since Korobi told her about the journey. What if Korobi doesn't return when her month is up? What if she chooses to remain with her father once she finds him? Fear makes Sarojini light-headed. Her bedclothes wind about her with suffocating intentness. Her heart feels like a pomegranate about to burst. Out of the black whirlpool of her mind another idea rises: Would it be such a terrible thing to die? To go where Bimal and Anu, reconciled now, wait for her? She tilts her head toward the chair where her husband liked to sit and thinks she sees his silhouette, waiting with more patience than he'd ever had while alive.

She opens her hands and feels her life beginning to slip through them. It is an easy movement, like a silk rope being pulled out of her. But when the rope almost reaches its end, she is caught by a knot: *I can't leave Korobi, not until she's married and has someone to share her grief.* And then another: *I need to know—who was the man Anu loved?* And finally: *Bimal died wanting forgiveness. I must try to obtain it for him.* She gropes around the bedside table with frantic fingers for her box of glucose tablets. Finally, finally, there they are. She slides two under her tongue, shuts her eyes tight. In a while she feels her breath easing. She sits up shakily, switches on the table lamp, finds the packet of biscuits she keeps in a drawer, chews her way carefully through four of them. She drinks a full glass of water and falls into a dreamless sleep.

Waking next morning, she isn't sure if she had truly been close to death, or if it was just a hallucination. Either way, something in her has shifted. She feels she has been given an extended lease for a reason. Infused with new determination, she goes over the monthly expenses. She combs through the bankbooks that Bimal had left, willing herself to make sense of his scribbles. She phones her lawyer and then the bank to find out the details of Bimal's pension. It is a substantial amount. Why then do they have so little money? She makes careful notes on a pad. If she cuts down on everything she can think of, will she be able to keep the house?

She enlists Bahadur and Cook in her mission. Cook decrees that she will make only one dal and one vegetable for their meals. A little rice, a few chapatis. No more of that expensive Darjeeling tea. They'll switch to plain black. She goes around the house like a policeman on a beat, turning off lights and fans in empty rooms. Bahadur threatens the gardener boy with dire consequences if he catches him watering the plants even a minute longer than necessary. He contracts with a local vendor to harvest the jaam trees in the backyard—they have too many, and every year heaps of luscious purple fruit lie rotting on the ground.

Sarojini's job is to make an inventory of heirlooms that can be sold: the ancient, handmade mahogany furniture of which there is so much in the spare bedrooms; the heavy brass dishes used on feast days in Bimal's grandfather's time. She starts with the china and the silver; her mother-in-law had a weakness for expensive British tea services, many of which have never been used.

She is admiring a gold-rimmed pink cup, so thin that light shines through it, when the phone rings. She hurries to the machine, her heart hammering with hope, and there, finally, is her granddaughter, her words tumbling over each other as they did when she made her monthly call from boarding school. Sarojini tries to control her sudden tears.

"Grandma, I'm sorry I couldn't call earlier! I have so much to tell you, but I didn't have a phone. I miss you! Are you okay, all alone?"

"I'm fine. Rajat calls me every day and comes over whenever he can. He's a special young man, that one. He tells me all your news, too."

"Now that I have my phone, I'll call you every day, promise."

A shiver goes through Sarojini. "Don't promise, shona. Promises only lead to trouble. Tell me all about what you did today so that for once I can surprise Rajat with your news!"

She listens mostly for the sound of her granddaughter's voice, waterfall and rainbow mixed together, describing how she ate lunch in Desai's surprisingly large and airy kitchen, with African violets on the windowsill because they used to be his dead wife's favorite flowers. That's why he never moved out of that place even though the neighborhood went bad—because it was where they started their married life. And then Vic, Desai's nephew, took her sightseeing to calm her down because she's so nervous—wasn't that kind? She's nervous because she's going up to Boston tomorrow to meet the architect who might turn out to be her father. What if he doesn't like her?

"Not like you!" Sarojini scoffs. "Impossible."

"You're biased! Besides, what if I don't like him?"

Sarojini doesn't have a response to that.

"Vic took me to the top of the Empire State Building. I'd always wanted to go there! Do you know, I've never been sightseeing in my life!"

Sarojini wants to protest, but then she realizes it's true. In Kolkata, the child only saw those attractions—the Shaheed Minar, Howrah Bridge—that were situated along roads she traveled for other reasons. In the city of one's birth, one can never be a tourist. Sarojini tries to visualize the spaces her granddaughter is traveling through, the smell of the new dish, the exact purple of the flowers, the city radiating out from the foot of the Empire State Building in every direction. Wherever you turned, skyscrapers sprouted, housing lives and histories beyond your ability to imagine. To the left, a river; beyond that, the start of an ocean. Ahead, the green gash of Central Park, beautiful and dangerous. The cold, exhilarating wind whipping her granddaughter's hair into her face. She is glad Korobi is getting to see something of the world, for this moment of respite in a minefield of uncertainty. Why then the prick, like a thorn beneath her skin?

She catches a different note in Korobi's voice, a hesitation. "Vic and I, we're going to pretend to be newlyweds, looking for an architect to build a home for us. That's how we were able to make an appointment with him."

Sarojini is shocked. "Does Rajat know about this—this pretense?"

There's a pause. "I didn't tell him. I knew he'd be angry—nowadays he gets angry so easily—even though it doesn't mean anything. I didn't want to get into a fight right before my trip to Boston. It bothers me that I have to hide an innocent detail like this from the man I'm planning to spend my life with. But don't say anything to Rajat. He won't understand, and I don't want to add to his stress. He's already going through so much at the warehouse."

Twin spirals of worry twinge through Sarojini. Something in the girl's tone, in her need to explain her innocence, bespeaks trouble. And what's this about problems at Rajat's work? Why has he kept it from Sarojini? Oh, these young people, with their penchant for secrets.

"Grandma, are you upset with me?"

Sarojini sighs. "No," she says, but she's not being completely honest. To change the subject, she adds, "So you finally got your phone."

"Yes! I must tell you how. When I got back to the apartment, Seema was lying on the couch with a quilt pulled up to her neck, looking like she'd been there all day. I cajoled her into coming for a walk—just a little one, because it scares her to leave the apartment. She didn't want to, but I insisted that she needed to get some fresh air for the baby's sake. On the way I saw her looking at some mangoes in a bin outside a store, so I bought a couple because she doesn't have much money. We were eating mangoes and laughing about something silly when Mitra walked in. I became quiet because he is such a grinch, but Seema told him all about the walk and how the baby must have liked being outside, he kicked and kicked. Mitra didn't say anything; he just called her into the bedroom. I thought he was going to shout at her for going out with me—he loses his temper with her quite often, though I do believe he loves her in his way. But when she came out, she was holding a package in her hands, and it was my cell phone! Do you think he had it all this while and wouldn't give it to me, just to spite the

Boses? But today when he saw I'd made his wife so happy, he changed his mind?"

"Best not try to figure out such things, shona. It'll only drive you crazy. Your grandfather was that way, always analyzing, trying to learn what people were like underneath their faces. Me, I say, who can tell what's in a man's heart? You have the phone. That's enough."

"I forgot to tell you." Korobi's voice dips into a whisper. "I asked Vic to take me to the Boses' gallery. It was a shock. The place looks abandoned. I got down from the car and peered through the front door. The lights were off, and dust covered everything, thick enough that I could see no one had been in there for a while. No wonder there haven't been any sales lately! Worse, there were quite a few blank spaces on the wall—not just the couple I'd expected from what Seema had told me about the vandalism. It's as though someone's been removing the paintings."

Sarojini doesn't like the sound of this. "Maybe you went to the wrong place?"

"It said Mumtaz, in gold letters right above the door. I was so angry. All this time the Boses have been trusting Mitra, paying him extra to turn the business around, losing money every day. And he's cheating them. I need to tell them what's going on, but I'm afraid."

Sarojini's knees feel weak. She has to sit down. She has a bad feeling about the whole business, and Mitra in particular. If the Boses confront him, Mitra would know Korobi told them. What might he do in retaliation?

"Shona, don't say anything to the Boses until you get back from your trip."

"Okay. In any case, Vic will help me figure out what to do. I'll bring it up on my way back from Boston. He's really smart. Even Mr. Desai, who has so much experience, listens to him. And he's funny, too. The other day when I got really frustrated from making those useless phone queries, he made this hilarious joke—"

Sarojini does not like how her granddaughter's voice sparks with enthusiasm when she speaks of Vic. "Be careful," she interrupts.

"I will! Don't worry!"

Sentences swirl inside Sarojini's head. *Remember who you are. Remember the world that waits for you here, its privileges and obligations. What happens in America isn't your life; it's only an interlude.* Who had said those words? It was Bimal, at the airport. Anu had touched his feet and said, *I will.* She had said, *Don't worry!*

"I love you, Grandma. I got to go now. I'll use up all my minutes otherwise. Wish me good luck in Boston."

When she was a child in her parents' home, a bee had once bitten Sarojini's face. Her lips had swollen up. For a whole day, she could hardly speak. Her mouth feels like that right now. What is good luck for Korobi? Sarojini is no longer sure. The best she can do is to say, with stiff effort, "I pray the goddess keeps you on the righteous path."

EIGHT

Evening has descended upon Kolkata. Mrs. Bose turns on the recessed lights and gives the elegantly arranged dining table a considering look. But instead of the satisfaction she usually feels, she is nagged by doubt. She has walked a razor's edge trying to create the right mix of taste and wealth: enough but not too much. Mr. and Mrs. Bhattacharya are coming to dinner, an event signaling a new intimacy between the families that Mrs. Bose desires yet shrinks from. It is a crucial night. She hopes that by the end of the evening, Bhattacharya will sign the partnership papers the Boses have drawn up based on previous discussions. This is why the right impression is so important. If Bhattacharya thinks their finances are precarious (and they are, more each day), he might shy away. If he thinks they're too well-off to be appropriately appreciative of his contribution (because that's what Mr. Bhattacharya likes, to be appreciated and preferably revered), then, too, he might decline. With that in mind, she has chosen her second-best Wedgwood set rather than the Spode. The goblets are glass, not crystal; the tableware merely stainless steel. She hopes she has not made a mistake. The menu is Italian, accompanied by French wine. Mr. Bhattacharya, for all his professions of Hindu purity, has a great fondness for French wines—in seclusion, of course.

The doorbell rings. Mrs. Bose calls out a warning to Mr. Bose, who is in the kitchen, putting the final touches to a platter of bruschetta. He is the gourmet cook of this household and the architect of tonight's dinner, but that will have to be concealed, because Mr. Bhattacharya has definite notions about a man's role in the home. Mrs. Bose smooths the edge of her chiffon sari (should she have worn a more traditional silk?), gives her hair a quick shake, and puts on a suitable smile. But it is only Rajat, who has brought Sarojini over for the evening.

At first Sarojini had declined, saying that she did not have the energy to go out, but Rajat cajoled her until she yielded. Mrs. Bose watches how attentively he leads the older woman to a chair, and a different kind of smile takes over her face.This is the way Rajat would have been with his own grandmother, she thinks, if she had lived. Mrs. Bose is grateful to Sarojini for awakening this tenderness in her son.

She is grateful to Sarojini for another reason, too. Bhattacharya has mentioned, several times, his admiration for the Roy family's heritage. Seeing Sarojini here tonight, integrated into the Bose household, will give him another incentive to become their partner. He has also mentioned a desire to see the Roys' family temple. Perhaps Mrs. Bose can set up that visit tonight.

"Pia," Rajat calls. "Come and say hello to Grandma."

Pia comes running from her room. Always so impulsive, this girl, holding nothing back! Was Mrs. Bose ever this way? She watches Pia throw her arms around Sarojini and hopes this sweetness will not cause her daughter too much heartache as she grows into adulthood.

"How thin you've become," Pia says, smoothing back Sarojini's hair, kissing both her cheeks. "I can feel all the bones of your face. It must be hard for you, alone at home with Grandfather gone and Korobi-didi so far away. You must miss her. We do, too—Dada especially, though he won't admit it. But I'm upset with Didi! She hasn't called me even once."

"Pia!" Rajat interjects. "You know Korobi didn't have a phone."

Sarojini hugs Pia. "I will certainly scold her for that. How pretty you look in this mauve salwar kameez, all grown-up. Did you get it recently?"

Pia makes a face. "Oh, no. I've had it for ages. Actually, I wanted to wear my new birthday dress. It's sleeveless and has these neat psychedelic colors. But Mom said the Bhattacharyas won't approve. They're very old-fashioned."

"Pia!" Mrs. Bose cries, half-laughing, half-exasperated.

"Don't worry! I'll be one hundred percent diplomatic when they come. Even better, I'll stay in my room until dinner. Grandma, you can come, too, if you get bored with all their business talk. I'll teach you how to play *Zelda*—it's a video game about a princess. And, Grandma, we have to feed you well, put some weight on you, otherwise what will Korobi-didi say when she comes back!"

"Listen to the girl," Sarojini says with a fond smile. "Taking care of me like she's a grandmother herself!"

"When is she coming back, anyway?" Pia continues. "Doesn't she need to get ready for the wedding?"

An awkward silence follows, adult glances meeting above her head, but Pia has already plunged into her next thought.

"Dinner's going to be grand! Dad made it all: bruschetta, salad with olives and tomatoes and three kinds of cheese, baked pasta with chicken, vegetarian pasta for you, and tiramisu for dessert. He is just the best cook! But we mustn't let Mr. Bhattacharya know that, either. Come to the kitchen, come, you and I can be the first to sample the bruschetta."

The doorbell rings again. This time it really is the Bhattacharyas, foiling Pia's plans. Bhattacharya is expansive and dazzling in white pants, a white silk bush shirt, and a Cartier watch, which he only wears for intimate social occasions. (For public events he sports a made-in-India Titan, which doesn't keep the best time but earns him loads of goodwill.) He shakes hands with Mr. Bose, nods to the others, and kisses Mrs. Bose on both cheeks, European fashion. Mrs. Bhattacharya hangs back a little, perhaps because she is weighed down by a sari with too much goldwork on it, or perhaps because of the kiss. She scrutinizes the decor with a small frown. "An orange wall," she finally says. "How very—unusual!"

Drinks are served, pleasantries exchanged, platters of appetizers passed around by Pushpa. Bhattacharya walks up and down the living room, glass in hand, as though the place belongs to him.

"Ah, there's that superb Jamini Roy mother-and-child I never tire of looking at," he exclaims, walking over to the painting. He admires the precise two-dimensionalism the artist is famed for and waxes eloquent on Roy's vision, at once magical and modern, sophisticated and innocent. Mrs. Bose feels a smile—her first genuine one since the Bhattacharyas arrived—taking over her face. Whatever his shortcomings, the man understands and loves art.

"Let me know if you ever plan to sell this one."

Mrs. Bose's smile slips. The Roy is her most prized possession. By amazing luck, Mr. Bose had discovered it in the back of a godown when an old estate was being liquidated. He had bargained shrewdly and bought it secretly, without her knowledge. She had found it waiting in their bed, wrapped in silk. That was the night, she believes, that Pia was conceived.

Fortunately, Mr. Bose comes to her rescue—as he always does—responding with utmost politeness that should such a situation arise, Bhattacharya would be the first to be informed.

"And what's this?" Bhattacharya is pointing to the framed engagement photograph hanging beside the Roy.

Mrs. Bose curses herself. She should have put away that photo before the Bhattacharyas came, so that there wouldn't be questions that led to other questions: where is Korobi now, what she is up to. She must do it as soon as her guests leave, so this never happens again.

"It's a photo of my brother's engagement," Pia says, eyes sparkling at having had her creation noticed, for once, instead of being upstaged by that stupid Jamini Roy.

"Lovely!" Bhattacharya says. But he's looking at Pia instead of the photo. "I can tell the photographer has a real eye for composition, the way the subjects have been placed within the frame."

Mrs. Bose's heart begins a heavy, arrhythmic beat.

"I arranged them," Pia says, delighted. "It took forever. Everyone complained."

"You did absolutely the right thing. Why don't you come here and explain who's who to me."

"Sure!"

Pia jumps up, but before she can move, Mrs. Bose cries, her voice too loud to her ears, "Here's one of the subjects in the flesh!"

She knows she's overreacting; Bhattacharya wouldn't really do anything; but even the thought of his fleshy hand on her daughter's shoulder is unbearable. She pulls Sarojini forward with a wide, fake smile.

"This is Korobi's grandmother. She lives in the ancestral mansion of the Roys, the one you wanted to see, with the historic Durga temple."

For a moment, annoyance at the interruption darkens Bhattacharya's face—he's aware, Mrs. Bose suspects, of her ploy. But the lure of the temple wins him over. He turns to Sarojini, asking if it's true that Netaji Subhash visited the temple for blessings.

"That's what my father-in-law always said," Sarojini replies. If she's aware of the underlying tension in the room and its cause, she gives no indication of it. She launches into a dramatic description of Netaji's visit to the temple before he left India for Japan, hoping for military aid. It gives Mrs. Bose a chance to whisper to Pia to go do her homework.

Sarojini ends by inviting Bhattacharya to the temple.

"Come on the next no-moon night, when we have a special puja for the goddess. It is supposed to bring the attendees great good luck."

Bhattacharya's eyes light up and his face takes on a boyish anticipation that surprises Mrs. Bose. "A wonderful idea," he says. "I'll do it even if I have to cancel a couple of appointments."

Mrs. Bhattacharya, who has been scrutinizing the photo with a sour expression, asks Sarojini, "And where's the bride-to-be tonight? Why isn't she with you? Have the lovebirds"—here she throws a sly glance at Rajat—"had a tiff?"

Mrs. Bose stiffens again. But Sarojini, bless her, has learned from her lawyer husband how to deal with malicious queries.

"Nothing like that, my dear! The children get along beautifully. But poor Korobi has taken her grandfather's death very hard, so I've sent her for a month to America, to spend some time with family friends."

Mrs. Bhattacharya seems deflated by this firm, no-nonsense explanation, but Mr. Bhattacharya wrinkles his brow. "With all due respect," he tells Sarojini, "it's a bad idea to send an unmarried girl abroad by herself. In fact it's downright dangerous. Who knows what temptations might come her way?"

Sarojini murmurs politely about her being in good hands, but Mrs. Bose notices Rajat's flushed face, his pained expression. Has Bhattacharya hit upon something? Is there a problem with Korobi that she doesn't know of? She feels a constriction in her chest. Oh, it's hard to accept that children come with their own fates. That a parent can do only so much to make them happy.

"Dinner is ready," she announces brightly. Thank God, the distraction works.

The meal proceeds excellently. Mr. Bhattacharya takes seconds of everything and praises Mrs. Bose. Beauty, business acumen, and now this—the ability to produce a gourmet dinner while looking as though she hasn't even stepped into the kitchen! Mrs. Bose inclines her head in modest acceptance, sending Mr. Bose a tiny, private smile. Bhattacharya drinks several glasses of chardonnay. His wife puts a restraining hand on his arm, but he shakes it off with a quelling frown and she doesn't do it again.

The tiramisu is served and complimented. Pia takes Sarojini off to her room. Pushpa brings coffee. It is time.

"Mr. Bhattacharya, shall we look at the partnership documents I've drawn up, based on our earlier discussion?" Mr. Bose asks.

Mrs. Bose holds her breath. They have decided that Mr. Bose will lead this conversation while Mrs. Bose gives him the necessary input through minute gestures they have perfected over years.

"We can look," Bhattacharya says, "but we'll have to change some of the clauses. I made some recent inquiries and found that your business isn't doing as well as I had thought. You're okay in India, thanks mostly to the Park Street gallery and your orders from the hotel chains, but you're losing a lot of money in America. And now I hear you have troubles at your warehouse."

Mrs. Bose curses inwardly. Bhattacharya must have a formidable network of informers. Thinking about the warehouse makes her feel ill. Last night, Mr. Bose and she had discussed the situation in the privacy of their bedroom. They agreed that Rajat had been too harsh. Alauddin, who had used the box cutter, shouldn't have been fired. Now he was stirring up the Muslim union members. The Hindu members were currently undecided, but in Bengal the ties of class were often stronger than religion. Unless the Boses took care of the problem rapidly, there might well be a labor strike. Shipments would get delayed, orders canceled, one mishap setting off another like a chain of firecrackers. Mrs. Bose's head spun just to think of them.

But what should they do? Mr. Bose wanted to compensate the injured Hindu worker and hire Alauddin back, thus appeasing the union. The workstations would be put back where they had been. When Mrs. Bose said that would undercut Rajat's authority, Mr. Bose suggested that they could move him away from the warehouse. He could help in the Park Street gallery and focus on putting together that website he was so excited about. They could make it seem like a promotion. Mrs. Bose wasn't convinced that would work. Hadn't they been delighted when Rajat had decided to finally settle down, after years of wildness, and help with the family business? Could they deny that he was working hard and doing well, except for this one error? If they moved him away, everyone would recognize it as a slap in the face, no matter what the Boses said. The workers wouldn't respect Rajat after that, and he would never forgive his parents.

They had talked late into the night but failed to come to a conclusion.

Lost in her worries, Mrs. Bose has missed part of the conversation at the table. She hears Bhattacharya say, "Mr. Bose, I'm willing to become a partner—but in light of the recent developments, you'll have to make some additional concessions. I want fifty percent ownership of the Park Street gallery and a hand in its operations."

"That's a significant change," Mr. Bose replies in his calm voice. But Mrs. Bose can see a telltale pulsing at his temple. "You'll have to give us a little time to discuss this."

"Take all the time you want." Bhattacharya smiles expansively. "I'm in no hurry, though I do believe you might be."

The phone rings, making Mrs. Bose jump. The shrill sound is like the cry of a cicada, amplified. Only Sonia ever calls at this hour. The family stares at each other, uncertain about how to handle this situation. "Well, aren't you going to answer it?" Bhattacharya asks.

"I don't want to interrupt the meal—or your conversation," Mrs. Bose says, stretching her lips with effort in the approximation of a smile. "The caller can leave a message." She is counting on how, whenever the answering machine clicks on, Sonia hangs up. She doesn't want Sarojini to think Rajat might be involved with another woman while Korobi is away. And if Bhattacharya knew that Rajat was being stalked—no other word for it—by an ex-girlfriend, that this possible scandal, too, loomed on the family's horizon, he'd surely drive a harder bargain.

"I'm done with conversing." Bhattacharya nods at Rajat. "Why don't you take care of the call, young man, while your mother gives me one last tiny piece of that sinfully delicious dessert."

Rajat has no choice but to pick up the phone. The caller says something brief and crackly. Mrs. Bose listens as hard as she can, but fortunately no words can be deciphered. Why won't Sonia leave her son alone? They'd been very much in love, Mrs. Bose had seen that, but it was over now. Rajat was engaged. Though used to getting her way (a trait Mrs. Bose understood well), Sonia needed to realize that it was time to move on. Or had Rajat been encouraging her in some way? Mrs. Bose decides she will have a talk with Rajat about it. In the past, he's shied away from such conversations, but this time she'll insist. In the kitchen doorway, Pushpa stands gawking. Mrs. Bose must chide her as soon as the guests leave. Servants! Sometimes they're enough to drive you crazy.

"Wrong number," Rajat says, replacing the receiver. His face is flushed again.

Bhattacharya raises an eyebrow but concentrates on the piece of tiramisu Mrs. Bose has managed to cut into a perfect square and serve him.

Finally, finally, the Bhattacharyas leave. Sarojini says she, too, must go. Mrs. Bose would like to tell her how much she appreciates her help with Bhattacharya, but that would entail long and complicated explanations. Instead, she gives Sarojini a hug, holding her an extra moment. The old woman must understand something because she whispers, "I'll pray for your family's peace of mind."

Once Pushpa, sulky from having been admonished, has cleaned up and left, Mr. and Mrs. Bose say good-night to their children and retire to bed. Though it is a warm night, Mrs. Bose feels chilled. Even her favorite silk Jaipuri bedspread, pulled up to her chin, doesn't help. In the dark, she clutches Mr. Bose's nightshirt lapels and cries fiercely that the thought of

Bhattacharya owning part of her beloved gallery, showing up whenever he wants with that proprietorial attitude, makes her feel physically ill.

"Then we won't do it, dearest. We'll find another way."

"But how?" Her voice spirals up in desperation. "We've been unable to find anyone else willing to invest in art. The banks won't loan us more money—"

"Hush, Joyu." He holds her close. "Remember the time I caught dengue fever out near Bankura District, in that remote village where there was no phone line to call you?"

"Shanto, this is no time to—"

"Remember?"

"Yes," she whispers, giving in. It's her favorite story, one they've told each other many times. She loops an arm around his neck. "I sensed you were in trouble. I left baby Rajat with Ma. I had to travel alone all the way on a bullock cart. I was so scared. I wasn't even sure I was going to the right place. There were no guesthouses out there. I had no idea where you were staying."

"But you found me. You nursed me until I could be moved and brought me back on that rickety bullock cart. I was so weak, I had to stay in bed for a month. We had no money. The landlord was determined to evict us."

She gives a little chuckle. "But I managed to persuade him to give us a month's grace. I even talked him into buying something from the store for his wife's birthday—embroidered pillowcases, I think it was."

"If we could make it through that, we can get through this, too."

"Yes," she says, though her voice is tinged with doubt.

"We'll think about it in the morning. We'll figure something out."

He holds her, running his fingers in soothing circles on her back until she relaxes into his chest, into sleep.

On the way to Boston, Vic makes me practice my lies. Along the freeway bordered by chain stores whose names appear again and again as though I'm caught in a looping dream, I tell him how excited I am to be in America, where my wonderful new husband has promised to build me the house of my dreams. We pass gas stations that sell slushy coffee and empty fields patched with tired gray snow. I make shapes in the air describing the L-shaped family room that needs to open to the dining area because I plan to throw lots of parties, the inner courtyard I want to fill with oleanders. I know I need to focus on this, but from time to time, my errant thoughts flit back to our time together yesterday.

When we were at the Empire State Building, Vic asked, "So, how does Kolkata compare to New York?"

I was silent. I've never looked down upon Kolkata from up high, so I had no idea how far the city sprawled, which shape it took. On the ground, I knew its contradictions: lavish wedding halls behind which beggars waited for leftovers; red-bannered, slogan-shouting protesters marching by a house where a musician practiced classical flute. But Kolkata's spirit, at once vibrant and desperate—I had no words to describe it to someone who has never lived there.

"It's complicated," I said finally. "Most Indian cities are. You must have noticed that yourself."

"I've never been to India."

"Never? Didn't you want to see where your people came from?"

He shrugged, a bit defensive. "When I was young, we didn't have the money to go. By the time we could afford it, I was a teenager and refused to waste my summers that way. I guess I really didn't think of myself as Indian."

"How did you think of yourself? As American?"

"Yes. Though after 9/11, I had some difficulties with that, too. Anyhow, my mother always asked me to accompany her, but she'd have to end up going alone. And then she died. Maybe one of these days, if I get enough money together, I might go visit her hometown. Might look you up in Kolkata, too. Though you'll be a rich man's wife by then and won't want to see me!"

I had given him a pale smile. He'd hit too close to the truth. Once I was married, Rajat would make sure this chapter of my life was closed for good.

The lanes swell; the Boston skyline with its high-rises looms over us.

We skirt the Common, with its statues of men in three-cornered hats. We pass colleges with stained-glass windows that, Vic tells me, are as old as anything white people built in America.

"You went to Berkeley?" I enunciate brightly. "Amazing! So did my mother! Did you happen to know a girl named Anu Roy?"

"Your voice sounds like you murdered someone and hid the body!" Vic tells me. "Say her name again and again until it becomes like any other word. Oh, never mind. Rest for a bit. Otherwise you'll be worn-out by the time we get to Evanston's office."

Gratefully, I turn my face to the window. We pass by a park with its daffodil beds. Yesterday, I asked Vic to take me to where the Towers used to be.

"Not you, too! Why?"

I wasn't sure. I only knew that it wasn't the impulse to gawk at disaster. Perhaps it was a mosaic of desires. To acknowledge tragedy. To pay respect. To understand Mitra's meltdown. To apologize for Grandfather, who had said that finally America was learning how the rest of the world suffers.

Through the chain-link I saw the piles of rubble still to be cleared, smashed concrete, mangled iron rods. Yellow machines like steel dinosaurs clamped piles of debris in their jaws. I tried to superimpose on the scene what I'd seen in my dream: the buildings collapsing, dust and fire, stampeding crowds, people falling like meteors out of the sky. Nothing matched. A supervisor in a hard hat motioned in annoyance for us to move on.

A part of me is still standing there.

We enter a tunnel, the dark punctuated by yellow globes of light. I can see Vic's face reflected on my window glass, close to mine. He's humming to a song on the radio.

"It was a bad time all around," Vic said when I told him about what happened to Mitra after the Towers fell. "I remember how terrified and furious I felt right after. That's when my own restaurant business—which had been doing quite well—started going under. People just stopped coming. Nine-eleven injured the people of this city in so many ways—we still haven't been able to tally up the casualties. We aren't used to shit like this happening inside our own borders, America the protected. We needed to find an enemy to lash out at. Some people did, and folks like Mitra became the casualties. But there were other kinds of casualties, too. A friend of mine who was in construction was hired to clean up Ground Zero. One night after a few beers, he started describing how it was. Imagine finding bodies everywhere, pieces of people half-cooked by the heat. Sometimes recognizing a friend. You didn't know when a patch of fire would flare up from below. And the stench. He'd come home exhausted but couldn't sleep. Started drinking. His marriage broke up soon after."

The car lurches to a stop. We are at one of the ubiquitous McDonald's.

"Time to change into your rich-and-fashionable clothes," Vic says.

When I come out of the women's restroom dressed in a sleek cream pantsuit, he purses his lips in a soundless whistle. The admiration in his eyes makes my heart lurch guiltily.

"Wow, didn't know you owned something this chic! Isn't it a Prada? They sell those in India?"

I give him a smile. The suit has a story, but it isn't mine to tell.

Last evening, when I was packing, Seema had come and perched on my bed.

"Boston! Wish I could go with you. I always wanted to visit Boston, but we never had the time—and then we didn't have the money. What will you do there?"

If it weren't for Mitra, I would have told her. There was no guile in Seema.

"Sorry," Seema said. "I know you told me you promised someone special you wouldn't talk about it. Bet I know who that is! Rajat-babu. He's the one who gave you that gorgeous diamond ring, right? I hope you remember to turn it inside out when you're on the subway, like I told you. You don't want people to see something so expensive. You love him very much, don't you? I remember how dashing he was. All the girls used to be after him. I think it would worry me if my fiancé was so attractive. What are you packing?"

I showed her a green silk salwar kameez with gold embroidery at the neck.

"Wow! That's very fancy."

"It's for an important meeting—"

"With white people? It's too gaudy! They won't take you seriously. Wait just a moment."

She ran to her bedroom and returned with the pantsuit. It was rich, understated, perfect. It made me realize more than anything else how far the Mitras had fallen. I looked at Seema in her shapeless polyester pants stretched over her enormous belly, holding up the suit with a tremulous smile, and understood a little of the anger Mitra must feel.

"You can borrow it. I'll probably never manage to fit into it again, and even if I did, where would I wear it? Only, let's keep it a secret. Mr. Mitra might get upset if he found out. He gave it to me for our first anniversary in this country. This year he's so preoccupied, he probably won't even remember the date."

She brought out shoes, a purse, earrings. The shoes were a bit tight, but I couldn't resist them. In the mirror I looked transformed, a sophisticate that men would line up to claim as their daughter. How could I thank Seema for such generosity? How could I console her for the longing in her eyes? We wrapped everything in a beach towel that said PEACE OUT and hid it in my carry-on.

It is snowing when we reach Rob Evanston's office. My first snowfall, and I'm too nervous to enjoy it. Inside, the furniture is overstuffed and has a mournful look. Evanston does not seem to be doing too well. The only occupant of the office is a stocky young redhead in a sweater meant for someone of less robust proportions, buffing her nails. She puts away her nail file with reluctance and informs us that Mr. Evanston is running late with his morning meeting.

The wall is crowded with photos of houses designed by my potential father. They are all of a type: large and rectangular, with crisscrossed wood beams and chimneys that rise up like fat exclamation marks. I dislike them all. I wonder if this means I will dislike him, too.

Finally, Mr. Evanston enters in a flurry of wind and snow and apologies, throwing down an armload of plans on a sofa in a manner that suggests his morning meeting has not gone well. He invites us into his office. Seated across from him at his table, I find it hard to concentrate on my spiel. Is this my father, this balding man with light brown hair and pale blue eyes, a little overweight, earnestly promising to do an outstanding job for us? He looks so—foreign. I can't relate to him. I must be staring; he looks at me with a puzzled smile. The photograph on his desk shows him standing outside a house similar to those on his wall, his arms around a red-haired woman and a plump girl—the same girl who was at the reception desk. The woman holds on to a boy who looks as if he's trying to squirm away. It strikes me that I might be on the verge of making all these good people significantly unhappy.

"Honey? Babe?" Vic is calling.

With a wide, fake smile, I launch again into the description of my dream house. Halfway through, I realize I'm describing my grandfather's house. A flood of homesickness chokes me. Suddenly I don't want to be here.

Mr. Evanston busily takes notes, interrupting only to point out features—the flat terrace, the enclosed courtyard—that wouldn't work in this climate. His daughter comes in with coffee and cookies and such a look of hope on her face that I feel worse than ever about my deception. I plunge into the part about Berkeley, but when I mention my mother, Evanston shakes his head.

"I don't recall anyone named Anu. I did have several South Asian friends at Berkeley, though. And even a girlfriend for a while, a Pakistani. Her name was Shahnaz." He smiles ruefully. "Halfway through her studies, her family found out about us and married her off to a distant cousin from Toledo. Broke my heart. But maybe it was for the best, because the next year, I met the missus. We've been married eighteen years now. After graduation, we decided to move back East—her family's from this area—and I'm glad we did. People are more dependable in this part of the country. The only thing I hate is the winter. By the way, you can't plant oleanders here. The snow will kill them right away. And speaking of snow, it's supposed to be coming down pretty hard this afternoon."

I believe his story. It's too mundane to be untrue. The men are discussing the weather.

"Really? Heavy snow this late in the year?" Vic asks.

"Yep. Freak snowstorm coming this way all of a sudden."

Failure has carved a pit in my stomach; I can't gauge how deep it goes. I'd like to leave the office so I can nurse my wounds in private, but I must continue with the charade. Mr. Evanston goes over blueprints of houses he has designed, pointing out features he's particularly proud of and advising us on the best appliance brands. Finally, Vic extricates us with our first true statement of the day: we have a long drive ahead.

Outside, big, wet flakes are pouring from the sky. Vic glances up with some anxiety. Inside the car, I can't stop shivering, even though the heat is on. I huddle in the black coat Maman gave me, but it's no match for the American Northeast. I'll have to start my search all over again, and now I have less than three weeks left.

"Are you upset that he isn't your father?" Vic asks.

I nod and turn away, not ready to talk. I am disappointed—and am not. I badly want to find the man to whom my mother had written that romantic and tragic love letter, which I carried in my purse. I know with the passing of each day, my chances of discovering him are growing slimmer. But I hadn't wanted Evanston, so comfortable in his mediocrity, to be him. What was it I longed for in a father? What doomed, romantic idea was I harboring?

We drive slowly on the slick road. Vic leaves me alone to worry. In the failing, melancholy light, the buildings look old and empty. A traveler's advisory comes on the radio.

"Shit!" says Vic. "We should probably stay in Boston tonight. This is not a good car for a snowstorm."

Panic makes me clutch his arm. "No! We've got to get back tonight."

He glances over in surprise. "I know you're short on money—I'll look for the cheapest motel. Heck, I'll even pay for it."

"Money's not the issue. You don't know how people think back in India! I can't spend the night alone with you. Well, not *with* you—ah, you know what I mean. Engagements have been broken for far less."

He shakes his head. "It's dangerous to drive any further. Tell your fiancé what's going on with the weather. He must trust you—and surely your safety matters more to him than a foolish social convention."

I recall how Rajat had spat Vic's name out in anger, and I'm not sure. Exhaustion hits me. The last few times we spoke, we seemed to be at cross-purposes. I couldn't shake the suspicion that Rajat was keeping something from me. We love each other, I know that. That's why we're getting married, isn't it? But I can't remember back beyond the tension to the tenderness. I just know that I am not up to facing more of his anger tonight.

"Oh, very well," Vic says, peering into my face. "If we must get back to New York, I'll give it my best try, in spite of having been dubbed the villain of our little drama. The worst part is, I don't even get to do anything fun for it!"

But an hour later, after the car skids and ends up inches short of a guardrail, even I have to agree that we must give up. I'm afraid that we will not find a place to stay, here in the middle of nowhere. But, ah, the wonders of America! A motel appears almost immediately, like an enchanted palace out of a fairy tale, its red-and-blue sign blinking through the fast-falling sleet. We struggle through the snow to the front desk, where a bored clerk hands us keys to two rooms. They're the cheapest available, but to me they're still shockingly expensive. I try to hide my consternation as I calculate how deeply they'll cut into my resources.

Once in my room, I phone the Mitras, hoping to get Seema. But of course Mitra picks up.

"Strange! It's not snowing in New York."

I'm infuriated by the insinuation in his voice. "Take a look at the Weather Channel," I retort, then hang up. My teeth chatter. The room is freezing, but I can't figure out how to work the thermostat. Seema's beautiful suit is bedraggled, the legs distressingly muddy. I would love to take a hot shower and collapse into bed. But first I must take care of my most difficult task. As I dial Rajat's number, I notice that my phone battery is low. And of course I have no charger with me.

On his way to the warehouse, Rajat makes an effort to stare out the window, but each time his eyes are drawn to the back of Asif's head. He tries to keep his mind on the momentous task ahead, but he can't stop replaying Sonia's voice from the phone call last night. *Ask your driver why he*

hasn't given you my letter, she had said before he had replaced the receiver with a shaky hand. He had been shocked to learn of the existence of this letter (what could possibly be in it?), but more shocked to realize that Asif was capable of such duplicity. He has decided not to confront the driver until after the meeting. He needs to keep his wits about him, and bringing up Sonia's letter now will sabotage any hope he has of remaining calm.

They were eating breakfast this morning when Subroto, the foreman, called home. Papa's face tightened as they conversed. The Muslim workers had filed a discrimination complaint with the union. They were planning to picket outside the warehouse today. The union had supported them in this, though they hadn't yet agreed to their demands for a full-fledged strike. But if the situation wasn't defused immediately, that would be the next development. Mr. Bose needed to come in right away to pacify the union leaders.

The blood pounded in Rajat's ears. He had caused this problem. He'd been a fool, dictatorial when leniency was needed, weak where strength was required. For a moment he thought it would be best to let his father go, as the foreman suggested. But he couldn't stand the thought of Papa having to clean up Rajat's shit. Plus, if his father took over now, the men would lose all respect for Rajat, the spoiled rich boy who ran to daddy when things got too hot. He'd never be able to work in the warehouse again. Then it would just be a matter of time before he slid back into his old lifestyle with his carousing friends. And that lifestyle had no place for Cara in it.

He reached across the table and gripped his mother's hand. "Let me go. Give me a chance to repair the mess I made. I'll do exactly what Dad and you tell me—but I have to show the workers that I'm man enough to face them."

Those other fears, unspoken, hummed inside him. It seemed to him that his mother felt them along her own nerves. It had always been this way between them. He felt her thoughts, too. She was weighing the risks at the warehouse against the shame that would spiral him downward.

She chose him. When had she not? As he watched her whispering fiercely to his father, he promised himself that this time he would repay her trust.

Having made their decision, his parents gave him detailed instructions. He must remember he was the ambassador of the Bose family. His job was to listen, take notes, and bring back the union's demands. He was to be polite no matter what they said, to show no emotion and offer no opinions. He was not to apologize; nor was he to defend his actions.

"But they're in the wrong, and they know it. I fined the Hindu workers, too. I—"

"It's no longer a question of who's in the wrong," his father said. "Now we must only focus on how to defuse this situation. The union doesn't really want that. They would prefer to assert their power through a shutdown. Some of them might try to incite you. Get you to say something rash. Maybe even get into a fight."

"That would give them the ammunition they need to start the strike," his mother explained. "They might even have someone ready with a hidden camera—that's what they did to the Manchandanis last year. Be alert."

"I'll be careful," Rajat promised. He felt like a warrior. Energy rushed through him.

As the lift doors closed, he saw his mother's hand find his father's and grip it tightly.

Rajat's buoyancy lasted only until he got to the car and saw Asif. The driver was waiting in the circular driveway, dusting the Mercedes, chatting with another chauffeur. His uniform was perfectly ironed. His sunglasses gleamed. His teeth sparkled as he laughed at something the other man said. When he saw Rajat, he wished him good morning and opened the door with a flourish. As though he were a film star playing at being a chauffeur. As though he hadn't deceived Rajat, hadn't stolen something crucial and intimate that belonged to him.

"Take off those ridiculous sunglasses," Rajat snapped.

Asif's features stiffened. Wordlessly, he did what he was told. Rajat could see the skin stretching tight across the man's knuckles as he gripped the steering wheel.

Had Asif read the letter? He couldn't have. He didn't know enough English. Still, the suspicion wound itself tight around Rajat's throat.

Since Rajat can't talk about what's bothering him, he finds other ways to express his displeasure. When Asif is about to take a back way to the warehouse, he insists on going along the main road. When they get caught at an intersection where the lights aren't functioning, Rajat curses aloud. A part of him despises himself for this behavior—he has always prided himself on treating retainers well. But he can't stop himself.

Why hadn't Asif handed the letter to him right away? What had he done with it?

Finally, they get through the backed-up traffic. With luck, they'll be at the warehouse in another ten minutes. That's when the phone rings. It's Korobi. He's glad she caught him before he got into the meeting with the union officials. He couldn't have stopped to talk to her then.

Because he has so little time, he gets directly to the point—as much as one can with the driver listening.

"What happened in Boston? Was he the one? Can you come home now?"

"No, he wasn't." He can hear the disappointment in her voice. But there's something else. Is it apprehension?

"Maybe you should come back to Kolkata anyway," he says. "Everything's gone wrong since you left—it's like you were my talisman."

"Oh, Rajat. I'm sorry you're going through so many troubles." She sighs—mournfully, he would like to think. Does she sound distracted? "You know I can't go back yet. I've invested too much in this. I've got to stay until I've checked out at least a couple of other possibilities."

They're interrupted by a beeping.

"Oh, dear. I think my phone battery's dying. I don't know why. I charged it last night. And I didn't bring the charger."

"Aren't you back in New York yet?"

"Actually—I'm still outside Boston."

"What do you mean?" His voice goes high, though he tries to control it. "Isn't it night there already? Why aren't you back?"

"We got caught in a snowstorm. We had to check into a motel."

"You and that man? He's there, too?"

Irritation sharpens her voice. "Where would he go?"

The phone gives more beeps. It's going to fail any moment. He knows he shouldn't ask, but he can't stop himself. "Is he there? In your room? Is he with you right now?"

There's a cold silence. "No, he's not," Korobi finally says quietly. "He's in his own room. Don't you trust me?"

Of course he trusts her. The snowstorm is not her fault. What else could she have done? Still, suspicion eats at him.

It's because he doesn't trust the guy she's with. Slick Vic. But, no. It's really because he doesn't trust himself. Because a part of him can't rest until it discovers what Sonia wrote. Because a part of him is thinking, right now, of his final conversation with Sonia.

Before he can put any of this into words, they're disconnected. He calls her back, but there's no response. Is her phone dead, or did she hang up on him? He curses again, punches the seat, feeling Asif wince.

No time now. They're at the warehouse gates; a large group of men swarm around the car, waving placards and shouting. BOSES UNFAIR TO MUSLIM WORKERS, the placards announce. Rajat's palms are clammy. He has to wipe them on his pants. A concerned Asif asks if he should turn the car around. It doesn't seem safe for Rajat-saab to go in there. The men have worked themselves up to such a frenzy, they're incapable of listening to reason. Now they're banging on the car windows. Not so hard that it'll break the glass, but hard enough to show who has the power.

Rajat has seen these men regularly for the last few months. Has made it a point to speak pleasantly to them whenever the occasion arose. But today they glare at him as though he's a stranger—no, not a stranger. A familiar enemy. One of them shouts through the window at Asif, "Brother, quit eating the salt of these Muslim-haters!" Asif wears his impassive chauffeur expression and looks into the distance. Against his will, Rajat must admire how calm Asif is. He himself is far from calm. But he thinks of his parents, who are taking a chance on him, and rolls down the window.

"Please permit me to speak to the union leaders."

If his voice shakes, no one is aware of it in the din. Amazingly, the crowd parts for him. As he steps out, it surrounds him again and presses him toward the entrance of the warehouse.

I stare at the phone, stubbornly mute in my hand. It's as though the universe conspired to cut off communication between Rajat and me at the most crucial moment, to further our misunderstanding. I punch the green button several times. Nothing. I long to fling the phone across the room, but I can't afford to break it. So instead I fling myself on the bed. Why did the phone have to die at exactly this moment? If only I'd had another minute to explain—

But then the truth strikes me, shocking as a slap. The real problem isn't the dead phone. Even if I could have talked to Rajat, what would I have said after he accused me—so crassly, so easily—of unfaithfulness? Where would I have found the words to convey how hurt I am that he could think I'd let go so lightly of my betrothal vows? If that's what he thinks of me, he doesn't know me. He doesn't know me at all.

And maybe I don't know him. The Rajat branded into my heart—who placed his steady palm on my back and taught my stumbling self to dance at Mimi's party, who tried to pull me from the quicksand of depression after Grandfather's death, who pressed his face against my throat one drunken night and said he couldn't live without me—would never have had such a low opinion of me. Or would he? Had I rushed into this engagement too quickly, putting my trust in gestures?

Or was it that even the best of relationships withered if people were separated too soon? Did early love, which grew out of the body's needs, require the body's presence to nurture it? Without those wordless glances that made the heart race, without the touch of lips that sent electricity through the body, without a shoulder to lay the dispirited head on and arms to shore us up against the world's cruelties, even the most affectionate words weren't enough. But the cruel words—paradoxically, those gained power as they flew across the miles to stab at a listener's heart.

Still, my mother had done it. She had kept faith with a husband half a world away, when she was pregnant and fighting with my grandfather. She had held my father in her heart until she died. And I was her daughter.

But what if my love for Rajat simply wasn't enough?

All these thoughts tumble through my exhausted brain as I press my face against a brown motel bedspread that smells of the loneliness of strangers and give way to tears. My life feels too heavy for me to shoulder alone. I'd thought myself strong and brave, smart and adventurous—but I wasn't any of those things. I was just a girl who needed someone to hold me.

I'm crying so hard that I almost don't hear the knocking at the door. But the knocker is persistent; I realize he isn't going to go away. Through the peephole, I see that it's Vic, holding two steaming cups and some packaged sandwiches. I dry my eyes carefully. I don't want the additional humiliation of his knowing that I broke down.

He sets everything down on the rickety bedside table—that's all the furniture the room has, except for the bed.

"I got them from the machines downstairs. Sorry, they don't have a diner. But the hot chocolate smells pretty good, and the egg-salad sandwiches look safe. It's freezing in here! Why haven't you turned up the heat?" He strides over to the thermostat, but even he can't get it to work. Finally, he gives up and calls the desk to demand another room.

I drink the hot chocolate in huge gulps even though it burns my mouth. I can feel its welcome warmth traveling through my body. It's the most comforting drink I've ever had. I'm touched by Vic's caring, especially in the wake of Rajat's suspicion. But that suspicion has made me newly awkward. I'm acutely aware of our situation: we're in my motel room at night, sitting on my bed. It's exactly the kind of compromising scenario Rajat had imagined. The irony of it makes me want to laugh.

I mumble my thanks into my cup, aware that I sound ungracious. But I can't risk Vic's mistaking my gratitude for a different kind of emotion. And he has a history. I remember Desai cautioning him to keep things professional, and it strikes me that he'd been cautioning me, too.

"Why were you crying?"

I look up, startled and chagrined. Loyalty to Rajat battles with my longing for sympathy.

"What did he say to you?"

"Please," I manage. "I don't want to talk about it."

He's silent. I feel my face growing hot. Finally he says, "It's been a hell of a day for you. Let's get you that new room. You'll feel better after you take a hot shower and eat something."

He leans forward. I feel his lips on my forehead, a moment's touch, like a falling petal. Somewhere there's a memory of a similar kiss, its sweetness now turned to pain. I push it away. I keep my eyes closed. It takes all my willpower not to collapse into Vic's chest. I must be faithful. I will be faithful. Is it wrong for me to want this moment not to end?

NINE

Sarojini is supervising a cleanup of the temple in preparation for Bhattacharya's visit tomorrow night. The gardener boy scrubs the floor, coaxes spiderwebs from corners, and changes a burned-out bulb while Bahadur instructs him vociferously. The wicker chairs used for Korobi's engagement, carried from the main house, create an ache inside Sarojini. The brass lamps are taken to the outdoor tap to be scrubbed with tamarind paste. Where is the large copper plate on which fruits are offered? No one seems to know. Beokoof! Bahadur yells at the boy in terrifying tones. But the boy is used to Bahadur and merely scratches his head. Sarojini wonders if other things are lost or stolen, things she has forgotten about. She finds she doesn't care. Far bigger things in her life have gone missing, and, look, she has survived them.

Their work done, the servants leave. Sarojini indulges her knee and sits on a chair to pray. The priest is late. Perhaps he's late every day, and Sarojini hasn't noticed. Since Bimal passed away, she only comes to the temple intermittently. The goddess, she feels, has let her down. It isn't right, she tells her sometimes. After all the pujas I offered you, asking you to take me first, this just isn't right.

Sarojini chants the names of the goddess, but her truant mind wanders. This visit of Bhattacharya's, it's like a rock heaved into the still pond of her life. She's not used to guests anymore. Over the last years,

Bimal had grown reclusive and abrupt, so that only his oldest, most persistent friends ventured to visit them. After his death, Sarojini let even that fall away. She has made an exception for Bhattacharya because of the Boses. She has gathered, by interrogating a reluctant Rajat, that they need Bhattacharya's assistance for their business to survive. Rajat, dear boy, would never ask for help, but Sarojini is determined to do what she can to further their cause.

She abandons the flowery Sanskrit mantras for homespun Bengali importunings. Goddess, Mother of Miracles, could you soften up Bhattacharya a bit? And while you're at it, throw the shawl of your protection over Rajat. The boy's in trouble of some kind, something serious, I can feel it, though he won't tell me the details.

Sarojini thinks back on the dinner at the Boses', tension hanging thick over that beautifully appointed dinner table like mist over the pond at sunrise behind her parents' village home. Suddenly, a great homesickness comes over her. For her childhood, that simple, happy time when all her needs were taken care of; for her parents' village, now across the border in another country she'll never visit; for the dust from cattle hooves glowing in the setting sun as herds returned from the fields. As if to intensify her yearning, a car honks irately outside her gate, and other drivers join in the cacophony.

She claps her hands over her ears and makes a decision. As soon as the no-moon puja is over tomorrow, she will go to Bimal's ancestral village for a fortnight. There's no need for her to languish here while Korobi is in the United States. She thinks of the village home, the old brick bungalow set deep in a mango orchard that she hasn't seen for seventeen years because Bimal refused to visit it, and is struck by resolution. She puts away her prayer beads and hurries to the house to make arrangements. Cook will come with her, like last time. And Bahadur—she'll send him ahead, to clean up the house.

From the doorway, Cook shouts, "Ma, Ma. Come quickly. Something terrible has happened."

Sarojini sighs. Ever since Bimal's death, Cook has been skittery. The least little thing puts her in a panic. The other night, she awoke Sarojini, certain that someone was trying to break into the house, but when they checked (Cook armed with the fish-cutting bonti), they discovered it was only a branch scraping against a window. As Sarojini walks to the house, favoring her bad knee, she considers what to pack. Will she need her heavy shawl? Quilts, certainly, because the nights are colder in the village. A set of dishes, complete with utensils. Mosquito nets. The village mosquitoes, superior in size and aggression to their Kolkata cousins, are not to be taken lightly. She remembers the palm trees in the back, how the leaves whispered when the wind blew. So many nights she listened to them as she paced the terrace, carrying a colicky Korobi, her own insides still raw from having Anu ripped away. Still and all, it had been a healing place.

But when Cook, wringing her hands, hurries Sarojini into one of the spare downstairs bedrooms, she sees that something terrible has, indeed, happened this time. Water is pouring down one of the walls. A pipe has obviously broken somewhere upstairs. It must have happened a good while back, because the water has pooled on the floor, too. She stares, aghast, at the Turkish carpet that has been in the family since before her marriage, now soggy and ruined beyond repair. Is this a bad omen? Finally she recovers enough to summon Bahadur to turn off the main water pipe and call a plumber. She paces in a fever of anxiety until the man arrives.

The plumber's news is as bad as Sarojini feared: large segments of pipe—not just the broken one—have corroded and will have to be replaced. Several walls in the house will have to be opened up to allow this. The job will take weeks and cost thousands of rupees, money she does not have.

After the plumber does a few makeshift repairs and leaves, Sarojini sits down heavily on the bed, the edge of her sari trailing in the ankle-deep water. She sits there for a long time, and then she goes to the drawer where she usually throws miscellaneous items she doesn't know what to do with. Cook comes by to ask how she is expected to cook lunch, now that the water is turned off, but Sarojini barely hears her. Her muscles ache with tension as she rummages through the debris of years. She knows she put the card in here, the card belonging to that man, what was his name, the one who came by, asking to buy the house? All she can remember is how much she had disliked him. Finally, frustrated to tears, she upends the drawer, scattering items all over the floor. There it is, the card with its glaring-red logo. She dials the number with a hand that shakes as though she had suddenly developed palsy.

"Mr. Vikas Saxena, please."

"He is not in, madam," a secretary intones. "May I take a message?"

"It's Mrs. Roy from twenty-six Tarak Prasad Roy Road, the old house that he wanted to buy and tear down. I'm ready to discuss his offer. But I need to talk to someone right away. Isn't there anyone in the office?"

"I will check, madam," the girl says, her voice bored. "Please hold."

Sarojini holds—what choice does she have?—for an interminable period. Then, just when she is convinced that the girl has forgotten about her, a man comes on the line.

"This is Mrs. Roy, calling from twenty-six Tarak Prasad Roy Road," she starts again, but the man interrupts her.

"Sarojini-ma, namaskar to you."

He speaks in Bengali, his accent thick but comprehensible. And familiar. Sarojini knows that voice from a long time ago.

"Sardarji?" she whispers. "Is it you? Are you here in Kolkata?"

"Yes, ma."

"But Bimal-babu told me that you had retired and gone back to your native place!"

"I did go back to Ludhiana for some time, but I missed Kolkata—I'd lived here so long. So I came back, and now I'm one of Saxena's overseers."

Sarojini braces herself and says, "Babu—passed away suddenly." Talking about her loss still hurts.

"I heard that from Saxena. I am so sorry. I wanted to call you, but I had promised Babu. That's why I hesitated, even today—"

"Promised Babu what?"

"That I would stay away from the family."

"Why would he want you to do that?" Sarojini asks, confused. "You were the best driver we ever had."

"Babu wanted to make sure no one found out—especially you. Of course, I wouldn't have said a word, but he thought that this way there was no chance of a slip."

"Found out what?" Sarojini's body grows hot, then ice-cold. Not another secret, just when she thought she was finally done with them! "Tell me now. Whatever it was, I deserve to know it."

Sardarji doesn't protest. Perhaps he agrees. "Soon after you went to the village, Korobi-baby's father came to Kolkata. He started asking a lot of uncomfortable questions, about how Anu-missybaba died, and what happened to Baby. But Bimal-babu was ready for him. He gave him a fake certificate, stating Baby had also died in childbirth. He had it forged and stamped with court stamps, so that it would look official enough to fool Baby's father. Babu hoped that then he would go back to America, and you folks could keep Baby. He had to pay a lot of people to keep their mouths shut—the forgers, the nurses in the infant-care ward, who knows how many others. He paid all of us servants handsomely, too—though we would never have said anything to that foreigner. None of us wanted you to have to give up Baby, who was the only family you had left."

"Oh," says Sarojini. It is a sound that one might make if punched in the stomach. Sardarji's words bring back the ache of those days, of losing Anu, of being terrified that she would lose the tiny, premature baby, too. But there's another kind of pain she feels. The reason for so many things that she attributed to Bimal's idiosyncrasy is becoming clear to her. Why she was so hurriedly sent to the village with the baby. Why she was made to stay there so long. Why most of the servants—including Sardarji—were gone by the time she returned. Why Bimal cut himself off from their social circle. Why he left so little money behind when he died.

Still she cannot believe it completely. Still she must ask.

"Korobi's father came all the way to Kolkata?"

"Oh, yes, ma. Just after you went to the village. Babu must have known he was coming because he'd already commissioned the forgers to create the fake certificate. I drove him to pick it up, and then I drove him to a big hotel. He had two certificates with him, and an urn of ashes."

Whose ashes could they have been? Sarojini wonders distractedly. Not Anu's—those had already been offered into Ganga Sagar by then.

"He gave it all to Baby's father."

A sudden hope spikes in Sarojini's chest. Here, perhaps, was some of the information Korobi so desperately needed. "Did you see—him? Did you hear anything they said?"

"No. Babu was very careful, a true lawyer." There's admiration in Sardarji's tone. "But when he got out of the hotel and into the car, he was really upset. He was cursing Baby's father, using gutter language, words I didn't even think he knew. That shocked me. As you know, babu despised people who couldn't control their mouths. At one point he covered his face with his hands and cried out, 'O Goddess, why this, on top of everything I've had to suffer? Of all the people in America, why should she have chosen him?' Then he remembered me and didn't say any more. Privacy and dignity were always most important to Bimal-babu."

"Was he angry because they'd had an argument?"

"I don't know. I think it must have been something worse, because Babu was upset the entire way home. Whatever it was, he kept tabs on the man until he left India—hired a detective, even. He was like a crazy man those days, Bimal-babu, snapping at everyone, not sleeping, spending money like water. I was worried he would have a heart attack. Anumissy's death had already taken a toll on him. Only after that man got on the plane did Babu breathe easily.

"It all paid off, though, in the end. Babu never heard from Baby's father again, and Baby grew up safe with you."

Sarojini doesn't trust herself to speak. She is overcome by shock and rage and a deep sorrow that Bimal had kept all this from her. That he had so little trust.

"How is Baby now?" Sardarji says. "I would like to come and see her one of these days, if I may. And is it true that you are thinking of selling the house? If so, I can make sure Saxena gives you a fair deal."

Sarojini must have made the right responses—though she can't remember what they were—because Sardarji sets up a date to come over with a preliminary contract and says his good-byes. After she hangs up, she sits with her head in her hands, unconsciously mimicking her husband from that fateful day long ago. Her mind moves in slow, fitful circles, like the grinding stone they used in her parents' home to make lentil paste. Why had Bimal been so upset with Korobi's father? What could have been so wrong with the man her daughter had loved to her death?

Three days have passed since I returned from Boston, three days of misery and silence. Rajat hasn't called, and though I long to hear his voice, I've vowed not to phone him. I'm afraid that if I do so, I'll capitulate and tell him I love him. And I do. But I refuse to be treated as someone who can't be trusted. He needs to admit the unfairness of his accusation, otherwise it'll set a harmful pattern for our married life. I can't let that happen.

Things at Desai's have been gloomy. No one at the university has given us any leads. No one has answered the newspaper ads, which are cutting deeper each week into my finances. At this rate, my money is going to run out long before it's time for me to return to India. Even Desai's losing hope; I can see it in his face.

To add to my problems, matters have escalated at Mitra's apartment. Since I've been back from Boston, each night I hear them arguing in their bedroom. Once Seema shouted, "Send me home! Send me home so I can have my baby in peace away from you!" When I'm there, she follows me around, mournful as an abandoned kitten. I sense that she wants to tell me something, but I force myself not to ask. I can't afford to enmesh myself in Seema's difficulties while my own life is in such disarray. As it is, Mitra, who hasn't spoken to me since our telephone altercation, glares at me when we run into each other as though their marital discord is my fault.

In this dark time, Vic is my only brightness. Something shifted between us that night at the motel. Driving back from Boston, as I slumped dejected in a corner of the car, he told me about his life. He was planning to leave New York—that was what he and Desai had been arguing about the day I met them. His restaurant, which had been doing so well even a year ago, was on the verge of bankruptcy because people no longer wanted to eat at a place named Lazeez. The unfairness of it had hit him hard, particularly because he'd always loved this city and felt proud of its cosmopolitanness. His failure made him belligerent and difficult to be around, and his girlfriend had broken up with him. The only thing keeping him in New York now was his reluctance to abandon his uncle, who had been swamped with work since 9/11, as people looked for loved ones who were lost.

"I'm glad I waited, though. Otherwise I wouldn't have met you."

I didn't know how to respond. I looked out of the window, embarrassed and pleased. Perhaps Vic didn't mean anything special because he went on, casually, to other topics. His college roommate had opened a nightclub in the San Francisco area and was doing well. He'd asked if Vic would like to come to work with him. What did I think of the idea?

I felt strangely betrayed at the thought of Vic's leaving New York, but I couldn't say that. It was illogical. Wouldn't I be going back to India myself in about two weeks? Still, a sigh escaped me.

"Cheer up! It's not the end of the world if you don't find your father. You made it all these years without him, didn't you?"

I wanted Vic to understand my longing. I considered telling him about my mother's intimate note, interrupted by death. The dream vision in which she yearned for me to meet the man she loved. But he had moved on to a more disconcerting issue.

"As for your troubles with Rajat, maybe this separation is a good thing. It's giving you both a chance to put things in perspective. It's better than rushing into marriage and regretting it later."

Vic's life trajectory seemed so simple, so American, fueled only by his own desires. How could I explain to him all the obligations that fettered me because I was the granddaughter of Bimal Roy, barrister, of 26 Tarak Prasad Roy Road? Because—like my mother—I had made certain promises?

"Remember last night on the road? We could have been in a really bad accident. But we came out okay, didn't we? Things have a way of working out. So stop worrying and give me one of those fabulous smiles."

I let him cajole me into laughter, to persuade me that I was lucky. The "fabulous" bit helped. But underneath I was thinking of his kiss. It had been a human gesture of comfort, no more. Immediately afterward, he had escorted me to my new room and left. Why couldn't I forget it, then?

What ironic coincidence had made Vic kiss me on the same spot on my forehead that Rajat's lips had touched? Everything was confusing me. Had I made a mistake by agreeing to marry Rajat, as Vic implied? Or was I on the verge of making a bigger mistake?

Today when I enter the office, Desai slides a thick file across his desk at me with a grin. He has located two Robs who live in Northern California who might be contenders. One is an estate lawyer in San Francisco, the other a writer in the Santa Cruz hills. Both had gone to Berkeley at the same time as my mother and might have taken some of the same courses, in political science or communication. They were both members of an international-student club that she, too, may have joined. He hadn't found any specific information about girlfriends.

"It's a long shot. Want to give it a try?"

How can I not? It feels like my last opportunity.

We formulate plans. I would call the lawyer and set up an initial appointment, pretending that I needed legal advice about some money I was about to inherit. To the writer, who was known to be reclusive, I would send an e-mail stating I needed to hire an editor for help with a family memoir I was writing. Once we met and finished the business discussion, I would go for honesty—partial honesty, at least. I'd explain that I was searching for people who had known my dead mother.

"You'll have to play it by ear," Desai advises, "depending on what they say. Even if neither of them is your father, maybe they can give you other leads."

Neither of us mentions my return ticket, hanging over my head, just two weeks away now.

More plans: Vic will fly to California with me, rent a car, and drive me around. Desai has a relative who owns a modest motel. He's arranged with her to give us a discounted weekly rate. He adds up the costs: airfare, motel room, the car rental, inconvenient incidentals such as food and gas. Vic's room and fee. But even though Desai has budgeted strictly, the total is significantly higher than the amount I have left.

"You don't have to pay me," Vic says. "I've been meaning to go out to California anyway. This'll give me a chance to meet up with Sid."

Mr. Desai purses his lips at his nephew's feckless ways but doesn't contradict him. I suspect he isn't totally displeased to discover Vic's altruistic side. He glances shrewdly from Vic to me and back again, then busies himself with recalculating costs.

But even with Vic's generosity, I don't have enough money for a week in California, and it'll take us at least that long. Desai wants to leave enough time for follow-up visits with the two Robs, if necessary. And he wants me to go to the university and talk to people in person. Face-to-face, people are less likely to turn you away. Face-to-face, you think of different questions that might lead to crucial answers.

"Call your young man," Desai says. "Ask him to wire you some more funds."

"I'll get the money," I say with jaunty rashness, though I have no idea how. I know this much, though: I'm not going to ask Rajat.

Once outside, I turn to Vic. Does he know a way of making some money quickly?

"How about selling your ring? It looks pretty expensive."

"No!" The word is out of my mouth before I realize it.

"Attached to our jewelry, aren't we?"

I want to laugh bitterly. I think of my grandmother's jewels, ancient, irreplaceable, that I sold without compunction. But this ring—I remember the touch of Rajat's hand as he slid it onto my finger. He'd kissed my hand afterward, his lips lingering on the stone. Giving it up would mean I'd given up on him.

"There's always one other possibility for a good-looking woman like you!" Vic says, grinning.

Later I'll wonder why his outrageous remarks didn't offend me. Was it that I had different standards for judging Vic because he was brought up here? Was it because he never meant harm? Was it because, in a world that seemed increasingly volatile, I knew he was one of the few people I could count on?

In the bloodred evening, Rajat paces the riverbank, where he has driven against his mother's wishes. Maman didn't want him to go out because matters have escalated at the warehouse, but staying at home was making him stir-crazy.

Rajat has always loved this part of the city. The old river, slow, brown, carrying its detritus with dignity, has something for everyone. When Pia was a toddler, Papa and Maman used to bring them to the less expensive side of the promenade to eat ice cream from the street vendors. The children shared a single cone, while the parents did without. Rajat always chose vanilla because he knew it was Pia's favorite, although he preferred pistachio himself. How simple things were then, the littlest objects imbued with happiness. Now he can't remember the last occasion when they were all out here together. All week Pia has been begging him to bring her to the riverside for dinner, to a new Moroccan restaurant her friends have been raving about, as her birthday treat. He promises himself he'll make time for it.

Today the river fails to soothe him. Like a scab that he can't stop picking at, he keeps returning to the warehouse. His visit had started well. The picketers had shouted and shaken their fists, but he had been calm. I am an ambassador for the Bose family, he had repeated silently as he was escorted inside. The president of the union, a Hindu who had been with the company for many years, had been civil. He had presented Rajat with a written list. Rajat thought the demands exorbitant—hire a Muslim foreman, hire back the man he had fired and pay him a compensation, return the workstations to their original state—but he didn't let himself react. Then came the final item: the Bose family must meet with the workers and offer a public apology for mishandling the incident.

Rajat felt a buzz of anger electrify his body. It was an insult—not just to him, which he could handle, but to his parents. Still, he remembered his promise. In order to leave before his control crumbled, he pulled the sheets from the president's hand and stood up while the man was still speaking. The vice president, a young man, took exception to this and raised his voice at Rajat, asking him to show some respect. The office-holders of the union weren't his household servants. Did he realize that they had the power to shut down the warehouse for a long time?

The threat was too much. Rajat forgot what his parents had said about the union's trying to incite him. Furious, he stalked out. A member caught him by his shirt. *You'll leave when we're done with you.* Rajat shouted at him to take his hands off him. Others yelled back in response, banging on the tables. Noise reverberated off the walls, deafening. A group of men rushed at him. Someone's hand grabbed his collar. He must have flailed out in response, though he can't remember it. He remembers the sickening-soft thwack of flesh against his fist.

Finally, the president intervened, restoring order, telling his men to let the babu go. But he'd taken back the list. In light of what had just happened, that list was no longer valid. Further compensation would now be due. The union would meet again and inform the Boses of their decision. A humiliated Rajat—his collar torn, a scratch burning his cheek, his heart feeling as if it might explode—was escorted to the car by a couple of musclemen while the picketeers jeered. The shock in Asif's eyes only angered Rajat further.

He should have waited until he was calm, but they were barely outside the factory compound when he shouted at the driver, asking why he hadn't delivered Sonia's letter. How dare he hold on to something like that, something private that belonged to Rajat! Asif had answered with more dignity than guilt. He'd kept it because he believed Sonia intended no good. She was trying to break up Rajat-saab's engagement. Rajat-saab should forget about Sonia. She was only trouble. Rajat had yelled that it wasn't Asif's job to make those decisions. That wasn't what the Boses were paying him for. Who did Asif think he was, to give advice to Rajat? A bloody relationship counselor? Asif hadn't said anything more. Upon reaching the building, he had gone to his quarters right away and brought Rajat the letter, securely sealed in an expensive, unmarked envelope.

Rajat knew he had been too harsh. He tried to speak normally with Asif the next day. Asif responded politely, but with a chill formality. Rajat knew Asif wouldn't forgive him so fast.

Now he takes Sonia's letter out of his pocket for the hundredth time. He should have burned it without reading it, but he couldn't do it. This weakness irks him. The sun has disappeared into the river, and the light is too weak for reading, but Rajat has memorized the letter already. He recalls perfectly those days Sonia is reminding him of, the heady secrecy of having her waiting in the hotel room, the way he rushed back there between meetings for delicious, mindless sex. But she was right, it wasn't just that. In between, he had talked to her about his fears and fantasies. Confessed his shortcomings. He can't remember if she had shared hers, but she had listened, holding his hand. No matter how wrong things went later, those days remained among his happiest memories.

Could it be true, what she says, that the real Rajat is the man in that bedroom? That with Korobi he is merely a wishful persona, bound to crumble over time? The need to call Sonia just once rises in him like the craving for a drug. He reaches for his phone, then curls his hands into fists. What happened between them afterward ruined everything that came before, like a fire that scorches a beautiful house and makes it uninhabitable.

He remembers the day he found out as a dark, headachy haze. He'd received a phone call from one of his ex-girlfriends. She asked if he knew where Sonia was.

"She's gone to a resort in Digha for a weekend with a couple of her girlfriends," he said, thinking it to be a genuine question.

"She's in Digha, all right." The girl laughed, a tinkly sound laced with venom. "But who's she with?" She hung up before he could ask her what she meant.

Sick with suspicion, he had driven the entire way at breakneck speed. He found them lounging by the hotel's swimming pool, Sonia in a bikini with a guy he'd seen at parties, a Punjabi executive she had gone out with before she and Rajat became serious about each other. When Rajat accused her, she pointed out that she was, indeed, here with her girlfriends. He could check with the hotel desk if he didn't believe her. Could she help it if Gurcharan had showed up, too? She claimed that she wasn't doing anything wrong and accused Rajat, in turn, of spying on her. She reminded him that he didn't own her. Rajat lost his head and made a terrible scene. Sonia called the hotel security, who escorted him from the premises.

Thinking about it mortifies him all over again. That he'd been naive enough to care so deeply while she had just been interested in flitting from flower to flower. How can he believe anything such a woman writes? How dare she claim that their relationship meant anything to her. How dare she assume that he'll run back to her just because she wants him now. How dare she compare herself to Cara. There's no similarity at all between them. He sees, suddenly and clearly, how unjustified his suspicions were the night Cara called from Boston—and why he'd had them. His knee-jerk reaction was a spillover from his history with Sonia. Cara had told him the truth about the snowstorm—he'd checked it out on the Internet. He should have put aside his pride and called her back the same day to apologize. He'll do it now. He crushes Sonia's letter into a ball, throws it into the river, and takes out his phone.

That's when he sees the three men walking toward him. They're working-class, he can tell by their clothes. Are they from the warehouse? He doesn't recognize their faces. But then, the Boses employ a lot of men. Hindu or Muslim? There are no visible signs. He's annoyed that the thought even entered his mind. But something about them is unusual. They move tautly, purposefully, not like people out to enjoy a river evening. He remembers his mother's uneasiness.

"Best to stay home for the next few days until we settle the matter at the warehouse," she'd told him.

"Maman, you worry too much about Pia and me. I'll be careful."

He hurries toward his car, keeping an eye on the men. Slides in and locks the doors. Starts the engine so that he can swing away fast if necessary. But the men continue at the same pace. They pass him without sparing him a glance.

He was wrong about them—another miscalculation to feel foolish about.

He considers getting out of the car again. A beautiful breeze has come up, and the moon hangs above the girders of Howrah Bridge like a thick gold coin. The men have receded into the dark, and the bank is quiet. The decision not to contact Sonia has calmed his mind. Finally, now, he can enjoy the river. But he thinks of Maman and starts for home. He'll call Cara tomorrow.

If someone had told me when I stepped out of Desai's office yesterday where I'd find myself this morning, I would have laughed. But here I am, fidgeting in a white plastic chair, guilty, overwrought. A few minutes ago, a woman emerged from the back room, all business in her lab coat and pursed mouth, snipped a few strands from my head, and disappeared into the depths of the facility to evaluate their quality. Depending on what she termed the "purity" of my hair, she'll decide how much to pay me.

Vic had called me last night. "There's a place. They buy human hair for scientific instruments. Are you sure you want to do this?'

When the woman asked me to unbraid my hair, it fell past my waist in glossy curls. The glint of admiration in her eyes went through me like a knife. Grandmother loved my hair. She would massage coconut oil into it, wash it out with ritha pulp, and braid it into different designs. One of my happiest memories is the feel of her fingers on my scalp. I try not to think of what she'd say if she knew what I was doing.

Stay focused on the moment, I order myself. On the necessity of now.

The woman calls me into the back room. The cold of her scissors burns the nape of my neck. I keep my eyes turned away from the mirror. I feel light-headed, untethered. But once the money is in my hand, I am somewhat consoled. I now have enough for California, and I've done it without having to beg anyone.

Vic narrows his eyes and stares when he picks me up. "I like it. Makes you look modern and confident." His voice grows admiring. "It was a big step to take. I must say, I didn't expect you to go through with it."

I angle his rearview mirror to examine myself. Once I get over the shock, I decide that I, too, like the new me. A mass of curls, barely reaching my shoulders, have transformed me into a stranger, glamorous and a little dangerous.

My high spirits take a tumble, though, when Seema opens the door to the flat.

"Oh my God! What have you done! All your beautiful hair, gone! Does your grandmother know? Did your in-laws give you permission?"

All my doubts come rushing back. I remember the pride with which Grandmother had pinned the sunburst hairpiece to my braid. And Maman—would she consider me damaged goods now?

"It's my hair," I say defiantly. But my statement is only half-true. That hair belonged to Bimal and Sarojini's granddaughter, to Rajat's fiancée, to Papa and Maman Bose's daughter-in-law to-be.

"Why, you won't even look like a proper bride!"

Visions of my shorn self, incongruous in red silk under the wedding canopy, invade me. Then I shrug. The way things are proceeding, who knows if the wedding will even take place?

"Why would you do such a thing?" Seema must have had a bad day; she's on the verge of tears.

"If I hadn't sold my hair, I wouldn't have the money to go to California. I would have had to go back to India without—without doing what I had come all the way to do."

Seema's eyes widen. "They paid you? How much?"

I tell her.

"That much!" I can see she's thinking hard. "Do you think they'd give me as much for mine? It's about as long as yours."

"You want to cut your hair?" I ask, shocked.

Seema nods resolutely. "I'll sell it, too. Then I'll sell my jewelry and whatever valuables I have left to the pawnshop guy. I'll go to India with the money, to my mother's house, to have my baby."

I can see she means it. This worries me. "Discuss it with Mitra before you rush into things."

"No! If I ask, he'll never allow it. He doesn't have to know until after I've done it. I waited all this while because I didn't want to leave him by himself, but he's changed. I don't think he cares much whether I'm here or not. He's involved in something—he won't tell me what—but it's become an addiction. I can't even count on him to be with me when the baby comes."

I don't have a good feeling about this. Seema is wrong in thinking that Mitra wouldn't care if she left. Like many controlling men, he would be furious. With her—and with me, because he'll surely blame me for giving her ideas.

"How will you arrange the getaway? As soon as he sees your haircut, Mitra will grow suspicious. Especially if it's right after I've cut my hair."

"I have an idea." But before Seema can explain, I hear Mitra's key in the door.

"Be very careful," I whisper as I slip into my room.

TEN

Seema lays the Prada suit, cleaned and lovingly folded, in my suitcase.

"I want you to have this. Yes, I'm sure. I hope it'll bring you good fortune."

In an hour, I'll be on my way to the airport, to San Francisco. With any luck, I'll miss Mitra, who is out. With any luck, I'll never see him again. If it weren't for my anxieties about Seema, I'd be ecstatic.

Seema has told me her plans. Tonight she'll give Mitra one more chance. She wipes her eyes as she says this, and I can see it is hard for her, the way it is to cut off a part of the body even when it might be diseased. She'll ask him where he went each day, what he did. She'll ask him when she can go to India. If his answers don't satisfy her, she'll proceed with her plan. When Mitra leaves the apartment tomorrow, she'll call the downstairs neighbor, Janki, who doesn't like Mitra because he's rude. Janki has agreed to drive Seema to the hair buyers, where Seema has an appointment. After the haircut, they'll go to a pawnshop. Once she has the money, she'll pick up her ticket to Kolkata—Janki's cousin, a travel agent, is holding it for her. Janki will take her straight to the airport. She'll be in the air before Mitra knows she's out of the house.

I gaze at her flushed cheeks and resolute eyes, amazed at this transformation. I can't believe this is the same woman who spent her days curled in a cloud of depression on the couch. What if Mitra notices it and grows suspicious?

Seema smiles a bitter smile. "Don't worry. If he can hide things, so can I."

Still, I'm filled with misgivings. Seema's plan has so many contingencies, each segment precariously balanced on the previous one. If one slips, all of it will come crashing down. What will Mitra do to her, then?

"I'll be careful." She gives me a hug. "You be careful, too—"

"What's going on?"

I jump at Mitra's voice, pulling away guiltily. He's leaning on the doorjamb, watching us with narrowed eyes. When had he entered the apartment? He must have been intentionally quiet. How much of Seema's plans has he heard?

But Seema is calm. She says, in her usual docile voice, "Korobi was worried about my health. She wants me to be careful, to keep in good spirits. One of her cousins who was given to worrying had a miscarriage, so—"

"You're not that stupid," Mitra interrupts. "Besides, I'm here to look after you."

"That's what I told Korobi!"

He fixes his suspicious eyes on me but lets it go. Perhaps he's as glad to be rid of me as I am of him. Seema offers to make him tea, and he follows her to the kitchen. I should go for my shower, but instead I take out the folder Desai has given me and take a quick look, once again, at the two photographs in there. Both men are handsome: one rugged-looking, the other more suave. In their youth they must have been dangerously attractive. I try to gauge their characters from their faces, but I'm handicapped by longing. *Please,* I beg. *One of you, please be my father.*

I hide the folder in my carry-on, under my nightclothes, and rush into the bathroom. By the time I'm dressed, I hear the honking of the cab that signals Vic's arrival. I thank the Mitras for their hospitality and politely refuse Mitra's halfhearted offer to carry my luggage down. I dare not look at Seema; I send her a prayer. And a thank-you. Seema's courage has bolstered my own.

Dashing in aviator glasses and a leather jacket, Vic hurries to take the bags from me. "The bastard didn't even help you with your luggage?"

"To be fair, he offered. But I don't want to take anything from him that I don't have to."

Vic nods appreciatively. "When Uncle first told me about you, I expected a spoilt heiress. But you've got spirit!"

I smile up at him, ridiculously pleased. It is a beautiful afternoon, warm, with plump clouds floating overhead. One is shaped like a heart. A breeze sets my curls dancing as though it were a holiday. I know I'll find my father in California. I just know it! Vic tells me a joke as he helps me off with my overcoat, and though it isn't that funny, we both laugh and laugh.

"Hey, look! Mitra's on the balcony, watching us."

I peer through the rear window as the cab pulls away. He certainly is, standing stiff and dark like a blemish against the afternoon. Why would he do that? I would have thought he'd seen more of me than he wanted.

My phone rings as we're approaching the airport. When I see Rajat's number, my heart expands, though part of me is apprehensive. But Rajat apologizes right away. He wants me to know that he'd trust me with his life. Indeed, I am his life. Every word he says is as intimate as a kiss. I listen hungrily. I didn't realize how starved I'd been for his endearments. But I'm embarrassed, too. Although Vic has politely turned toward the window, I'm sure he can hear Rajat. So I have to interrupt Rajat to tell him that Vic and I are on our way to the airport.

Tense silence. Then Rajat says, "I'm glad you won't be alone in a strange city. Just be careful, okay?"

That word, *careful,* holds a subterranean significance, but I'm determined to be positive. "You be careful, too! Now that I'm away, your old girlfriends are probably trying to get their hooks into you!"

Rajat is quiet. I'm afraid I've offended him with my clichéd joke. The cab pulls up to the terminal. I realize in sudden guilt that I've forgotten to tell him about the abandoned gallery. I rush to describe it—the dust, the disuse, the empty wall.

Once he gets over his incredulity, Rajat's furious. "I'm going to call

Mitra right away and get to the bottom of this! What kind of game does he think he's playing?"

"No, don't call him!" I say urgently as I juggle the phone, count out bills for the cabdriver and try to think like Mitra, all at the same time. "That'll give him the chance to cover things up. Papa or you should personally come to New York. Surprise him."

Rajat sighs. "I'd love to. That way I could be with you as well. But there are too many troubles brewing here. The warehouse is on the verge of being closed down by the union. I don't think either of us can leave."

I'm shocked and chastened. I had no idea that matters at the warehouse had escalated that far. I want to ask for details, but a policeman tells me to get moving. I bid Rajat a hasty good-bye, promising to call before boarding.

The security line is extremely long and slow. There is, apparently, an alert of some kind. Both Vic and I are pulled out of line and made to wait over to one side, even though we walked through the detector without any problems. Almost everyone waiting with us is brown-skinned. I point this out to Vic, but he motions to me to be quiet. By the time we are checked all over with an electronic device ironically called a wand, our flight is about to leave. We run through the airport, breathless, and get to the plane just as the gate is closing. The other passengers glare at us accusingly. In all this confusion, there's no opportunity to call Rajat.

"It isn't fair," I hiss in Vic's ear once we're seated. "We were in line before many of these people. And did you notice how many Indians were pulled out for security check?"

"Welcome to flying while brown in post 9/11 America!"

"Doesn't it bother you, being treated like this? You're a US citizen. You shouldn't have to—"

Vic shrugs. "I choose my battles. Things could be worse."

I'm dismayed by his offhand dismissal of an injustice that clearly needs to be addressed. The easygoing attitude that I'd found so attractive in him has its drawbacks. Rajat would never have let things go like this.

Stop right there! I tell my mind. I open my carry-on to pull out the father folder. That's what I should be doing: getting a better sense of the two men I'm going to meet, figuring out what matters most to each, instead of comparing my fiancé to someone I'll never see again after two weeks. The thought depresses me. I focus on the folder, which is, luckily, right on top so I don't have to rummage around. I spread out the sheets on my tray table.

Suddenly, though, I remember something. The folder should have been at the bottom of the bag, under my nightie. Someone took it out while I was in the shower. Mitra. I'm furious—with him but also with myself for not having been more careful. All these days of secrecy, gone to waste.

I tell Vic, who is troubled, too, but he attempts to reassure me. "What Mitra really wants is to blackmail the Boses. Unless you actually find your father, there isn't enough proof for him to blackmail them with."

I hope he's right. It's scant comfort, though, to think of Mitra waiting, vulturelike, to swoop down on me when the moment's ripe.

It is an hour before dinner, and the flat is empty. Papa and Maman have gone to the gallery, Pia to her badminton lesson, Pushpa down to the servants' quarters. Rajat turns on the stereo and lies down on the living-room sofa, thankful for this reprieve from anxious, watchful eyes. The soft strains of jazz wash over him, holding him in their weightless embrace. For now, no one expects anything of him. For now, he can allow his worries to recede.

But his mind refuses to cooperate. It demands to know why Cara didn't call back from the airport as she'd promised. Sonia has left another message on his mobile. How should he respond so she won't call again? Can Mitra really be double-crossing them? Rajat needs to be certain before burdening his parents with a new worry. There has been no news from the union leaders yet. What are they planning?

His parents must have been disappointed by the fiasco at the warehouse, but they hid it well. They assured him that it wasn't his fault—the union had obviously planned for matters to escalate so they'd have a valid reason to call for a strike. But Rajat knows otherwise. If he had kept his cool, they would have been on the road to reconciliation by now.

What can Rajat do to stop the downward spiral of his family's fortunes? New York—that's where he must concentrate. The gallery is a sinkhole into which their assets are disappearing, more each day. He must call Mitra, make a few, discreet inquiries, figure out what's really going on. He knows Korobi doesn't want him to do this, but she doesn't understand the situation here. Rajat can't ask his father to make the long, expensive journey to America—or to send Rajat there—when their finances are so precarious, the situation with the union so volatile. Not unless he's certain that Korobi's fears are valid. And for that, he needs to hear how Mitra responds to his questions.

It must be early morning in New York, but Mitra picks up his cell phone right away. He sounds alert and polite. In answer to Rajat's queries, he explains that business is slow. Indian art isn't popular at this time, unfortunately. All Eastern things are associated in people's mind with 9/11. Still, he's trying, faithfully opening the gallery every morning, placing ads in the newspapers, leaving brochures with organizations whose clientele might be interested. All by himself, too, because as Rajat may have heard, Mitra's wife is in the family way and not keeping well.

"I heard from some friends who went to the gallery that it was closed in the middle of the day."

Rajat listens carefully for a defensive tone, but Mitra's voice is equable. "Sometimes I have to step out to pick up lunch or meet with a potential customer. Even if I'm gone for just a few minutes, the place has to be locked up. I was just thinking about this problem the other day. Maybe I could hire someone part-time, for just a couple hours a day, to cover me while I take a break? I know a good person."

Mitra sounds so reasonable that Rajat has to fight to recall Korobi's concern, the insistence in her voice as she told him the Boses were being cheated.

"I was told the place was dusty. That some of the paintings are gone from the walls."

For the first time, Mitra's voice has an edge. "Who told you that? Let me guess: It was Miss Korobi, wasn't it? Maybe she looked in the wrong place. There's another gallery on the same street that's been closed down. I wish she had mentioned it to me. I would have set her straight." His voice dips confidentially. "I hate to say this to you, sir, but the young lady took a dislike to me from day one. She has been—how shall I say it?—difficult to deal with. I invited her on several occasions to visit the gallery, but she never had the time. Too busy going around sightseeing with that young fellow in the leather jacket."

"Sightseeing?" Rajat can't help repeating, even though he knows he's handing Mitra the advantage.

"Ah, yes, several times." Mitra's voice grows sonorous. "And visiting beauty salons. Just a couple days back, don't know what came over her, she cut off all her hair. My wife tried to talk her out of it, but—"

"Cut off her hair?"

"You didn't know? There's a lot she's been keeping from you, looks like. I would inquire into them, if I were you."

Rajat rallies. He remembers what he said to Korobi, *I would trust you with my life*. He tries to hold on to that feeling. "I'm sorry, Mitra, but I don't believe you."

"I'll send you a photo, if you like. I took one just today, as she was leaving for California. Thought it wasn't right, how she was out here having a good time with some other man while you worried about her. Check your e-mail in about five minutes. You can see for yourself."

Rajat takes deep, shaky breaths after he hangs up. He doesn't believe what Mitra said about the Mumtaz, about Korobi confusing it with another gallery on the same street, conveniently shut down. But the accusations about his fiancée—there Mitra had seemed disturbingly confident, certain that he could deliver.

Rajat goes to his room and flips the switch on his computer. Yes, the message from Mitra has arrived. Rajat stares at it for a while. A voice inside him warns, *Delete the message without opening it. Remember Korobi, the way she is: straightforward through and through. She wouldn't cheat you.* But another voice says, *People lie; photos don't.*

He clicks on the attachment and there she is, in her chin-length, curly hair, so different from the Korobi whose image is stamped on his brain that for a moment he thinks Mitra is playing a trick on him. But it *is* her. He recognizes, with a pang, the tilt of her neck as she looks up at a young man in a leather jacket—good-looking, Rajat must admit, even if it's in a raffish way—who is standing far too close to her. Recognizes the smile—how he never tired of watching it, how he loved the way it transformed her face. Now she's offering the same smile to this guy! Vic is helping her off with her coat—the black coat that Maman gave her. Such an intimate gesture. Rajat stares at the photo until the faces blur; then he reaches for his mobile.

Once again Asif is driving the long stretch to the airport, past the lit billboards that depict perfect families shored up by their perfect accessories, past the mosquito-infested lakes edged by slums, past the amusement park, which, Pia-missy has told him, houses Asia's largest roller coaster. Tonight there are only two of them in the car: Barasaab and Memsaab. Pia-missy has an algebra test tomorrow, and Rajat-saab has stayed home to help her study for it. Saab and Memsaab are mostly silent. In the intermittent flashes from the billboards, Asif notices that their hands are clasped. The detail touches him. It is not the flighty romantic gesture of young lovers in Bollywood movies, but the sturdy grip of longtime companions comforting each other in the face of tribulations. And tribulations they certainly have.

The workers haven't gone on strike yet at the warehouse, but things are tenser each day. Asif had driven Barasaab by the main entrance this afternoon. The Boses had hired extra security, and men in dark blue uniforms stood around the front, armed with batons. For the first time ever, the enormous black metal main gate was chained and padlocked in the middle of the day, and only the side entrance was open. When he saw that, Saab leaned back against the seat and closed his eyes. Stakes carrying placards with violent red lettering were planted along the ground.

Workers with red bandannas clustered around the small gate, harassing anyone who tried to enter the warehouse. They watched the Mercedes closely, and one of the men spat on the ground and said something. But Asif had taken care to roll up the windows ahead of time so Saab wouldn't have to listen to low-class vermin like that. He sneaked a look backward and felt a pang. Saab looked so old and tired. He was a good man, a decent employer. He didn't deserve trouble like this.

Pushpa had told Asif about the strained dinner with Bhattacharya, and how afterward Memsaab had broken down. Asif had difficulty imagining Memsaab, who was tough as buffalo hide, in tears, but now, as she lays her head on Bose-saab's shoulder and closes her eyes, he can believe it. What a weight it must be on her to be left in charge at this hazardous time—because the truth, whether anyone admitted it or not, was that Rajat-saab wasn't much help in such situations.

Saab asks for some music, and Asif puts in a classical sitar CD, Memsaab's favorite. The music, he knows, is so that they can converse without being overheard, but through his many years of chauffeurship, Asif has become adept at hearing past such camouflage.

"I'll call you as soon as I've visited the gallery."

"I can't believe Mitra has really closed it down. Why would he do such a thing? Maybe Korobi's mistaken—"

Saab shakes his head. "I trust Korobi's assessment. She's a smart girl. Mitra's up to something, but until I go there, I won't know what."

"Be careful. I had a bad dream the other night. Guns, blood." She shudders. "If he's cheating us in a major way, he might be dangerous. He might try to do something to you."

"Now you're being fanciful! But I'll take precautions."

"And Bhattacharya? What are we to do about him?"

"Joyu, you can't beat your head against every wall at once. We'll deal with Bhattacharya after I get back. Focus on the union for now. They're about to send us a new set of demands. As soon as you get it, let me know, and we'll figure out how to negotiate. You're a strong woman. I know you can handle things until I get back."

"I'm not sure. I feel so tired, so afraid. It's as though everything I spent my life building up is disintegrating. The headmistress from Pia's school called today. She asked why Pia hasn't returned the Darjeeling excursion form, the girl had been so excited about it before. I questioned Pia. She said she didn't tell us because we can't afford it right now. She gave me a hug and said, 'It doesn't matter, Mama.' I tell you, it broke my heart. And Rajat hasn't been sleeping the last few days. I heard him in the kitchen at three a.m., getting water. It's not just the warehouse situation—there's something else. But he won't tell me what. Oh, it's hard to see your children's pain!"

"He's a man now, Joyu. You can't protect him from his life."

"Oh, Shanto, come back quickly. I really need you."

He raises her hand to his lips. "I'll come back as soon as I can. And meanwhile, I'm with you in your heart."

Asif drops them off at the entrance to the airport and waits in the parking lot for Memsaab to call him when she's ready to leave. But when the phone rings, it isn't her.

"I was starting to get upset with you," Sonia says in her husky voice. "Really upset. But now I see your strategy. You were smart to hold on to the letter until the right time. Rajat is meeting me tomorrow evening for dinner. Look for your reward when you get home." She hangs up before Asif can fully process what she has said.

A text message is on his phone, too, from Mahmoud, Sheikh Rehman's contact man. The sheikh is getting annoyed. He needs to know Asif's answer, yes or no, by the weekend. *Meet me at Akbar Kebab House Friday night, brother,* Mahmoud writes. *The sheikh's a good employer—don't throw away this opportunity.*

Asif thinks about Mahmoud's message while he drives Memsaab home. She rests her head against the window glass and doesn't say anything, not even when, along a dark stretch of road, he hits a giant pothole. Asif should be relieved, but he finds himself wishing for her to revert to her old, fiery self. When they reach home, instead of giving him a hundred instructions, she says good night in a small voice and walks heavily toward the lift.

Asif makes his way to his room, ruminating on the problems of the rich, how they are more complicated than those of the poor. Only when he reaches his door does he remember Sonia. He looks around.

There's nothing in his doorway. Maybe she had something slipped under the door? But the floor's bare. Then he sees it, an envelope on his pillow. It's fat with money, more than he's ever held in his hand. Even as he counts the notes in wonder, a part of him is afraid. Today he's been rewarded, yes, but there had been a threat in Sonia's voice, too. What kind of woman is this Sonia, and what might she do if people don't give her what she wants?

It is the night of no moon, and Sarojini is waiting for Bhattacharya to arrive. In spite of the coil that she has lit, the temple is full of mosquitoes, and she must pause her prayer beads to swat at them. She asks the goddess's pardon—they are her creatures, too, though Sarojini cannot quite see the reason for their existence. Unless it is to teach her forbearance. But hasn't the goddess given her plenty of humans in her life already to teach her that admirable quality? Her life with Bimal was a saga of forbearance, and even after his death, she has to call upon it as she gets ready to sell the house. Things are moving more quickly than she anticipated; in three short days, Sardarji is bringing a sale contract for her to look at.

Afraid that she wouldn't understand it, she had phoned Rajat, whom she has not—surprisingly—seen for some days now, and asked if he'd have the time to help her with something.

He gave a bitter laugh. "I have all the time in the world, except for one evening when I've promised to take Pia out to dinner. What is this regarding, anyway?"

She wouldn't tell him over the phone. The boy loved this house even more than Korobi did. He once said he thought it the most beautiful house in the world.

In the midst of prayer, her mind wanders. *Beautiful.* Yes, the house is that. It has the desolate beauty of fragile things, a desperate glimmer, the lamp brightening before it dies. Would she be sad if it was gone? She isn't sure. True, it holds many memories, many traditions. But some of them she would be happy to release into the void.

Bhattacharya whispers that word, too, when he enters the temple. *Beautiful.* Sarojini almost doesn't recognize him, he looks so different. He has taken off his chains and rings, his watch. He wears a simple dhoti. Throughout the service, he sits very still, his eyes focused on the goddess. Even the mosquitoes fail to distract him. At the end, he wipes his eyes with the edge of his dhoti, surprising Sarojini, who had not taken him to be a devout man. Impulsively, she invites him for dinner, explaining that it'll be makeshift because of the plumbing problems, but he asks if he can instead sit with her on the temple veranda for a while.

"I could feel the goddess's presence," he says, lowering himself onto the old, cracked steps. "I can see why Netaji would visit here. Do you know, he was one of my heroes when I was a child. I would dress up like him in a khaki uniform, with a toy pistol tucked into my belt. I wanted to dedicate my life to doing good for India. That's why, once I made enough money, I decided to join politics." He exhales deeply. "It didn't quite work out the way I imagined."

This confession, too, she hadn't expected. Is it the enveloping darkness, comforting as a womb? Is it the intermittent chorus of frogs, punctuated by firefly light, reminiscent of younger years when one had the ability to marvel at every minute miracle?

"Sometimes I feel the party is controlling my life—what I eat, wear, say. People I mix with. They'd even like to shape my thoughts, and once in a while I'm afraid they do. I joined them because I loved my religion and was sad to see our young people falling away from it. I was excited about the Hindutva platform, which I believed would bring back its glory. But—" He sighs again. "I don't want to burden you with my problems, Ma."

She is touched that he calls her mother, though it is a common enough practice among Bengalis. "It's no burden. I'm an old woman alone, and happy for your company."

He must hear, in her tone, that she means what she says, for he begins, haltingly, to tell her about his growing-up years. Deep into the night, he talks about his father's modest career as a teacher; his mother, who worked late into the night as a seamstress so she could scrape together the money to send him to a decent school; how they often had to do without necessities so he could get an education. He'd tried to repay them by doing as well as he possibly could in school and later in college. But soon he learned that wasn't enough, that you needed the favor of the powerful. The things he had to do to gain that. And the things he's done to others, now that he's the powerful one.

When he finally stumbles to a stop, she says, "I think you're too harsh on yourself. There's good in you—I could see it during the puja. It's never too late to change. Ask the goddess for help."

"I did feel something tonight that I haven't felt in years. It was like a dead part of me came alive. I have to thank you for it. It's a special place, this temple. Do you think I might come again?"

"Of course, my son. It's an old temple, nothing fancy, and falling apart in places. But if it gives you peace, you can come whenever you want."

He touches her feet in appreciation as he gets up to leave. "It's a great gift you've given me tonight, Ma. I can't wait to come again."

"It might not be as peaceful once the construction starts, though," Sarojini says. At the questioning look on his face, she explains that she must sell the house. "Don't worry," she ends. "Saxena has promised he won't touch the temple."

Bhattacharya shakes his head forcefully. "It just won't be the same! Part of the charm of the temple is the grounds—those big, hundred-year-old tamarind trees, the old house in the background, the gates that shut out the twenty-first century. We can't let this happen! I'll help you with the repairs, for both the house and the temple."

Sarojini's heart gives a leap. It is as though the goddess has taken this man by the hand and brought him to her. If she accepts Bhattacharya's offer, her problems would be solved. Still, she hesitates.

He takes hold of her hand. "Don't say no, Ma. It'll make me happy to give you this gift. I waste my money in so many useless ways." He grins, his teeth white in the dark. "Maybe this way I can keep the wife from buying more jewelry! The party would like it, too, my role in preserving a historic Hindu temple and its pristine surroundings. They're bound to get a lot of publicity out of it. So you see, you'll be helping my career."

He's so persuasive that Sarojini is on the verge of saying yes. Oh, how wonderful it would be not to worry about losing the house. But he has the ability to provide a more important present, and she must ask him for that instead.

She takes a deep breath. "I do want you to give me something—but it isn't this. I would like you to help the Boses, who are going through such a rough time. You have the power to save them, I know you do. That would make me happier than anything else."

He's silent for so long that she is afraid she has angered him. Finally he sighs and says, "You've set me a hard task, Ma. It cuts into some big plans I'd made. It would have been easier—and more satisfying—to have done something directly for you. But I'll try. I can't promise much more than that."

As he walks her to the house, holding her by the elbow to make sure she doesn't stumble in the dark, Sarojini thinks how many layers there are to a man's heart, tender spots beneath the calluses, hidden even from himself.

ELEVEN

I'm dressed perfectly for deception in my Prada suit. Still, I hesitate at the entrance to Rob Mariner's office, my brain a nervous buzz. The bursts of pink oleanders along the freeway have disoriented me. My mother must have traveled this same freeway when she first came to California, seen the same flowers, felt the same stab of homesickness. I sense her around me, that yearning I'd felt long ago in my bedroom, but when I reach out, there's nothing to grasp.

Yesterday I took the train up to the Berkeley campus. Vic had offered to drive me, but I wanted to do it alone. I spent all day going where my mother would have gone, asking questions, showing the photograph. People were kind—perhaps something deep in us responds to the search for a lost parent. They offered tea and sympathy and sometimes hugs, but no one remembered her. I walked up and down the campus, longing, most illogically, to turn a sudden corner and be faced with the girl in the photo, her straight, serious eyebrows, her improvident smile. The sprawling, sparkling lawns dotted with happy young people only compounded my dejection.

Last night I emerged from the shower to find a message on my phone. It was Seema, breathless with elation and tears, calling from a public phone in Kennedy airport. She would board her flight in just a few minutes. Her plan had worked. She was sorry to trick Mr. Mitra like this, but she had no choice. They'd had a bitter quarrel last night. He had grabbed her and shouted into her face, his features distorted until they seemed those of a stranger. The shock had caused cramping pains in her stomach; she was terrified that she would lose the baby. But she was fine now. Her family was coming to pick her up from the airport in Kolkata. They would take good care of her and her child.

"I can't thank you enough," she ended. "Without you, I'd never have had the courage."

Mitra, too, had called me last night, and again this morning. In the first message, he sounded worried. Did I know where Seema was? Had she told me she would be going out? I'd felt an unexpected jolt of sympathy as I imagined him entering the apartment and calling out his wife's name, asking for tea. The second message had him breathing hard on the line before he said, "You made her do this. I know you made her do this." His voice gave me a chill; I didn't say anything to Vic about the calls.

Mariner's offices are more elegant than I'd imagined: the spare lines of the furniture; the recessed lighting; the walls hung with original abstracts, intimidating in their inscrutability. I hide my nervousness to follow a slim, blond assistant to his private domain. He has agreed to a twenty-minute free consultation—too little time, I fear, for my true purposes. I wish Vic were with me. Dropping me off, he said, "Remember, whether you're his daughter or not, you're still yourself." I wish I had his ability to reduce things to their simplest denomination.

Rob Mariner's photo—taken from the website of a charity gala—had shown me a lean, dark man in an expensive suit, his arm around a woman in a lavish gown that displayed a considerable portion of her assets. Not his wife. He was divorced, though his name had been linked since then with a couple of high-society ladies. His smile had seemed world-weary in an attractive way. I feared he would be a hard man to fool.

But he is surprisingly easy to talk to, exchanging pleasantries to put me at ease. When I offer him my story of being the sole beneficiary of a rich, elderly relative who lives in California, he takes attentive notes. When I stammer that I can't reveal the name of my relative, he nods equably. It's now time to ask my most important question—only I don't know how to broach the subject.

Then he leads me right to it, asking how I chose his office.

I tell him it's his reputation—but also where he went to law school. "My mother went to Berkeley, too."

"Really?" He looks interested, and that's enough for me. I plunge into the details: her name, how she died in childbirth, what she studied, how I'm searching for people who might have known her. I know I should be more restrained, but I can't help it. I slide her photo across the table and lean forward to look into his face.

Something's going on inside him. He looks at me in a whole new way, not happy or sad, but with an intense, almost triumphant interest. Then he picks up the photo.

"Her name sounds familiar." I can tell he's not saying everything he's thinking. "We might have had a class together. I did know several Indian students when—"

The phone rings. His secretary reminds him that his next client is waiting.

"I have to go," he says regretfully. "But I'd love to talk further." He looks into my eyes—meaningfully I think. "I do have some photo albums from my college days. We could look through those and see if she's there. The only time I have free in the next few days is six p.m. tomorrow, for about a half hour, if you'd like to stop by my place." He scribbles his address on the back of a card and slides it toward me.

I run across the parking lot.

"I'm sure he knows my mother! When I said her name, his face changed."

Vic is more cautious. "Maybe you imagined it because you want it so much."

"I don't think so. There was something special in his eyes as he looked at me after that. Really looked, you know, like he was trying to recognize something."

"Did he say anything particular?"

"No. But he wouldn't admit to something like that right away, would he? He's a lawyer, after all. Maybe that's why he invited me over, to get to know me better. Make sure I'm the genuine article."

"I don't like you going to his home by yourself. Why don't you call and ask to meet in a coffee shop."

"I can't! That would be like saying I didn't trust him. He might get offended and call off the meeting. Stop frowning! You're acting like—like my grandfather, insisting I have a chaperone! It's just for half an hour. And anyway, aren't you going to be lurking close by, just in case?"

Vic responds, but I don't hear his answer. I'm too busy thinking of what I'd almost said to him before I caught myself: *You're acting like Rajat.* Is that how I see my fiancé when I'm not guarding my thoughts? Someone who draws a tight circle around me and wants to keep me inside it? From being the dashing prince who kissed me boldly behind the oleanders, how has he come to this?

Late at night Rajat drives to Harry's Bar and Grill. Sonia has suggested the place, a favorite from their early days, with quiet, dim alcoves for couples who want to talk. It's not on the usual circuit of partygoers, and that suits him. He doesn't want to run into anyone he knows.

Did he call Sonia too hastily after seeing the photograph that Mitra had e-mailed him? He evicts the question from his mind, rolling down the window for the cool wind. He loves this strip of road by the river. If only his life could be as calm and unhurried as the Hooghly, as uncaring of what fortune throws into it.

His mother had tried to stop him again. She had put her hand on his arm as he was at the door and told him that Abinash, the assistant foreman, had overheard a group of workers complaining that the union was too mild in their demands. They'd talked of taking matters into their own hands. Abinash suspected they might belong to the Naxal party. He had advised her to keep the family close to home, not to offer easy targets. Rajat hated seeing the new lines on Maman's forehead. She had always taken such pride in her appearance. Now, gray showed at the roots of her hair because she had skipped her visit to the salon. He would have listened to her, but Sonia was already on her way.

"I'll be back as soon as I can, Maman."

"Where are you going? You know it's not my habit to pry. But for safety reasons I need to know."

He couldn't lie to her.

She clasped her hands in agitation. "That Sonia's nothing but trouble! Don't you remember the heartache she made you go through?"

He weakened. She was right about the heartache. Maybe he should call Sonia. Back out, at least for tonight.

Then his mother said, "It's not fair to Korobi, either."

Her name brought back the photo, as clear as though it were branded into his brain: Korobi smiling over her shoulder at Vic, leaning into him as he removed her coat, flirtatiousness rife in every line of her body. His heart burned as if someone had cut it open and rubbed it with salt.

"At least take Asif—"

"No, Maman. I need some privacy." He put his arms around her—the one woman he could always count on—to soften the refusal. "I'll be careful, I promise."

A car is behind him on the otherwise empty road, its headlights bobbing in his rearview mirror. How long has it been there? Why doesn't it turn onto a side street? His heart tightens. He thinks he sees two silhouettes, bulky, muscular. Through the camouflage of darkness it's hard to tell. But here's Harry's, looming up all of a sudden because he hasn't been paying attention. He pulls into the parking lot, tires squealing as though he were a teenage driver. The other car pulls in, too, but with more control. A man in a suit and a tall woman with a head scarf climb out, throwing him disapproving glances as they enter the restaurant.

Inside, Sonia's at the bar, wearing a knee-length black dress shot through with silver threads, a new outfit, demure for her. He's afraid she'll do something flamboyant, such as throw herself into his arms, but she only offers him her hand with an uncertain smile. She is thinner—and nervous. He can see her neck muscles working as she swallows. She really wants this meeting to work. He feels ashamed because his own motives are questionable.

They go to one of the back alcoves. He orders for them: grilled chicken wings and beer, which they both love. He's determined to stick to one drink. He isn't sure what he's going to say to Sonia, but he'll need a clear head to say it right. There's an awkward silence; then they both start speaking at once, break off, and laugh embarrassedly.

"How are you?" Sonia finally asks. "You look good."

This, he knows, is untrue. Between worrying about the upcoming strike, the ailing New York gallery, and what Korobi is up to in the United States, he's not getting much rest. At night he finds himself startled awake by troubling, garbled dreams. Sonia's calls haven't helped, either. Recently Pia told him that he was getting raccoon eyes. He glanced into the mirror before leaving home tonight; his sister had a point. He hadn't made any efforts to hide them. He's done with trying to impress women. It's got to be on his terms, this time, whatever Sonia and he decide to do together. But what is that? What does he want?

"You look good, too."

They smile wryly at the mutual lies and pick at their food.

"I'm sorry you're having so much trouble at the warehouse. They're about to go on strike, aren't they?"

He nods, displeased. Are the Bose family's problems common knowledge in all of Kolkata?

She gives up the pretense of eating. "I know you feel I'm intruding—but it's just that I care. I miss you terribly. We fit so well together, like two pieces of a complicated jigsaw puzzle. I was too stupid to realize how special that was." In a rush she adds, "Like I wrote, I'm sorry about what went wrong. I don't want you to waste your life in a marriage that isn't right for you. I feel responsible—like I pushed you into it. I'm asking you to give us one more try."

She worries the tablecloth with her fork. How difficult it must be for her, a woman used to getting everything she wants, to make a request like this. He's struck by an unexpected wave of admiration. If their situations were reversed, could he have done the same?

And what of the opportunity she's offering? It's true: they understood each other's dark side—deeply, intuitively, with a startled recognition. With her, he never had to strive to be admirable. To go back to that—he can't deny it would be a relief.

"As I wrote, I'd be happy to help with your family's finances. I have money of my own, and Dad would loan me the rest. All I'm asking is that we give this a try. If it doesn't work"—she shrugs—"I'll accept it."

It's a generous offer. Temptation sweeps through him like a monsoon storm. Bhattacharya out of their lives for good; the union appeased by extra compensation for the workers; the smile back on his mother's face; her beloved Park Street gallery her own again. Maybe even the New York operation could be salvaged. And he, Rajat, would be the savior of the family.

And what about himself? The possibilities are endless. A new car—or two, why not? A Beamer for everyday use, a Lamborghini for going out with friends. The look on Khushwant's face when he saw it! Suits tailored in London. Skiing in Switzerland. Shopping in Dubai. Gambling in Monte Carlo. But more than that, power and autonomy. He had gotten along famously with Sonia's dad from the beginning. The old man had promised to make him vice president of his Delhi operations. Rajat would never again have to face those damned workers at the warehouse, judging him against the achievements of his father.

Then like a shock Korobi's face comes up in his mind—not that damned photo but the way she'd looked at the airport, frowning a little, staring at his face as though she were memorizing it. It scatters all the other images, which he sees aren't so important after all. And Sonia herself—the way she is today, though she means it right now, that's not her real self, that's her making an effort, wanting to win him back because she's seen she's about to lose him forever. It can't last. He knows her well. The default Sonia is drama and tantrums, rushing from party to party, adventure to adventure, a constant bungee jumping. Just thinking of it makes him tired.

"I'm sorry. I love Korobi."

The words startle him. He hadn't meant to say them. He'd intended to leave Cara out of the discussion, guessing that her name would rile Sonia up—and he can see that it has. But he feels the heft of what he has just said, its truth.

"You can't love her!" Sonia cries. "It'll never last. You're like fish and fowl. Why would you love her, anyway, that pale, boring, anemic—ah! Why?"

He examines his statement and is surprised to find it has nothing to do with whether Korobi is a better person than Sonia (which she is), or prettier (which she isn't). It has nothing to do with her innocence, or her courage, or her enthusiasm for the world, though these are all good reasons to love someone. For him—as perhaps for others, too, because why else is Sonia here?—there's no logical explanation for love. It just is.

"You don't have to decide on this tonight," Sonia entreats. "Let's go out a couple of times as friends. Let me give you the money you need. No strings attached."

She's like a person who's running and a bullet hits her and she keeps on running, believing that if she can just continue acting as though this terrible thing hasn't happened, she can erase the reality of it. It hurts him to see her this way.

He stands up, pushes back his chair. His coming here tonight has been a mistake. He'll try to redeem it by giving Sonia the truth. He owes her that much. She's spoiled, yes, and selfish, but except for that one episode in Digha, she's always been a straight shooter.

"It'll never work out for us, Sonia. Don't get me wrong. You're an amazing person, magnetic as a meteor. No wonder I was mad about you. But now I know it wasn't love. I'm sorry for any false hopes I raised in you tonight. All I can say in my defense is that I didn't know myself very well until just now. Please, Sonia, let's break it off cleanly and move on with our lives."

He braces himself. She'll probably swear. Maybe throw the heavy beer stein at him. He hopes she will not shout. He hates it when people shout.

But she's totally, astonishingly silent. He cannot read the stillness on her face. Is it heartbreak, or fury so deep she doesn't have the words to express it? She pushes past him without looking at him.

On the way back, he watches for cars in his rearview mirror. He's annoyed at how paranoid he's growing. But no one's following him. Why would they? He's not some Tata or Ambani heir, just an ordinary man—he feels a small relief as he admits this—with a failing family business. He opens the windows, speeds up so the air rushes through him. He's done the right thing tonight. Once Sonia gets over her pique, she'll see it, too. Meanwhile, he's going to call Korobi as soon as he gets home.

He's going to tell her how Mitra tried to use the photo to turn him against her, and in the telling he'll foil that ruse. He's not going to ask her to explain, either. Not the haircut, not Vic. For better or worse, he's thrown in his lot with Cara, and he must learn to trust her.

At 6:00 p.m. sharp, I call Rob Mariner from the lobby of his high-rise. He presses a button somewhere; the security gate opens; I pass through and take the elevator to his penthouse. He's dressed casually in slacks and a sweater that make him look more like an older brother than a father. I'm in my Prada again—I have nothing else that's suitable—and I blush as I see he realizes this. To hide my embarrassment, I walk over to the floor-length windows, which boast a gorgeous view, a bridge studded with lights against the deepening evening. Everything in this apartment gleams with richness. The carpet under my feet is thick and luxurious. Even the door that Mariner (I'm tempted to think of him as Dad) is locking behind me swings shut with an expensive, hushed click. Only the photo albums with their scuffed covers that he has set out on the coffee table indicate that they belong to a different era of his life. My heart speeds up as I stare at them.

Mariner pours wine for us—an excellent cabernet from Napa, he explains. I don't want any, but to be polite I sip a little. It's metallic and leaves a hot aftertaste. He raises his glass and wishes me luck with the inheritance. I force myself to smile. Is it my guilt, or is there a glint in his eye? The lighting is too dim to tell. Soon, I hope, my lie will not matter. The photo albums sit on the table like enigmas. I want so badly to look through them, my hands tingle.

"Let me see that photo again," Mr. Mariner says. He holds it up next to my face. "You're more beautiful than she was." His scrutiny embarrasses me.

"I know you only have a little time," I say. "Could we take a look at the albums?"

"Actually, I'm in no rush. I freed up my evening for you."

I'm surprised. Then my heart speeds up even more. Why would someone go to all this trouble? For a long-lost daughter, of course.

"That's very kind of you." I look into his eyes; I want him to see my appreciation. But more than that, I want to see what my mother saw, what made her write that letter.

He opens the album and moves closer so we can look at it together. I scrutinize the photos, small and faded, and hold up my own photo of her against them, for comparison. They're mostly of students with paper hats drinking at parties, or squinting against the sun on beaches. There are a couple of Indian women, but none of them is my mother.

I look up to tell him this and find that his face is very close. His hand is suddenly on my back, pulling me to him. My whole body stiffens in shock and I pull away.

"What are you doing?"

"Don't pretend! Isn't this why you came to my place?"

I hurry to explain. "I came because I'm looking for people who knew my mother."

"Why me, out of the hundreds in this area who went to Berkeley? Is it because I have money?"

Desperate, I let go of all pretense. "My father—all I know about him is his first name, Rob, and that my mother met him in Berkeley. I'm searching for him."

His voice is hard. "Why? So you can blackmail the poor sucker?"

My face grows hot at the insult. "I'd like to leave now," I say as calmly as I can. I reach for my purse, but he grabs it and puts it behind him.

"Oh, I can't let you leave so soon." He puts out a finger and starts to trace the outline of my lips. I snap my head away in horror. When I try to back away, he grabs my hand.

"Let me go," I cry. "You lied to me!"

He holds me tight. "No more than you did, honey, with that ridiculous fairy tale about your inheritance. Did you think I got this far in my career without being able to sense it when someone tries to deceive me? I knew the kind of person you were even before I was alerted. No one gets away with trying to pull something over on me."

Stupid! I've been stupid and gullible. Both Vic and Rajat had warned me. Why hadn't I listened?

He lowers his mouth on mine, hard, bruising. I strike out with my fists; it doesn't seem to bother him. The thrust of his tongue makes me want to throw up. I pull away with all my might. When he lets go, it's so unexpected, I lose my balance and fall back on the sofa. I steel myself for another attack, but surprisingly, he only watches me. His mouth is twisted—is it with contempt, or a dark amusement? How had I ever thought him handsome? How had I hoped he might be my father?

I don't know what kind of game he's playing, and I'm not waiting to find out. I lunge for my purse and run toward the door on shaky legs. I expect him to come after me, but he remains on the sofa. Malice glitters in his smile.

I twist the knob, but the door won't open.

"It's locked." He takes a key out of his pocket and swings it tauntingly on its chain.

My mind spins. He walks toward me slowly, enjoying the situation.

Fury rises up through my panic. If he touches me, I'm going to fight him with my last breath. I'll get a knife from the kitchen. I'll—

I grab my cell phone from my purse, dial 911, and hold it up, my finger lingering over the call button.

"If you don't open the door, I'm going to call the police."

A tight grin appears on his face. "Go ahead! In fact, why don't I call them myself? I'll tell them that you came here to seduce and then blackmail me. That you turned ugly and started threatening me when I wouldn't give in to your demands. Who do you think they'll believe? A reputable lawyer who has lived in this city for twenty years—or you, a foreigner from nowhere with only one decent set of clothes? I wouldn't be surprised if you end up in jail."

I'm no match for Mariner, his convoluted thinking. I don't think he's going to call the police, but I don't want to take a chance. I back away and do the only thing I can think of: punch in Vic's number. He picks up at once, bless him!

"I need some help," I cry.

"You want me to come up?" he shouts, loudly enough so Mariner can hear. "I'm on my way right now. A deliveryman is going into the lobby—"

I can see from Mariner's displeased eyes that he hadn't expected this particular development. We've cut short the little game he was enjoying so much. He strides toward me, a black look on his face. I force myself not to back away.

He throws the door open and flings a slew of expletives at my back as I stumble out.

There's no deliveryman in sight when I lurch from the building. I suspect there never was. Vic has the car idling in the driveway, but when he sees how distraught I am, he jumps out.

"Did he do something to you? The bastard! I'm going up there—"

"Please, let's just leave." I grip his arm with trembling fingers until he gives in.

"It's my fault," he says as the car roars away. "I should have insisted—I didn't imagine! You sure you're not hurt?"

"No, thank God. I don't think he ever intended to physically harm me. But he wanted to frighten me, and he certainly succeeded in that." To my dismay, I find that I'm crying. "Oh, Vic, I feel so dirty, inside and out. I don't want to do this anymore. I've never come across anyone who hated me so much. What I did wasn't totally honest, I admit it, but did it deserve that kind of hate?"

"No, it didn't. Like I said, he's a bastard. Don't let him get to you."

"I can't face another person like that, Vic. I don't want to meet Rob Davis. I just want to go home."

"Hush, sweetheart. You're too upset to make any decisions. Let's go to the motel. You take a long shower, wash away that SOB's touch. We'll get dinner and a decent night's sleep, and tomorrow we'll figure out what to do." Vic takes my hand, kisses it, and holds it to his chest. "I want you to know that you were brave and quick-witted in a situation where most women would have fallen apart. You deserve to be proud of yourself."

I'm grateful for his words, even if I don't fully believe them. I can feel his heart beating against my palm. *Sweetheart,* he called me. I want to say, I couldn't have done it if you hadn't been there for me. But I remain silent. Mariner has taught me a lesson in caution that goes deep.

In the backseat of the Mercedes, Mrs. Bose rubs her tired, stinging eyes. All morning she tried to reach her husband at his New York hotel—that's the only number she has until he procures a mobile—growing more worried each time he didn't answer. It's nighttime in America. Where is he? Recently, to her annoyance, she finds herself getting anxious at the smallest things. This morning it seemed that Pushpa was hanging around the flat too much, watching her. Finally Mrs. Bose couldn't stand it and told her to go to the servants' quarters and stay there until she was called.

Partly this is because Mrs. Bose didn't sleep last night. She had paced up and down, imagining ridiculous scenes—car wrecks and kidnappings—all the time while Rajat was gone. When he returned late, she turned away, angry that he had put her through the wringer like that. Children had no idea what a mother went through, obsessing over the risks they took in such cavalier fashion.

But last night, after weeks of silent brooding, Rajat was jubilant. He kissed her on both cheeks, sat her down at the dining table, made them coffee with Kahlúa and whipped cream—one of her weaknesses—and told her about how happy he was to finally have Sonia out of his life, and his heart. He said he'd explained to Sonia that there was no hope of their getting back together. The whole experience had taken a load off his chest and made him realize how much he loved Korobi. He went off to bed whistling.

Mrs. Bose went to bed, too, but she wasn't able to sleep. The coffee and the alcohol buzzed through her system, making her more jittery than ever. The big bed was empty and cold even after she draped a satin quilt over the Jaipuri bedspread. She longed to burrow her face into Shanto's shoulder, confess all her anxious imaginings, have him laugh at her irrational fears. Be careful, she whispered into the pillow. She was speaking to both the men in her life—Mr. Bose because she didn't trust Mitra, and Rajat because she was afraid of what a rejected Sonia might do in retaliation.

Her mobile rings, pulling her back to the car. She scrabbles for it in her purse, catching a nail in a zipper and breaking it. Damn! But it's not important because Mr. Bose, who must have procured a cell phone with amazing efficiency, is on the line. Just hearing his voice is like standing under a hot shower on a freezing morning.

He catches her up quickly on his news. The gallery was just as Korobi had warned: locked up, dusty, paintings missing. What a sad change from when they'd opened it with a splendid, scintillating reception! Hiding his fury, he called Mitra, saying that he was in town on sudden business and would like to meet him. Surly with surprise, Mitra claimed to be sick in bed. When Mr. Bose indicated that he would be happy to come over to Mitra's flat, he admitted, grudgingly, that he wasn't that sick. They agreed to meet at the Mumtaz in an hour's time. But Mitra never showed up. Mr. Bose had half-expected that, though his other half—his optimistic, saintly half, Mrs. Bose thinks—had been hoping for a reasonable explanation.

Tomorrow he would need to file a police report, ask the alarm company for a fresh code, and find a reliable locksmith to install new locks so Mitra can't get in there and wreak more damage.

"I wish I could be there to help you!" Mrs. Bose says.

"The best help you can give me is to take care of yourself. By the way, I called Korobi today."

"How is she?" Mrs. Bose asks, making an effort to be interested in the girl in light of what Rajat had said last night.

"Disappointed. Yesterday she'd gone to see one of her main leads, but it turned out that he wasn't her father."

Mrs. Bose cannot with any honesty say she is unhappy about this, so she remains silent.

"She didn't give me details, but I gathered he wasn't particularly pleasant."

"I wish she'd get over this obsession and come back home," Mrs. Bose says. "She belongs to a perfectly fine family already. If she hadn't been so headstrong, she could have been a support to Rajat at this time. The poor boy misses her."

"Actually, she's been more helpful to us in America than she would have been back home. We owe her."

Mr. Bose is too softhearted, Mrs. Bose thinks. If it weren't for her guarding his interests, people would walk all over him.

"If she hadn't alerted Rajat, Mitra would still be milking us. Plus she phoned Mr. Desai from California and requested him to help me. Without him, I'd be stumped. He found the locksmith and called the police. Tomorrow he'll come over when we enter the gallery. But Joyu, even from outside I could see that three paintings are missing. Two aren't that special, but the third is the Anjolie Ela Menon. We're going to Mitra's apartment tomorrow. He's gone, I'm sure, but his wife might still be there. Maybe we can find out what he did with the paintings."

Mrs. Bose is too upset to respond. She shuts her eyes tight and sees the Menon, the gold oval of a woman's face blending into black. It was one of their best pieces. She had handpicked it to send abroad because she loved it so much.

Only after Mr. Bose hangs up does it strike her that Mitra is a worse danger now because he has nothing to lose. Maybe, fueled by vindictiveness, he'll follow Mr. Bose as he makes his way to his hotel, to his room even. She calls Mr. Bose to tell him this, punching the digits frantically. But she only gets a mechanized voice informing her that her call cannot be completed at this time.

Reaching the gallery, Mrs. Bose is further annoyed to see that the parking spots in front have been dug up by the corporation so that Asif has to drop her at the end of the block. As soon as she enters the gallery, Shikha hands her a fat stack of messages that Abinash has sent over from the warehouse, mostly queries about orders that should have reached customers by now. The most urgent one is from the buyer for Khazana, a five-star hotel chain that had ordered two hundred large brass statues for their lobbies and hallways. If the statues don't reach them in two weeks, Khazana will regretfully have to cancel the order and go with a competitor.

Mrs. Bose sinks heavily into her chair.

"Madam, also Mr. Bhattacharya left a message for you to phone him when you get in. Subroto the foreman needs to speak with you urgently. And you have a lunch appointment with Utsab Lal."

Mrs. Bose feels a migraine descending upon her. She massages the worry lines on her forehead. The half-broken nail snags on a lock of hair and she has to make an effort not to swear. She wants to go back to the flat, curl up under her comforter, and stay there until her husband returns. But Shikha is waiting.

"Did Subroto say anything to you?"

"The strike started this morning. They've padlocked all the gates. Subroto's waiting outside the warehouse, on the street, for your call."

Mrs. Bose slumps down farther. Yet, it's almost a relief, as when a boil that has been swelling with pus for days finally bursts.

"Madam, shall I cancel the lunch?"

"I can't do that." She has been wooing Utsab, a young abstract painter who, she predicts, is going to be one of the next greats. He's skittish, though. He hasn't agreed to let her hold an exhibition of his works yet. And touchy. The kind of man likely to take a broken lunch appointment as a serious insult.

"I'll do the lunch. And I'll call Subroto. But I can't deal with Bhattacharya right now. Oh, Shikha, would you happen to have a nail file?"

"Yes, madam. Oh, dear, your beautiful nail, just look at it! Part of it needs to be clipped first. I'll take care of it for you while you make those calls."

Mrs. Bose gratefully surrenders her hand to Shikha. She calls the foreman and winces at the cacophony that immediately assails her over the line. But Subroto is less distraught than she feared. A robust demonstration is going on outside the gates, but overall things are under control. The security guards are on hand. Though they've been told not to engage with the demonstrators except in a dire emergency, Subroto has good hope that their presence will prevent vandalism. A few young men are more belligerent than the foreman would like, but they'll calm down after a few days of shouting and placard waving and going home to wives who are annoyed by the salary loss. Most important, the union has presented a new list of demands, which Subroto will hand-carry to the gallery as soon as possible.

She calls Delhi next, cajoling and sweet-talking until she gets the buyer from Khazana to give her two extra weeks. By now it's time for lunch. She rises from the table with the first smile she's been able to muster since morning. Shikha has made reservations at a Thai restaurant nearby, a quiet, elegant place, and Mrs. Bose feels she might actually manage to eat something.

Lunch progresses excellently. Utsab has just completed a painting he is pleased with, and that puts him in an expansive mood. He doesn't mention the strike—perhaps, immersed in the world of the imagination, he doesn't pay attention to such plebeian things. Before they part, he agrees to give Mrs. Bose ten paintings to show at the gallery next month. She can't wait to tell Shikha!

Ebullient, she hasn't been paying attention to her surroundings. She doesn't see the two men until after she steps out at the end of the block, dismisses Asif, and begins walking toward the gallery. Nondescript in cotton pants and cheap sandals, they suddenly flank her, one on either side, uncomfortably close, though they don't touch her or prevent her from walking. She doesn't recognize them, but she can feel the threat that emanates from them like heat from a machine that's been left running too long.

They speak to each other in soft voices, as though continuing a conversation.

"See how the rich are, bhai? The memsaab just went and ate a hearty meal in that expensive restaurant. Does she care that her employees have been forced to go on strike, giving up their meager salary? That their families will get only rice and water, if that much, at the end of the day? Does she care that their children will cry for milk?"

"Of course not. Why should she? Even if our brothers go on strike until they starve, she'll have enough money. For years the Boses have sucked us dry so their son can drive a foreign car and drink at fancy bars, so their daughter can go to a high-class Christian school and wear silk dresses and makeup."

Mrs. Bose knows she should remain silent and keep walking. They won't hurt her, not today. They only want to scare her. But the accusations are so unfair that her pride won't let them go unchallenged.

"We've always been generous to our workers," she says through stiff lips. "Our men are paid premium wages. They get vacation and sick leave and new clothes on Durga Puja—"

"And why only on Durga Puja day?" One of the men blocks her way. "Why not on Eid? Why is the Bose family partial to its Hindu workers? Why do they hobnob with Bibhuti Bhattacharya and his Hindutva party? Why have the Muslims been targeted after the trouble at the warehouse? Why has Alauddin-uncle been fired while no Hindus have been let go?"

"Let me pass. I'll discuss these matters with the union, not with you."

"The union," says the other man, and spits on the pavement, purposely close to her foot. Mrs. Bose can't take her eyes from the glob of spit. It pulls her back to a time when she was young and unsure, with a heart anyone could reach in and wound. *A shopkeeper's scheming daughter*, her father-in-law had called her. She begins to shake.

"The union limps like a toothless old tiger," the man snarls. "We want quicker answers. We want payment for the mental anguish our brothers suffered. And we'll get them. Oh, yes, one way or another, we'll—"

She hears the rapid thud of footsteps behind her. Her heart flings itself against her ribs.

"Brothers, brothers!" It's Asif, breathless from running. "What are you doing? Let Memsaab be. How can you fall so low, bullying a woman who is by herself?"

"Stay out of this," one of the men growls. "She'll take our message to the right place once she knows we mean business. If her family is in danger, she'll make her husband see things our way."

"And why are you on their side, Asif Ali?" the other asks. "Is it because they let you sit in a fancy air-conditioned car while we carry backbreaking loads and pound nails into crates? Don't you realize they think of you the same way as they do us—cockroaches to be crushed under their chappal when the time is right? Don't you care that they fired Alauddin-uncle, who gave them the best years of his life, without a second thought, just because he was trying to protect his own flesh and blood? You're more of an enemy to us workingmen than the rich babus—"

A part of Mrs. Bose's mind, which has detached itself from her shaking body, wonders how Asif will respond to this accusation. But she will never know because at that moment the guard from the jewelry store next door to the gallery hurries up, his baton out and ready.

"Madam, is there a problem? Are these goondas giving you trouble?"

But the two men have melted away.

"Are you okay, Memsaab?" Asif asks.

She nods, incapable of speech.

Shikha rushes up, too, wringing her hands. Fortunately, she had stepped out to check if Mrs. Bose had returned, seen what was going on, and run to the jewelry store for help. Now she leads Mrs. Bose to her office.

"Oh, madam, how absolutely horrible! Sit here and drink this water. Why, you're shivering. That must have been terrifying! I was shaking, myself, and I was only seeing it from a distance. Here's a towelette to wipe your face. To approach you like this in broad daylight, right on Park Street! Is there no limit to the audacity of these criminals?"

Mrs. Bose can't hold back her tears. Other things she can handle, but that spit—it has undone her. "They're following us around," she says through sobs. "They knew where I'd gone to eat. And they mentioned Rajat being at a bar—that's where he was last night. They know where Pia goes to school. Who knows when they'll show up next, or whom they'll target! Oh, Shikha, how can we live like this?"

"It's not right, madam." Shikha pats Mrs. Bose's back timidly, in tears herself. "I know you've been a good employer to the men in the warehouse."

"There's no justice to their thinking. Remember the Deorah family four or five years ago? It was in all the papers. Their youngest son was kidnapped, right here in Kolkata, their car hijacked on his way back from tennis class. The kidnappers asked for a ransom of one crore rupees. The family gave it, but the boy was never returned. The police weren't able to catch the kidnappers, but they suspected that the chauffeur had been part of—" A horrifying thought strikes Mrs. Bose in mid-sentence. "What if those men today are part of a group that's planning something like that?"

"Madam, madam, calm down please, you'll make yourself ill."

"That Asif—" Mrs. Bose gasps. "He tried to stop them, it's true, but why did it take him so long to reach me?"

"I don't know, madam. It does seem strange."

"Is he with them, but pretending not to be, so I'll trust him? I heard them—they called him by his name. Oh, God, Shikha, what if their next plan is to kidnap Pia? I can't let her go in the car with Asif by herself anymore!"

"Your maidservant could go with her—"

"Pushpa? She would be useless. She and Asif, I've seen them together. She'll do whatever he says. Oh, why isn't Mr. Bose here to support me when I need him the most!"

"Madam, please don't be so upset. I can't stand to see you like this!" Shikha's face is splotched with distress. "I'm here. I'll support you." She pauses, chewing on her lip, thinking furiously. "What if I come to the flat each morning and ride to the school with Miss Pia? The school's not so far from here—I can walk to the gallery after that. In the afternoon, I'll meet Miss Pia at school and do the same thing. I'll be vigilant every minute. I'll keep my mobile in my hand, and if I need to, I'll call the police. I promise you, madam, as long as I'm with her, you don't need to worry."

"Would you do that for me?" Mrs. Bose sits up, infused with grateful energy. "That would make me feel so much safer." How loyal the girl is, she thinks. How dependable. And a quick thinker, too. As soon as things settle down, she'll give Shikha the biggest bonus ever.

TWELVE

For two days I've been lying on my bed in Motel 6, staring at the listless beige curtains pulled shut over the window. Two precious days lost. At another time, I would have fretted; now I don't care. In the shower, I scrubbed myself until my skin was raw. The soap smelled like resignation. Messages from Rajat have piled up on my cell phone, but my tongue is incapable of performing the gymnastics of explanation. I can't let go of what happened with Mariner. His eyes changed, in his office, when I said my mother's name. You can't mistake recognition. He knew her name even though he later claimed he had never met her. What could that mean?

I've asked Vic to use the rest of my money to change my ticket. I want to go home, to bury my face in Grandmother's chest, in the smell of her starched cotton sari. But Vic is being difficult. He brings me trays of food: rice and dal and Gujarati karhi spiced with ginger, cooked by Desai's cousin. He tells me I can't give up—that would mean Mariner has won. He tries to get me to go with him to karaoke night at Mystic City, his friend Sid's nightclub. He reminds me that Rob Davis the writer has confirmed our appointment for tomorrow morning. He'll wake me early. It's a long drive to the mountains. When I shake my head, he acts as if he didn't notice.

Something Mariner said when I was in the apartment has been bothering me. If only I could remember what it was. I've replayed the scene in my head as many times as I could bear, but the details shied away from me.

Now we're in Vic's car, winding through pine and eucalyptus on our way to see Rob Davis the writer because Vic has insisted that I must. I wear jeans and a full-sleeved shirt buttoned to my neck. No more Prada for me. Vic has bought me coffee; I sip its welcome bitterness in silence. Through my open window the smell of the land seeps into me, mossy and damp and clean. It reminds me of the hills where Grandfather had sent me—to keep me safe from men like Mariner, I see that now. I never appreciated them, grumbling when the teachers took us on steep weekend walks among the deodar trees to see the ice sparkle of the Kanchenjunga peak. Sorry, Grandfather. Then I realize that it's the first time I've remembered him without anger since I learned what he'd done to my mother—and to me. Perhaps it is because of my terrifying experience with Mariner that I feel more sympathetic toward Grandfather's desire to protect the women of his family.

The trees around us are tall, with thick, reddish trunks. Vic tells me they are redwoods; in some parts of these hills they are thousands of years old. If we have time, he'll take me to see them. Everyone needs to see a thousand-year-old tree at least once. I say nothing, but I don't think I'll have the time. If Rob Davis the writer turns out to be my father—and these enchanted woods make me feel that such a thing is perhaps possible—I'll spend the rest of my stay with him. If not, it's time I went home.

I've memorized Rob Davis: his age; his education; his intelligent eyes behind frameless glasses; his controversial books, which received awards and hate mail; his craggy, sunburned face; his temper; his divorce from a famous magazine editor; his love of solitude; his tousled brown hair threaded with gray; his drinking problem, now overcome; his money problem, still present; his inability to write in recent years. Coming from her predestined, predictable life, my mother would have been amazed by a man like him.

The road narrows; the ocean sends intermittent sapphire sparkles over the distance; the fog is draped across the tops of trees like fairy lace. When Vic turns off the engine, the silence, punctuated only by birdcalls, is like nothing I've experienced before.

I see him right away, to the side of a cabin, piling firewood. He wears jeans and a green plaid shirt and is thinner than I had guessed. His face is leathery from being outdoors. Laugh lines radiate from the corners of his eyes. Hope overcomes the flimsy ramparts I'd built around my heart. Maybe I'll be third-time lucky, like in the fairy tales.

"I'm Korobi," I say with a smile. "The one who's writing the book." I put out my hand and guess that his grip will be strong and calloused. But I don't find out because he steps back with a frown.

Vic, who's waiting in the car, jumps out. "Is there a problem?"

"You know there is!" His gaze rakes us. "She lied to me. She isn't writing a book. She's a fraud, going around the country milking men she can con into believing that she's their daughter."

I'm shocked into silence.

"That's not true," Vic says hotly. "Who told you this?"

"An anonymous caller. I didn't believe him, but here you are, exactly the way he warned you'd be. Next you'll ask me about Anu Roy. I can tell you right now I've never known anyone by that name. Now get off my property."

A trembling goes through my body. I remember what Mariner had said: *I was alerted.*

The reach of Mitra's vengeance was long, indeed. He would be ecstatic if he ever discovered its consequences.

There's nothing for me to do except turn around, my face burning, and get into the car.

"What now?" Vic asks on our way down.

I stare out the window, too crushed to answer. All this time, against all logic, I'd been convinced I'd find my father. I'd believed that my mother, who had started me on this quest, would help me. At last, because I must, I call Rajat.

"I failed."

I'm afraid that he will deluge me with kindness, and then I'll break down completely, but he only says sleepily, "You must be disappointed. But you did your best and now you can come home. God, Cara, I need you so much."

How about what I *need?* I want to ask.

"Go to Papa," he adds. "Stay with him in New York until he can get you a new ticket. He'll put you on your flight, and I'll pick you up in Kolkata. You'll never have to be alone again."

Safe forever in the care of the men of the family. A month ago, I would have been grateful.

"I'll tell Maman to start the wedding preparations. She'll be delighted."

"Okay," I manage to say.

Rajat waits—perhaps for a greater show of enthusiasm. Finally he says good night.

But it isn't night for me.

Vic, who has heard everything, raises an eyebrow.

"No one cares that I didn't find my father," I say. "All the troubles I went through, searching, the dangers I faced—no one even wants to know about it. All they want—even Grandmother—is for me to go back, pull the blanket of status quo over myself, and dwindle into a wife."

"I agree with Rajat," Vic says, shocking me. When I turn to him angrily, he adds, "About one thing: It's time you stopped searching. Why are you so obsessed with it, anyway? You need to look away from someone else's past into your own future. You think that if you learn who your father and mother were, it'll teach you who you are? But you are someone already. You'd see it if you weren't so busy focusing elsewhere."

He pulls the car over and takes my hands.

"I've been falling in love over the past weeks, watching the brave, loyal, headstrong woman you are struggling against odds that would have defeated most people a long time ago. I've held back because you're engaged to be married. But I can't let you go back into a life that may no longer fit you without pointing out that you have other choices." He waves at the wooded hills blueing into the distance. "You can stay with me in California."

I look at him, surprised and yet not so. Somewhere deep inside, I must have felt this coming. My heart unfurls, a sudden red flower.

"Sid wants to make me a partner at Mystic City," Vic continues. "I can tell him to take you on, too. I know I'll love the work—and I'd love to have you by my side. You'll enjoy the adventure of turning the place into something unforgettable. Plus you'll have your own money—earned by yourself, not handed to you by family. If you want, you can even continue searching for your father. What do you think?"

It's tempting. In spite of the troubles I've faced here, I love what I've seen of America. And there's so much more, unbounded and bristling with possibility. Here I could become a new Korobi. Vic—easygoing, good-humored—wouldn't try to mold me into his concept of sweetheart or wife. It would be so easy to fall in love with him. Maybe I am already half in love.

But what I feel for Rajat is true, too. The morning in the temple when he slipped his ring onto my finger is etched deep into my being. When he kissed me in the driveway, under Grandfather's disapproving eye, wasn't that a breaking of boundaries? He shared his dreams for his business with me, asked me to be his partner in creation. Things have not gone the way we hoped, but when the storm settles, as sooner or later it must, can we not resume our interrupted adventure?

"Don't answer now," Vic says, kissing my palms. "You've been on an emotional seesaw. I wouldn't even have brought this up if that phone conversation didn't make me fear that time was running out. Think carefully about what kind of life would make you happy. That's what I really want."

Now I must call Mr. Desai to give him my news.

"All our leads have turned into dead ends," I say. "What now?"

If the pragmatic Desai also tells me to stop searching, I'll have to make my next decision: Vic or Rajat, America or India.

"Someone called yesterday," Desai says. "A Meera Anand from Phoenix. She claims she's the other woman in the photo. She left a number. Would you like to phone her?"

Rajat has come to hear Sarojini's news. But first he makes his own triumphant announcement: Korobi's coming home! When Sarojini looks saddened by Korobi's triple failure, he shrugs. "It's for the best, isn't it?"

Sarojini nods dubiously.

"Now tell me your deep, dark mystery."

There's no good way to broach the subject, so she says baldly, "I need to sell the house."

His voice cracks in outrage. "Sell this beautiful, historic home and have it destroyed? Why would you want to do such a terrible thing?"

She gives him a faint, bitter smile. "Why do people sell their belongings?"

"You need money? Tell me how much. I'll get it for you! Never mind from where! Why do you need it anyway?"

She sighs. He would, too. He's that kind of man. To prevent him from embarking on a foolhardy and dangerous endeavor, she lies and says she isn't unhappy about it. The old house was becoming too much for her, anyway. What will she do with it, once Korobi is married and has gone to live with Rajat? But then, because it's too much to hold inside her, and because he's part of the family now and sooner or later must deal with its secrets, she tells him about her conversation with Sardarji.

He sits staring, his tea cold and forgotten.

"So that's where all the money went," he finally says. "To pay off people to keep their mouth shut about Korobi so her father would never know. And Grandfather never told you any of this?"

She shakes her head. The humiliation of Bimal's having withheld the news of Korobi's father's visit from her when all kinds of other people knew about it stings her hard, once again. To prevent more questions, she pushes the house contract toward Rajat. He examines it carefully. The details seem reasonable to him, but he's not willing to take a chance, not where Sarojini is concerned. He suggests they show it to Papa, who will return in just a few more days. Then Rajat hesitates, something else clearly on his mind.

"Your old driver said Grandfather was really upset after meeting Korobi's father. What do you think the—uh, problem was?"

"I can't imagine," Sarojini says. But that's not entirely true. Imagining that terrible problem is exactly what she's been doing, over and over.

At the door, as Rajat wishes her good-bye, she lays a hand on his arm. "By the way, has Bhattacharya contacted your parents recently?"

"Not that I know of. Why?"

"No reason," says Sarojini, suppressing her disappointment. "I was just wondering."

"I can't believe I'm talking to Anu Roy's daughter, after so many years," Mrs. Anand says over the phone in her gravelly, cigarette smoker's voice. "I didn't even know Anu had a daughter. I thought she—Oh, never mind! It's quite by chance that I picked up a paper at the Indian grocery. Usually I never read that stuff. Tell me, do you look like your mom? . . . Only her eyebrows? I remember them! She was so serious, your mother—at least in the beginning, when we lived in the same student co-op. Whenever she needed to make a decision, those thick eyebrows would scrunch up. I'd make fun of her for being so meticulous with the tiniest things, like what to wear to class or whether to go out with a group of friends if some of them were guys. She told me her family had taken a big risk in sending her to the US and she wanted to make sure she didn't let them down. She never let me forget that a lot of eyes were on her, all the way from Kolkata, because she was the first daughter of the Roys who was allowed to go so far from home. It sure made me thankful that I didn't come from a famous family. Especially later, when the shit hit the fan.

"Don't get me wrong. She was fun, too. She always had the wittiest comments, though often she would only whisper them into my ear. She liked trying new things. I remember she went to International House to learn folk dancing on Fridays. She'd come back all flushed and happy and show me the new steps and try to get me to go with her. But I was a bit of a couch potato and never made it. Oh, yes, that's where she met your dad.

"Your mother had strong values. If she thought something was wrong, she wouldn't take part in it. Sometimes we'd all get together and smoke pot—it was normal. She didn't say anything—she was never preachy—but she'd walk out of the room. She annoyed the heck out of me at those times, but deep down I admired her, I really did.

"That's why the incident with your father was such a shock. You see, she'd already told me about her promise not to marry against her father's wishes. But even the strongest of us has a chink in our armor. Hers was love. She'd never experienced it in India. Never had a chance, I guess, the way she was guarded, and that's a dangerous condition for any grown woman to be in. She was swept away. Those early days after she met your father, she'd walk around dazed, like she was on something stronger than pot. I guess she was, really.

"I tried to warn her, to get her to break it off before it was too late. But from the moment she kissed your dad, it was already too late. Worst thing was, she knew what she was doing would bring pain to a lot of people she loved. I could see it tearing her apart. That's when she told your grandpa, hoping he'd understand. But that didn't turn out so well, did it?

"Right after, she lost a lot of weight. Couldn't sleep. Her grades went down. She told your dad she couldn't see him again. I think they tried that for a while. Then one day she was gone from the co-op without a word. That upset me because I thought we were friends. I was sure she'd gone back to India, but later I heard she'd moved in with your dad. . . . No, I don't know when they got married, or where. I don't think they invited anyone. I didn't see much of her after that. It's a big campus, and she may have been avoiding people.

"I ran into her one last time on Sproul Plaza. She was walking with your dad. She was pregnant with you by then and looked pretty happy. She told me she was going to India as soon as the semester ended, that she'd talked to her father. This was her chance to make up with her family, and she was determined to succeed. Rob stood there with his arm around her, smiling in his ignorance. He had no idea about Indian families. I said good luck, though I didn't have much hope. There's no one as stubborn as a traditional Hindu father—I should know. He doesn't forgive easily, not when you choose the kind of man she'd chosen. Your dad was a nice person—I'm not saying otherwise—and educated, too. But still . . ."

"What do you mean by 'that kind of man'?"

"You mean you don't know?"

The first day that Shikha rode with Pia-missy to her school, Asif thought nothing of it. He even enjoyed hearing the two of them chatting in the back, Pia telling Shikha about a new music DVD, and Shikha describing the young painter Mrs. Bose would be exhibiting next month. To tell the truth, Asif felt sorry for Shikha. She was so pinched and plain, not like Pushpa with her come-hither eyes. She'd probably never get herself a husband. Let the poor woman laugh at Pia-missy's jokes, he thought magnanimously. I doubt she gets many opportunities. He was a little surprised when she returned to the house with Pia in the afternoon. Perhaps she needed to pick up something for Memsaab? But Shikha only walked Pia to the elevator and then asked Asif to take her back to the gallery.

Asif is no one's fool. When Shikha shows up again the next morning, he catches on at once. So this is what Memsaab thinks of him. He drives to the school through a red haze, and during his lunch break he contacts Mahmoud. He'll take the job with Sheikh Rehman if it's still open.

It is. He can start as soon as he wishes.

"I'll begin tomorrow, then."

On the way back from school, Asif's eyes keep straying to Pia, who is bobbing her head to the beat of a song. He longs to explain why he's quitting this job, to tell her how insulted he feels, that he would have stayed for her, if he could have. He's furious, too, that this is coming so soon after he put himself in danger to protect Memsaab from the goondas at the gallery. That man called him a traitor to his own kind. Maybe he *had* been.

But Pia—how he'll miss her smile, her small, sweet demands, her confidences, her innocent faith in his intelligence. He clears his throat as he pulls up to the apartment. He must say something before she goes in. Who knows when he'll see her again, if ever? He remembers the last time he saw his sister, as she climbed into the train that was to take her to her husband's village. He had wanted to tell her he would miss her, that he was there for her if she ever ran into trouble. But the platform had been full of the bridegroom's relatives, bustling around self-importantly, and he didn't get a chance. He's not going to make the same mistake again. At the very least, he must tell Pia-missy that he's leaving. He wishes Shikha would get down so he can have a moment alone with Pia. But Shikha is watching him, brows jammed together, mobile clutched like a weapon in her hand. She pushes at Pia. *You go first*. His chest tightens with rage. He imagines driving very fast, taking Shikha not to the gallery but to the deserted river road. Scare the life out of her. That would serve her right.

From outside the car, Pia-missy gives him a wave, just like every day. "See you later, Asif," she says, using his formal name because Shikha is listening.

It's his cue to respond, *See you later, Missy*. But today he cannot. A scorpion is squeezing his heart with its pincers.

"God bless you, Pia-missy, and keep you safe always."

Her eyes widen. He has never said anything like this to her. "God bless you, too, Asif."

Then she's gone. He stares after her until Shikha, still clutching the mobile, asks in a testy voice if he might possibly get her to the gallery sometime before it closes.

Night has long ago settled over 26 Tarak Prasad Roy Road. The birds in the tamarind trees have tucked their heads under motionless wings. The street dogs are curled into balls of silence. Bahadur rides the train of slumber back to the Kathmandu of his childhood. Cook is transported to the Roys' village home, where she sits on the porch frying fish, each as large as her forearm. Lying in Korobi's bed, where she has moved because she misses the girl so much, Sarojini is mired in her own dream. In the dream, the roof of the house has been transformed into glass and she can see through it to a bright blue expanse, where a blimp hangs. The banner suspended from it reads KOROBI ROY'S FATHER IS A LEPER.

As she watches in horror, the blimp swings around. On its other side is another banner: BIMAL ROY'S PRIDE KILLED HIS DAUGHTER.

No! cries Sarojini. *Lies!* But at least one of the statements is true—she knows this. She weeps so hard, she cannot breathe. Maybe she's dying. That's good. It's the best thing that could happen to her. But with that thought, she wakes up. The phone is ringing. Let it ring until the caller gives up! But the ringing continues until finally she gropes through the unaccustomed dark to the corridor and picks it up. It's her granddaughter.

"I'm sorry about your failure but glad you're coming home soon, shona," she says sleepily. "Rajat gave me the news. It did my heart good to see how happy he was. You're lucky to have a man who loves you so much. . . . What was that? Slow down! I can't understand a word you're saying."

"Grandma, I think I've found my father!"

Sarojini's hands begin to shake. Just when she had hoped it was all safely over. Folly to think that. Nothing was ever safely over. By this stage of her life, she should have known it.

"Mother's friend, the one in the photo, saw our ad and contacted us. She told me so many things about my mother in America! I'll tell you later. Some of it was sad. But most importantly, she knew my father. His name is Robin Lacey. He was a history major at another university in the area. She heard he took a job teaching somewhere in the South. Desai is searching for him right now."

This Lacey, he doesn't sound too disreputable. But Sarojini's heart is still beating hard, her fear metamorphosing into irritation.

"He's not too good at his job, your Desai. Why couldn't he locate him all this time?"

"Because we all made a huge wrong assumption. Grandma, I want you to sit down on the little stool by the telephone before I tell you. My father's not white. He's black."

"Speak up. The line's garbled. It sounded like you said *my father's black*."

"That is what I said. My father's African-American."

Is Sarojini still dreaming? Or has Korobi gone crazy, over there in

America? "That can't be," she explains in her most reasonable voice. "Then you would have looked African, too."

"Mrs. Ahuja explained that my dad was very light skinned. But his features and especially his hair—they were African-American."

"Hair," Sarojini repeats. She tries to visualize the kind of hair Korobi's father might have. It takes a moment because she has only seen black people in movies. But things that mystified her for years begin suddenly to make sense. Why Korobi has such curly hair. Why Bimal was livid when he met Korobi's father. She remembers how carefully Bimal would examine Korobi all through her first year in the village. So it wasn't purely out of concern for the baby's health, or for love of his only grandchild.

"Grandma, are you there? Are you upset?"

She appraises the question, turning it around in her mind. "No, shona. But I'm afraid a lot of people will be shocked if they find out." She swallows. It is hard for her to say the next part, but she must. "Mrs. Bose. Maybe even Rajat."

"Rajat? You think *Rajat*—"

Sarojini wants to explain the complicated gradations of race prejudice in India, how deep its roots reach back. Why, for so many people, having Korobi's father turn out to be black would be far worse than if he were merely a foreigner. But it's beyond the present capacities of her muddled brain. "Don't open that can of worms," she begs her granddaughter. "Just come home."

"Please don't ask that of me." Korobi's voice is tortured. "I can't! Not after getting this far!"

Sarojini sighs. What other answer could she have expected from Anu's daughter?

"I'll call my father as soon as Mr. Desai finds his number," Korobi says. "I don't have the money to fly to him. Is it too much to hope that he'll come out to California to meet me?"

Sarojini doesn't answer that question, which is more of a prayer than a query. Or that other unspoken query: *What if he doesn't want anything at all to do with me?*

"Who else knows?" Sarojini asks briskly, hiding her trepidation.

"Only Vic. But he's very discreet, a true friend."

"Mr. Bose?"

"No. Mr. Desai says, I'm his client, and whatever he discovers is confidential until I inform him otherwise."

Sarojini can feel her shoulder muscles loosen a little. Maybe the situation can still be salvaged.

"Do a kindness to an old woman—don't tell anyone about this father of yours until you've talked to him. Not even Rajat. If Lacey isn't keen on meeting you, you should just forget about the whole thing."

"How can I forget?" Korobi's voice is bitter. "I'll never forget! My whole world has been turned upside down all over again. Today I was looking at myself in the mirror, my skin, my hair—I'm seeing everything differently now. Every detail has taken on a new meaning. But since you ask, I won't say anything, not even to Rajat. For the moment."

Sarojini must satisfy herself with that. "Thank you," she says formally.

"You're welcome," Korobi says just as formally. "I'm sorry I woke you. But I *had* to tell you."

"I understand."

Korobi lets out her breath in a ragged sigh. "I love you, Grandma! It matters so much to me that you aren't upset because my father is black. That I am half-black myself."

Sarojini weighs the statement. Amazingly, it's true. She's astounded, worried—but not upset.

"I've kept you up too long. Go back to sleep now!"

Sarojini hadn't thought she would ever again find anything funny, or at least not for a long time. But her granddaughter's blithe supposition that she can sleep after this conversation—it makes her laugh out loud.

THIRTEEN

Sheikh Rehman is an amalgamation of opposites that continue to surprise Asif. He finds himself enjoying the experience more than he had expected. The sheikh prays five times a day, though not necessarily at the prescribed hours. An oversize, handsome man, he has a hearty laugh. His servants—many of whom have been with him for decades—adore him in spite of what they affectionately term his "short fuse." Already, within three days of being hired, Asif can understand why. Rehman never holds a grudge, is generous with money, and takes care to learn the details of his servants' lives. A shrewd businessman, he is ruthless with dishonesty or incompetence, but if someone is in genuine trouble, he's likely to bail him out. When alone in the car with Asif, he likes to chat. One of his favorite topics is the interpretation of Islam. Yesterday he told Asif about the trip he made two years ago to Mecca. It was a life-changing experience, something every Mussalman should undertake. If Asif ever decides to visit, Rehman would be willing to pay for his journey.

The sheikh is not married. Plus he loves good food and wine. As a result, almost every night he visits one of the best restaurants in the city. Sometimes it's a business dinner, but often the reason is unabashed pleasure. He has a bevy of glamorous girlfriends, models or starlets who, Asif is surprised to learn, coexist quite peacefully. Rehman, who likes to lay things out, has informed them that he isn't serious about any of them, but he's happy to make sure they have a good time whenever they're with him. In return, he asks that they don't get possessive and dramatic, because he hates drama. It also helps that one of his lawyers has the women sign an agreement.

Rehman likes lawyers. Several work full-time for him, handling the varied and complex facets of his life. He likes chauffeurs, too. He employs four of them because, he has told Asif, he wants them to be there for him 100 percent, alert and cheerful. They can't do that if they don't get enough rest. Whenever Asif has night duty, he will get the next day off until noon. What a luxury it will be to sleep in late—Asif can't remember when he's ever been able to do that! At the Boses, he always had to be ready by 7:00 a.m. to take Pia-missy to school. Even on weekends, there were extra classes, badminton, or dance. He tells himself he's lucky; this job is really a step up.

But the truth remains that Asif misses Pia deeply and illogically, even though he has tried to stop himself. He'd give up all the mornings of sleeping late, present and future, just to hear her say, *Come on, A.A.! I know you can go faster than this!* When he's alone in the car, he finds himself tuning in to her favorite station. If one of her special songs comes on, he turns the volume up loud, the way she liked it, and imagines he hears her singing along.

Tonight Asif is on restaurant duty for the first time and determined to do an outstanding job. Rehman has brought an associate from Hyderabad to the recently opened El Jadida, on the river, which has been garnering excellent reviews. It'll be work and fun combined: he's invited two models to join him. Asif has been warned by his fellow chauffeurs that he's not to step away from the car, not even for a minute, not even if his bladder's bursting. It'll probably be a long night. But it's also probable that the sheikh will suddenly decide to bring the party home. If Asif isn't standing ready when he does, Asif will be out of a job.

The sheikh owns four cars, which for a man of his financial status shows immense restraint. Asif admires him for that. He admires Rehman's choice of cars, too: a red Hummer for strenuous trips to beach resorts or countryside villas; a black Rolls to demonstrate his appreciation of special visitors; a gray Honda for when he wants to go around town incognito, like Haroun al-Rashid; and a tiny white Bugatti Veyron, kept shrouded in Lycra in the air-conditioned garage, just because.

Tonight, Rehman has chosen the Rolls. The car moves like a razor through silk, making Asif shiver with pleasure. Once Rehman and his party disembark, Asif maneuvers the car to the far corner of the lot to protect it and buffs it lovingly with a piece of chamois. How Bahadur would have appreciated this car! But he'll never be able to show it to the old man.

Then his eyes are caught by a vehicle he knows too well, a Mercedes that cruises the lot looking for parking and ends up a few rows away. Asif tenses as he sees Rajat and Pia get out. His first impulse is to turn his back so they don't notice him. But why? He hasn't done anything wrong. It's the Boses that have insulted him, forcing him to quit.

Pia-missy is wearing black pants, a sequined, black kurti, and high heels, looking "very glam," as she would say. What's she doing here on a school night when she should be finishing homework? Really, sometimes her family is so irresponsible.

Stop! he tells himself. You have no right anymore to think like this. And no need.

Whatever the reason for this midweek escapade, Asif has to admit they make an eye-catching pair, brother and sister, laughing together. Suddenly, he remembers: it was her birthday yesterday. This dinner celebration is a birthday treat.

How could Asif have forgotten! Every year on her birthday, he gives Pia a gift—something that, based on her chatter through the year, he knows she wants. Nothing expensive, maybe a CD or chocolates or a book, but Pia-missy always makes a big deal of it. When she cuts her birthday cake, she saves a piece for him and sends it down through Pushpa. He had bought this year's gift from the Air Conditioned Market a couple of months back, after Pia mentioned how cool it would be to have a mood ring. It's packed away in his painted trunk, under his bed in his new room, along with the photograph she took of him. Now he'll never get the chance to give it to her.

As he stands, not sure what would be worse—her not knowing he's there, or her noticing him—she turns. Her eyes widen. She pulls at

Rajat's sleeve, whispering. Does she want to say hello? Rajat shakes his head firmly and starts moving toward the restaurant. But Pia digs in her heels and stands with her hands on her hips, a stubborn stance that Asif knows well. They argue. Rajat throws up his hands. Then he softens—it is her birthday, after all—and puts his arm around her shoulder. He brings his mouth close to her ear. He's explaining something. Is he telling her why Asif left them? Indignation rises in Asif like heartburn. He wants to inform Pia that whatever Rajat is saying is inaccurate. Even if Rajat has good intentions, how would he know Asif's truth? Has he ever seen Asif, really *seen* him? Only Pia has, and that's why what she believes matters to him. He wants to shout this across the rows of cars. But she's turning away, walking with her brother toward the restaurant. The big doors swing open, light and music pour out, a chorus of fun-filled voices, and into that Pia disappears.

Asif yanks open the door of the Rolls and sits heavily in the driver's seat. Forget her, forget her. He's better off with Rehman. Maybe in a few months he'll ask to go on that pilgrimage. His life could do with a transformation.

A car drives slowly across his line of vision. This one, too, is familiar, with its silver sheen. Sonia's? Yes, there she is at the wheel, talking on her mobile. Did she see Rajat and Pia enter the restaurant? Of course she did. Clearly she followed them here. And now she's going to go in and make sure they see her, too. Maybe create a scene. Spoil poor Pia's birthday treat. Asif feels indignant. Then he's just tired. He's had it with the rich, their self-created, egotistical theatrics. Let her do what she wants. What is it to Asif?

But Sonia doesn't go into the restaurant. She doesn't even get out of her car. She drives slowly past the Mercedes, examining it intently. Asif stiffens. Is she planning to sabotage it? Visions of slit tires, even car bombs, whirl frantically through his head. But he's overreacting. What's wrong with him this evening? In another moment, she has passed the Mercedes. She turns her car sharply, exits the parking lot, and disappears into the dark.

What was that about?

I don't care, Asif tells himself. It's none of my business. He thinks of Pia again, how docilely she had nodded at her brother's explanation of Asif's perfidy. How easily she was convinced. She hadn't looked back, not even once. He's a fool to care, to think that there was a bond between them, an affection powerful and real, cutting across the compartments society had constructed. In the end, he's just a chauffeur, easy to replace.

Every time I think of calling Rob Lacey, I grow dizzy. Twice I punch in the number and delete it. This is the most important call of my life, and I have only one chance. If I come across wrong—I'm not sure what he'll do then. Hang up on me? Block me from calling again? Report me to the police for harassment?

"Stop stressing!" Vic says as he watches me chew on my lip. "Just be yourself."

But I'm not sure my self is enough. "Take me to the ocean, please," I say.

We cross a park with windmills and buffaloes and cascading nasturtiums. Finally we're on a beach, the sands sprinkled with driftwood. I can see purple jellyfish and scuba divers in gleaming black suits. Circling gulls cry a raucous warning. Rocks like lopsided pyramids glint in the setting sun. And, yes, there are oleanders. Windswept, dusty, but still beautiful.

"Want me to stay?" Vic asks.

He's brought me this far on my quest, and I'm grateful. But what I need to do now must be done alone.

"I'll call you when I'm finished," I say, then shiver at the word I thoughtlessly chose.

I unfold the material Mr. Desai faxed to the motel, information I still haven't digested. Here's a blurry photo. Professor Lacey—I don't want to jinx my chances by thinking of him as *father*—has woolly hair cut close to his scalp. His glasses glint in the camera's flash, obscuring his eyes, as he stands at a lectern, wearing a dark suit. His expression is pleasant but businesslike, a man who has places to go and doesn't wish to waste time getting there. Not the kind of man who would drop all his responsibilities and fly out to meet a maybe-daughter.

The information about him is generic; Desai hasn't had time to dig up anything eccentric or intimate. Lacey graduated from San Francisco State the year I was born and moved to Texas a year later. He has stayed with the same university all these years. He has a couple of books and several articles on ancient civilizations. He's married—my heart twists a little at this—and has three children. His wife, also African-American, is a nurse-practitioner at a local hospital. They are active in their church and well regarded in the community.

In short, he's crafted for himself a complete, productive life. The last thing he needs is a grown daughter, an Indian, appearing out of the woodwork.

It's not as if I have anything to lose, I tell myself. But that's not true. I have something frail and precious right now: hope. I wonder how my life will feel if that's gone. I punch in the numbers.

If he doesn't pick up, I might never get up the nerve to call him again.

A deep, raspy voice answers, "Rob Lacey here."

I have neither the desire nor the energy for subterfuge. I say, "Hi. My mother was Anu Roy, from Kolkata. I'm looking for my father, Rob Lacey. Are you him?"

There's silence at the other end. Uneven breathing, as when someone climbs up a steep staircase.

"My name is Korobi, after the oleander."

He makes a sound that could be a swift, soft curse. Then he says, "My daughter is dead."

"Not really," I say, feeling absurdly apologetic.

"No. I saw my daughter's ashes when I went to India. I still have the death certificate somewhere."

I'm at once taken aback and jubilant. So my father didn't just continue with his life when informed of the deaths of his wife and daughter. He made an effort to find out what had happened. The knowledge is an unexpected gift, although I'm confused about the death certificate and the ashes. I look out across the ocean at the setting sun, with my father's voice in my ear, and feel a sense of resolution at last. This is the view, I realize all at once, that my mother had shown me in my dream, the night before the engagement.

"You came to India? When?"

"Didn't know that, did you, miss? Does this change your script? What kind of con game is this?" His tone is well on its way to hostility. "Are you trying to get some sort of paternity suit started? Let me tell you, you've come to the wrong—"

I'm suddenly exhausted. Why was everyone in America convinced that I was out to deceive him? After so much searching, was it too much to have expected a little excitement in my father's voice? A spark of cautious joy at the possibility that I wasn't dead?

"All I wanted was to meet the man my mother had loved. In a letter she never got to send to you, a letter I found by chance, she had written that you made her feel complete. I wanted to ask you about that, about her. There's so much I don't know—"

"How did you find me?" he interrupts, his voice hard.

I'm speechless for a moment, trying to find the words to describe the shock of discovering that my beloved grandfather had lied to me all my life. Grandmother's sad retelling of my mother's last days. Rajat's unwillingness to let me go. Maman's anger at what she saw as my fickleness. My American odyssey, with all its expenses, insults, and assaults. How my engagement—and my future—is at breaking point.

"Trying to come up with a convincing story, are you?" Lacey taunts.

What's the use of baring my heart to such a man? Whatever disappointments he's experienced over the past eighteen years, in addition to the deaths of his wife and daughter, have made him distrustful. He has closed himself away. He's no longer the man my mother had loved so fiercely. I have no future with such a father.

It's oddly freeing to have nothing left to lose. "Never mind," I say, surprising myself. "Go back to your wife and children and your comfortable job. You won't hear from me again. I've wasted enough of my life on you."

I press the end button and drop to my knees. The wind has turned; the sun has disappeared behind clouds. It's freezing. My teeth begin to chatter. The ocean roars and roars in my head. I fling the phone down and squeeze my eyes shut. When I feel an arm around my shoulder, I hit out in all my fury.

"Ow! You're more dangerous than I thought!"

It's Vic, come to check on me. He sees right away how things went and sits beside me on the sand. He lets me weep because sometimes that's the best thing a friend can do. He's the one who hears when my phone begins to ring. He's the one who scrambles in the sand and hands it to me.

The food at El Jadida is as superb as the reviewers have claimed and worth the long wait, though more expensive than Rajat had expected. He hides his concern and passes his charge card to the waitress with a flourish that makes Pia giggle. He has only one sister, and she has only one birthday a year. He'll practice frugality elsewhere. Although what's the point? The strike has sunk its teeth so deep into the Boses' bank account that no amount of personal frugality can staunch that wound.

It's late by the time they leave the restaurant, the parking lot three-quarters empty. Pia is in high spirits. She cradles a bag of pastries that she has bought to take home. She's telling him a joke. He loves how she's so amused by it that she cracks up before the punch line. Suddenly she comes to a stop.

"Dada, Asif's still here. Look, he's standing next to that black car."

"Ignore him. If he couldn't bother to give us even a day's notice, he doesn't deserve our attention now. You know how much trouble he caused us, disappearing just like that. If I wasn't home because the warehouse is closed down, how'd you even be getting to school?"

"It's not like Asif to behave that way. You know it. He's been with us since"—she counts on her fingers—"since I was in class four. I have to find out what happened."

"Pia! I forbid it. Pia! Maman's told me to be extra careful with you. You know what happened to her outside the gallery just the other day. Those men—"

"This is our Asif! He would never hurt me. Please? For my birthday?"

She makes use of his hesitation to run across the lot. He follows close behind. Maman described for him, in graphic detail, the kidnapping of the Deorahs' grandson, and though he doesn't want to admit it, it's made him nervous.

"A.A.!" Pia's smiling, Rajat can tell. An answering grin spills across Asif's face. They're completely focused on each other, oblivious of Rajat's presence.

She goes right up to their ex-driver, her voice plaintive. "A.A., why did you leave us? It's horrible with you gone. Dada is so grumpy in the morning when he drives me to school. He gets irritated if I say even two words. And he hates my music."

"Sorry, Pia-missy. I had no choice."

"Maman said it's because someone offered you a lot more money."

Asif swallows, his face pained. "It wasn't the money, Pia-missy. I would never leave you for money. You know that. But I couldn't stay on."

"Why not?"

"It's—complicated."

"It's because of Shikha being in the car with us, isn't it?"

He says nothing.

"I'm sorry, A.A. I'm so sorry! That wasn't right of Maman."

"Pia!" Rajat's voice holds a warning. She should know better than to criticize a family member to a servant.

"Please don't be, Pia-missy. You never did anything to be sorry about. Never in all these years. You were always so kind."

"Maman's really anxious right now, with Papa gone to America and the problems in the warehouse, so you mustn't hold it against her."

Rajat doesn't like the way this conversation is progressing, as though between equals. "That's enough, Pia!" he says sternly. "It's almost midnight. Time to go. You have school tomorrow."

"Coming, Dada." She reaches in the bag and hands Asif a pastry.

"Happy birthday, Pia-missy." Their ex-driver sounds choked up.

"You didn't forget!"

"Forget? Never. I got you a gift, but I don't know how to—"

This drama has gone far enough. Rajat starts the car. He honks and throws open the passenger door. "Get in the car, Pia. Now!"

She gets in, flinging him a mutinous glance. She waves at Asif while Rajat swings the car around.

"You didn't have to be rude like that. Half a minute to let him complete his sentence wouldn't have hurt."

Rajat's surprised at how grown-up she sounds. Guilt twinges through him. To quell it, he says, "You don't know your boundaries. He's a servant—and not even our servant anymore. Left us for some Muslim high-flier. You're a girl from a good family. You're growing up now. You need to learn how to behave in society."

"He may be a servant, but he's a person first. A good person. Better than a lot of society people I know."

"That doesn't matter. He's not of your class." She gives him such a withering glance—his little sister who's always adored him—that he's stung into adding, "And giving him that expensive pastry was completely unnecessary."

"I don't care about class. He's my friend. I'll give him a pastry if I want. I'll give him ten pastries."

He's about to remind her that Asif can never be her friend. But he sees that she's overexcited and on the verge of tears. He doesn't want to ruin her birthday treat, this evening that has gone so well, by arguing about that damned driver. It'll do no good, anyway, when she's in this stubborn mood. He sighs. Why has God chosen to fill his life with headstrong females? He turns the radio dial until he finds Pia's favorite station, even though he dislikes the mindless pop it plays.

"You're tired out, Sweet P. Sleep for a bit. I'll wake you when we get home."

Asif takes a small, appreciative bite of the pastry, then rewraps it in the crinkly gold paper it came in and places it delicately in his pocket. Paper-thin layers of crispy dough, soaked with honey and studded with crunchy nuts. It's delicious and different, the best thing he's ever eaten, mostly because Pia-missy gave it to him. She's probably being scolded for her generosity right now—he'd seen them arguing in the car as Rajat took off, tires screeching, driving too fast as usual. The pastry looks as if it won't spoil soon, not like the soft milk-sweets Bengalis favor. Asif has a small fridge in his room, empty so far because he eats in the servants' kitchen; he'll save the pastry in there and eat it a tiny bit at a time.

The last sweetness melts on his tongue. His eyes idly follow a dark brown Maruti van driving across the lot, also going too fast, also screeching at turns. What is it with these rich people? Midnight seems to bring out the crazy in them. The van disappears in the same direction as the Boses' car. Loud laughter and off-key drunken singing as a group of revelers exit the restaurant. Asif peers at them. No Rehman yet. It's getting cold, a fog coming in from the river, obscuring the stars, so he gets back in the car. Then it strikes him: the Page 3 types who frequent this restaurant would rather be boiled in oil than caught driving the stolidly middle-class Maruti.

His heart begins to thump. Stop it, Asif! It's a coincidence that the van left the parking lot right after the Mercedes. That it turned in the same direction. A lot of people live in South Kolkata. It could be some celebrity's backup vehicle for when his Jaguar is in the shop. But even as he thinks this, Asif has already wiped his sweaty palms on his pants and turned on the engine, he's already on his way, driving just as fast, though he's too proficient for his tires to squeal. He'll follow the van for a few minutes, just to make sure he's wrong. Then he'll hurry back to the restaurant. Rehman will never know.

In a couple of minutes he sees the van and, ahead of that, the Mercedes, which is no longer going fast. Rajat must have cooled down. The van could easily overtake him if its driver wished to. The road is wide-open, no other traffic in sight. But for some reason it has slowed, too. Something else is not right. It takes Asif a moment to figure it out: the van's headlights are turned off. Has Rajat noticed? Probably not. He's not the most observant of men. The scene reminds Asif of a movie he'd seen about an underwater adventure, a shark swimming up silently behind an unsuspecting diver.

Perhaps the van's occupants—two of them, Asif can see their silhouettes—can be deterred from whatever they're planning if they know someone's aware of them. He speeds up until he's close behind the van, switches on his brights, and honks. Maybe the noise will alert Rajat, too. The man on the passenger side turns to look. Asif tries to see his face—does he know him? Is he from the warehouse?—but it's too dark. The driver unrolls his window and signals impatiently for Asif to pass, but Asif remains where he is, leaning into the horn.

The maneuver has had one positive result: Rajat realizes there's trouble of some sort behind him and speeds up. But the van speeds up, too. Then, without warning, it rams the Mercedes from the back. Asif hears the thud and clang, sees the car shudder, and winces. That car—he'd taken care of it as if it were his own body. No, better than he'd ever taken care of his body. Rajat is honking, too, sticking his arm out the window, shaking his fist while trying to speed up. A bad idea. The Mercedes weaves wildly, almost going off the road. The van rams the Mercedes again, from the driver's side now. Asif hopes Rajat was able to pull back his arm in time. The bastards are trying to force him into the ditch that runs alongside the road. Asif imagines Pia-missy clutching the dashboard, her mouth open in a scream.

Asif has to act, he has to *do* something. If he calls the police, he knows they wouldn't arrive in time even if they hurried. And it's doubtful that they'll hurry, because Asif is a nobody. For a wild moment he thinks of calling Sheikh Rehman—the number is programmed into his mobile, which is in his shirt pocket—and asking him to send help. The van rams the Mercedes again. There's a terrible scraping sound. A bumper has come loose and is dragging on the road. Sparks fly. One of the car's wheels goes over the edge of the road. Rajat is struggling to get it back on the road, but the car's on the verge of flipping. The van readies itself for one last collision.

Asif grips the steering wheel of the Rolls as hard as he can. He's bathed in sweat. Crazy, crazy. He slams down on the accelerator and hits the van from the back at an angle, propelling it away from the Mercedes. Again. Forgive me, Sheikh. The front of the Rolls is dented beyond redemption; the hood tents up; the headlights are smashed so that he can't see too well. Or is the problem with his eyes? The back of his neck is on fire. Something thuds into his windshield, and cracks sunburst across it, further obscuring his vision. Now the van is teetering, too. The man on the passenger's side leans out of the window, his mouth open in a yell, pointing a gun. He hits something—is it the front grille of the Rolls? There's a sound like an explosion. Asif attempts to maneuver over to the driver's side of the van, but the Rolls wobbles uncontrollably. He must have blown a tire.

The van's to his side now, getting ready to pound him. I'll take you with me, you son of a pig. He smashes into the van as hard as he can and feels the impact go through his spine. Then he's weightless, airborne. It's like flying. No, it's like being dead. He gropes for the mobile. Come on, A.A., you can do it, press the 1. His fingers clench. His head strikes the dashboard. All turns black.

FOURTEEN

That seat in the front-left corner," Rob Lacey says, pointing, "was—for some reason I never understood—your mother's favorite. She'd come in early so she could claim it. And where we're standing in the corridor right now, this is where I used to wait for her to get done with class. I'm afraid I was a terrible distraction. She'd complain later that she missed half the lecture because she kept glancing at me and trying not to smile. But she was a terrible distraction, too. Some days I wouldn't even go to my classes—my university was all the way across the bay, in San Francisco—because I couldn't bear to be away from her for so long."

I peer through the oblong of glass into the room, where a lecture is in progress. The wooden desk-chairs are old and gouged. I long to sit in the chair my father has pointed out, to place my hands where my mother's had been, to learn through osmosis what she would have taught me had she lived. Ironically, I'd walked through this very building a few days ago. But it had no more meaning than when one leafs through a book in a foreign language, intrigued by the strange shapes but mostly frustrated. Now I had a translator, and it made all the difference. I want to tell my father this, but I'm still shy with him, although I'm beginning to like him a great deal. Perhaps too much, considering we haven't yet discussed the future.

When he called me back on the beach, he'd said, calmly, "You shouldn't hang up on people like that. Your mother used to do the same thing when she got mad at me. Where are you staying? I'll fly out tomorrow to meet you."

Vic and I picked him up him from the airport yesterday evening and took him to our motel—he'd opted to stay there, though surely he could afford fancier lodgings—and then on to Mystic City. Sid, a tall, thin man with an earring and a shaved head, shook my father's hand and welcomed me with a hug and a knowing grin: *So you're the one!* He settled us in a quiet corner with drinks and steered a protesting Vic away.

Alone with this man, my father, I felt excruciatingly awkward, a gangly teenager again. Under the pretext of sipping my drink I glanced at him from under my eyelashes. He looked older than in the photo, his hair grayer than I had expected. Twice he ran his hands over it and said, "Damn! If someone had told me yesterday morning that I'd be sitting today with a daughter I didn't even know I had!" His skin was, indeed, light. He had big, beat-up knuckles. Did that mean he liked working with his hands? There was so much I needed to know about him, and so little time. In two days he'd have to return to his other life, where people continued their activities in blithe ignorance of my existence.

We spoke stiltedly, courting each other with little, likable pieces of ourselves, delaying our difficult questions, our subterranean, complicated truths. By unspoken consent, we turned off our cell phones, not wanting anything to encroach upon our brief moment together. He handed me an envelope full of old photos: my mother outside a tall, domed building, mock-curtsying in a bright, frilly skirt; laughing in an apron in a tiny kitchen, flour dusting her cheek; looking doubtful under a sign that promised her a happy birthday; and finally, thinner and sadder, with shadows in her eyes, cradling her curved belly.

"You can have them. I made copies."

I wanted to laugh and weep, both at once. I remembered Mariner's apartment, my hunger for a single glimpse of my mother's lost life that had nearly led me to disaster. And now, unlooked-for, this treasure trove! The universe had a strange sense of humor.

We walk across campus to the domed building I had seen in one of the photos.

"This is the International House, where we met, in this hall, at a folk-dance class. She was standing right here."

I imagine her in a red, frilled dress, a world of anticipation in her eyes.

"It was a difficult time in my life. I'd recently switched majors from engineering to history, which upset my family. They'd worked hard to put me through college, and they felt I was reneging on an unspoken contract. They were particularly displeased with my area, ancient civilizations, not even something meaningful like African-American history. I was going through a lot of soul-searching, a lot of guilt. I'd never have come here—I'm a terrible dancer—if a friend hadn't forced me because she thought I needed cheering up. Your mother wasn't that great a dancer, either, thank God—because otherwise I'd have been too intimidated to approach her. What I liked about her right away was that she was enthusiastic and unafraid, laughing at herself when she messed up. She had a mass of beautiful hair that flowed all the way down her back. Later she told me she'd never cut it—it was a family tradition. I kind of thought you'd have long hair, too."

He looks at me for a moment, and I return the gaze. I want to tell him how much I've given up to find him, but that's a story for another time.

"I kept going back to that class because of her. I'd maneuver my way around the room so I could be her partner. We started talking. She wanted to know where I came from, what I liked to do, what books I read. She had a genuine interest in people, your mother. And she was arrow-straight. When I asked her out, she told me right away we could only be friends. She explained the promise she'd made. When love ambushed her, she fought it every step of the way. But finally she had to call your grandfather. We both knew by then that it would be wrong for her to marry someone else."

My father breaks off, unwilling to enter that dark wood yet. Instead, he takes me to the building where they lived.

We walk down Telegraph, past vendors and street people and leftover hippies, secondhand clothing stores jostling for space beside upscale eateries, and turn into a narrow street. The building is dilapidated, its stucco a disheartening, crumbly gray.

"Ugly as sin, isn't it? It looked just like this even then. We had that tiny studio on the top floor, in the corner, see? It was cheap because the elevator didn't work. We were dirt-poor. Your grandfather had cut your mother off. Her scholarship covered her school expenses, but not much more. I didn't feel I could ask my family for help. They weren't well-off, and besides, they weren't pleased about us getting together, either. They thought—"

He breaks off, a pained look on his face.

"I worked a couple of part-time jobs and Anu tutored. That's how we managed to make ends meet. We had one secondhand mattress and one dining table with mismatched chairs that we used for eating and studying, both. Though we had no nursery for you, we were so excited for you to be born. I'd never been happier than I was there. Or sadder, when I received news from your grandfather that she had died, that you both had died. It seemed impossible that so much joy could vanish so quickly."

I wonder about his journey from grief to acceptance, to his present life with his new family that I'm jealous of. I wonder if my mother had been equally happy in that apartment. On the scales of joy, could even the best husband equal the weight of everyone you'd loved as far back as you could remember? But the gulf between 26 Tarak Prasad Roy Road and this building is so wide, perhaps joy meant something else here.

But then I think back to the note I'd found. My mother *had* been equally happy with him, even if that happiness was tinged with loss. Sometimes we appreciate something more because of the price we've had to pay for it. I consider showing him the letter, but I'm not ready, not yet, to share the one piece of her that I hold.

"She was a terrible cook, your mother. I'm the one who fixed dinner—I even learned some Indian dishes because she'd get homesick for them. But she made the best tea. We'd drink it in bed while we read each other snippets of what we were studying. Anu had a way of looking into you, of giving you her complete attention, that made you want to be the best person you could be. She's the one who turned me on to poetry. I've kept a couple of her favorite anthologies. When I read certain poems in there, I hear her voice. Sometimes we'd just sit quietly, gazing at this jacaranda tree. That's the best kind of silent, when you're with someone you love so much that you don't need to talk to them. And she loved flowers. It bothered her to be shut up in a small apartment. Her dream was to move to a little place with a patio—that's the best we could imagine in those times—and get some oleanders in pots. Now I have a half acre where I've planted row upon row of oleanders. I had a struggle with my wife about those. She was scared that the kids, who were little then, might put the poisonous leaves in their mouths."

"Did she know why you planted them?"

He looks down. "Selena doesn't know about your mother. When I met her, about two years after Anu died, I wasn't ready to rake up those painful memories again. I thought, 'Let some time pass; then I'll tell her.' And one day it was too late."

Is he going to tell her about me? That's another question I can't ask.

He says he must show me one final place, so we take the bus up the hill. On the way he describes his long-ago trip to India: how shell-shocked he was in the hot confusion of Kolkata, how Bimal Roy met him in the hotel lobby with the two death certificates and an urn of ashes. When Lacey asked how my mother died, Bimal Roy had turned on him in fury. It's because of you they're both dead, he said. He asked Rob Lacey never to contact them again.

I wait for rage at my grandfather to wash over me, but there is only sadness. What he did, it was because of love. Isn't that why most people do what they do? Out of their mistaken notions of love, their fear of its loss?

We disembark, and suddenly we're in the midst of roses, a multicolored, flowering amphitheater on the hillside. My father takes my arm as we descend to the trellises heavy with yellow blossoms. It's the first time he has touched me. I clasp his hand as a child might. How many times have I longed for this! He limps a little. Will we ever know the injuries that lie in our pasts?

"The Rose Garden was special to Anu. This is where we made our vows to each other."

"You got married here?"

He hesitates. His face flushes, then pales. He squares his shoulders. "Your mother and I were never married."

For a moment, the words hover in the air between us, meaningless.

Then I stare at him, aghast. "I'm illegitimate?" I whisper. Now it makes sense, why Desai was having such a hard time finding wedding records. "I'm a—bastard?"

He winces at the word but forces himself to meet my eyes. "I begged her, again and again. Especially when she became pregnant, which we hadn't planned on. But my asking only made her more upset. She took the promise she'd made in the temple—that she wouldn't marry against her father's wishes—very seriously. I couldn't understand it, but there it was. That was one of the reasons she went to India—to ask her father to release her from her promise so we could marry before you were born."

The air is cloying, burdened with the scent of too many roses. I can't come to terms with this new, shameful me. I feel a great, dizzying anger toward my parents, that they should have marked me like this. I don't know a single person among all my friends, relatives, acquaintances, even servants, who is outcast in this way. I envision myself telling Rajat of this stigma. The news traveling to Papa and Maman. To Bhattacharya. I can't even imagine the fallout from that.

"I'm sorry," he says, his face stricken. He comes toward me, but I back away.

"Please. I need to be alone." Something of the horror I feel must be in my face because it stops him short.

In my motel room, I'm unable to remain still. I turn on my cell phone. Two messages from the Boses' apartment. But how can I talk to Rajat while this new information burns inside me like a disease? The last number is Vic's. I would ignore that, too, but he'll keep calling. I dial his number and, thankfully, get a recording. I leave a message saying that my father and I had a long talk, and that I'm absorbing all the things I've learned. Please, I end, don't call me again tonight. I need to think things through.

I'm suffocating in the room. I need air. In the lobby, Desai's cousin tells me, reluctantly, that an elementary school down a side road has a playground. But it's not the best part of town. I should hurry back before dark.

I walk around the deserted playground until I come up against the school building. I lean my forehead against the discolored stucco wall, its rough, nubby surface. Some kinds of success are worse than failure. It would have been better not to have found my father than to live with this profound shame. I'm furious with everyone—my mother, my father, my grandfather.

When I hear footsteps behind me, I don't turn. Whatever's about to happen, let it.

A hand grabs me, swiveling me around. It's Vic, angrier than he's ever been.

"What are you doing here? What's wrong with you? Didn't Nayna tell you to get back before dark? Didn't she tell you it isn't safe? Get in the car."

In the car, he questions me until I let my shameful secret spill out. I keep my face turned away. I can't bear to see the disappointment—perhaps even distaste—in his face. But he takes hold of my shoulders and swings me around.

"I know you've had a shock, but quit acting like you committed a crime! It's not as terrible as you're making it out to be, not these days."

"It is, where I come from."

"People won't judge you for something that you had no control over. Not the people who love you."

He's thinking of Rajat, I know this. What I don't know is whether I can count on Rajat. He might stand by me—he's too decent a man to let me down—but what would he be feeling in his heart?

"And if they do fault you, maybe they don't love you the right way. Better to know this sooner rather than later. Call Rajat and tell him. See what he says. You know my offer still stands."

I'm grateful that Vic has spread himself like a net beneath my fall. But I can't hit Rajat with something so huge over the phone. Since I came to America, even my efforts to tell him simple things have been problematic, rife with miscommunication. When I give him this disconcerting information, I need to be in the same room, looking into his face. The truth of how he feels about the new me will be in his eyes, not his words. That's the truth I need to know.

"Let's talk about your father instead," Vic says.

"There's nothing to discuss."

"Aren't you being a bit too harsh?"

I stare stubbornly at the dashboard, but Vic keeps speaking in his easygoing, reasonable voice about how Lacey put his life on hold, took a big chance, and came all the way out to California to meet me. He didn't have to do that. Then again, he could have told me a lie about the marriage, but he trusted me with the truth. In any case, it had been my mother's decision not to marry him. That probably hurt him a lot. Vic talks until he can see, in my eyes, that my anger's melting. That I admit the truth of what he says.

"He's waiting in the motel. Are you going to continue pouting, or are you going to go talk to him?"

I have one more day, one more chance. I will not waste it on resentment. I will not add to all the wrong decisions my family has made.

"Take me back to the motel," I say.

Sarojini distrusts the sunset hour, when the dying day collapses around 26 Tarak Prasad Roy Road. To stave off its melancholy, she lights the evening lamp. She must pray for Korobi, but what should she petition the goddess for? That the girl has a happy reunion? Or that the meeting is a disaster so that she returns home for good, having cauterized this folly from her system?

The phone shrills, startling her so that she almost drops the lamp. She picks up the receiver with misgiving. She can't remember when last the phone brought her good news.

Mrs. Bose is on the line. It takes Sarojini a moment to recognize her voice, jerky with tears. Mrs. Bose, always so confident and polished, begging her to please come and be with her at the hospital, the children were both in an accident last night, she's beside herself with fear because Rajat is still unconscious.

"Of course, my child! I'll come right away. You should have called me sooner. Which hospital is it?" But Sarojini knows already by the prickling on her skin. It is the Pantheon, once again the site of her family's reckoning and loss.

The hospital is a labyrinth of corridors stacked one above another. People in uniforms rush around importantly, their instruments gleaming in the blinding lights, too busy to address an old woman's confusion. Finally a janitor takes pity on her, leans his mop against the wall, and leads her to the ward where Pia and Rajat have been admitted. Sarojini is shocked at Mrs. Bose's wild, uncombed hair, the hollows gouged under her eyes. Her kurta hangs limp around her. A streak of salt is on her cheek, dried tears. Sarojini rubs it away gently with her finger.

The children have been placed in separate rooms so that Pia, who is now awake, will not be upset by Rajat's condition. Rajat's left hand is fractured in two places. He had a concussion when he came in and is on oxygen. He moves in and out of consciousness, groggy from painkillers. Luckily, Pia's injuries were minor—bruises and a dislocated shoulder. She'll be released tomorrow, but the doctors want to observe Rajat a while longer. The concussion is bad. Mrs. Bose is exhausted from running back and forth between the rooms and updating Mr. Bose and staving off the police, who want to get statements. What is she going to do when Pia is discharged while Rajat remains here?

"Don't spare it another thought, Jayashree! Pia shall come home with me. She loves the house and has been begging to come and stay. She'll sleep beside me. I'll make sure she eats well and rests. . . . No, no, you must not thank me. What is this westernized formality? Aren't we family? Now let me see the children."

Pia has a purple bump on her forehead and her arm in a sling, but she seems quite recovered otherwise. She complains bitterly to Sarojini because they will not let her see her brother—or Asif. An unwary attendant has let it slip that the chauffeur has also been admitted here—in the general ward, of course—and that he was banged up pretty bad, and since then Pia has been begging to see him.

"He saved us, Grandma. We were on our way back from the restaurant when this horrible van suddenly rammed into us for no reason. At first I thought it was an accident, but then it kept hitting us. We almost flipped over. It was the scariest thing. I screamed and screamed for help, but the road was completely empty. Then A.A. came out of nowhere, just like a superhero, and crashed his car into the van to get them away from us. That made them mad, so they started ramming him. I didn't see anything after that—we'd landed in the ditch by then—but I'm pretty sure I heard gunshots. I can't tell you how horrible it was, being trapped in that car with Dada moaning and half-passed-out. If A.A. hadn't scared them off, I bet those men would have hurt us much worse. A.A. must have called the police, too, because they showed up soon after. Grandma, please tell Maman to let me see him!"

Sarojini assures Pia that she will do her best. Once outside, she asks for details. Is it not a simple road accident, then? Mrs. Bose shakes her head. The police have confirmed what Pia said. But by the time they arrived, there were only two cars, the Mercedes and the Rolls, both in the ditch. Broken glass and tire marks indicated the presence of a third, larger vehicle. They have no leads yet.

Mrs. Bose wrings her hands. "I should never have let them go out that night. But it was Pia's birthday and she asked so many times that I weakened. I should have known they were planning something."

"Who?"

"Some of the workers at the warehouse are Naxalites. It must have been them. Two men had threatened me outside the gallery a couple of days back. Oh, why was I so stupid? The signs were all there. My children, my darling babies. Why didn't I pay more attention?" Mrs. Bose's voice rises hysterically.

It takes Sarojini significant effort to coax her into calmness. People who seem most in charge, not a crack visible, sometimes fall apart totally in a mishap. It had been the same way with Bimal. Finally, she gets to see Rajat, who is sleeping fitfully, his arm in a huge cast. There's a swelling above his left eye that makes Sarojini cringe; his entire forehead is discolored with bruises. She touches his unhurt hand and whispers a prayer.

He stirs. His eyes fly open, dart from side to side, unseeing. "Korobi?" he whispers. "Cara?" The sedatives take over again.

Mrs. Bose bites her lip, trying to control her tears. "He keeps asking for her. I wish she were here for him. She belongs here, by his side. I phoned her twice, but she didn't pick up, and I was too distressed to leave a message."

"I'll call her as soon as I get home," Sarojini says. She bends over

Rajat and whispers, "I'll make sure Korobi comes home to you." She hopes she hasn't promised more than she can deliver.

His eyes shift under his lids, but he doesn't open them.

With a sigh she asks Mrs. Bose, "Can I see your driver now?"

Asif is down the hall in a double cabin. He'd been put into a ward in a cheaper wing, with a roomful of other patients, but when Mrs. Bose heard Pia's story, she moved him here. Once in the room, Mrs. Bose stands behind Sarojini as though she doesn't want him to see her. Sarojini is shocked at Asif's appearance. He's unconscious, a bloody bandage around his head. His face is a mass of bruises, far worse than Rajat's. One arm is in a cast. Restraints have been placed around him. Mrs. Bose whispers that he has a couple of broken ribs and has to be kept from moving. His breath comes unevenly, noisily; an oxygen tube is attached to his nose. He has not regained consciousness since they admitted him.

"Thank God the police came on time!" Sarojini says to Mrs. Bose. "Did another motorist call in the accident?"

Mrs. Bose shakes her head. Asif's new employer had phoned the police. Apparently Asif had punched his number on his speed dial before his car flipped over.

"New employer? Isn't Asif working for you anymore?"

"He quit a couple days ago." Mrs. Bose lowers her eyes.

There's a story here, but Sarojini doesn't have the heart to interrogate her. "Go home and get some sleep, Jayashree. Bahadur is downstairs—he'll drive you. I'll watch all three of them until you get back."

In the morning when I come out of the shower, more messages are on my phone. This time, I listen to them all. Yesterday's messages from the Bose residence hadn't been from Rajat, after all, but from his mother. The machine has distorted Maman's voice, which sounds wobbly. "Korobi?" she says. "Korobi?" But she doesn't leave a message. I wonder why she called. We've only spoken twice since I left India, stilted conversations about how my search is going, punctuated with awkward silences. She probably wants to discuss wedding preparations.

The next message is from Grandmother. Again no details, just asking me to call. Her voice, too, sounds distorted. Waterlogged. I sigh. The wedding, which in India had felt like a gift box tied with a satin ribbon, waiting to be opened, no longer seems real to me. All its attendant busyness feels meaningless. Especially since there's a distinct possibility that, after I divulge my double secret, there will be no wedding.

I turn off the phone. I'll call them back, but not yet. This last day is for my father.

Last night we had an emotional reconciliation, with apologies on both sides. Now we feverishly ask each other questions, wanting to know everything possible in the few hours left to us. I learn that my father is an avid woodworker. He has built three feeders in his backyard for hummingbirds and shyly hands me a pen he made out of cedar, with my name carved on it. He must have stayed up late to finish it before he flew out.

He asks me about our house, which he always wanted to visit. "Your mother spoke of it so many times. When I came to India, I asked your grandfather's permission to come and see the room where Anu grew up."

"What did he say?" But already I can guess.

"He said, 'You'll enter my house over my dead body.'"

I'm angry for my father, but unexpectedly, I feel a jolt of sympathy for Grandfather, too. While my father had been longing for something to connect him to his sweetheart, Grandfather had been desperate to protect the last bit of his daughter that was left to him.

Because he has the right to know, I tell my father what I learned from Grandmother about my mother's last visit. Afterward, as he sits holding his head in his hands, I whisper, "You must hate Grandfather very much. All I can say is that he suffered, too."

Lacey gives a sigh. "I did hate him at first, with a deep, corrosive hatred that ate into me. I hated what he did to Anu by forcing her to choose between her family and our love, the life we could have made together. It broke a beautiful, intelligent woman in two. I don't think I can ever forgive him for that—and for keeping you and me apart. But over the years I've come to see that Anu, too, was responsible for her situation. She knew what he did was wrong, but she couldn't shuck off her guilt. Couldn't break away from his control. Her childhood conditioning went too deep."

We sit in silence, thinking of many things. Hesitantly, I tell him about the dream that started off this whole search for me, my mother's visit. I've held on to it until now, afraid he might scoff. But he nods and says, "I believe." He says, "You were lucky. What I wouldn't give to see her one more time, even if it's in a dream."

The slump of his shoulders is so forlorn that, even though I had not intended it, I open my purse and take out my mother's love letter and slide it across the table to him. As he reads it, an expression of tremulous joy takes over his face. He reads the note several times, smoothing out the worn sheet with a reverent forefinger. For a moment, he has forgotten me. When he finally raises his head, a dazed, faraway look is on his face as though the note had pulled him back in time.

"Thank you," he says, a little shakily, as he passes the note back to me.

I hold it, the talisman that has brought me this far, the only thing of my mother's that I possess. Then, quickly, before I can change my mind, I press it into my father's palm. "She would want you to have it."

At the airport I ask, "Will you come for my wedding? If I get married, that is? You could stay in the house, sleep in my mother's bed."

He shakes his head. "It wouldn't be the same without Anu. Besides, I'd only cause you trouble. With your in-laws—and that politician they're courting. I know how people feel about mixed-race relationships. Anu and I faced a bit of that in California, even. You've seen me and I've seen you. We've had this time together and spoken the words that needed to be said. We've promised to keep in touch. That's enough for now."

As we walk to the security area, a question I hadn't intended to ask tumbles out of me. "What if I stay on here? With Vic? What would you think of that?"

That brings him to a standstill. He cups my face in his hands and looks into my eyes. "I'd love to have you closer to me, you know that. Make you part of my life, make up for some of the lost years. I'm going to tell Selena about you as soon as I return. But I don't know you enough yet to judge if staying here would be the best for you. This much I will say: never choose something because it's easier. That's what I did when

Bimal Roy handed me those death certificates. I should have investigated further instead of getting on the plane home. A part of me wanted to, but I squashed it because it would have been too painful to stay on and search."

At the security line, I hug him and hold my breath so I can keep the smell of his cologne with me a little longer. He turns on his cell phone. Soon I must do the same. We can't fend off the jealous world any longer.

A crush of people presses him forward. Soon I'll lose sight of him. I raise my voice to ask him the question that has plagued me all my life, though I don't think he'll have the answer. After all, even Grandmother didn't know.

"Did my mother ever tell you why she wanted to name me Korobi?"

"She did, actually," he calls out over the heads of the other passengers. "Because the oleander was beautiful—but also tough. It knew how to protect itself from predators. Anu wanted that toughness for you because she didn't have enough of it herself."

This time when the phone rings, Sarojini is ready. She has been waiting all morning, in fact, beside the phone, waiting and fretting and nodding off from time to time because she spent the night in the hospital.

"Grandma! Sorry I'm late calling you back. I'd turned off my phone because I was with my father. Oh, there's so much to tell you, good and bad both, I don't know where to start!"

The girl babbles on about the day the two of them spent at Berkeley, visiting places where Anu had lived, walked, eaten, studied. All the amazing new things she has learned about Anu. Part of Sarojini hungers to hear more. What kind of a person is this Lacey, what was his life with Anu like, what does he intend to do about his newfound daughter? But she has a more urgent agenda.

"Korobi, I must tell you something, too—something really important," she cries, but it's like trying to stop an avalanche.

"I love him, Grandma. I refuse to lose him again. I need to tell Rajat all about him. But you were right, I must wait until I get back. Because I learned something else about myself, something—terrible. Well, at least the world would consider it terrible. I don't even know how to tell it to you."

Sarojini feels a spiral of nausea rising in her. She wonders if her sugar has fallen again. What now, Goddess? What else can there be?

"I tried to call Rajat several times, but I can't seem to get hold of him. Where is he?"

The accumulated stress of last night crests and breaks, and suddenly Sarojini's furious. "If you had thought for a moment beyond your own plans and pleasure and returned my phone call—or Jayashree's—you'd know that Rajat is in the hospital. So is Pia."

There's a long silence. Korobi's voice, when she speaks again, is so abashed that Sarojini feels the sting of compunction.

"What happened?"

Sarojini explains what little she knows. She tells Korobi how Rajat has been asking for her.

"I'll call Maman right now," Korobi says. "I'll change my ticket and come home as soon as possible."

Only after she hangs up does Sarojini realize that she never got to hear Korobi's terrible news.

Mrs. Bose, too, is waiting for the phone to ring as she paces the hospital corridor with her mobile. She hasn't talked to Mr. Bose since yesterday. She sifts through the latest updates that she needs to give him. For once, they are good.

He'll be pleased to hear that Pia is being discharged in a couple of hours, and that she'll stay with Sarojini. Pia was so delighted at this news that she didn't get overly upset when she saw Rajat. She wrote her name in large purple letters on his cast. She still insists on visiting Asif before she leaves, but Mrs. Bose has told the doctor that such a visit would be traumatic for her sensitive daughter, and the doctor has agreed to officially forbid it.

Rajat's news is good, too. He was able to sit up this morning and eat a light breakfast. His painkillers have been reduced. He isn't talking much, but Mr. Bose doesn't need to know that right now. Subroto the foreman came over to the hospital this morning. He informed her that the union leaders are shocked at what happened and are investigating the matter. The accident, unfortunate though it was, has roused significant sympathy among the workers for the Boses, and Subroto believes this will help the negotiations.

She hopes Mr. Bose has equally good news to give her.

Who says a watched phone never rings? The mobile buzzes in Mrs. Bose's hand. "Shanto?" she says eagerly. "Sweetheart?"

A woman clears her throat. "Maman? This is Korobi here."

"Oh, it's you." Disappointment flattens her tone. As soon as the words come out, she realizes how unfriendly they sound, though she hadn't meant them in that way. She knows, from personal experience, what can happen if one is not on good terms with a son's intended. But she cannot shake off her resentment toward the girl for not responding sooner to her inarticulate cry for help.

"Maman, I'm so sorry I took so long to phone you back." Korobi's voice sounds tortured. "My phone—it—got turned off. Grandmother told me about Rajat and Pia. I'm so sorry! I wish I were there to give you support."

Tiredness and tension make Mrs. Bose want to snap, *But you aren't, are you? Even though my poor boy keeps calling for you*. She closes her eyes tight and imagines what her husband would say: *Come on, Joyu, you're better than that*. She makes herself smile so that her voice will sound sweeter. "It's okay. Your grandmother has done a lot for us."

"How is Rajat? Grandma said he—asked for me." Korobi's voice is shaky with tears.

Something about that must be contagious because Mrs. Bose finds herself tearing up, too.

"Tell him I love him. I'm so sorry I'm not there by his side. Tell him I'm changing my ticket and coming back as soon as I can. I'll never go anywhere without him again."

"I'll tell him," Mrs. Bose says, wiping her eyes.

"I love you, Maman."

"I love you, too." Words they've never said to each other until now.

After Korobi hangs up, Mrs. Bose thinks with regret, I should have asked her what's happening with her search. Probably she found nothing, or she would have mentioned it. Poor child, she must be disheartened.

But Mrs. Bose doesn't have time to dwell on her oversight because the phone rings again. This time, ah, Blessed Goddess, it is Mr. Bose, asking about the children. But he's concerned, most of all, about her. How is she handling all this stress? If it's too much, he'll drop everything and come home. She just has to say the word.

Tenderness wells up in her. "No, Shanto. You finish what you went there to do. Otherwise the entire journey will be wasted. I can manage. I know you're with me in my heart."

She gives him, proudly, her news, and he gives her his, which is also better than expected. The meetings with the insurance company have been promising. They've agreed to pay a percentage of the damages and even the theft. Only the amount remains to be negotiated. Desai has been of immense help in setting up a moving sale. That should make them some more money. Once that's over, Mr. Bose can ship the remainder of the inventory and return to Kolkata.

"How about Mitra?"

"No sign of him. The police discovered that he was involved with an illegal gambling concern. That must be where all the money we were sending him went. Desai and I accompanied them to his apartment. We were shocked to find that it was completely trashed, the dishes shattered on the floor, the sofa ripped as though with a knife. At first we thought intruders had done it, but the police think he did it himself."

"How very strange! What about his wife?"

"The police questioned the neighbors. One of them said that a few days ago she left for India without telling Mitra. Mitra was beside himself with fury when he figured out that she was gone. He came over to this woman's apartment, yelling, threatening her for conspiring against him, until her husband threw him out. They haven't seen him since. The police think he's skipped town."

"I hope so. Be careful, though. Please."

"I will. About Rajat's accident—did the police discover anything else?"

"No. They're waiting to question Asif. The doctor said he's regained consciousness, but he's still very weak."

"Have you been to see him since then?"

Mrs. Bose is silent.

"You need to go, Joyu. He probably saved our children's lives by scaring off those goondas."

"I feel so ashamed, Shanto, for distrusting him with Pia."

"You can't change that. But at least you can thank him. Reassure him that we'll take care of all his medical expenses, and that we'll speak on his behalf to his employer. If Asif's out of a job because of what he did, tell him he can come back and work for us. If, God forbid, he's disabled, we'll take care of him."

"How will we pay for all this?"

"We'll just have to. And, Joyu, you can't keep Pia away from him. What he did, risking his life—I have a feeling he did it for her. She needs to see him, and it'll do him good to see her. Take her with you."

He speaks softly, but she hears the steel in his voice. He waits until she says meekly, "All right, Shanto. I'll do as you say."

FIFTEEN

Late at night I'm pulled bleary-eyed from sleep by the insistent ringing of the phone. I'd been awake until late, worrying about Rajat, and had just fallen into a doze. Who could be calling at this ungodly hour?

"Sorry to wake you," Desai says, "but it's urgent. My office was broken into when I was helping Mr. Bose with the art sale. By the time I got back after dinner, most of the files had been torn up. My computer was smashed, as were disks with client information. Whoever did it was smart enough to figure out the alarm and disconnect it."

I'm so shocked I can't speak for a few seconds. "I'm terribly sorry," I finally stammer. I can't even imagine how Desai must feel. Hundreds of hours of work, destroyed. His whole business, probably. What will he do?

Desai gives a mirthless bark of a laugh. "It's not as bad as it sounds, though I have to confess it gave me quite a turn. It's the first time I've been vandalized like this. Luckily, I'd taken precautions. I have client information backed up off-site, and insurance will cover most of the damage. The reason I'm calling you is because I realized something just a few minutes ago, after I went through the debris. Your file and disk aren't here."

I feel even worse. I'm the cause of his troubles. "Mitra?" I whisper.

"Definitely. He's desperate. I bet within a day or so he'll try to blackmail your in-laws with the information he stole. And now he has more ammunition than what he hoped for—he knows your father's black, and that your parents weren't married."

I'm still in shock. I'd guessed that Mitra was dangerous. I'd warned Rajat that he might try to harm the gallery, or even Papa. But I'd never guessed that he'd choose me as the vehicle of his revenge. How one-eyed I'd been, like the deer in the fable.

"You need to forestall Mitra. That's why I disturbed you so late at night. Call your fiancé immediately and tell him about your father."

"I can't! Rajat is in the hospital with a concussion. I changed my ticket to get back to him as soon as I can."

"It might be too late by the time you get to Kolkata. If Mitra gets to the Boses with the information before you do, he could convince them that you meant to deceive them. If you can't talk to Rajat, tell Mr. Bose. He's a levelheaded man—"

"No!" I cry. "Rajat has to be the first to know. I can't let him hear this news from anyone else. I owe him that much. And I have to be with him when I tell him. If he has reservations, I'll see them in his face. Then I'll know I can't marry him."

"Korobi, forgive me, but you're making a big mistake. And you're being too idealistic. Any man would be shocked by this news—even a man who really cares for you. If he loves you, he'll get over it. You've got to give him that chance."

But I remain silent until Desai lets out a sigh. "That pigheaded Vic has been a bad influence on you, I can tell."

Lying in bed, Rajat meditates on the softness of his pillow, the crisp, clean smell of his sheets. How wonderful to be back in the privacy of his own room, with a feathery strain of jazz floating through the air. He can hear Pia in the kitchen, begging Maman to let her stay home from school today in honor of Rajat's release from the hospital. Rajat does not expect Maman to agree. She's a stickler about Pia's studies. Perhaps she's making up for having been too indulgent with Rajat. But to his surprise, she says yes with a distracted air and goes off to answer the phone. It is probably the foreman again. Negotiations are proceeding favorably with the union; following the incident on the river road, and in light of Rajat's injuries, they've modified their demands. Finally, Rajat thinks, with some irony, he's been of use to the family!

A triumphant Pia settles herself at the foot of Rajat's bed. She has taken upon herself the task of making him drink the pomegranate juice the doctor has prescribed. She tells him sternly not to dillydally with the glass she has handed him. Why is he so quiet? Is he still groggy from the painkillers?

He nods because it's hard to explain. The painkillers, which have been reduced, have little to do with his mental state. A strange calm, different from anything else he has ever experienced, has descended on him. Through its filter, the world appears dappled, like sunlight through leaves. Pia's voice is like a treeful of birds, more music than meaning. The various dramas surrounding his life—the strike, Korobi's search for her father, the night attack—all seem part of an intricate design, not fully comprehensible but engrossingly interesting.

This calm had descended on him at the very moment the car flipped over, even as a part of him was screaming in agony and terror. The painkillers had shrouded it, but it has now spread itself across this beautiful day, this turquoise sky outside his window, stippled with possibility. He recalls a line from a song he heard on the radio when visiting Sarojini: *Anondo dhara bohiche bhubonay.* A river of joy flows through the world. He'll have to ask her how the rest of the song goes.

"Never mind," Pia says. "You don't have to talk. You just rest. I'll tell you everything you've missed in the last few days." She launches into a dramatic description of her time in the hospital, the hateful smell of disinfectant, the terrifying tetanus shot, the awful food the nurses forced her to ingest. They were scary, especially the head nurse, who with her saucer eyes and big, crooked teeth resembled the demonesses in the *Amar Chitra Katha* picture books Pia used to have as a child.

The police had been to see her, too, she adds importantly. They brought a detective with them, a mousy man who didn't look anything like a detective should. He asked her a slew of questions. He was so disappointed because she hadn't seen the men's faces or a license-plate number that Pia had considered making something up.

"Pia! I hope you didn't!"

"No," she says regretfully. "Anyway, they'd taken off the license plate—that's what Asif told them—and he would know, because he's very observant."

Rajat's body is made of glass and filled with colors. Asif's name stirs them up until they are a rainbow.

"You've seen Asif?"

"Oh, yes, I went to see him twice, and Maman came, too. We took him flowers the first time and a big basket of fruits the second time, because now he can eat regular food as long as it's cut up into little pieces. Next I'll take him some Cadbury's. He likes the orange chocolate bar the best. Maman made me wait outside while she talked to him. I don't know what she said. I almost eavesdropped, but then I thought it wouldn't be right. Plus I knew A.A. would tell me if I asked. I think she said sorry and thank-you. She was crying when she came out. I've never seen Maman cry before. Have you? Then she let me go in by myself, which was good because A.A. won't really talk if she's there. I could tell A.A. wasn't angry with her anymore. I stayed with him until visiting hours were over, and she didn't try to rush me out."

"How is he doing? I want to go see him, too."

"You can come with me as soon as you're stronger. Bahadur will take us. Grandma has loaned him to us for now. A.A. looks terrible. His head is still bandaged up, all his bruises have turned purple, and they've put a big black collar around his neck. But his nurse, who was quite friendly with me—I guess they treat you better when you're not a patient—said it looks a lot worse than it is. She said he's really lucky. A.A. made a face at me from behind her back when she said that. He broke a couple of ribs, but they're healing well, and they didn't puncture a lung, which they could easily have done when he hit the steering wheel. Oh, he has a cast, just like you. I wrote on his cast, too.

"So, anyway, those same policemen came in to question him while I was there. They asked me to step outside but I wouldn't because you know how police can be sometimes with people who don't have money.

Plus A.A. said I could hear anything he had to say. They asked him if he had any idea who those men might be. Were they workers from the warehouse? A.A. said he couldn't recognize any faces, it was too dark and too much was going on. Then . . ."

Pia hesitates.

"What is it?"

"Nothing."

"Come on, Sweet P. You never were any good at keeping secrets!"

"I am, too!" But she lowers her voice. "A.A. told them that he saw Sonia in the parking lot that night."

"Sonia?" The colors inside Rajat coagulate into a muddy brown.

"Yes! At first the detective said it could be a coincidence, she could have been there for the restaurant. But A.A. said she didn't go in, she just stopped near our car, made a phone call, and left. The police got quite excited when they heard that, though the detective said it would be hard to prove anything. Anyway, they told me I must not mention it to anyone because word can travel and they don't want to alert her. Plus it might be dangerous for A.A. if someone finds out that he talked. So I didn't say anything, not even to Maman. I wasn't going to tell you, either, but I'm glad you made me. It was hard, keeping it all to myself. What do you think was going on?"

Rajat shakes his head, unready to conjecture. At some point, he knows, outrage will overtake him. But he doesn't want Sonia to ruin this silent, calm happiness that envelops him.

Pia continues with her adventures. "I hardly got any time to talk to Asif because right after that his employer—who is a sheikh and very powerful, A.A. told me later—came in. He was this big man in an expensive white suit and had two bodyguards. He was so angry, his face was red and his nostrils all puffed up. His voice was quiet but it was scarier than if he had shouted. He asked what the hell had A.A. done, did he know how much the car that he had totaled cost? Even if he worked all his life for the sheikh for free, A.A. wouldn't be able to pay for it. AA kept saying, 'Sorry, Huzoor.' He got so upset that his blood-pressure machine started beeping. So I held his hand and told the sheikh to please not stress him, couldn't he see that A.A. was just coming back from death's door. I explained that A.A. had saved my life and yours. He still looked furious, so I added that I would ask my parents to pay for the car."

"God, Pia! That car is unbelievably expensive. We don't have the money—"

"But I couldn't not offer! It was only right. A.A. almost died for us, didn't he? Anyway, the sheikh turned to me with a huge scowl and said in a booming genie kind of voice, 'Who is this person?' A.A. and I answered at the same time. AA said, 'This is Pia-missy, I used to work for her,' and I said, 'I'm his friend.' Then the sheikh asked if I was such good friends with Asif, how come he didn't work for us anymore? I told him there had been a misunderstanding, but it was cleared up now and we would really like A.A. to come back—if the sheikh allowed it, of course. I would like you to know I was most polite."

"You took a lot upon yourself. What are Maman and Papa going to say?"

"I think I can talk them into it. The sheikh thinks I'm pretty persuasive."

"He does?"

"Oh, yes. After he'd asked me some more questions, he said, 'You are quite an outspoken young woman and persuasive as well as stubborn. I can tell that your husband will have his work cut out for him.' I wasn't sure if it was a compliment, but I thanked him very nicely and he laughed. Then he took our names and address and said he would be in touch."

Rajat hopes Pia has not landed them in new trouble with her impulsive behavior. He's proud of how brave she has been, though. Her face, backlit by the window, seems to have acquired a golden sheen. But he's tired. "You are all those things, and loyal, too. I'm sure A.A. appreciated your championship. Now I have to take a nap."

"That's an excellent idea," she says in a matronly voice. "I'll wake you when it's time for lunch and help you to the table. The doctor said it's important for you to move around."

Then she's Pia again. "I can't wait to tell you about my adventures at Grandma's! You know I stayed with her while you were in the hospital? It was such fun. I'm so glad we're inheriting a Grandma from Korobi-didi. The pipes weren't working right, so Bahadur and Cook brought water for us in buckets from the outside tap, and I helped them. At night Grandma and I slept together in a big, high bed with posts and stairs to climb up, and she told me all kinds of stories. Did you know, that house is supposed to have a secret room behind a bookshelf where they used to hide revolutionaries during the independence struggle! She said I can search for it next time I visit. That temple has a lot of stories, too. One evening Mr. Bhattacharya stopped by for the evening puja, and he was really different and nice. I'll tell you everything at lunch."

From the doorway she adds, "Korobi-didi called twice, but you were sleeping and she told Maman not to wake you. She bought a new ticket. She should be on her way home already. If she makes all the connections, she'll be in Kolkata tomorrow."

Korobi's name is like a sea wind. He remembers calling out for her. Was it in the hospital? Was it during the crash? It's good of her to cut her search short and return for his sake. The wind blows through him, cleansing. Salt and distance, smell of the deep. He realizes he has never seen the ocean except tamed and touristy at Digha. When Korobi returns, he'll ask if she'd be willing to travel to a real ocean with him. Maybe when they are there, he'll be able to describe how it felt when he thought he was going to die, and afterward, this calm. At the ocean, they will talk to each other truly, and listen.

"She called Grandma's house while I was there. She talked to me, too. She asked all about your injuries. Oh, I forgot! She said to give you a big hug for her—here it is—and tell you she has something very important to share with you, face-to-face, as soon as she gets back."

Mrs. Bose has shut herself in her bedroom with the phone because she does not want the children to know how agitated she is. "What do you mean, Mitra's trying to blackmail us about Korobi's father?" she asks her husband. "Has he gone crazy? He knows he'll go to jail if the police get hold of him, so now he's clutching at straws?"

Mr. Bose says, "You're right about him being desperate. But he isn't crazy. Quite the opposite. He seems to have planned everything out. He sent me a fax with all the relevant information. He said that if we don't respond within a week, he'll send it to Bhattacharya. I checked with Desai. At first he was reluctant to break confidentiality, but when I explained what Mitra was trying to do, he admitted that the information is authentic. Mitra broke into Desai's office and stole the file. Korobi's father is some history professor named Rob Lacey. But, Joyu, listen: he's black."

"Impossible! Why, you just have to look at Korobi to know—"

"That's what I said, but Desai explained that Korobi's father is very light-skinned. And there's more. Apparently Korobi's parents never got married."

"What are you saying? Korobi's illegitimate? How can that be? Korobi's mother would never do such a—such a horribly immoral thing! Why, she comes from one of the oldest—"

"It's true, unfortunately. Desai said something about a promise Anu had made to her father in the temple. I didn't have the time to get into all the details."

"Oh, God! What will we do, Shanto? Never in my wildest nightmares could I have imagined something this terrible. How can we have our son marry a girl of mixed blood who has, moreover, such a scandal in her past? Here we were so delighted to be making an alliance with one of Kolkata's most respected families, and now we discover—this?"

"Times are changing, Joyu. I'm not pleased, either. But such things matter less now."

"They still matter a great deal!" Then Mrs. Bose is distracted by another thought. "Did Desai get a chance to tell the poor girl any of this before she boarded her plane?"

There's a pause. Then Mr. Bose says, "Mitra told me quite clearly that Korobi has met her father. It was all in the folder. Lacey flew to California and met with Korobi two days ago."

"Two days ago? He must be lying!"

Mr. Bose hesitates, then says, "I don't think so."

"Korobi saw her father two days ago? But she's talked to me since then. Twice. She didn't say anything about this. She talked to you, too, didn't she? Did she mention her father to you?"

Mr. Bose is silent.

"She let us assume that she failed to find him! How could she be so—duplicitous?"

"Calm down, Joyu!"

But Mrs. Bose can't calm down. "How can I trust her again? It's bad enough that she has all this—dirt in her background, but on top of that, she's a lying, cheating—"

"I was upset, too. But try to see it from her point of view. Maybe she's scared about how we'll react."

"And so she plans to hide such a huge thing from us? To deceive her own husband?"

"Let's set aside the issue of Korobi for a little while. Right now we have to decide what to do about Mitra. He's demanding that we withdraw our charges, call off the police. He's asking for money—a lot of it. Additionally, we have to provide him with a positive recommendation so he can look for a new job. If word of what has happened here gets around—now or later—he's going to leak the story to the press. They're always interested in skeletons hidden in the cupboards of the newly rich—though maybe we've fallen out of that category now!"

"How can you joke at a time like this? If Bhattacharya—or his party members—got wind of this, it would be the end of any kind of partnership, any possibility of saving the business. I don't understand—why should Mitra harbor such a grudge against us? We helped him as much as we could, in spite of all the losses we suffered."

"He sees it differently. He went on and on about how we wouldn't let him return to India after 9/11, even after the police arrested him and his wife was so terrified. How they had to move into a tiny, bug-infested apartment in a bad neighborhood because he didn't have enough money to pay rent. How depressed his wife became there. Our behavior pushed him into gambling—to try and make some quick money to send her to India—though obviously that didn't work out well. But most of all, he blames Korobi for destroying his marriage. Says she turned his wife, who loved him dearly, against him. Korobi put ideas into her head and encouraged her to run off. Mitra says his life is ruined because of her."

"Korobi! She's the reason why he turned on us?"

"You can't take what he says seriously, Joyu. He's not rational right now. But he is extremely shrewd, and therefore dangerous. I've told him I can't do anything until I get the money from the sale of the paintings—and he knows I can't—so that buys us a few days. Then you and I will have to make a decision."

"This engagement must be broken. That's my decision. It'll solve all our problems."

"Sweet, that decision is not ours to make. It's up to Rajat."

"The poor boy! I can't even imagine how upset he's going to be when he learns how Korobi's trying to deceive him."

"Jayashree, listen to me! You can't say anything to him right now. First, because he's just recovering, and it'll be too much of a shock. Remember, he loves her. And second, you have to give Korobi a chance to meet with him. Who knows, maybe she's looking for the right way to tell him this news, which must have shocked her as much as it did us."

Mrs. Bose disagrees. That girl was not planning to tell them anything—she can feel it in her bones. If Korobi does confess now, it'll only be because Mitra has already spilled the beans. Mrs. Bose loves Mr. Bose more than she loves anyone else in the world, but when will he learn the folly of trusting too much?

"I don't know if I can keep such an upsetting thing inside me, Shanto, when I'm already so weighed down with other matters. However, I'll try. For Rajat's sake."

And she does. Each time she sees Rajat and the words come into her mouth, she swallows them. Each time he expresses his delight because Korobi will be returning tomorrow, she turns away, though she longs to warn him. She can't help wondering if Sarojini is in on this scam, too; the possibility upsets her further. Since the accident, when Sarojini was such a rock of support, she has begun to think of the old woman as a mother. All day the unspoken sentences build inside her chest like steam. Blood pounds in her temples. Her entire body aches. She takes a shower; perhaps it'll loosen those tight shoulder muscles. But the hot water only makes her feverish. When she comes out and finds that Bhattacharya has left another message asking her to call, saying they need to speak urgently, she's ready to snap.

Just as dinner is served, Pia says, "We'd better hang up the engagement photo again! We don't want Korobi-didi to see that we'd put it away. It would hurt her feelings."

"Do it later," Mrs. Bose says. "Come and eat now."

"We don't have much time! She told me she's planning to come here straight from the airport." And with that, Pia is off. She searches the spare room until she finds the photo in a drawer, where Mrs. Bose has stuffed it. In her dramatic way, Pia makes a big to-do, calling to Pushpa to bring the hammer and nails, telling Rajat to stand back and watch if the photo is straight. Mrs. Bose has to press her lips together to keep from yelling at her. It's not the child's fault, all these problems, she tells herself. I should be thankful that she's recovered so quickly from the trauma of the accident.

Once it's up, Pia turns to Rajat for approval.

"It's an amazing picture," he says. "I wonder who the photographer is?"

Mrs. Bose does not find this amusing. She tells them to come to the table, the food's getting cold. Still they dawdle.

"What beautiful hair Korobi-didi has," Pia says, touching the picture with a loving finger. "You think Maman will let me get mine curled like hers for the wedding reception? Of course mine won't look as nice because hers is so much longer."

"Not anymore," Rajat says.

Mrs. Bose stops ladling dal into their bowls. "What do you mean?"

Rajat looks awkward. Clearly the words slipped from him when he wasn't paying attention.

"Tell me," she persists, folding her arms as though he were a guilty teenager.

Perhaps the accident has lowered his resistance. Or maybe he's startled by her insistence. He tells her about Mitra, the photo he had e-mailed.

"Mitra was involved in that, too?" Her voice rises though she knows she should control it—Rajat hates people who yell. *Stop, Joyu,* Shanto would have said. *The boy isn't well. Don't rant at him.* "That man's obviously been planning to get us for a while. Why didn't you tell me earlier? We could have been proactive, prevented worse things."

"I didn't tell you because it's my private business," he tells her coldly. "Mine and Cara's."

Her hands begin to shake. The tone, the words, the ridiculous name he's given Korobi—they push her over the edge. That scheming, deceiving girl—and now he's taking her side against his own mother?

The words have been waiting all day. They explode out of her like soda from a can that has been violently shaken.

"Oh, really? If you two are that close, you must already know what your papa called to tell me today. The truth about your darling Cara's father—surely that's your business, too, what Mitra is using to blackmail us? No? Looks like she forgot to mention a couple of little facts."

I step outside the airport terminal into the early morning, the sky just lighting up, surely a good omen. Bahadur is waiting with the car. He glances at me and glances away. I see, with a lurch of the heart, that he doesn't recognize me. Is it just my hair, or some deeper sea change I've undergone? I put a hand on his arm and smile. His leathery face breaks open in an astonished grin.

"Korobi-baby! Welcome home! We've all been waiting for you to come back. The house is like a graveyard without you. But you look like a little girl!" He lifts my suitcase, struggling a little, and looks scandalized when I take it from his hand. "You shouldn't do that, baby. That's my job."

I smile and put the case into the trunk, help him shut it.

As the Bentley speeds down the still-sleeping streets, I'm amazed at how different the city appears. I've taken this road from the airport every year upon my return from boarding school, have looked at the same scenes. But today it's as though a cover has been whisked away. The piled garbage leaps out at me; the street dwellers lighting cow-dung fires next to gleaming apartment buildings seem at once pathetic and brave;

outside soot-streaked temples, flower sellers hang up their bright, hopeful garlands. And the smell of the city, even this early, overwhelms me: incense sticks lit by shopkeepers before they start the day's business; oil heating in woks outside the street shops for frying samosas; dust and phenol as sweepers clean the entrances of banks. Did any place in America assail me with such larger-than-life odors?

Layer upon unseen layer, how this complicated city holds me. For better or worse, I've chosen it over the cities of America. I've decided to fulfill the promises I made here. Love rushes through me as I think this—and worry. I'm not sure the city will love me back. That it will accept the secrets I'm carrying. At the airport, Vic held my hands tight and said, "Come back if there are problems. I'll wait for you." But I know there's no going back to some things.

All the way in the airplane, I fidgeted, unable to sleep. I pictured the look on Rajat's face when I tell him who I really am. But his face, it kept changing, like water in wind. I want that trial to be over as soon as possible. I call Grandmother from the car to tell her that I'm going to visit Rajat first, before coming home.

"Of course. Your first responsibility is to your husband and his family."

I don't agree. My first responsibility is toward whoever among my loved ones needs me most. Today it's Rajat. Tomorrow it might be Grandma. If at another time it's my father, I hope I can go to him, too.

But this is not a time for arguing. So I only say, "I'm not married yet! And after I talk to Rajat, who knows what will happen?"

"Don't think bad-luck thoughts!" Grandmother says, but she sounds nervous. I called her about the illegitimacy before leaving America. I think she's still in shock. "I'll let Jayashree know you're on your way."

I lean back and close my eyes, rehearsing what to say to Rajat. Every speech I construct sounds wrong. I'll just have to offer him the unadorned truth. Better to spend this sliver of time remembering how much I love him. How, when Grandmother told me about the accident, I felt as if I were about to die myself. That was when I knew for sure, at last, that we completed each other. When I realized where I needed to be.

Grandmother is back on the phone. "Something's very wrong! When I told Jayashree you were on your way, I thought she'd be all excited. Instead she told me they didn't want to see you. I was so shocked I could hardly speak. When I asked what the matter was, she said, 'Ask your deceitful granddaughter.' Then she hung up on me."

The car is like a boat on a stormy sea, rising and falling, making me nauseous. Just as Mr. Desai feared, Mitra must have contacted the Boses, preempting me.

"Oh, you foolish girl!" Grandmother cries when I explain. "What are we going to do now? You should have listened to Mr. Desai. Thanks to your stubbornness, you may have ruined your future. Once trust is broken, it's almost impossible to repair—you know that yourself! Tell Bahadur to bring you home. The only thing we can do now is to wait for the Boses to calm down."

I think longingly of the beloved familiarity of 26 Tarak Prasad Roy Road, the old house waiting to shield me from the unjust angers of the world. I want it so much. For so long I've been a stranger in hostile places. It would be a relief to collapse into Grandmother's arms, into my childhood. But I know I must see Rajat right now, in his anger. If he isn't willing to listen when I tell him the truth, if his love can't overcome the mistrust Mitra has ignited in him, if he's unable to accept me as I am, there's no future for us.

SIXTEEN

I ring the bell of the Boses' apartment twice before Pushpa opens the door. Instead of greeting me effusively as on other days and leading me to the living room, she asks me to wait at the door—like an unwelcome salesperson. I don't allow myself to get upset. I'm playing a game of strategy, and I can't allow Maman to defeat me even before I step into the arena.

After a long time I hear Maman's voice asking Pushpa to send me in. I step into the chill quiet of the hall, and there she is on the couch, wearing an elegant silk designer robe that makes me newly conscious of my crumpled state. Rajat is nowhere to be seen. I realize with a sinking heart that Maman has appointed herself gatekeeper. In response to my hello, she merely looks at me, eyes pausing for a second of additional disapproval on my hair. No teacups are set out, no snacks, not even a glass of water in spite of my long journey. A tribunal of one, she has already judged me guilty.

Resentment rises in me, but I can also see the circles under Maman's eyes, the new wrinkles etched into her face. Since I saw her last, she seems to have aged years. Some of this is due to me.

"I know you didn't want to see me," I say, "but I have to talk to you—and especially to Rajat—and explain things. After that, if you want me to leave, I will."

"Rajat isn't well. The shock of discovering your duplicity was too much for him. He had a relapse and suffered all night with a terrible migraine. Finally he took sedatives and is sleeping now. I can't wake him just so you can weep on his shoulder and try to gain back his sympathy."

"Maman, I'm sorry Mitra broke the news to you before I could. I know that has upset you—"

"Don't call me Maman. You no longer have the right."

The harshness of her words is like a punch to the stomach. It takes a moment before I can steel myself to continue. "I only discovered my father's identity a few days ago. And the fact that my mother never married him—I learned that from him even later. Please try to imagine how devastating it was for me. My entire notion of who I am was shaken up. I felt betrayed. Unworthy. I didn't know how to tell something so big to Rajat over the phone." Even to my own ears, the words sound stilted. They convey nothing of my complicated desperation.

"And so you decided not to tell him at all."

"That's not true. I planned to tell him everything the moment I got back. That's why I was coming here."

"Why should I believe you? You're only saying this because we already know your secret. Where's the proof that you weren't just planning to hide this information—these things that could affect future generations of our family—from us?" Maman's voice grows strident. "I think you were hoping to trap Rajat into marriage before the truth came to light."

That stings. "I'm not that kind of person. You know it!"

"I know nothing of the sort."

There's a movement in the corridor. It's Rajat, holding on to the wall, pale and haggard, the large white L of his cast intersecting his body.

"What's all this noise?" He asks, his voice groggy. Then his eyes widen—I'm not sure if it's with joy or with astonishment at my effrontery at being here.

"It's me, Rajat. I came as quickly as I could."

I want to run across the room and throw my arms around him, to touch the bruises on his forehead, the hard foreignness of his cast. I'd returned because I thought he needed me. Now I see I need him just as much. But an invisible electric fence has been erected between us.

Maman hurries to Rajat's side and helps him to the sofa. She calls to Pushpa to fetch a glass of water and a quilt.

"You shouldn't be out of bed, Son. Don't you remember how dizzy you were last night, and weak with vomiting?"

She launches a dagger glance at me. "As you can see, you've done us enough harm. Please leave. Now."

I fight against the guilt piling up like cinder blocks on my chest. I address myself to Rajat. "I was going to tell you everything, Rajat. You must believe me. But I needed to do it face-to-face. I needed to hold your hands and look into your eyes and make sure my race and my illegitimacy hadn't changed things between—"

"It's very convenient for you to say that now," Mrs. Bose cries, "now that you know Mitra has given you away. I say it again—you cannot prove it!"

I ignore her and place all my attention on Rajat. "Remember what I said when I first told you that my father was American? I said that I refused to go through life with a secret hanging between us, separating us. Do you think I'd lie to you now about something so huge that the weight of it would crush our love? Because if you do, then it's all been for nothing—my giving up my father and rushing back to be with you."

Rajat holds his head. His eyes are tortured. "I don't know what to think! Korobi, do you realize that Mitra's trying to blackmail us now because of this?"

"If she really intended to tell us," Maman says again, "there must be some proof. Ask her for it."

My head is pounding. My throat is so dry I can hardly speak. "If you don't trust me, Rajat, if you need proof, then it's over between us."

"She's threatening you with an ultimatum because she doesn't have anything else," Maman declares.

Rajat looks away. "Maman is right. If you didn't intend to deceive us, you must have evidence of that. And if you do, why should you mind being asked to share it?"

There's a rushing noise, like waves crashing inside my head. I hold on to the back of the chair. I will not faint here. I will make it to the car. I'm Korobi, Oleander, capable of surviving drought and frost and the loss of love. I pull the engagement ring from my finger, set it on the table. *Goodbye, Rajat.* I walk, one precise foot after another, to the door. When I reach it, I say, without turning, "Call Desai. He'll tell you."

In the kitchen of 26 Tarak Prasad Roy Road, Sarojini is teaching Korobi to make singaras. The cauliflower has been chopped and sautéed, along with diced potatoes and fresh green peas. While this filling cools on a large stainless-steel platter, Korobi writes down, in a blue notebook she has purchased for this purpose, the precise combination of spices—cloves, coriander, black pepper, cinnamon—that has been roasted, ground, and added into the half-cooked filling. Next, Sarojini demonstrates how to roll out the skin: thin flour circles to be shaped into cones and stuffed, then fried in hot oil, then drained on newspapers. When the oil sputters, Korobi jumps back, and they laugh.

"You'll get used to it," Cook says. "Look how many burns I have on my arms. That's the only way to become a good cook. See, see, this one has come out perfect, all puffy and golden. Quick, drain it with the slotted spoon. Why, I couldn't have done better myself!"

The cooking lessons are part of the self-improvement regimen that Korobi has resolutely busied herself with since she came back from the Boses' apartment and spoke those death-knell words: "I'm not getting married."

Sarojini had remonstrated with her. Rajat was ill. He was in shock. They were both in shock. Korobi shouldn't have reacted in such haste. "Let me ask him to come over, talk out the misunderstandings. I'm sure things would work out if you—"

Korobi lifted her face, blotchy from the tears she had shed in the car, but her voice was steady. "If you contact him, I'm going to leave."

And she could leave. Sarojini knows she has options. Rob Lacey phones Korobi every couple of days. After finding out how matters turned out with Rajat, he invited her to come to America to study. Her grades are good enough for her to gain admission at his university. He'll get her a campus job, help with the expenses. Vic, too, has phoned several times. Korobi doesn't tell Sarojini the details of those calls, but Sarojini can guess.

It is only love and stubbornness that keeps Korobi here, Sarojini guesses. Love for her grandmother, and a stubborn desire to succeed in spite of the Boses. To that end, she contacted the principal of her college. Sarojini listened to the conversation from the other room, marveling at the easy roll of Korobi's voice—neither abject nor overly confident—as she explained her situation. The girl Sarojini had seen off at the airport could never have managed it.

The principal must have been impressed by this new Korobi because she said she would make an exception for her, taking into account her good grades and the sudden tragedy in her family. If Korobi can study, on her own, the material she has missed, she'll be allowed to take the half-yearly exams. If she passes, she can return to class after the summer holidays along with her batchmates. So Korobi has been poring over her textbooks and phoning classmates, asking to borrow notes. If, in between, Sarojini catches her staring into the distance with a bleak expression, if at night she hears muffled sobs from the girl's bedroom, she holds back and does not interfere. Sometimes—she knows this from her own life—to get to the other side, you must travel through grief. No detours are possible.

In the evening, they have an unexpected visitor—well, not so unexpected, perhaps, for Bhattacharya has taken to stopping at the temple each week. If he's not too busy with election meetings, he stays over and has dinner. Each time he brings gifts—chocolate-filled sandesh from Ganguram's Desserts, or hefty sprays of tuberoses, enough for the temple and for Sarojini's bedroom so she can fall asleep to their fragrance. Sarojini has protested about such unnecessary lavishness, but he says, "Let me do it, Ma. My own mother died before I could afford to get her such things."

This evening he dines with them on fried eggplants, gram dal, fine basmati rice, and the singaras Korobi made a little while ago. "Wedding fare!" he exclaims, turning to Korobi. "What delicious singaras! I can tell you have an excellent teacher. It does my heart good to see a modern young woman taking the trouble to learn our traditional Bengali cuisine. So, when is the happy day to be?"

Sarojini tenses. The girl has such obstinate notions about honesty. But perhaps out of consideration for her grandmother's feelings, or some residual loyalty toward the Boses, Korobi only says, "We don't have a date right now."

"Could you do something for me?" Bhattacharya asks Sarojini. "I've been trying to contact Mrs. Bose all week, but she hasn't returned my calls. She's probably preoccupied with that terrible accident. This city is becoming most unsafe—something I'm going to change if I'm elected. Could you tell her that I've decided that I don't need to become a partner in their gallery? Too many complications. I'll just loan the Boses the money they need—a private loan, with you as witness. No one else will know. They'll have five years to repay it. Will that make you happy?"

For a few moments, Sarojini cannot speak, she's so taken aback. Finally she manages to say, with a smile, "Yes, my son. It makes me happy."

And it does. In spite of that last disastrous meeting between Korobi and Rajat, and the icy silence from his end since then, Sarojini finds that she still loves the boy. She misses him, especially in the evenings, when he used to drop by to check on her. If the phone rings, her unreasonable heart knocks about in the hope that it might be him calling. She cannot phone him—not even with this welcome news—because of the promise she made to Korobi. But tomorrow morning she will send the Boses a courier letter.

"Now you must let me do something for my own happiness," Bhattacharya says. "Let me pay for the temple's yearly expenses, as I mentioned earlier. And the repairs for this house. Please don't say no. I'm doing it for myself, really, because I plan to visit you regularly, and I'm getting tired of having to use bucket water for washing up."

Sarojini stares at him with such astonishment—her genie with a bonus wish—that he bursts out laughing. It is an infectious sound; after a moment, Korobi and she cannot help but join in.

It seems that the goddess has finally paid attention to Sarojini's importunities and turned her grace-filled eyes on them all, for next morning, while Korobi is at the library and Sarojini is composing the letter to the Boses, the phone rings. It is Rajat. He sounds defensive as he greets Sarojini with a formal namaskar, but Sarojini will have none of that. She scolds him roundly for having ignored her all these days. "No matter what happens between you and Korobi, is that any reason to cut yourself off from me? Is that all I am to you, Korobi's grandmother?"

"No," he says in a small voice. "You are my grandmother, too."

"And don't you forget that. You come and visit me, you hear! I haven't seen you since that night I spent with you in the hospital. If you prefer, you can come while Korobi's at the college."

"Actually, I called to ask if I can come over this evening—to see her as well as you. Do you think she'll agree to meet me? Will you ask her?"

"Just come. That child is too stubborn to say yes, even though I know she's hurting for you."

"I'm hurting for her, too, Grandma."

They are the sweetest words she has heard in a long while.

When the doorbell rings, Grandmother is in the temple for evening puja and Cook has gone to the market, so I must interrupt my studies to answer it. My first impulse, upon seeing Rajat, is to slam the door, but he has inserted his cast—now decorated with Pia's artwork—into the opening.

"Please leave," I whisper through numb lips, but perhaps I've only imagined the words, because he steps in. I notice that he has lost weight. Stubble shadows his hollow cheeks. The look on his face is that of a first-time diver standing on the edge of a steep sea-cliff.

"I've come to apologize."

"Not necessary," I make myself say. "We're done with each other."

He swallows. He keeps his eyes on me. "Even so, I must apologize for my bad behavior. It took a lot of courage on your part to visit us, especially after Maman had asked you not to come. It took courage, too, to want to tell me your difficult news face-to-face. Phoning would have been easier. Or e-mail."

I appreciate that he doesn't make excuses for himself. He has some valid ones: his ill health, the sudden shock of the news, Mitra's incitement, Maman's pressure. I give a small nod, not knowing what to say. A part of me wants to fling my arms around his neck, but another part warns me that I've only just started to heal. Do I want to open up that wound again?

"I want you to know," Rajat says, "that I do trust you. No matter what I blurted out the other day—or said in jealousy over the phone when you were in America—I trust you. I'm sorry that I gave you the impression that you couldn't trust me to accept the news of your parentage. That it would matter more than my love for you."

"It's a big thing to accept," I whisper. "Even I feel shocked, from time to time, when I think of who I really am. It's so different from who I thought I was. Illegitimacy. A mixed-race heritage that might surface in our children. Most Indian families would have a hard time accepting these problems. How could I demand that of you?"

"Because of love. Isn't that what we do for the people we care for? Accept their problems because there are so many other wonderful things we love about them? And in your case, these aren't even your problems. They're just the circumstances you were handed."

He looks down, and I realize the next part is hard for him to say. "So, here's my question to you. Will you forgive me for being such a brute? Will you accept me with my own sack of problems—the ones I hid all this time because I was afraid I wouldn't be worthy of you otherwise? Would you be willing for us to try again to build a life together?"

In answer, I rub my palm along his stubbled jaw, the way I've been longing to ever since he entered the house. When I maneuver my way around the cast to kiss him, his mouth tastes bittersweet, like almonds and mint.

"Here's what was really bothering me on that morning," Rajat tells me, "though I recognized it only after you walked away. I didn't know if you still really loved me, or if you'd returned out of a sense of duty—or even worse, pity—because of the accident. You seemed so distant while you were in America. I know how attractive life there can seem. Your mother gave in to it."

I feel a twinge. I can't deny that America's siren song had pulled at me. But I came back, of my own choice. Surely that counts for something. "I love my mother. But I am not her. My journey has taught me that."

"I was jealous of Vic, too."

Vic. His name pulses warm in my chest. I can't deny the attraction that bloomed briefly between us. I'll always be grateful to him for being my friend when I didn't have anyone else, for pulling me across chasms where I would otherwise have fallen. Someday I hope to tell Rajat more about him. But we've had enough doom and gloom for now. I mock-punch his cast. "Vic again! What if I tease you about Sonia?"

A dark shame flits over his face. "I have some things to tell you."

"Let's save our confessions for another time. Except this one: I should have trusted you with my news—you're right about that."

His lips find mine. For a while there's no need for talk.

Later, as we sit on the sofa, my head on his shoulder, I say, "Your mother hates me now! How will we handle that?"

"Maman's bark is worse than her bite. But I'm ready to stand up to her. I'm pretty sure Pia and Papa will take my side."

"What if people find out about my background?"

"We'll just have to live with the gossip, for there's sure to be some. If we accept it calmly, they'll lose interest. Fortunately, we need not worry about Bhattacharya—Grandma told me about his generosity when I called. Who would have thought! Speaking of Grandma, we had better go and release her from the temple—the mosquitoes must be destroying her. She's been waiting there to hear our news."

"She's in on this? What about Cook? She's been gone to the market for a suspiciously long while."

"Actually, she's in the gatehouse with Bahadur. Grandma instructed her to stay there until she called her. We might as well tell her, too. Maybe she'll make us some of her special mihidana dessert in celebration."

"Why do I feel like I'm the victim of a conspiracy here?"

"Because you are." He grins. "A conspiracy of love."

I aim my most ferocious frown at him. "I can see I was premature in declaring that I should have trusted you."

SEVENTEEN

Asif Ali sits in the front passenger seat of the Boses' new Toyota, dressed in a cream kurta embroidered in gold. He is not used to wearing Indian clothes to work (although it's unclear whether today qualifies as work) and tugs self-consciously at the kurta's neck. The cloth is very fine. Memsaab picked it out for him with Pia-missy's help.

When they presented it to him, he protested that it was too expensive.

Pia-missy said, "Nonsense, A.A. Remember, you'll have to be in the wedding photograph."

It's strange to be riding up front in the passenger seat, like a driver trainee—or a boss. He hasn't sat here since he was a whippersnapper, recently arrived in Kolkata, acting as though he knew everything but secretly terrified of the big city. How much he has learned since then. When they hit a traffic snarl and Ram Mohan, the young man whom the Boses have temporarily hired, looks panicked, Asif, without even having to look around, advises him to take the third left and then the second right. And it's a good thing that he doesn't need to look around because he can't turn his head too well. His neck is still encased in a whiplash collar—cream colored, to match his kurta—though his cast, along with Rajat-saab's, came off earlier this week.

"Thank God," said Pia-missy. "Those ugly things would have quite ruined the photo."

She doesn't know that in Asif's room, in the painted trunk under his bed, lies a piece from his cast, the part where she wrote in purple, *Asif is my friend.*

In the back are seated the rest of the wedding party: Memsaab in the middle, resplendent in a traditional Bengali cream-and-red silk, Rajat-saab and Barasaab on either side. Pia-missy is already at 26 Tarak Prasad Roy Road—she went over last night so she could help Sarojini-ma dress Korobi-madam for the ceremony. In the car, she'd showed Asif her brand-new curls.

"Do you like them, A.A.?"

His sister used to tilt her head in the same way and wait, confident of his approval. For the first time, he's surprised to discover, the memory doesn't hurt. "They're very becoming, Missy."

"Mama didn't want me to get real curls, so these will only last until I wash my hair. I'm planning not to wash my hair for a long time."

Asif hides his smile. He's afraid that her scheme is destined for failure—but who knows? Recently Pia-missy has managed to get her way in some unlikely situations. She's the reason why Asif is back working for the Boses.

When Asif was about to be released from hospital, Sheikh Rehman sent a man to the Boses with a letter for Pia-missy. He wrote that she had made him realize that some bonds were stronger even than religion. If she wanted Asif back as her chauffeur, the sheikh would not stand in her way. But since Asif was still in the sheikh's service, the sheikh hoped she wouldn't mind if he took care of the driver's medical costs. It would be the honorable thing to do. In a postscript he added that her parents need not worry about replacing the Rolls. For years the sheikh had been doling out criminally large sums to the insurance company. It was time for them to pay him back.

In response, Pia had sent her own letter to the sheikh. Through the chauffeur grapevine, Asif heard that when the sheikh read it, he laughed out loud, then folded the note carefully and put it away. No one knows what the letter said. Asif wonders if, one of these days, he might ask Pia about it.

Here they are, at 26 Tarak Prasad Roy Road, a few minutes late, but nobody minds. Here's the tamarind-shaded, bird-dropping-spattered driveway that he hadn't expected to see again. Here's old Bahadur, grinning broadly as he strains to pull open the gate.

"Get down and help him!" Asif tells Ram Mohan. "Hurry up, can't you see him struggling? Then run back and hold the door open for Rajat-saab." Asif himself takes care of the door for Barasaab and Memsaab, who thank him and give him the rest of the morning off.

"Don't be late for the wedding photo, though. You know how particular Pia is."

"Yes, Memsaab, I'll be on time."

And he will. Because he isn't planning on going anywhere far. He and Bahadur have a lot of catching up to do. The stories Asif has to tell will make the hair stand up on the old man's arms. He can already smell the masala chai brewing on Bahadur's porch.

The priest has asked Sarojini to sit on his right because she is to give away the bride, but she says no because that is Bimal's seat. She unrolls his mat on that spot, leaves it unoccupied, and positions herself beside it. Throughout the ceremony she feels he is sitting by her, enunciating the mantras far better than the priest can, silently correcting him where necessary. The temple is full of the smell of sandalwood incense and the wild odor from bunches of oleander—Pia's idea—in large jars. The garlands have been exchanged, the mantras repeated, the bride's forehead marked with vermilion, the puffed rice thrown into the fire. The in-laws have blessed the newlyweds. The neighbor ladies ululate to frighten away demons. A wind rises in the bamboo. Sarojini's mother wipes her eyes because soon her daughter will be gone—not just from her home, but from this little town of coconut groves and ponds filled with red shaluk flowers, surrounded by fields of sugarcane. Gone to Kolkata, with its frighteningly high buildings all clumped together, its clanging trams, its men and women always in a rush. They will never see each other again—

Sarojini gives herself a shake. How the mind tricks us, flying back in a moment to another country, another lifetime. Bimal, do you remember the way you took my hand that night, in our flower-carpeted bed, the younger cousins giggling and eavesdropping outside our door, the way you touched my face? We learned each other one limb at a time. There was so much rain that night, the courtyard was flooded; the old women said it was a good sign, our life to overflow with happiness.

Look now at our granddaughter, strong and beautiful. She has traveled the world and chosen to come back home. Perhaps her mother would have, too, if we had let her. See her hand in the hand of her husband. He, too, has traveled, gone astray, swung back. He has stepped on that dark road you know already and I soon will—only he has been allowed to return. They've chosen each other again, after having known each other's faults. They've decided to live with me in this house, which we will not have to sell, after all. In the evening we'll sit on the balcony. The old marble will resonate with the young people's stories, their jokes. Bimal, are you watching? Korobi told me that your last word was an apology, an admission of wrong. Do you agree that we have made atonement?

Mrs. Bose sits beside her husband on the same wicker chairs they used a lifetime ago and observes the wedding ceremony. For years she had dreamed that Rajat's wedding would be held in the most luxurious marriage hall in Kolkata. She had a fat leather binder in which she had listed the names of all the people she would invite—every one of her friends, and several enemies, whom she would present with such luxurious guest-gifts that they would never forget the occasion. And the outfits of the bride and the groom! Cloth of gold studded with Swarovski rhinestones, sherwanis and blouses embellished with cutdana and pearl danglers! Instead, because of the couple's wishes, here they are in this crumbling temple, dressed in simple silk, not one designer label among the lot of them. The bride wears only the diamonds the Boses gave her for the engagement. The gorgeous dowry pieces belonging to Sarojini that Mrs.

Bose had so admired at the engagement ceremony are gone. Sold. When Mrs. Bose found out about that, she couldn't sleep for a night. All that history, all those classic designs that goldsmiths no longer knew how to make! But Korobi had merely shrugged. They were too heavy, she said.

She's a good soul, Mrs. Bose thinks, watching Korobi now. A little simplistic perhaps, but honest, and kind. After she had left that day, Mrs. Bose had phoned Desai. When he confirmed Korobi's story, Mrs. Bose had regretted the things she had said. When they next met, she had taken Korobi aside and—hard though it was—apologized. The girl could have said something harsh—she had the right—but instead she had thrown her arms around Mrs. Bose and told her to put it out of her mind. It took largeheartedness to do that, Mrs. Bose admitted to herself. The girl was courageous, too, going all across America like that. From the few details Korobi has mentioned about her trip, it's clear that she hadn't let anyone push her around. She's like Mrs. Bose that way. Perhaps they will get along better than she had expected.

This temple grows on one after a while, Mrs. Bose thinks: the peaceful cooing of the pigeons on the porch; the smell of wholesome, home-cooked Bengali food wafting in (is that fish fry she smells, slightly scorched?); a flash once in a while as Pia takes a photo. With nothing to distract her, Mrs. Bose listens to the Sanskrit mantras and actually understands some of them. *May your heart be mine, may my heart be yours. May your sorrows be mine, may my joys be yours.* Yes. She takes Shanto's hand in hers, and joy fills her body. There's much to be thankful for. The New York operation lost them money, but not as much as they had feared. The warehouse is open again, operating cautiously, with some changes. Rajat still handles the accounts—but remotely now, from the Park Street gallery. The Boses have cut down on their lifestyle, buying a Toyota—a Toyota!—to replace the totaled Mercedes and giving up their coveted club memberships. Shanto doesn't seem to mind; he says he was getting tired of all those late nights anyway. They have not heard from Mitra since Shanto informed him that they would not pay, though they did receive news that his wife has given birth to a healthy girl. Shanto says they must remain watchful and not grow complacent about Mitra, but Mrs. Bose is optimistic.

Rajat's flat has been sold. Rajat and Korobi insisted on it, saying they would rather live with Sarojini, they didn't want her to be alone in this big house. The money from the sale has helped to shore up Barua & Bose, as has the unexpected loan Bhattacharya gave them, with no strings attached. Mrs. Bose cannot understand his change of heart, though she is certainly grateful. The world, as Shanto says, is full of mystery.

Most of all, how thankful she feels as she watches her children, who might have been dead today. Her mind lights briefly on Sonia, who almost destroyed them, and rage spirals up for a moment. Let it go, let it go. She has heard rumors that Sonia is in Europe now. She was ready to pursue the inquiry, but Shanto persuaded her to drop it. There was too little proof of Sonia's involvement. A billionaire's daughter's word against a chauffeur's, that's what it came down to in the end.

The ceremony has ended. The groom kisses Korobi's cheek and then of course Pia must do the same. *Take a picture, Maman!* Through the lens Mrs. Bose sees her children kissing Korobi on either cheek as if she were a queen. The film captures the soft pleasure in the girl's eyes. All right, Mrs. Bose admits it: she feels a twinge of jealousy. She isn't a saint, she's a mother-in-law.

The reception will be held tonight in a small, classy restaurant in South Kolkata—the bride and groom have balked at anything bigger. But at least the place has a five-star rating. Assisted by the vigilant Shikha, Mrs. Bose has personally overseen the arrangements: the decorations are most elegant, the menu very fine, the background music subtle yet original, the restaurant manager ready to have a nervous breakdown. The entire event is exclusive—only fifty of their closest friends invited. Mrs. Bose was surprised at how pleased each one was, once they knew how few of them had been called. If the uninvited are gossiping—Mrs. Bose is astonished to discover this—she doesn't care! No entertainment has been planned, and a minimum of speeches. The hostess will actually have time to talk to guests, the newlyweds be able to make meaningful conversation with friends. A novel idea. Who knows, it might become all the rage! Besides, there's still next year. If the website Rajat and Korobi are designing takes off the way they hope, Mrs. Bose plans to throw the most amazing first-anniversary party.

For the wedding photo we stand once again on the veranda overlooking the garden. So much has changed since we gathered here less than three months ago. This time Pia puts Rajat and me in the center, with Grandmother on one side and Maman on the other. Papa stands next to Maman, while the servants form a periphery around us. Next to Grandmother is a gap deep as a canyon. No one has mentioned Grandfather, but each of us is thinking of him. How pleased he would have been by the whole event. How loudly he would have complained. How regally he would have inclined his head at Cook and Asif and Bahadur as they came forward bearing gifts and received envelopes of money in turn.

Along the length of the arm Rajat has put around me, the arm that had been in the cast, runs a scar. It's covered by the sleeve of his kurta, but I know its presence acutely. How fragile is the happiness we carve for ourselves. This morning Grandmother dressed me in a sky-blue sari she had bought twenty-five years ago, hoping that my mother would wear it for her marriage. The sight of the sari sent up a tendril of disappointment. Though I have said this to no one, I'd dearly hoped for another visitation. Perhaps now that her secret was known, my mother would be voiceless no more. Maybe she would tell me how proud she was of my journey. Perhaps she would give me a blessing-advice for my married life.

My bridal toilette was pleasantly complicated by Pia, who insisted on taking photos at every stage, and Cook, who kept bringing drinks of various kinds—milk, hot tea, barley water with lemon and honey—to keep up my strength during the ceremony. In the midst of all this commotion, Bahadur ran in with an overnight package that had arrived from my father. It contained a hefty check, which did not surprise me, and a book, which did. It was an anthology of poetry, its pages thin with use. In my hands, it fell open at a particular page, dog-eared, containing a short poem. I bent over the page, breathing in the smell of old paper, like anise. My mother's fingers had taken the edge and turned it down so she could find the poem whenever she needed to. All morning, my thoughts returned to that poem, its four short lines. In the things we love lie clues to who we are. What we want for those we love.

Pia instructs me sternly to quit daydreaming and look into the lens. The camera flashes and flashes again. *Smile, everyone. Don't stop smiling!* She makes me turn toward Rajat. She wants a portrait of just the two of us.

"Korobi-didi, look into his eyes. One hand on his shoulder. Dada, come on, put your arms around her. Don't be shy. Folks? Can we have a little romance here?" She clicks the shutter, illuminating us.

Later, peering at the photo on the camera's screen, I discover two small ovals of light above our heads. A reflection from the flash? I choose to believe otherwise.

Tonight, when we're finally alone in our flower-filled bedroom, I'll take out the book I've hidden under our wedding pillow. I'll read to Rajat the poem my mother has sent to us:

He who binds to himself a Joy
Doth the wingèd life destroy;
But he who kisses the Joy as it flies
Lives in Eternity's sunrise.

ACKNOWLEDGMENTS

MY DEEPEST THANKS TO:

My agent, Sandra Dijkstra, for her enthusiastic championship from the beginning.

My editor, Millicent Bennett, for her astute vision.

My publisher, Martha Levin, for her faith in my work.

Friends Robert Boswell, Alex Parsons, Irene Keliher, Gabrielle Burton, and Kerry Creelman for their valuable suggestions.

My mother, Tatini Banerjee, and my mother-in-law, Sita Divakaruni, whose encouragement remains with me even after they are gone.

Swami Vidyadhishananda, Swami Chinmayananda, Swami Tejomayananda, and Baba Muktananda for their blessings.

And most of all, my family: Murthy, Anand, Abhay, and Juno, for their love and forbearance (because it isn't always easy to live with a writer).

ABOUT THE AUTHOR

Chitra Banerjee Divakaruni is the author of six acclaimed novels, including *The Mistress of Spices*, *Sister of My Heart*, and *One Amazing Thing*; two short story collections, *Arranged Marriage* and *The Unknown Errors of Our Lives*; four volumes of poetry; and several novels for young readers, including *The Conch Bearer* and *Neela: Victory Song*. Her work has appeared in *The New Yorker*, *The Atlantic*, and *The New York Times*. Born in India, she currently lives in Texas, where she teaches creative writing at the University of Houston.